The Discovery of the East Pole

Shiboruto

Nippon Trilogy

Part One

By

Reginald Grünenberg

Higashi kyouku no hakken

PERLEN VERLAG

To Anne,

with love & gratitude

"Lucifer sought to be an artist. He saw the Creation and understood the reason why he ought to be a separate God on his own in it; and reign with the Centralic Fire-Power in all things and form himself into all things and turn into any form of things that he wanted, and not what the Creator wanted."

Jakob Böhme, *Quaestiones theosophicae*, 1624

"Hence when the name of the Christian religion had but been received with some seeming approbation in the country of Japan, Satan immediately, as if alarm'd at the thing, and dreading what the consequence of it might be, arm'd the Japoneses against it with such fury, that they expell'd it at once [...] Some have suggested, that there is yet a Time to come, when the Devil shall exert more Rage, and do more Mischief than ever yet he has been permitted to do; whether he shall break his Chain, or be unchain'd for a Time, they cannot tell, nor I neither."

Daniel Defoe, *The Political History of the Devil*, 1726

Prologue

During the first month of the fourth year of the regency *Kansei*, on a late afternoon on the peninsula of Shimabara in southern Japan, flocks of screaming birds rose from the treetops. The sun sank towards the mountains in the west and the wind blew freshly from the sea through the streets of the fishing village Himi. The calyces of flowers were wide open, the azaleas were whispering in the salty breeze and the cicadas, exhausted by their frantic chant in the heat of the afternoon, yearned twilight and slid into a slower minor. Everything witnessed the arrival of a warm spring evening on the Ariake Bay. The old volcano Unzen lay silently behind the village. Only the swarms of barn swallows and sparrows swelled up and their cries grew ever louder.

The blind seer of the village groped her way out the door, wiggled on the road supporting herself on a cane and shouted with a strong voice in direction of the store where her daughter-in-law worked. She sold all that her husband, the fisherman Tatsu, brought on by-catch and what could be preserved by drying, mostly brown algae, sea cucumbers and sometimes even abalone.

"Natsu-chan, come quickly. Something just happened. Come on! Hurry up!"

Then she spoke in a lower voice to herself.

"Ohohoh, I feel it. I feel it so strongly."

Her daughter pushed the curtains in the entrance of the store aside and came out with haste. She, too, had heard the unusual concert of panicking birds and was troubled.

"*Okā-san*, what's that?" she cried, as she ran across the street and offered the old woman her arm as an additional support, something that she otherwise would have rejected. Not this time. Her mother-in-law clutched hard with wiry fingers the forearm offered to her.

"Listen to the birds! They are afraid, they say! Something big and bad is coming up. Oh, my bones ache as if I were buried under rocks. Daughter, I know that feeling. It does not bode well. Where is Tatsu?"

"He has put up with Habu for night fishing. They want to catch squid."

At this moment a tremor shot through the earth… then the air boomed.

"What do you see?" asked the old woman, ripping her milky eyes wide open.

"Nothing! Nothing!"

"Look after the Unzen. Tell me what's there!"

Natsu looked up to the summit of the volcano as her mother had told her. First, no words came from her lips. Then she screamed. The old woman stared in the same direction at the fire mountain with her dead eyes. She seemed to see more than her daughter as her face petrified. The pinnacle smoked and trembled, then it rose, as if the whole mountain was drunk and wanted to try to get up from its throne of rocks but invisible chains held it there. From a distance, avalanches of debris became recognizable, pouring out of rock bumps and silently gliding down the slopes. After a short pause, the summit began to wobble, and its tip drew a circle into the sky. The old woman whispered all to herself, while her daughter screamed frantically in the rousing chorus with the neighbors who had meanwhile hurried out of their homes on the street.

"Oh, you Gods of the Earth and the Skies, stand with me! Something terrible is coming up. Something terrible! Destruction and doom! I do not know this strange spirit. Please, help me! I'm afraid."

Suddenly she sat up, her crooked back tensed, she grinned with her toothless mouth, turned slowly on her axis, and began to scream horribly.

"Hara hara hara memosama! Sukkurebusu gogamu, sukkurebusu *Abaddonu*! Sukkurebusu kollokami!"

Horrified, the daughter stared at the spastic dance. The neighbors also looked confused back and forth between the mountain and the crazed old woman. No one understood her words. They were not Japanese. Her dance got wilder as she repeated the dreadful verses louder and with a screeching, inhuman laugh. Then her prophecy entered fulfillment and the work of destruction began. The rocky dome of the old fire-mountain Unzen collapsed, the summit sank slowly in an opening throat. The landscape, for a hundred generations familiar to the people, changed its face forever in just a few breaths. Smoke ascended from the mountain's gorge. The old woman collapsed, fell unnaturally twisted into the dust and died shivering. Nauseating fumes crept slowly into the valley.

Many weeks passed. Meanwhile, tremendous masses of magma were cooking up in the caldera of the truncated Unzen. With increasing frequency, the fire mountain spew ashes and fountains of liquid stone which flowed down like vomit on its craggy slopes. Thus, the quakes began, quietly but steadily. After dark, screaming ravens fluttered in panic through the night. People were pale and exhausted. The evil whispers of the earth didn't let them sleep. At night, they were lying on their *futons* with eyes open, pressing their ears again and again on the ground in feverish attempts to understand the message of the *kami* in the depths of the mountain. The roof of the old volcano having collapsed, the 'good' kami who had lived there under the top until then, had dropped down into the crowded dungeon of Hell, where they were now at the mercy of their 'evil' counterparts.

In Nagasaki, at an eight-hour walk distance from the scene, surrounded by mountains in a fjord, people made pilgrimages every day on the hills to look from afar in prayers and in awe at the rumbling Unzen. The narrow paths east of the city up to the lookout points on the peaks of Hokazan, Hikosan and Tomachidake were broadened by the trampling of the spectators. The only people who could not go there themselves were the Dutch. Their delegation of merchants and officials was gated on the artificial island of *Dejima* in Nagasaki harbor. Since two hundred years ago they lived during their individual periods of residence in barracks under strict surveillance of Japanese authorities and they were forbidden to leave the island. The inhabitants of the city were so much troubled by the ongoing quakes that they lost no thought of the 'barbarians', as they called the foreigners, on the island. The hardships of these days became legible also on the faces of the Dutch. The lack of sleep and the increasing uncertainty afflicted them and aggravated the dreary, monotonous existence on the tiny colony in the harbor.

Around noon on the first day of the fourth month Kansei, about eight weeks after the collapse of the summit of Unzen, the earth in Shimabara began to tremble slightly. Successively irregular fine and dull shocks were just felt, but not yet heard. Then the spans between them grew shorter and seemed to build up a rhythm: Loud shock ... long pause ... quieter shock ... short break ... still louder shock. The knocks gradually swelled to quakes as if a huge mattock worked its way from the bottom up through the soil, more violent and finally so strong that the first houses collapsed. People could no longer stand on their feet. Men, women, children, and the elderly fell whimpering and crying into the dust. The fishing boats off the coast on the return from catching felt the dull blows of the deep seabed against their hulls. No breath of wind stirred. Only rippling waves lifted in time to the quake and drove the boats slowly to the coast. The fishermen stared in the direction of the evil mountain, as if he would call them. Tatsu, whose mother had been the only victim to be lamented at the onset of the volcanic activity, bobbed with Habu on their boat out there in the doldrums and harvested seaweed with long poles. When they felt the quakes, Tatsu grew afraid for his pregnant wife Natsu.

"Come on, Habu, let us go back soon."

"Are you insane? Swim back, if you want! I stay on the boat. Here on the water, we are safe."

"Habu, I need to save Natsu! Let us pick her up. We also go right back out into the bay." Habu, wearing only a linen loincloth and a large sun hat made of straw, rose with a violent jerk that made the small boat totter, and erected himself in front of Tatsu.

"Do what you want. This boat does not go back to the coast in any case. I don't put my life at risk for Natsu. You should be grateful that I save your life, you fool!" Habu hissed at him.

Tatsu knew that he had no chance against the strong, stocky Habu. He was shocked by the cold that glared at him through the eyes of his friend. Desperately, he looked over to the village, behind which stood the desert ruins of the collapsed volcano. While he initially only heard an ominous rumbling in the distance, which crept over the peaceful shimmering sea, the air on land was ripped by titanic thunders. The wooden huts buckled one by one like toys. The bewildered villagers ran about, screaming and reeling until they fell, and they came no more on the legs. The beats shaking the earth seemed to approach a climax, when suddenly this infernal rhythm rushed into the void. Silence. The waves in the bay flattened. Soon, people dared to stand up again, their faces still full of terror and wet with tears. Some thought it was over, stood in front of their sunken huts and wept for their belongings. The sentimental and the fearful ones remained silent and listened tensely toward the mountain. The sun was almost at its zenith and shone with all its strength on the battered face of the landscape. The heat drove a sweet stench from the *Shintō* shrines through the streets of Himi. For weeks, the villagers had performed services to plead for mercy with excessive food offerings. With the time passing, these slumped to piles from fermented rice, slimy vegetables, maggoty, rotten fish, and venomous wilted flowers, usually blurred by clouds of fat, metallic-blue blowflies. Now, in the heat of midday, the latter stayed almost motionless. Even the cicadas, whose chirping at this hour was otherwise the flashiest, were silent as if they had ceased to exist. Nature was torpid, and the world seemed to have stopped breathing. Only the exhausted cries of some children, the soft moaning of their mothers and detached lumps of rock rolling downhill could be heard here and there.

Then the mountain exploded. The whole landscape seemed to rise, to stir up and to throw itself into a wild warp of surreal waves running through the ground. Boulders as large as houses, fertile soil clods and islands of dried lava flew high in the air, darkened the sky, and stayed there as if weightless for a moment. The blow was so powerful that the villager's eardrums burst. The explosion was heard on the Chinese mainland beyond the sea. Korean coast guards, seized by panic, sent at once a messenger to the royal court with the most urgent warning that the Japanese, now in league with demonic forces, were preparing for war. The deafened villagers at the foot of the mountain were slain by the masses of falling rocks in a brutally roaring rumble. Brimstone and fire rained from the sky. The end of the world began.

The huge magma chamber that had filled up for weeks blew away the previously sunken summit which had stuck like a giant cork in the mountain's gorge. Its explosion tore a rapidly growing gap in the east slope, which eventually ate into the plane, down to the beach and finally below the waterline into the sea. The beach, which had fallen to the extent that the mountain had risen, was flooded by the sucked-in sea water. It rushed inland towards the torn edge of the mountain and poured down over the whole length into the huge gap. When it hit on the magma inside the volcano, the mixture of water and liquid stone detonated. Huge, demonic howling fountains of vapor shot out of the gap that widened into a canyon and tore glowing lava bombs with it into the sky. The tide swelled up to a thundering waterfall. Shortly after, the huge reflux of the now boiling water into the bay met the cooler seawater.

Vortices formed, swirling deep funnels into the water until they reached the seabed and stirred it up. They had the same direction of flow and danced separately along the coast. After a short while, they united into a single maelstrom that pulled everything into the depth. Like a wild, wavering spinning top the water rose above the shoreline, towered over the tops of the highest trees, and ripped everything away that it touched. The coastal people around the peninsula found themselves trapped between the further exploding mountain, and the rushing sea. The noise was so outrageous that no one could hear his own voice anymore. The quivering air grabbed them with fists of steel and shook them like mindless straw dolls. Meanwhile, *pyroclastic* flows, avalanches and clouds of glowing rock dust, shot down the slopes of the Unzen. Where they could not reach, because the ground led them through other channels, invisible gas vapors crawled in and choked all life. At last, with a terrible eruption, the mountain threw up the viscous magmas from its crater. They came down like a roller and sealed under a glowing coat the dead gorges which its vanguard had left. The remaining fields and sods on the slopes burned to white ashes.

As the mountain fell back into his shattered throne, the seabed around the peninsula rose over its entire surface. This movement of the ground unleashed furtively the greatest of all the forces of nature. Whole mountains of water were raised like nothing from the ascending sea floor and had to run off. They formed a gigantic undersea wave that raced through the dark depths at the speed of an arrow. The quietly shimmering water surface betrayed nothing of the planetary force that was unleashed underneath. The Shimabara peninsula does not extend out into the open sea but is at a distance of some miles enclosed by the mainland. Thus, the inhabitants of the surrounding coastal areas could watch the event of the outbreak from the first moment on. The onlookers from the villages of Kumamoto and Saga gathered on the beaches to pursue the further eruption of the volcano from a supposedly safe distance. They felt the earth tremble, heard the thunder and rumble of the mountain, and they saw the column of smoke that rose vertically from the massif, its slopes and its secondary peaks into the afternoon sky. Also, people from the hinterland had come to the beaches to witness the drama. As the sea retreated, they did not know whether and how this related to the volcanic eruption.

Within a short time, the sea level fell by several meters, always on and so fast that you could watch it. The fishing boats were suddenly grounded, seagrass lay limp around in large piles, fish jumped gasping in the mud, giant spider crabs sought shelter in the emerged rocks and a steep underwater cliff appeared. The coastal residents watched aghast in the open belly of the sea which released a bottom they had never seen before. Some of them approached this curious alien landscape, some even climbed down and began to gather once sunken objects. Others were frightened and shouted, "The mountain drinks the sea!" They described well what they saw, but they could not see the cause of this mysterious motion of the sea. Around the volcanic island spread a circular underwater wave. It reached through the Ariake, the Tachibana and the Shimabara Bay the opposite bank first with a trough. Immense masses of water were sucked away from the coast and built up in an invisible submarine force. The more cautious women that didn't want to approach the denuded stinking seabed stayed slightly higher on the beach where they kept an eye on the mountain. They noticed it first and shouted.

"Look! Over there! There is something coming."

The men stopped, looked back out to the sea, and saw now far outside a delicate white line that quickly moved to the beach. From then on, it only took moments until it swelled into a mighty head of foam on a large wave crest. A roar began to shake the air that did not come from the Unzen. No one had ever heard this noise before. This rolling thunder expanded further and let the earth tremble now, while the horizon with the smoking mountain disappeared behind the ever-growing wall of water. Until then, people hadn't budged, so much fascination and horror had them detained on their spots. But now they recognized the mortal danger. From the calm waters in the bay rose a gigantic tidal wave. This view, that spook of nature, was counterintuitive, illogical, and undecipherable to them. They could never have imagined an enraged sea without the presence of a hurricane. In a panic, the men in the mud hurried back and climbed over the rocks out of the still further emptying ocean basin. Those who stood on higher ground ran away screaming from the beach, hoping to be safe if they only reached their huts. The falling water levels had opened an abyss, and those who had not yet fled were transfixed by this dark valley of yawning depth. Behind it, the vertical wall of a mountain of water had built up. There was no escape. It was not a tidal wave, as one might have seen them before. It was an elemental, a primordial force from which no man could tell, because no one who ever saw it had survived. Stunned and paralyzed with fear, those tiny people stared into the face of this deluge which towered before their eyes amid deafening rumble and now also darkened the sky. That was the end of the world. The wall of water had now gathered all its strength and rose almost vertically above the empty soaked seabed. Like an angry God this mountain climbed up from the depths and hit against the coast with unimaginable violence. The speed of the outraged sea made it hard as stone and it ripped away all things it touched. The wall of water raced across the beach inland, shaved away villages, uprooted trees, and lifted rocks from their bases. There was no escape. Seconds later, the whole country was under water for miles. As the first wave had completed its work of destruction, the ebb tide drew the drowning ones into the depths. They returned several times back to shore–as corpses. The second and the third wave, which already no living eye saw anymore, rinsed them again as flotsam inland and finally took most of them along to let them disappear forever in the belly of the sea.

Towards evening, silence wrapped the Unzen and the shattered landscape all around. Clouds of ash, pumice dust and stinking sulfur darkened the skies. The fishermen who, like Tatsu and Habu, were out at sea during the outbreak, were the only ones who survived. They had had to watch the cruel spectacle of the volcano from a distance and ventured out back to shore only at dusk. There, only the silent witnesses of the devastation awaited them. Where once stood their huts, rose fuming petrifacts as monuments of an evil nature. Tatsu found Natsu, crushed and half-charred by a lava bomb. It was still burning hot, so he could not even approach her. This sight took his mind. Screaming and full of hatred, eyes veiled by tears, he ran up the slope against the Unzen, threatened the fire mountain with waving fists and wild curses. His bare feet got burned on the hot stones, but he did not feel it. On a ridge he lost his footing, slipped, and fell into a trough filled with odorless, deadly volcanic gas. He died agonizing in delusion. During the night, clouds moved up from the sea, built compounds with the toxic gases and rained off as sulfuric acid. No one could remove the bodies. The few survivors were forced to flee at once, so as not to suffocate or to be decomposed alive in the acid bath. The next morning, a leaden smell of corroded carcasses filled the air. The corpses on the beach or floating in the water were eaten away by crabs and fish.

The fishermen of the surrounding coastal areas could not find their villages on their return. All they encountered were uprooted trees and a few scattered corpses of the drowned. On a spot where two hundred souls previously dwelled, now a giant beached coral block towered over the alluvial sand. They had thought until then, the evil drama had only happened at the foot of the Unzen and that they could safely watch it as spectators from afar. Now, they knew they were betrayed. The huge, devastating ground wave which destroyed their homes and families passed unnoticed under their boats. These fishermen called it then 'tsunami', the 'harbor wave', because they believed it had appeared as a punishment of the gods only on their coast. This event, which occurred according to the Christian calendar on the 12th of June in the year of our Lord 1792, erased twelve thousand names from the Book of Life.

Before that happened, just shortly after the first eruption, the prefect of Nagasaki, in anticipation of a major disaster, had sent a message to the *Bakufu*, the government in the capital *Edo*. It was ruled by the young *shogun Ienari Tokugawa*, just nineteen years old and for four years in office. He immediately dispatched his experienced minister *Sadanobu Matsudaira* to Nagasaki. On a sailing ship he dared the dangerous sea voyage along Japan's wild Pacific coast to the south. He reached Nagasaki two weeks earlier than if he had travelled overland. Sadanobu had immediately arranged for the mobilization of the rice stockpiles from the neighboring fiefs in case of an emergency. He had seen too much during the regency *Temmei*: the eruption of the volcano *Asama* in Shinano and the ensuing famine; the drought in the Central Provinces and the floods in *Kantō*. He knew the will of the gods was unfathomable and could only rarely be appeased by prayers. But he and his administration could alleviate the consequences for the victims of such ordeals. It was his duty to save as many souls as he could to anticipate any unrest and to preserve the eternal peace in the empire of Japan. That was his conviction. Now he could prove what a wise administration is able of. Without his preparations, the death toll would have been much higher.

Barely older than the shogun in Edo, *Tennō* Morohito held watch over the events from the imperial city of Kyōtō. He attended the ceremonies of the *Shintō* priests and meditated. The *kuge,* the imperial court council, meanwhile began to establish a fine and extensive web of correspondence, spun from letters imbued with maudlin grievances and ominous mythical poems. Like political spiders they worked silently and pulled the strings of their cocoon from Kyōtō all through the empire. They felt that their hour might have come. In the struggle for power between the shogunate, the military government in Edo, and the spiritual leader of the country, the Tennō in Kyōtō, the angry volcano in the south of the country seemed to usher in a new round. When the gods showed their displeasure in this way, then that was possibly an opportunity for a reorganization of the state. If the shogun did not get this thing under control, an elder, a mystical power would have to be called, the Tennō on the chrysanthemum throne. The gods were the ancestors of Morohito. He, the Tennō, was the direct descendant of the supreme sun goddess *Amaterasu* and the only human being who could speak directly to her and all other divine beings. But even His Imperial Majesty, following the tradition by searching for divine counsel in his dreams, could not fathom the alien demon that had entered his realm.

The morning after the cataclysm, sunlight pierced pale and cold through the bell from toxic dust and gas. No groan. No motion. No more sighing over the charnel grounds and not a single bird. Only the muffled gurgling of boiling hot springs among the rocks in the rugged southern slopes of the mountain pervades this wasteland. They are called 'jigoku', that means 'hell' and shall remind everybody of the earlier Japanese Christians who were cooked here by the authorities because they refused to renounce their faith. These traitors were loyal to the 'Goddo' from the West, his son, 'Kirisutosu' and a shogun who went by the name of 'Popu'. Therefore, they were lost as subjects of the Japanese emperor. Even by a proper execution they could not be handed over any more to the kami in the realm of death. Therefore, they should get at least an impression in this world of the nature of the afterlife they deserved in the Bakufu's view that was always strict and consistent in religious matters. The monologue of the softly hissing geysers accentuated the silence over the dead land. Suddenly, from a canyon west of the shattered mountain another murmur and rumble arose that did not originate from the rocky scree, nor from the faint crackling of crystallizing lava. It sounded like–a scolding. Regularly and eruptive as the outbreaks before, but not nearly as formidable. At another spot, the fog was ripped to shreds by a large figure that moved quickly uphill without even touching the rocky ground, as if no obstacles blocked its path. Below the huge crater, the eruption of the volcano had uncovered a cave. Its entrance was a fuming maw, surrounded by petrified tears of the earth. In quick succession two huge shadows swooshed into it. From there, several passages led down into a series of chambers inside the mountain. The main chamber, at the lowest point of this system, was larger than any building ever created by man and larger than any room that a man ever had seen. It rose like the interior of a cathedral above a lake of liquid, orange and yellow glowing lava, the flickering light illuminating the bizarre shapes on the walls and the ceiling, seemingly tortured creatures trapped in the rock. Several islands of solid rock floated on the lava lake, which in turn were connected by wide, solid ridges. On the largest of these islands, in the very center of the volcanic palace, there was a sparkling, black column which had such a vague form that it could have been a shadow. From different edges of the chamber forth, two great figures raced to the central island. Once there, both stopped with a heavy jerk in front of the column.

One of them was a huge, fierce-looking man with shaggy hair and wild eyes. The bare legs, protruding through the bottom of the shirred, coarse robe, were fat, hairy columns of marble and muscles. His beard was trimmed and the fingers of his hands as well as the toes of the feet had no nails, only bloody ends. His expression was furious and snorting. In his distorted mouth under the huge hooked nose stood to rows of ugly, pointed teeth. He turned to the column and said with a thundering voice that made the entire chamber tremble:

"I'm Takehaya *Susanoo* no Mikoto, the Master of Ceremonies and ruler of all lineages of spirits and souls since My sun-sister, the great Amaterasu, rose to the skies to separate the night form the day. To me is due the obedience of the spirits without number, the *kami* of the mountains, forests, winds, rivers and seas, plants, animals, and stones. I have slain the eight-headed dragon of Yamata. Humans honor Me and make sacrifices for Me since the dawn of time. Whether *Jōmon* or *Yayoi*, the tribes of *Yamato* or the *Ainu*, they obediently follow My rites. The dynasties of their people come and go, yet their service to my altars is without limits in time. I am the Way of the Gods and I have the power to return them to nature. I am the longing for peace in the unity of all animate and inanimate beings. The souls of men, I force them to obedience and soccage by the ancestral chains of their forbearers who had found their way into my kingdom. Man is nothing to Me before he serves Me as kami. Until then, I allow him to ask Me for protection from the evil spirits." Then he cried out: "And this here is MY WORK!" He stamped his bare, nail-less foot on the ground and not only the mountain, but the whole country was shaken by an earthquake. "I have raised this empire from the seabed to the sky. And now I want to know what thou, alien spirit, hast to do here!"

After this said, he let himself fall into a crouch with his mighty rump between his knees. Then also the second figure sat down, crossed his legs into the lotus position and began to speak. It was a colossus. The garment hanging in huge folds, held together by a simple cord, caressed his voluptuous forms. Everything about his appearance was even and soft. He had a round, thoughtful face with huge eyes. His earlobes hung almost down to the shoulders and his voice was deep and soft.

"I am *Buddha*. I am the way of goodness and love. I redeem those from all sufferings who can let go of suffering. I deliver those who can let go of themselves. I bring the message that the desire for bonding is a fatality. I know of Susanoos rule and I respect it. I show the souls that can let go of themselves a noble and beautiful way into His kingdom. To Me as well, man is nothing if he has not forgotten himself. And who are thou, new spirit from the earth?"

The column changed its shape and slimmed. A tall, dark figure with a pale face peeled out of it and the silhouette of the column turned into a long cloak of shadow. From the thin mouth a voice whispered:

"I am *Shatanu*, the fallen angel Satanael, Lucifer, the Light Bearer, the Deceiver, the Accuser and Prince of Darkness. I am the morning star, and I come down upon the world, first and last. Many names I wear. Belial, Beezebul, Gadreel, Azazel, Incubus, Succubus. Few serve Me in the rite, but I am the ruler of the passions of men. I want the part of the souls that

You despise. I live on the seeds of evil in these late beings. I cherish and care for them until they are ripe for harvest. My food is the weakness and wickedness of men, their desire to be great and important, their mistaken belief that the Gods were interested in them. When they have fallen into my kingdom, I torment their souls for eternity. The suffering of the hopeless in my hells is without equal."

The new spirit of the earth, who called himself Shatanu, made a long pause. His pale hands pulled the shadow cloak closer together.

"You, Brothers of the East, I bring You bad news from the West. I, once a mighty ruler, I am losing power over men. They forget the old religions, forget their passions for honor, revenge, and sacrifice. Scarcity, My strongest ally, begins to wane. It gives way to growing prosperity. Gone are the times when famines and plagues drove men to Me."

"What have We to do with it?" Susanoo grunted. "Your ridiculous Christian god does not exist anymore here for a long time."

"Yes, I treasure your Japanese Empire where it is the sacred duty of the subjects to step on the cross and to spit at the son of the desert god. Your *fumi-e* is a truly ingenious custom. Perhaps this is why I have so much confidence that We can achieve in the league more than every one of Us by Himself. And without knowing, You have already rewarded Me richly. Thousands of self-proclaimed Christians who You let be cooked here on the slopes of the mountain in your *jigoku*, they have unexpectedly gathered at the gates of My Kingdom. They did not understand the perverted message of the desert god and cloaked with his teaching only the wickedness of their small nature. Their souls were not admitted at the gates of the awaited paradise. Abaddon, My servant, angel of the abyss and administrator of the final darkness, he told Me of those legions of the fallen, whose kind was never seen in the depths of hell and were not followed by more. I examined and questioned them for one last time before the glowing chambers shut forever about them. It was them who gave Me the idea to visit You–to propose You a pact."

"What for do We need a pact with an ordinary earth spirit of the West? Shall We let Us get nailed to a cross as it seems to be the fashion where You come from? Unworthy, dishonorable reign of insane gods!" Susanoo snarled impatiently.

"Apparently You still do not know to whom You speak," Shatanu hissed softly, while his shadow grew enormously until it touched the ceiling of the chamber. Then his voice turned into thunder, so full of power and hatred that the mountain shook.

"You bloody fools! Bloated provincial spirits of the East! For too long You stewed in Your own Japanese juice. You know nothing about the battle with the God of revelation! To nail his son on the cross was MY plan! He was MY brother! I wanted to prepare a bloody feast for the end of the Christian God, who came out of the desert four thousand years ago. Cunning as a serpent, he divided himself up into a Holy Spirit, a Son of Man and Himself. A part of Him I let bleed on the cross, yet He transformed My deed into the most dangerous weapon ever directed against me. The God-Serpent still has three heads. Not one I could chop off!" His thundering shout filled the dome of the volcanic cathedral. Suddenly, a terrible howl rose from the depths of his infernal chest. He felt the nails on the cross, which now pierced him.

"The Christian God," he yelled, "commands an army that is now a hundred times larger than the number of both the living and the dead in Your empire. It sweeps over the earth like a plague. You cannot stop it. This time, they will submerge Your country like clouds of locusts darkening the sky." Then Shatanu lowered his voice again.

"You, Buddha, You had already to suffer centuries ago that my primitive sister Kali, the goddess of blood, drove You out of Your home in India. Do not forget that! That was truly not a great opponent against whom you had to exist–and yet You were not successful. Now, a very different and far bigger power comes to infest Your shores. This God of the Christians, he alienates men from nature, from the old ghosts, the venerable rites, and from faith itself. He hides deep in their hearts, holds their souls captive for paradise and requires from them nothing in exchange. He says, 'I am the goodness and the omnipotence; I love ye and ye ought to be benevolent and powerful as I am'. Each of them is made after His image. Everyone is a little god."

Susanoo looked disgusted. Buddha seemed petrified.

"They have gained deep insights into the fabric of nature. With science, technics and engineering they flatter themselves being the new creators of a second nature. Even that was initially My plan. I gave them weapons and made them greedy for power and immense wealth. I wanted them to chase for millennia after the secret of how to make gold. Instead, they quickly tamed the fire in any form, found laws in nature and sources of mechanical power. I told them 'Enrich yourselves and take what you want from this world!', but they understood 'Seek Me within My creation!' They took my generous invitation for a word of the desert God. Maybe it was even His ruse and He twisted my message. Now, the knowledge of nature makes them rich and their faithless faith strong. A generation ago, I shook the earth under a large *city on the coast of Yūroppa*, burying thousands and thousands I drowned. The suffering was great. So much so that every thinking being under the rule of God had to doubt his power and goodness. How could the Almighty allow such a misfortune? How could God love them and yet punish them so terribly? But the work could not be finished, its goal not reached. It was not enough to heal their sick optimism."

"When will His armies reach our shores?" Susanoo asked grimly.

"Soon. Very soon."

"What advice do you have?"

"I offer you an alliance. Only with joint forces we can curb that power. I have a plan. It will be a great punishment for mankind. "

Buddha awoke from his torpor.

"Truly, You are a mighty prince of darkness. I believe every word You say. But I am Buddha. I bring no harm and no penalty. It is not my nature. I teach humans to overcome sufferance by enduring it. No greater plague exists than this world itself. Existence and life are both like you. Both are united with you. Yet, God and Counter-God are one and the same for me. You are my enemy, Shatanu. And I, Buddha, I am laughing at You, because You have no power over Me! "

Buddha felt Shatanus glowing eyes resting on him and heard his voice whisper.

"Venerable Brother of the East, we have more in common than You think. Do You believe that I enjoy this human cesspool, this stinking, muddy world? Tell Me: who is responsible for this? No, oh Buddha, My friend, neither You, nor I, nor Susanoo or Our powerful Brothers in Ahurika are able to make the world as bad as it is. The desert God, He is the creator of this world that We do not want. He sets it so, without asking us. He disputes us all spheres in this world as in the hereafter. He is a trouble-maker who wants to conquer and to change everything. He will steal all souls from You, he will depopulate and lay waste your skies. He does not accept Your Nirvana, Buddha, not any more than He will leave the souls to rest as spirits in Your forests and fields, rivers, lakes and waterfalls, Susanoo. Wake up, damn! I predict You, Your end is near!"

"I tell you, I'm not a spirit of denial. My strength is tolerance, the endurance of suffering. In My realm come the souls once they are purged from negation, from the will to act, from thinking," Buddha replied and was silent for a moment.

"But I can agree with You on one thing. When the humans recognize supreme purposes in the revelation of the desert God that shackle them to the Great Wheel of Fate, their fatal need for bonding and meaning has triumphed again. They will not be able to step out of the eternally recurring flow of sufferance. I am always looking for a great sign of the futility of human endeavor. To fill the Nirvana, I need the power of images, which I am not able to create by myself. A picture, a thing or an act that makes them drop all ambition and hope, that I would be of great service to Me."

"You see, My Brother," Shatanu replied satisfied, "so we still find an agreement. I will not ask you anything that contradicts your nature. "

"And what is Your request?" Susanoo barked.

"Nothing big. Just give me some leeway so that I can run preparations in Your island empire. And don't expel those whom You call 'barbarians' prematurely from it. My plan shall not be interfered with. And You, great Susanoo, do not be surprised, for I will make You more powerful than ever. Watch over Your shrines and the observance of the rite. This is the help that I expect from You."

"What is Your plan?" Susanoo asked.

"At times You will know. You would not understand if I revealed it to you now. Only this: I will bring You a Sword of Fire, a weapon as it has not been seen since the beginning of the world. It will come from the chambers of Our enemy. Well, are You all right with this? Do We have a covenant?"

"I agree," Susanoo grunted. Buddha nodded silently.

"So be it! Here We meet again. My plan needs to evolve, precautions must be taken. To conclude and to seal on Our deal, I return to You the souls which I have taken from here. Among them, there are the best and the worst, the greatest and the least. I have made no difference. There are Yours and I respect Your reign in this place."

He knelt in front of Susanoo and Buddha, opened his hand, and blew into the ashes of souls lying therein.

"They shall live on in You, and Ye shall decide on their fate."

Susanoo sucked in those pertaining to him through his giant nostrils, Buddha inhaled his souls of the purified with his mouth. Both were satisfied and appeased with the gift. They left the place as they had come.

Shatanu sank down into the rocks to the fiery veins deep underground, where he found the dark channels. From there, he returned undisturbed to his kingdom in the west. Sinister thoughts were his company.

"I want to create an event, all after My fancy. There, I will incorporate the lessons from My defeats. The Good is to give birth to Evil, ailing and in pain. The two ends of the world and the time have to be tied together, so I'm not coming back as the paradox tormentor, who always wants Evil and only creates the Good. No betting anymore with the Creator. I have lost all of them. I have gotten myself to games whose rules He dictated. Even when I took possession of Judas' soul, I was not aware of God's plan. He has the power to look far ahead in time. And He sees something in the hearts of men, which remains hidden for me. Therefore, this plan that I have taken, is larger and bolder than any other before.

"I will reveal Myself. There shall be no doubt anymore about my existence. My revelation will shine above all the heavens and it will create a new humanity, far superior to today's poor version of it. If that plan fails, all humanity shall end. For they will not hear again the voice of God; and no Paraclete, no Phanuel will speak any more to their defense. The tablets of the commandments will crumble into dust, the cross is to break, the covenant shall perish, and no one will remember the madness that the desert God has brought to the world. At the end of time, We will see which revelation was stronger, whether my brother Jesus and our Father were not just a passage to prepare my own creation. My semen is cold, yes, but my thoughts are blazing fire, and I create with them a new world."

Chapter I

Würzburg

Napoleon's Wrath–Don Mastema–Alexander von Humboldt–Student's Duel–Siebold has Plans

"Now, Authors are much divided as to the manner how the *Devil* manages his proper Instruments for Mischief; for Satan has a great many Agents in the Dark, who neither have the Devil in them, nor are they much acquainted with him, and yet he serves himself of them, whether of their Folly, or of that other Frailty call'd Wit, 'tis all one, he makes them do his Work, when they think they are doing their own; nay, so cunning is he in his guiding the weak Part of the World, that even when they think they are serving God, they are doing nothing less or more than serving the *Devil*; nay, 'tis some of the nicest Part of his Operation, to make them believe they are serving God, when they do his Work."

Daniel Defoe, *The Political History of the Devil*, 1726

Napoleon's Wrath

At the time when the Unzendake broke out on the southern Japanese island Kyūshū, revolutionary France was still preparing for its first war with the European monarchies. A quarter of a century later, the shadows of restoration lay over the whole of Europe. After Napoleon's defeat at Waterloo in 1815, the Congress of Vienna redrew the map of the continent and declared the final failure of the French Revolution. The legitimacy of the nobility was restored, and in many countries, the old rulers were reinstated into their former offices. Germany was still a confusing swarm of small principalities and kingdoms, all with their own currencies, laws, customs duties and mostly ruled by incompetent despots. The Wars of Liberation against the French had not created a strong, united people of citizens who would have demanded freedom, constitutions and parliaments, but a coziness-conscious bourgeoisie that settled in this period, later to be called 'the Biedermeier'. The German language was stilted, and its verbal expression laborious, because there was no culture of free speech. French and English travelers who had read Madame de Staël's famous book *De l'Allemagne* and hoped to meet a "people of poets and thinkers"– her words–were surprised at the stink of spiritual narrowness that covered the country. A provincial spirit reigned, that avoided everything great, openly public, and sublime, especially feelings, ideas, and thoughts. Instead, it found its harmless happiness in the small stuff of private life. It was only at the universities that there was dissatisfaction with the advent of this reactionary attitude that suffocated the spirit of honor, any aspiration to heroism and the essence of freedom. Many students had served as volunteers in the Wars of Liberation and got an idea of the difference between a subject and a citizen. Hundreds of them met at the Wartburg for a great celebration, all from the newly founded fraternities, to celebrate in the light of the torches. With the call for the unity of all German countries they harangued themselves into national ecstasy. In the process, they burned the Code Napoleon together with Prussian uniforms and soldier's braids.

In the following year, tobacco smoke hung thickly in the air again at the *Smolensk* in Würzburg, a pub for regular student brawls. Singing and wild talk alternated, mixed with and intermittently gave up to loud laughter from two dozen men's throats. The student association Corps Moenania celebrated the birthday of one of its members.

"Wellmann, you owe it only to the fact that we must celebrate your birthday today, if I do not challenge you to a par force ride. I'll be happy to stuff your big mouth next week, though. Until then, rinse it thoroughly with beer. I'll go along with that, by the way. Cheers, Wellmann! My best brotherly wishes for your nineteenth birthday."

Corps brother Spegg sat down, everyone lifted the jugs and cheered Wellmann to "You shall live, live, live, three times longer!" For a moment it was quiet, except for the gurgling of the thirsty student throats.

Then von Siebold got up.

"Corps brother Wellmann, luckily I don't need to challenge you anymore. Everyone here knows that I have long since outstripped you in horse riding, just like everyone else here..." whereupon he took a dramatic pause to allow the "Heyda!" and "Hohoo!" shouts and the joyfully affected indignance of the table mates.

"...and two duels we have fought valiantly together. I appreciate you as a brave patriot and share your political views. This said, I also wish you a successful progress of your diligent studies–and above all a woman who has the power to finally stop you from roaming our streets at night".

The society cheered, beat itself on its bellies and some choked at their own laughter. The matter of the daughter of the university librarian and the widow of a recently deceased notary, whom Wellmann had hunted at the same time, had only come out the day before and it was the first opportunity for the members of the corps to exchange views with due liveliness. It would certainly have been too dangerous for a nasty official toast if Wellmann, as a love-hungry student, hadn't been so incompetent in his nocturnal advances and if they wouldn't have remained without consequences. Wellmann himself grinned broadly into the round and took the friendly mockery with humor.

All the members of the corps had expressed their congratulations in turn, had spiced them up with sarcastic remarks, reminiscences, and anecdotes and finally saluted the birthday child. Now it was Wellmann's turn to deliver a speech. Having already emptied three pitchers of beer, he felt called upon to present a great thought that had occupied him for a long time.

"Dear brothers, here we are sitting now, on this eighteenth June in the year of our Lord 1816, in a contemplative place and nothing seems to cloud our idyll. If you will allow me, I would like to rise from this place for a moment, like a big bird–preferably a majestic bird of prey that I would like to impersonate..." whereupon he also let pass a dramatic pause for applause and laughter to continue then all the more resolutely, "...from this place for a moment. I fly slowly higher and see the lovely Würzburg below me, the Residence, and the Botanical Garden, I see the house of my esteemed teacher Professor Schmeller and the bridges under which the Main flows through our city. Then the winds carry me higher and higher in circles until I see the German lands from the Alps in the south to the sea coast in the north. A movement of minds is going through this whole country. With my sharp bird eyes, I see the faces of people, beyond Bavaria in Saxony, in Holstein, in Hanover and of course in Prussia. These people are relieved that the great European war is over now, that the Congress of Vienna has given us all a reliable peace order and that Napoleon Bonaparte is banished forever. Then I fly even higher and now overlook the European kingdoms and principalities. There too, many people are satisfied that the lords are lords and the servants are servants again, that the transition of privileges by birth is reinstated and the will of the state is again identical with the will of its ruler.

"I fly even higher now, further and further, to where the outer space begins. Now I discover a small island on the horizon in the southwest. More than a thousand *miles* off the African coast, in the middle of the deep waters of the Atlantic Ocean, the seabed has risen as volcanic rocks into the cloudy skies of this region. There, on the island of Saint Helena, I see a man standing in the rain on the lip of a cliff, dropping steeply in front of him several hundred feet into the dark waves. He stares into the direction of Europe. It is the world spirit in its captivity. There Napoleon, the monster, the war genius who carried the torch of revolution throughout Europe, waits for his death. His gaze is angry, I see him scolding and raising his fist against Europe. Well, we don't have to be afraid of his threats anymore. Perhaps he wants to warn us in the offended way of a dethroned majesty about what will be lost and what will happen to us if we destroy his work. It is indeed, my dear brothers, my greatest concern that the French bloodhound could prove to be right beyond his grave with such a curse. Among the elders here at the table, I know that there is hardly anyone who would not have liked to have been a Frenchman when the armies of the German tyrants were overrun by the Marseillaise and by the revolutionary's burning desire for freedom, or when the human rights were proclaimed as a universal law in Paris. It could have been a wonderful time, a festival of nations!

"Yet, the revolutionaries could not abstain from turning history into a slaughterhouse. They first murdered their king, then their own people, and finally they ravaged Europe with war. I will not go into the details here of who started this war, for I can well imagine what the eloquent people of those days, those Dantons and Robespierres, but above all what the clever Napoleon could have rightly replied to me. The Europeans, above all the kings and princes of the Holy Roman Empire of the German nation, forced the war on revolutionary France under the leadership of the

Duke of Braunschweig. I am, however, concerned with something quite different. Napoleon showed with his conquest of the German Empire that we are weak. Why were we weak? Because we were not a real empire or a united nation, but a vast patchwork of kingdoms and principalities. What did Napoleon do after he overrun and conquered them? He has had their number of over a thousand imperial territories limited to just thirty. Under his administration, many customs barriers and regional mintings have disappeared. He has scrapped the clergy of its privileges and wanted to give us a uniform jurisdiction with the *Code Civile*.

"But the bloodthirsty genius did not want to completely abolish particularism, but only so far as it served him for the better control of the empire to be dissolved. Therefore, he preferred some dukes and princes by giving them kingdoms. He wanted a third force between Austria and Prussia. This is how our Kingdom of Bavaria came into being. Well, I don't want to say anything against our beloved King Maximilian, whom I already revered as a child, even if he was only an imperial elector at that time. It must also be acknowledged that good progress has been made under the government of his Minister Montgelas who granted more civil liberties and rights in our community. But the decisive step by which the Napoleonic work would have found its fulfilment beyond its creator's short-term quest for power, namely the unification of all the countries of German language in a single Germany, in a single nation, that was something they all thwarted. If I had been old and knowledgeable enough two years ago, one night I would have kidnapped brother von Siebold's beautiful mare. I would have ridden like hunted by the devil to the Congress in Vienna to prevent the emergence of the new order in Europe, and above all the inception of the mendacious German Federation, which we owe to Prince Metternich. Of course, I would not have been heard there. But I would have had my magic hood–the same I wear when you miss my presence in some lectures–and thus become the secret ventriloquist of all the envoys of the German states. They would have been surprised if they had heard themselves calling for a strong central government and the national unity of Germany against the orders of their selfish sovereigns.

"But oh, it all turned out differently and my speech just strikes like an impotent wave against the rocks of the new system, which unfortunately was decided upon without me. What do I want to say with all this?

Although we sit here comfortably in an inn named *Smolensk* to commemorate the battle that heralded the beginning of Napoleon's demise in the Russian campaign, we should stay awake enough to see how many promises of the French Revolution and its greatest propagator, who carried its torch to us, are still unfulfilled."

He sat down with it, visibly moved by his own speech. Applause swelled up, some beat the table with their fists to show their approval. Two seniors whispered to each other behind their hands.

"He's a really moderately gifted physician, except for the specimens, where he shows some skill. Yet, he's good at delivering speeches."

"Yes, his likes will eventually change the country more than we do with our legal or medical arts. We should recommend him to the student corps in Jena. They're looking for talented speakers and patriotic minds. Something's coming up."

Don Mastema

After he had applauded firmly, Siebold got up from the table. The beer pressed on his bladder and he went 'beating off water', as they said in these student circles. On the way to the lavatory he saw the light of the late afternoon sun fall through the window frame and shade a cross onto a table where a man read in a book. He stood out for his unusual costume and close-fitting, shiny hair. On the way back, emptied and raised by the enthusiasm of Wellmann's speech, Siebold let a prying look stroll over to the man. The stranger suddenly raised his head, beheld Siebold and addressed him friendly: "Herr von Siebold! What a pleasant coincidence. Please, keep me company for a moment." His left hand pointed to an empty chair at the table, while his right hand closed the book carefully. Siebold came to the table and introduced himself.

"*Philipp Franz von Siebold*, a student of medicine and member of the Corps Moenania, whom you can hear and see carousing over there. To whom do I have the privilege of speaking?"

The man rose from his place and towered over Siebold, who himself was of considerable stature, by more than one head. Siebold was surprised that he had to raise his eyes to be able to look his counterpart in the face as it should have been.

"Don Mastema, traveling trader and passionate friend of the sciences from the Basque Country." Whereupon his black velvet cloak opened, and a hand appeared that reached out to meet Siebold's. The young student had to look at it as he took it, for it was tall, incomparably beautiful and felt like cool ivory. The long, slender fingers covered his whole hand and appeared like that on its back so he could clearly see the almond-shaped fingernails. The pressure of this hand was strong, masculine, and yet almost intimate.

At that moment, Siebold noticed a peculiar smell that seemed to emanate from this person. It was sweet and tart at the same time, pleasant and stimulating. Siebold felt an indefinite memory rise and wondered whether it was only the vague idea of how musk smells, the secretion of the glands of the deer of the same name, of whose excellent qualities for the production of perfume he had read, yet which he had never smelled in its pure form. Maybe it was something completely different. They sat down, and Don Mastema gave him a friendly scrutinizing look, while Siebold noticed the refined shape of Mastema's remarkably pale face.

"You have become a handsome appearance, Siebold, a dashing man. I see that first dueling scars adorn you. There is probably nothing like a duel with a brave comrade", he said playfully. Siebold wondered whether he meant it seriously because nothing about Mr. Mastema's noble appearance suggested that he could be attached to those dangerous students' dares that were despised by the higher classes.

"You don't know me by name alone?"

"I don't want to confuse you. Yes, I know you. Your name was mentioned earlier in the social gathering, which I am now withholding you from. Last time I saw you, however, you were just a child. I was acquainted with your father."

"You have an advantage over me because unfortunately, I can't remember my father Christoph Siebold," he said, trying not to show the stranger any emotion.

"He died of consumption in January 1798, just before my second birthday."

"I'm aware of that. I didn't meet him until just before he died. It's unfortunate when a man must leave life at such a young age. He was only thirty-two years old if I remember correctly."

"That is right. What was your connection with him?"

"I would like to tell you that. However, I have one condition, namely that you will not tell anyone about the following. Can you promise me that?"

"Well, yes, I will," Siebold replied in surprise.

"I went to him because he had the reputation of being an ambitious man and highly interested in scientific innovations. I had already talked to a number of German doctors about a discovery I made on one of my journeys in England. The English have a gas they call *laughing gas*. The educated circles organize so-called 'parties', at which this gas is administered with preference to courageous ladies. They fall into a state of dizziness for the amusement of the other guests and begin to laugh uninhibitedly. In my opinion, however, this substance has a much more important quality. I think it is a potent painkiller. But most doctors did not take this hint seriously because I don't have a doctoral degree in medicine. I, therefore, sought a conversation with a capable surgeon who would scientifically investigate the effect of nitrous oxide and recommend it to his colleagues. Surgery of the bones and internal organs would undoubtedly be a major achievement for surgery. My interest in this matter was to import or to produce this gas. Your father could have been a rich man with that. We could have made a fortune."

Siebold was astonished and his senses suddenly turned almost painfully keen. Inquisitively he went on.

"This is a fascinating matter. Please be so kind as to tell me how my father reacted. And what was the reason for the failure of this project?"

"As I suspected, your father was more than open to the idea. We also agreed at the time to keep this a secret for some time to come. He at once began trials on severely wounded or terminally ill patients. Before he could systematically record the results, he died."

Yes, he died of exhaustion, which led to his consumption. I let him work day and night, always with the promise that he would be able to claim the fame of this groundbreaking discovery for himself. I spoiled the samples of the gas and always let the pain-relieving effect for his patients be just so strong that he had to continue with the experiments. He worked himself to death. I stood by his bed the night he died and blew out the last rest of his light. He left me this fatherless son, whom I needed and who will now prepare himself for his task. My plan to make somebody the first cause of a long and infallible chain of further causes and effects to a fulfilling and radiant end effect finally takes on a useful form in his person.

Siebold was moved. He was receptive to stronger emotions thanks to the beer he had previously drunk.

Honor and wealth, so close to his father and him? How much easier could he have had it in his studies if he had already owned a fortune on his father's side? His noble fellow students made life difficult for him by letting him feel his origins. Young nobility without land hardly counted and a fortune would have had to be considerable to elicit even the slightest gesture of recognition from a scion of the Thurn and Taxis or Battenberg family.

"By the way, I also knew your grandfather, Carl Caspar Siebold. That was at a time before your family was knighted. He was one of the few men in the German Reich who could meet me at eye level," Don Mastema smirked.

Siebold understood. In fact, his grandfather was almost a giant, a handsome man of almost seven feet to the top. A shining figure and a bon vivant with his own vineyard in the garden, a musician, and an exceptional dancer. Above all, however, he was one of the most respected surgeons in Germany. He received the extraordinarily honorific title 'Chirurgus inter Germanos princeps' from the medical faculties for his development of new surgical techniques and instruments. For his outstanding achievements during the Napoleonic Wars in the field hospitals, he was promoted to the imperial nobility by the emperor.

"I met him here in Würzburg at the ball of a family that has since been wiped out by the war. He was an impressive figure and I had great admiration for him. In conversation, he proved to be one of the warmest and brightest people I ever met in these latitudes. But may I tell you..." here he hesitated, "–and I don't want to be irreverent at all–that the aristocratic ladies saw it quite differently. They were almost afraid of him, despite his extraordinary masculine beauty."

"Yes, I have heard of this irritation. My uncle told me about it. Such things still exist today," Siebold explained reservedly. He didn't want to go into details. For him, it was a deep thorn that the better circles of society still considered a doctor, especially a surgeon, to be a craftsman pursuing a bloody business associated with misfortune and pain. Surgeons were occasionally even compared to butchers. In the case of his grandfather, the spite went on. The fine ladies never missed an opportunity to remind everybody that his own grandfather was only a count's cook. This wonderful man, who saved hundreds of lives in the hospital and on the battlefield, was a parvenu for them. His awards, medals, and his family, in which all the children attended the university and further innovations were made in science, his fortune and finally his title of nobility acquired through diligence and courage, all this only made it worse. Carl Caspar von Siebold himself couldn't have cared less. He did not listen to the gossips of the higher circles and felt independent of them.

Siebold's father Christoph, on the other hand, who himself at the age of twenty-four had made it to an extraordinary professorship in medicine and soon afterward became the first doctor at the Juliusspital, he indeed suffered from the contempt to which his father was often exposed. He was his larger-than-life role model, and he had made it his life's work to emulate him. Siebold's mother Apollonia had only revealed to him this undercurrent of their family history on the tenth anniversary of his father's death. He was not yet twelve years old, but his childish mind was already wide awake and consequently shaped by this impression. He could not forget a word she had said to him that evening after the common prayer. Because until then, there wasn't a shadow on his father's life.

Alexander von Humboldt

"What interesting reading have you been distracted from by me," Siebold asked so that he would no longer have to talk about those uncomfortable remains from the past.

"I have just received the latest volume of an extensive work on a famous scientific expedition to South America from the author's hands."

"You mean Alexander von Humboldt's *Voyage aux régions équinoxiales du Nouveau Continent*? Do you know the Baron von Humboldt personally?"

"To your first question: Yes, this is the book. So, you are familiar with his work–and I hear you speak French. That's remarkable for a young physician. Well, I can also answer your second question in the affirmative. I had the pleasure of several encounters with Mr. von Humboldt. Most recently, we met in London for his admission as Fellow of the Royal Society. I am more than a little proud of it because I think he is the greatest naturalist of our time."

"May I have a look at this book?"

"Of course, please."

Siebold took the volume wrapped in blue linen, on which the title and the name of the author were printed in golden embossing. He opened it with devotion. So, this was a book by the great *Alexander von Humboldt* that he himself had once held in his hands! The table of contents gave an impression of how diverse nature and life on the South American continent had to be, but also of Humboldt's powers of observation and encyclopedic education. Instinctively Siebold turned more page until he found what he had suspected and secretly hoped for, namely a dedication from the author's pen.

> *Pour mon cher ami Don Mastema, qui est un fin connaisseur de toutes les matières traitées ci-suivantes, qui a plus d'une fois dirigé ma curiosité dans la bonne direction, à qui je dois plus d'une faveur et qui est en même temps toujours resté un énigme moi car je n'ai jamais compris comment un seul homme peut en savoir autant !*

The signature was simply *"humboldt"*.

"That is a very flattering dedication, Don Mastema," Siebold exclaimed.

"You see, Humboldt's *Views of Nature* was the first scientific book I ever read. My uncle and legal guardian Pastor Lotz, who taught me mathematical geography at the age of eight and in whose place I spent my childhood, gave it to me on the occasion of my first day at school in the Würzburg grammar school. He said that I must have an unknown patron because the book was given to him by a courier with a note for me to begin studying nature."

Chance shall have no power over my plan. Everything has been well prepared.

"There must have been people who were convinced of your abilities from the beginning," said Don Mastema with a smile.

"I have read the book several times and learned a lot from it. Since I live in my teacher's place, the honorable Professor Ignaz Döllinger, I am studying not only medicine but also the other sciences that Humboldt considers helpful and even necessary to fully understand nature. I have been working in botany, zoology, and geology for some time now."

"What are your professional goals in your training?"

"I have only just begun my university studies. The immediate goal is, of course, a medical career, for example in the field of pediatrics. But I confide to you that I would also like to become an explorer. I was thinking of Brazil. Humboldt has not yet been there and yet, building on his work, I could travel and do research there as a physician trained in natural sciences."

It is the right time for this encounter. I must intervene here and now.

"Young friend, I'm sure your project will have a better chance if you devote your efforts to the Far East. Humboldt's travel companion Aimée Bonpland has just left for South America. I suspect that this time he will travel much further south, to Brazil and Argentina. And now I'm going to tell you a secret. Humboldt has been talking for years about an expedition to Asia. But he is not interested in *Java*, the Philippines or Korea, but Inner Mongolia. That is why I would like to give you some advice today, just as I did then with your dear father, who unfortunately could no longer make any profit from it. Go to Japan! There you can achieve fame and glory as a scientist, perhaps even your own fortune. The country has been closed off from the rest of the world for over two centuries and we know almost nothing about it."

Siebold looked at Don Mastema with thoughtful astonishment. Could this really be a workable idea? He knew of no connection between Bavaria or other southern German states and the Japanese Empire, so it was certainly difficult to reach. In fact, he himself knew almost nothing about this country. This would be indicative of the validity of Don Mastemas argument.

"In the business matter with my father, as you said, you had your own goal. What is your interest this time, if I may ask?"

That was cheeky. The man in the garment of a Basque nobleman had not expected so much importunity, rather a curiosity oriented towards the proposed travel destination, immediate gratitude for the reference or simple restraint. But this young man seemed to be filled with massive self-confidence, despite the seeds of doubt that had already been planted in his early life to make him grow up as a talented but easily influenced man.

However, Don Mastema was not embarrassed to answer.

"It is absolutely right that you should draw this parallel. Look, I'm just a merchant. And as such, as my nature dictates, I am constantly thinking about how I can further increase my not insignificant fortune. For this, I always need capable partners. In the case of Japan, it is quite possible that we could go into business if you decide to work there. So far, I have not found a way to import rare Japanese plants or the works of art. I read the reports of the Japanese researchers Thunberg and Kaempfer, who gave my imagination a strong impulse. I am sure that I could sell the products of this distant and exotic country profitably all over Europe. Is the motivation enough for you?" he asked coquettishly back.

"Yes, indeed", Siebold admitted a little shamed, because he too had noticed the audacity of his inquisitive question.

"I will go now and join my corps again. It would give me great pleasure if we could stay in touch. I would like to be able to keep you informed about the progress of my efforts, for I consider following your advice."

"Don't worry, I will get off in Würzburg more often. You shall be notified in advance every time. I will continue my journey now," he said, and both got up from the table. When Siebold wanted to say goodbye, something caught his eye.

"Ah, I see, pes equino-varus congenitus, or just clubfoot. Like Monsieur de Talleyrand, Napoleon's Foreign Minister, if I'm informed correctly. Didn't you receive the appropriate treatment as a child?" he asked with the routine of a born doctor.

"Yes, a clubfoot, young Siebold. No, I have not received the proper treatment. The deformation can also no longer be regulated surgically."

"May I take a look, maybe at the occasion of our next meeting?" Siebold asked thoughtfully.

"No, I'd rather not. Goodbye, young friend, and be diligent! I hope that you will soon be heard of for your successes", to which he bowed with perfect courtly elegance once more deeply before Siebold, turned around and walked off.

Student's Duel

"You met the Basque! Yes, I remember him. How could I forget? Your father spoke of him with amazement," said Apollonia von Siebold haltingly to her son. They sat together at breakfast on the shady terrace of the rectory. Siebold was reassured that Don Mastema's claim that he knew his father and had a promising business relationship with him was confirmed by his mother. On the very first weekend after his meeting with the fascinating stranger, he rode into the nearby Heidingsfeld in beautiful July weather to visit his mother. She had lived there with his uncle and guardian, the parish priest Franz Josef Lotz, since his father's death.

"What was your impression of him then," Siebold asked.

"Oh, I have exchanged only a few words with him. When he came, your father and he would lock themselves in the study and were not allowed to be disturbed. Every time they came out after long meetings and the stranger went away, your father glowed with enthusiasm. However, he did not want to comment on the content of his talks with the visitor. Therefore, I can only say that Mr. Mastema, as he is probably called, had an invigorating influence on him and that he had an obliging and extremely cultivated appearance." Siebold leaned back, crossed his arms in front of his chest and contemplated the blooming orchard of the parish, looking for a horizon to which his gradually higher-flying thoughts and plans could hold. Apollonia noticed how good he looked now that he was a student and lived with professor Döllinger. His appearance was extremely elegant. The flower-white shirt with moderate frills on the button placket and the short green jacket with border and high stand-up collar were flawlessly clean and flattened, the tight breeches underlined the muscular expression of the thighs and his knee-high boots shone like black gold. His brown hair was neatly cut, full and slightly wavy. He had a healthy face color and with the straight, slightly pointed nose, the curved lips, and the prominent chin he now seemed much stronger and manlier to her than his own father, whom she remembered as tall, thin, and hollow-cheeked. And just as he was sitting there in silence, he had great things in mind.

These were her short moments of happiness, for she was proud that at least her son is something, or rather someone, she has successfully achieved in her life. She had never gotten over her husband Christoph's early death and she felt so much indebted to her brother, the priest because she had been living in his house and at his expense for over sixteen years now. She was deeply grateful for him, for no father could have been better for her son than this caring and educated person. He was delighted to devote all his attention to the lively little Philipp since he had moved in with his mother. In the garden of the rectory, the boy got to know nature. His uncle spent hours and days there with him, explaining to him the names and peculiarities of each plant and together they observed the life of birds and insects. Lotz had for the first time in his life the leisure to do such things, and the presence of the insatiably curious boy was more than welcome. He also taught him Latin, geography, and history at an early age, so that young Philipp had no difficulty in following the demanding teaching of the Würzburg Latin school and later that of the grammar school.

Siebold was too much in thought to continue talking to his mother. She did not blame him, for she was not a person who made many words. His short visit was joy enough for her. He said goodbye to her and asked her to greet his uncle, who had already started an excursion with two boys from the village to the surrounding forests in the early morning. The following Monday, late in the afternoon and right after the lecture in pharmacy, Siebold and Baust, who was also a student of medicine and belonged to the same corps, had a verbal exchange. Siebold had come to the university on horseback because he wanted to ride out later. Just as he rewarded his beautiful mare Alexandra for the long wait with a few handfuls of oats and spoke quietly to her, Baust passed him with several fellow students.

"Hey, Siebold, is that the woman you always dress up for? I mean, isn't that a little exaggerated?" Everyone in Baust's company laughed.

"You know, Baust, walking around as unwashed as you are is not only an insult to humanity, but also a disrespect for animals", Siebold replied calmly, and again the bystanders laughed. He knew for a long time that he was a constant provocation for Conrad Baust. As an ambitious lad, Baust had a dangerous tendency to envy. At the same time, he was neither overly talented, hardworking nor wealthy. Siebold's always flawless fashionable appearance and the fact that as a student he could afford the luxury of having a horse, while Baust had to be content with a Saint Bernard dog, which he also let run wild until its fur became completely matted, these circumstances fomented with him, who was easily aroused by nature, a growing reluctance and unpredictable thrusts of hatred against Siebold.

"I think you're nothing but a fop and a vain dude who'd like to chase aprons but can only afford to stroke his horse's warm butt. Nothing quite serious. But there are quite a few people who say that you are an asshole."

Nobody laughed. That was an official insult. Even in indirect speech and formulated in the subjunctive, this expression was an intolerable gross affront, a classic libel that had to entail, among students, a demand for a duel. The rules of the Corps Moenania prescribed this act of honor for its members. Siebold approached him.

"Baust, did you call me an asshole?" he asked with a stern face. Baust couldn't go back. He wanted to mask his anger with this indirect speech, so as not to have to bear the consequences of an official insult. He wanted to make fun of Siebold and mock him safely. That had failed him thoroughly.

"Yes, I said that there are people who call you an asshole."

"Have you brought these people to justice? Or, if not, are you prepared to give me their names, so I can throw them down the gauntlet for this insult?"

"No, and once more no."

"Then I challenge you. Tomorrow at six o'clock in the evening at the duel course in the Guttenberg forest. My second is Spegg. The fencing weapon is the saber."

"Agreed. My second is Roxin. As impartial, I choose Wellmann."

"No, I refuse Wellmann. I have an open bet with him. He's not impartial."

"Well, then, Schwab."

"Agreed," replied Siebold, turned around, got elegantly on his horse, and rode off without further notice.

The next day, Siebold galloped in the early evening across the meadows and dirt tracks to the secret duel course in the forest.

The armed fights of the students, especially the duels with the dangerous saber, were forbidden by the police. Whoever was caught had to reckon with a large fine. It did not matter whether it was a question of measuring forces amicably between comrades or the serious regulation of a matter of honor, which much more often led to serious injuries. The student corps, therefore, held their duels in places where they could not be discovered.

Siebold hadn't thought of anything else since the incident at the university. Early in the morning, he trained again in the large attic of Döllinger's house. He was not allowed to be too loud, because Döllinger and his family were not to notice what he was preparing there. Most people outside the student corps had little or no consideration for this barbaric ritual. Above all, he wanted to defend the honor of his family. Baust, this common coolie, was not allowed to offend any of Siebold! After all, several generations of the Siebolds served the sciences at the university, and the medical faculty was often called the Facultas Sieboldiana. Siebold felt pugnacious and completely right, even though he feared that this serious dispute could become dangerous for the first time. Until then, his duels had been strictly regulated and restrained competitions with brothers of his corps. He had already gotten a few scars out of it. This was now his first real conflict of honor and he expected the blows to be harder and more vicious. Siebold felt a tension in his chest that had not subsided since his encounter with Don Mastema. He had a hunch that in this fight he could finally get rid of this besetting, nervous energy.

At the duel course, a small clearing in the middle of an oak grove, more than two dozen members of the corps were already gathered, including his friend and second Spegg. He at once began to dress Siebold in the heavy leather apron, which reached up to the heart pit. He put on the bracelets and the stiff neck ruff, then slipped over Siebold's right striking hand the leather glove. Siebold did not say a word and let his friend proceed. One could see that Spegg was worried this time. Baust had long since been dressed up and, with his saber, kept screaming and cutting the air in two with all his power. He intentionally enraged himself so that his bloodthirsty fuss frightened even those who had come as spectators and had nothing to fear from him. Then Schwab, the referee and impartial, ordered the duelists to take their positions. They were both well bandaged all over their bodies; only their heads had to remain unprotected. The referee asked them to greet him first and then each other honorably with their sabers held upright in front of their faces. Then they should, with their arms outstretched, let the tips of their sabers touch the leather armor on their opponent's chest to measure the standard distance at which they had to fight. From this position, they finally had to put their left leg as far back as possible, so that the seconds with a thin trace of flour could fix the rear line, which the duelists were not allowed to cross under any circumstances. Otherwise, this would be a dishonorable defeat.

"Duelists, I expect a correct and valid duel from you, strictly in accordance with the rules of our corps. The fight goes over six rounds, each ending with the first shot or blow that hits. The fight is stopped when one of the duelists receives a 'shit-stain', which corresponds to a wound of at least one inch in length. And now–*Silentio!–Pugnat!*"

The two combatants aligned the sabers and crossed them. With bent knees, bobbing on the spot and supported with their left hand in their hips, they looked for a favorable starting position for a sally and attack. Then the sabers clashed heavily in rhythmic blows. Baust rammed little and hit all the more violently, Siebold parried quickly and skillfully. He held back with sallies and moved sideways or backwards as far as he was allowed to. There have already been over thirty blows to Siebold when he was hit over his right cheekbone, dangerously close to the eye. The wound was less than an inch long and did not hurt but was bleeding heavily. The first round was over and Siebold had the wound treated with *alum* by the ringside doctor, another student of medicine. The *astringent* effect of the salt stopped the bleeding at once. Siebold was calm and satisfied. He now knew the style that Baust was fighting. In the next round, Siebold also hit Baust hard and let him feel the power of his muscular impact arm. Then he sallied and hit Baust hard with the tip on the leather armor just below the sternum, which was a 'hit'. Baust had to struggle for breath but was not injured. Now he thought he had recognized Siebold's technique again and prepared himself for an all-decisive 'hit' that he wanted to give him next. When they entered third round, however, Siebold unexpectedly came out of the reserve and showed his skills. He feinted, hit and parried in rapid succession. With fine tricks he attracted Baust and lured him out of his cover. He now showed the whole art of fencing, as his grandfather had secretly taught him. Carl Caspar Siebold, who was over sixty years old and of athletic stature, had learned fencing from the legendary Göttingen fencing master Christian Kastrop. And the young Philipp had been his most enthusiastic student. They also had to keep this lesson secret from the whole family, because above all Father Lotz would never have tolerated this warlike training of his ward. Siebold now had his opponent completely under control, tempted him with a quick feint to a careless bareness on his left and hit him with a blow that could have split a skull. With his face expressing a shock, Baust grabbed his head, but his severed ear was already on the ground. A scream went through the crowd. This was a heavy 'shit-stain', which put an end to the fight and Siebold's honor was restored. The ringside doctor placed Baust on a blanket, stopped the bleeding again, disinfected the wound with alcohol and at once began to sew on the ear again.

Siebold has Plans

From this day on, Siebold was only focused on his studies. The unrest after the encounter with Don Mastema had vanished. In Corps Moenania he was held in high esteem because he had undergone the duel fairly and with technical brilliance. The teasing about his fashionable appearance didn't stop, but no one dared to make a serious case out of it, neither in the corps, nor among the other students. Siebold now had one goal in mind. The first two semesters he had followed the tradition of his family and studied medicine because it seemed to have been passed on to him. Yet, he had always felt an excess of interest and passion that could not be accommodated in the fulfilment of some familial legacy. If his aim had always been to become a physician in a private practice, a hospital doctor or a professor of medicine, these ambitions would have been served easily by the standard university education in medicine. But there was a lack of evidence for him from the beginning. "Why should I be a doctor?" he asked himself. In the end, this would perhaps limit him so much that he could only work as a surgeon. Siebold was seriously concerned that the increasing specialization he saw could also determine his professional and life path. His scientific curiosity reached such an extent that it could no longer be satisfied by the medical faculty alone. There was no consolidation of the fields of knowledge that attracted him, but rather the constant addition of new scientific research topics and interests. Up to the memorable encounter with Don Mastema, he had not yet found a Polaris around which he could have circled the imaginary starry sky of his future life. He also knew that Don Mastema was right about the prospects of going to Brazil as an explorer. He did not want to tell him, but two months earlier he had contacted the recently founded Senckenberg Nature Research Society to enquire pro forma about such possibilities. He thought that a newly constituted scholarly society would have to be particularly advanced and interested in ambitious research projects. The good name Siebold opened the door for him at least to such an extent that he was given a detailed explanation for his refusal. However, there was no talk of Aimée Bonpland's journey. It was rather the hope or fear of the society that the famous Alexander von Humboldt himself would still undertake this research trip. This would mean that a young medical student's project, whether planned or already underway, would be meaningless. With this refusal, the much-admired Humboldt caused him his first defeat without any action and blocked the whole New World from his scientific ambition.

For a while, Siebold did not want to admit to himself that this path would now definitely be closed to him. Unlike Humboldt, whom his fortune made independent and who was able to finance his expeditions entirely from his own funds, Siebold had to obtain the financial support of universities, foundations, or princely patrons for the realization of a research trip. Of course, these were all dreams that he did not dare to share with anyone. He probably would have been accused of being mad. But then this Basque nobleman came out of nowhere and planted words into his heart, which he had wanted to hear for a long time.

Now that his goal had been redefined, his concern about how he could achieve it also vanished. Above all, he wanted to learn more about Asia in general and Japan in particular. He began to buy all available literature on travels to Asia from the money he had left after deducting expenses for food, accommodation, clothing and his horse. He ordered the books via his bookseller Knopp from far away and it sometimes took weeks until the delivery arrived. He was eagerly awaiting the three-volume reprint of 'Most Recent News from Asia' by Theophilius Friedrich Ehrmann and Friedrich Ludwig, published by the Diesbach bookshop in Prague. The third volume contained all the knowledge of his time about Japan. He didn't sleep for two nights because he had to read the book in one go. He also acquired original works from travelers to Japan such as *Engelbert Kaempfer's* 'History of Japan', published in London in 1727, and the famous travelogues 'Resa uti Europa, Africa, Asia förrat aren 1770-1779' by the Swede *Carl Peter Thunberg*, published in Uppsala in 1788. In this case, however, he was disappointed because he had dared to understand the Swedish language in writing to such an extent that he could read the book with benefit. But that was not the case. One day an unexpected package arrived. Siebold was excited. It was sent by Don Mastema with a short message.

> *Dear Doctor von Siebold,*
> *With the enclosed small finding I wanted to underline once again the advice given to you. You will not find the studies of Varenius quoted anywhere. Therefore, this is an exclusive knowledge from the beginning of all Japanese studies. I wish you every success in your further studies.*
> *Yours sincerely*
> *mastema*

The enclosed book was the 'Descriptio Regni Japoniae' by Bernhardus Varenius, published in Amsterdam in 1649. Siebold had never heard of this book. He devoured it. The author, who died shortly after the transcription at the age of twenty-eight, had dedicated his work to the senators of the city of Hamburg and told in detail about the customs and traditions of the Japanese. Siebold found the book touchingly unscientific, for all that Varenius had to report was embellished hearsay. Among other things, he referred to the testimonies of the Belgian ship's boy and cook François Caron. He had been left alone by his captain in Japan, where he learned the language so impeccably that at the time he could not only express himself fluently but could also write and translate documents. Nevertheless, Siebold read the book with great profit. He assumed that he was holding in his hands the oldest document in the world in which the beginnings of a physical and mathematical geography could be found.

While he quenched his thirst for knowledge of travel literature, he did not neglect his medical studies, for this was to be the basis of all his research plan in maturing. He was taught pathology by Professor Spindler, who was himself a pupil of his father Christoph Siebold, whom he remembered with nostalgia more than once in front of the assembled students. Siebold's father was, therefore, although long dead, but often present. But also, his still living relatives accompanied him through his studies. Professor d'Outrepont taught him obstetrics at the first German maternity hospital, which his uncle Elias von Siebold had founded before he followed a call to Berlin's Charité. From then on, Siebold closely followed the work of his brilliant uncle, who founded two further outpatient clinics for gynecology and obstetrics in Berlin and published important essays and textbooks in his field of research. In surgery, his major, he was taught by Professor Cajetan Textor, the undisputed authority in this field, and here Siebold demonstrated extraordinary craftsmanship. He was introduced to the medical sciences by Professor Ruland and studied chemistry and botany with Heller, Pickel, and Rau.

By far the greatest influence on him, however, was the professor and privy councilor Ignaz Döllinger, in whose house Siebold lived. More and more, this outstanding anatomist and physiologist, who cultivated an unusually warm and liberal relationship with his students, became his fatherly friend. Since the rooms in the university building were insufficient for the anatomy, Döllinger and the students carried out scientific exercises and studies on evolution in his own apartment. There he had also created various collections and an extensive *herbarium*. Siebold took part in this work by commissioning school children from the neighborhood to collect conspicuous insects, flowers and grasses from the surrounding fields and forests and present them to him for inspection. If there were specimens not yet included, the collection was enriched by them and the children received a small finder's fee. Siebold spent hours and days with Döllinger in the collections, in the adjacent greenhouse and in the systematically laid out garden of the museum. With a never-ending curiosity and attention to detail, they researched and discussed morphological differences and tried to illustrate clear lines of development of species and genera. Together with the students they went on excursions to the Gramschatzer or the Guttemberger forest. On other occasions they explored the botanically inexhaustible and exemplary cultivated palace gardens of Werneck and Veitshöchheim. Döllinger and his clever, alert wife Ilse were also extremely sociable people, whose generously furnished house was always open and often accommodated travelling scientists and dignitaries. Siebold got to know many well-known German, Dutch, French, English, and Swiss researchers from all scientific disciplines at lunchtime or over a beer in the evening. He then accompanied Ilse Döllinger on the piano, who played the violin in a spirited manner. He sometimes felt transported back to his childhood when he was still singing and making music with his mother and the many uncles and dancers in his grandfather's house. He slept little at night, because he continued reading in his books or in those he was allowed to take from Döllinger's library to the living room. His interests wandered all along a broad horizon, because he read everything about the history of the European state world, the development of physics since Sir Isaac Newton's 'Principiae mathematicae', the applications and apparatuses for exploiting vapor pressure, the discoveries and inventions in the field of optics, optical measuring instruments and telescopes, Lamarck's new theory of descent in his zoological philosophy or the news about the recently introduced gas lighting in London's city. The world of knowledge seemed to him to be in an extraordinarily fast and violent movement. He could not avoid the feeling of living on the threshold of an exciting and demanding age, which required excellent knowledge right at the beginning, if one wanted to keep up with it and perhaps even shape it with new insights, discoveries and inventions. His robust nature and the low need for restful sleep allowed him, in addition to this amazing workload, to cultivate his sporting exercises in fencing and riding as well as the sociability of the student corps life. In the following years he fought nearly thirty duels which garnered him over a dozen smaller injuries and scars as lasting memories. At the end of 1818, he fought the last duel with his senior brother doctor Vincenz Wachter. Shortly thereafter, Wachter bid his farewell with a proper carousal, because he was delegated to start his first job as a naval doctor in Holland. Wachter was happy about this, and Siebold, who had only fought amicably with him in the duel, asked him how he had managed to reach this coveted position. Since Wachter was more or less washed there by a stream of coincidences, however, he could not give any helpful information. For Siebold, time went by incredibly fast.

Soon another two years passed and on October 8, 1820 he stood perfectly dressed and not completely free of nervousness in the middle of the auditorium of the medical faculty. Opposite him sat the professors Textor and Ruland as well as three of his fellow students. The ranks were full of other professors and students, because nobody wanted to miss the event of the promotion of one of Siebolds. All eyes were on him.

It was the public disputation and thus the most important part of the doctorate, whereby a student could acquire the title of doctor. He had put forward thirty-five theses on the performance of surgical interventions on the tongue, which he now had to defend against the obvious or even less plausible objections of his examiners. He passed this scientific discussion with flying colors and received 'summa cum laude', with the highest praise, from the chairman of the doctoral committee. He promised to submit a written dissertation on the subject of 'De lingua'. Now he could call himself a doctor of medicine, surgery and the art of childbirth. The subsequent booze with the brothers of the Corps Moenania in the pub 'Harmonie' became popular. The carousing students and professors emptied barrels of beer and wine until the landlord had to confess at midnight that his supplies were exhausted. As he kept good relations with his professional colleagues, he was able to get supplies from the nearby 'Smolensk' and the guests continued to drink until the early hours of the morning. Siebold quickly recovered from the feast and the following weekend he proudly rode to his mother in Heidingsfeld. There was also a festively set table and parish priest Lotz had even invited the neighbors, because there was not every day such a big occasion to celebrate. Siebold's mother Apollonia glowed with happiness and bliss, all the more so because she or, to put it better, her brother had a surprise in store. When the society was gathered at the table and the young doctor had been offered sweet port and congratulations, Lotz opened up to him that the position of a doctor in the village was to be filled from now on and that the city magistrate would like to see it occupied by the newly graduated Philipp Franz von Siebold on the advice of the priest. Siebold could not believe it at first, because despite his academic success he had been worried about where he could work with his degree. Because there were not only many doctors and few vacancies in Würzburg. In any case, this secured his livelihood for the time being and he was able to live and work near his mother. Two weeks later he had moved out at Döllinger and had already opened his own practice in Heidingsfeld. After a strenuous student life, he now recovered during his work that felt like recreation and which gave him extraordinary pleasure.

The following year Siebold helped more than a dozen children to be born healthy, treated syphilitics and operated on many malignant ulcers. An accumulation of cases of various eye diseases brought him to a considerable deepening of his knowledge in *ophthalmology*. Among other things, he tested the latest surgical techniques and findings in the field of cataract surgery. Since the work in the small town was much less extensive than his earlier duties during his studies, he had considerably more time for his further scientific interests. He was satisfied that he could now also deal with geology, mineralogy, and applied physics in the evenings and on the weekends. About this contemplative life, in which Siebold's experiences as a doctor grew just as incessantly as his scientific knowledge, the second Christmas in Heidingsfeld passed, which he spent with his mother just like he always did. In this dark winter the restlessness that he had felt for the first time at the beginning of his studies came back to him. He was now financially secure at a low level and largely independent in shaping his profession and pursuing his interests. Gradually, however, the accumulated knowledge from his diverse scientific studies also hungered for practical application. He saw that the medical practice in this village offered no opportunities for such plans. Gradually he began to complain cautiously and the prospect of having to stay for an unforeseeable period of time in his current job began to strike at his mood. For the first time in his life he got to know and fear boredom. But then the events rolled over when a whole new perspective was opened to him in the spring of 1822. The good Lotz, meanwhile Canon of Würzburg, and Siebold's influential uncle Elias in Berlin agreed that the obviously highly gifted and meanwhile impatient young man had to be sent out into the world. They contacted Doctor *Franz Joseph Harbaur*, an old friend of the family, who had known Siebold's father and grandfather well and was now the chief inspector of medical services in the Netherlands. The benevolent conspiracy of the two uncles worked out. In mid-February, Siebold had already received a letter from Harbaur, who offered him the opportunity to join the Dutch colonial ministry as a military doctor and to embark for Java in the Dutch East Indies this year. That was the happiest moment of his life.

Chapter II

Sea Voyage to Java

Visit to the Luminaries–The Jonge Adriana Sets Sail–Lovis Verhoeven–The White Spot–Batavia

Visit to the Luminaries

Immediately after Siebold had sent the dispatch with the joyful approval to Harbaur, he began with the extensive preparations for the forthcoming journey. From years of studying scientific travel reports, he knew that he had to open up and cultivate many contacts in his home country so that the results of his research activities–whatever they were–could be published because that was still completely uncertain up to then. Six years earlier, as a student, he had received a rejection from the Senckenberg Society of Natural Sciences with his ambitious request for an expedition to Brazil. This time he wanted to act more cautiously to at least become a member of this circle of venerable scientists. To his surprise, interest was at once shown in the request, because the museum in Frankfurt, which had just been newly built by the society, was still looking for all kinds of natural objects for the further development of its collections. Thus, he was already a corresponding member of the Senckenberg Society at the end of March.

Siebold did the same at the Imperial Leopoldinian-Carolinian Academy of Natural Scientists, or Leopoldina for short, the oldest and most renowned society of German scholars. In the first step, he wrote to Christian Nees von Esenbeck, the president of the Academy, whom he had met at the Döllinger house on the occasion of his teacher's birthday party under the most favorable conditions. Back then, Nees von Esenbeck, who looked like an old sea bear with his ice-grey beard, discovered his alter ego in Siebold and promised to help him in every conceivable way if he could. Now it was time and he instructed Siebold to ask his teacher Döllinger or a member of the Academy known to him for a letter of recommendation.

Since he had not yet published any scientific papers or held any outstanding positions, a reference was the least he needed to be accepted into the illustrious circle. The rest would be taken care of by Nees von Esenbeck as president of the Academy. Siebold finally received the required reference from the botanist Ambrosius Rau, who recommended him warmly.

Siebold was relieved because he now had some certainty that he could make his future discoveries and treatises accessible to science and the public in Germany.

In May, the passport arrived, a laissez-passer for the many national borders he had to cross for the "scientific journey via Frankfurt am Main to the Netherlands to The Hague and back," as the wording said. But that was not all. He impatiently awaited the written permission of his regional government and its confirmation by his sovereign King Max I. Joseph of Bavaria that he could transfer to the services of the Netherlands. On the last day in May, he finally held the decisive document in his hands. It was also a formal military discharge certificate that contained a portrait in official medical terms that did not completely match with the image he had of himself.

Size 6 foot 1 inch (=177.5 cm), brown hair, oval forehead, brown eyebrows, blue eyes, average nose, average mouth, brown beard, oval chin, oval face, healthy complexion, strong build.

On June 7, he kissed his weeping mother Apollonia goodbye, in whose eyes fear and joy fought together, let old Lotz hug him fatherly again and climbed into the carriage to Frankfurt, the roof full of trunks and suitcases. For the first time, he crossed the borders of his country, which he knew well from his childhood through the multitude of hikes, rides, and excursions. The familiar landscape moved past him, and he was deeply moved. He had departed from home. Now he was on a great journey. It was supposed to take him halfway around the world. The nature of his homeland bid him farewell this summer morning with glowing colors and he wondered when he would ever see this picture again. Until then, he wanted to feel every foot of the planet passing under him, consider every minute and hour as a gift and remember it. Behind the Spessart, through the open window, he observed the gradual change in vegetation, the formation of the hills and the course of the rivers and streams.

His first stop was in Darmstadt. He visited friends of the family and former fellow students for a few days, because he could not tell enough people what a great mission he was on. In Frankfurt he met the anatomists *Samuel Thomas Sömmerring* and *Philipp Jakob Cretzschmar*, the latter of whom was an enthusiastic animal observer and initiator of the Senckenberg Foundation. Siebold was now rewarded for the extensive preparations of his trip. He was glad that he had planned so much time and stayed over a week. The encounter with these two scholars was invaluable to him. Sömmerring, a lively man of well over sixty years, was already a famous scientist before the turn of the century, for his dissertation on the brain was groundbreaking. His next ambitious work, 'On the Organ of the Soul', was surprisingly noticed and discussed by the 'Crusher-of-Everything', the famous philosopher *Immanuel Kant* in Königsberg. He made it a showpiece of the dispute between the medical and philosophical faculties–with the highest recognition of the new findings on the composition of the brain contained in the book–, explaining that doctors will never find a soul wherever they locate it and however they define it. With white wine and a pipe, the old Sömmerring amusedly told how much he had admired the strategy of the old fox and what a joy it was for him to have attracted the eyes of such a great spirit even for a short moment. He had sent him his work earlier on with a humble request for an opinion and without actually hoping to get any response from Kant. The Weimar Privy Councillor Goethe, with whom Sömmerring was in lively and friendly correspondence, also saw the idea that the soul could lie in the circulating brain fluid as an absurd mixture of philosophy and medicine. But Sömmerring considered Kant's critical assessment of his work to be unequally more elegant and sovereign, for his objections were well-founded. It was also too clear how Goethe wanted to take revenge in this way for the fact that Sömmerring had previously rejected his discovery of an alleged intermaxillary bone in humans for fundamental reasons. Siebold listened to these stories with admiration and felt irresistibly attracted by the company of the great spirits, which this cozy man seemed to cultivate completely casually. He had learned so much from him before. His almost poetic treatise on the beauty of embryos, the 'Icones embryonum humanorum' of 1799, was decisive for Siebold's interest in the art of childbirth and pediatrics. In addition, Sömmerring's rich and incomparably artfully illustrated standard work on the physiology of the sensory organs had been the basis for his disputation thesis about the tongue.

"You don't sound like you're actually preparing for a long-earned retirement. Do you currently have other scientific plans?" inquired Siebold.

The old man laughed wily.

"If you knew, young hero on a trip to India! The older I get, the crazier my ideas are. And since my reputation—only God knows how a trouble-maker like me could get this far—clears away each and any obstacle, I can literally do whatever I want. You see, I have been in Frankfurt for less than a year, but I have managed to get smallpox *vaccination* introduced here now. The serum for this is no longer extracted from the lymphatic fluid of the blisters of critically ill smallpox patients but from the blisters of patients who have caught the much more harmless cowpox. You can't imagine the resistance I met here at first! But obviously, you can't refuse anything to an old headstrong like me. I was able to convince people by first inoculating only strong and healthy volunteers who could easily cope with the symptoms of controlled infection. All the others came by themselves in the following months.

What the venerable *Edward Jenner* had done wrong in England and *Hufeland* in Weimar, in my opinion, was the choice of the weakest and neediest first. I also know of princely houses from all over Europe that liked to infect mentally and physically unstable orphans or the handi-capped in order to obtain more serum. That's what triggered the epide-mics! The magistrate of Frankfurt had first threatened me that I would have to pay the fifty Reichstaler fines, which are still related to the vaccina-tion. I negotiated with them that I will probably pay, but only if there are at least ten cases of acute pox disease. When some people became seriously ill from the vaccination, I isolated them at once on a specially established farm far out in the countryside. There they were intensively cared for and received the best food to strengthen their body's defenses. The close connection between food and illness should not be underestimated here either. They have all survived—and they will certainly never die of small-pox. I guess I won that bet.

Now I am more and more enthusiastic about astronomy. A few years ago, the great *Fraunhofer* in Munich impressed me with his studies on the decomposition of the spectrum of sunlight. He also told me about a crazy pharmacist from Dessau who gave up his profession to find yet another planet in the solar system within the Mercury orbit. Crazy people are exactly my case and I wrote the man, a certain *Samuel Schwabe*, he should tell me more about it. To my surprise, his comments on the spots on the solar disk were much more interesting than his planetary hunt. So, I got the best telescopes and since then I mainly watched the sun. Because Schwabe may be right that there are regularities. By the way, I consider my interest in outer space quite soberly–so, as sober as one can still be after so many glasses of wine–to be a result of my advanced age because I probably only explore the dimension into which I will soon evaporate. Yet only if, as Thomas Hobbes put it, I don't have to simply crawl out of the world through a hole."

Then he laughed until he almost threatened to suffocate. While Cretzschmar hit him therapeutically on the back so that he regains his composure, he turned to Siebold. "Well, we mean it seriously: Send us not only reports from distant countries but above all finds. *Java* is a highly interesting field of research, hardly developed scientifically yet, because the Dutch obviously have their trouble to settle there in a somewhat civilized way. Japan, which you mentioned earlier, is practically a white spot, not only on the maps but on the very globe of our knowledge. We are ignorant of the current state of culture and nature on this great island. Above all, we do not have a single material proof of the craftsmanship, artistic or scientific ability of this nation. Siebold, if you ever get there, you'll have a lot to do, I promise you."

With these words in mind, Siebold traveled on to Hanau, spent a few days there with the botanist Karl Friedrich von Gärtner, an expert on the sexuality of plants, and continued to Bonn, where he was received with a warm welcome that surprised him. Nees von Esenbeck had been waiting impatiently for him because he finally wanted to hand him over his diploma as a member of the Leopoldina. Siebold felt a kind of intellectual fear of heights that softened his knees for a moment when he received the document from the satisfied president of the honorable society. Within the Academy, he was now called Casserius. In Bonn, he also met the anatomist Joseph d'Alton and the philologist *August Wilhelm von Schlegel*, who told him about his travels through Germany with Madame de Staël. Siebold knew of the great achievement of his unsurpassable Shakespeare translation and was interested in his work in Ancient Indian philology, the subject Schlegel taught at the University of Bonn. But he noticed a certain worldly distance to this important man, who suspected in all appearances either sublime feelings, old spirits, or hidden living forces. Siebold was rather embarrassed by this tendency towards the wonderful and the fantastic, for he did not even know what to do about it. The world, as he looked at it through the glasses of his scientific curiosity, was mysterious and astonishing enough for him. Nevertheless, both von Schlegel and all the people he met in Bonn showed him so much interest and goodwill that he could not decide whether he should be satisfied or ashamed. Nees von Esenbeck and his brother, who was also a naturalist, promised him all conceivable help for the future. Before he left for Holland, he wrote to his mother with emotion.

"My family is known and respected here. It is like a connection that has existed for generations. I am amazed how much more the name Siebold is considered here than in my Bavarian homeland!"

When Siebold arrived in The Hague on 9 July 1823, he immediately approached the Office of the Inspector General, who was still on a mission. The secretary made several agreeable notifications to Siebold. Not only did Dr. Harbaur appoint him a surgeon-major with effect from June 11. He would also receive an annual salary of three thousand six hundred guilders, which was about four times his salary as a doctor in Heidingsfeld. He was also released until Harbour returned. So, he had time to get to know the city and above all to see the sea for the first time in his life. He also found the opportunity to travel to Amsterdam and was fascinated by the commercial vitality of this magnificent city, which seemed to accommodate people from all over the world. When Harbaur finally returned and received Siebold in The Hague, he made him a confession that moved Siebold deeply.

"Mr. von Siebold, you don't stand in front of me as a common suppliant. Conversely, I owe it to your grandfather and your father to be able to welcome you here in such a responsible position to help you. Your forefathers were my teachers and supporters. Now I'm here to finally pay a not insignificant debt to the Siebold family in your person." After this short speech, which Harbaur solemnly held in a standing position, they sat down in the deep leather chairs at the window of his cabinet and the jovial

Inspector General told about his encounters with Siebold's relatives. When Harbaur bid him farewell and wished him a good journey, he had wet eyes from the memories of his teachers.

Shortly before Siebold arrived in Utrecht, where he had been temporarily commanded to the 1st division, Colonel Casimir Murmann received him with the greatest joy and reverence, for he owed his life to Carl Caspar von Siebold. In 1800, the great surgeon and wound doctor in Würzburg treated Murmann with a terrible gunshot wound that would certainly have killed him elsewhere. The colonel's gratitude was now completely transferred from his savior to the grandson, and so he arranged for Siebold to remain on holiday so that he could visit Holland and still travel to Paris. Siebold wrote to Döllinger and told him about this wonderful chain of friendly and helpful encounters that had been forged two generations before him. Döllinger replied at once. "It is comforting to think how I started my zootomy so unprotected with a skeleton of a pigeon and how now a friend in East India and a son in Africa want to enrich science; just a shame I'm so old." Siebold also gave an account to his uncle Elias in Berlin, because he owed it to his initiative to be able to hold such a high rank in the Dutch army from a start, for which others must have served up to twenty years.

"In the circumstances I found in Holland, I am infinitely happy. I can finally turn unrestrictedly and independently to the medical practice or deal with the beloved subjects of natural science in easily acquired leisure, so that I believe that I can soon do something good in human knowledge and research; and all the more so as I have begun this work with inner peace and a high, always constant courage and will continue it likewise up to its still undetermined goal. Science, honor and fortune, brought onto the balance of human life, by far outweigh danger, renunciation, and deprivation!"

The *Jonge Adriana* Sets Sail

The planned voyages to Paris and Brussels did not happen anymore, because his ship was to leave earlier than planned. He went to Rotterdam, where on 23 September 1822 the *Jonge Adriana* laid inland in the sheltered harbor. There was a breath of fresh air. The first foliage danced over the jetty and shimmered in the light of the early morning autumn sun. Siebold had already had his suitcases and trunks stowed away the day before and spent the night in a comfortable inn. He was one of the first to come up the gangway at sunrise with light luggage. He had just had European soil under his feet for the last time for a still undetermined number of years. He was drunk with happiness that all his wishes had come true so quickly. He had to keep a low profile in order not to address everyone with enthusiasm and to share his joy. Concurrently, he entered a ship for the first time. Everything at that moment was new to him. His researcher's curiosity was at once fully occupied with the perception of all the mechanisms, devices and objects which he had never seen before. In addition, the strong smell of salt and algae, damp wood, fish and fresh tar somehow permeated him.

Around eight o'clock, the final preparations turned the ship into a termite mound. The members of the crew hurriedly ran back and forth and shouted rough instructions. When the soldiers arrived, it was the first clear and orderly process this morning. They came in a row, passed the gangway one by one and sorted themselves at once into four blocks of five times five men each. They were one of the many replacement continents for the troops stationed in the Dutch East Indies, which regularly had high losses due to illness. The officer ordered them to their quarters. Finally, some women came aboard with their children who followed their husbands because they had decided to stay in the colonies and build a new life there. Together with the crew and the soldiers, the ship now carried over one hundred and fifty passengers. When the frigate, weighing four hundred tons, set sail and departed under the encouraging shouts and waves of the spectators, Siebold was fascinated by the first movements of the huge, fully loaded ship as it moved inch by inch away from the pier. Carefully, the *Jonge Adriana* glided through the shallow Meuse, which gradually widened until it reached the open sea after an hour. Once they had left the estuary, the ship turned southwest and sailed along the coast towards the Strait of Dover. Siebold went to the starboard side, which lies to the right in the direction of travel, as he had learned in his travel literature, and looked out to sea. He was so overwhelmed that he had to hold on to the railing. He was moved not only by the view of the calm sea in front of him, which seemed much larger from the ship than from the land. The sight of this sparkling expanse, which he saw for the first time in his life, became to him as if in a sudden intoxication the inner image of his forthcoming adventures and the boundlessness of this panorama of nature produced in him a majestic feeling, which carried the thoughts of his future and his mission for a moment into dizzying heights.

After a few hours, he noticed how slowly the ship moved forward in a light breeze. After all, it was a frigate, a fast warship with a slim hull and three masts under full sails. He had the impression that a carriage on a paved country road would be about twice as fast. Pen and block at hand, he sat down and counted on the sizes he knew. From Rotterdam to *Batavia* it was about twenty-one thousand *nautical miles*. As a rule, these troop transports took between four and five months to reach their destination. He carefully set a travel time of one hundred and forty days and after appropriate division received an average travel speed of one hundred and fifty nautical miles per day or 6 ¼ nautical miles per hour, which is called 'knots' in seafaring. That was just more than a good walk! Siebold, who loved speed and was already so economical during his studies that he could afford a horse, was amazed at this slowness. Since the length of the route almost corresponded to the circumference of the equator on earth, the thought of having to cover this distance like a walker struck him.

The weather was sunny at first and there was still a pleasant, fresh autumn wind from the southwest. So, they couldn't just sail straight ahead but had to cross against the wind. Since the frigate was specially designed for courses close to the wind, the individual strokes of cruising were long and close to the line of the ideal route. On the morning of the third day, as they passed the English Channel, the sun no longer emerged from the grey of the low-hanging clouds. Siebold watched over starboard the coast of France and its offshore islands. He thought of St. Malo, further back in a bay and out of his sight, from where the dreaded corsairs left earlier on with the letters of caper of Louis XIV to ambush the English. The crews of these ships consisted almost exclusively of Maloins, who in civilian life were farmers, fishermen, and craftsmen, earning with His Majesty's permission a sometimes no-so-little extra income with such loot. Just like the Swiss farmers, who gathered in the valleys after the harvest and made their services available to the princes throughout Europe as well-fed, battle-tested, and dreaded mercenaries, and who were often given the right to plunder in addition to pay. The Maloins were, therefore, the Swiss of the seas. In winter, thousands of otherwise peaceful people turned into cruel robbers and murderers. All this was already part of history because the wild times of mercenaries and pirates had long gone.

The sea had turned dark. A cool, humid wind blew across the foredeck and the clouds were torn into grey stripes. The older sailors looked out at the water and silently shook their heavy skulls. The passengers, who noticed such harbingers but could not make sense of them, learned nothing of the shy sailors. The mate sent to control the moorings and the hatches that sealed the cargo; the chief officer suggested to reef the sails lightly as a precaution and to clear the storm sails; but the captain ordered his *Jonge Adriana* to continue under full sails. In Rotterdam, he had the reputation of a dull official in the sailors' bars, but also of a non-hazardous man in Christian seafaring. The places on his payroll were sought after. Seldom did sailors die on his ships. The deficiency diseases had taken a little toll since Cook's travels around the world, and his knowledge of food conservation in tropical waters was an important chapter in Captain Bonn's catechism of seafaring. He wanted to avoid the pull of the Straits of Gibraltar and see the North African coast to the east.

The soldiers were restless. It was their first sea voyage and they suspected that they were approaching an experience unlike anything before. For the first time they also felt the heeling of the ship, because with the rain a new wind had set in and it didn't hold the frigate in an upright position as it had since the departure. The threat of the invisible force of nature was still just a whisper, but it was already fiddling the planks of the ship with celebratory force. Since they had passed the Channel, where they still had to cross against the wind, the ship now made faster progress. When they reached the latitude of Portugal, the travelers were offered the magnificent spectacle of nature that had been announced for days and nights. The waves of the Atlantic pushed ever more powerfully like wide whalebacks, piled up slowly, rose above and below each other, devoured the horizon and the ever louder hissing wind soon tore the foam crowns from the crests, shooting with the spray through the air, chasing across deck or pelting down on the wooden walls of the horizontal superstructures. The hull of the ship became an instrument on which storm and sea played their hellish sounds. The hatches of the cabins were crowded by some soldiers who no longer wanted to stay below deck, if none of the officers expressly ordered it. The crew was not allowed to be hindered in their work, because now all winches had to be moored, all ropes put on standby and the tarpaulins put on. The thick weather took a few minutes to soak the curious. The widely reefed sails killed hard and their blows banged like lashes over the heads of the crew. The soldiers were relieved to notice a sign that took something of the extraordinary nature of the event. Smoke came out of the two point-roofed metal pipes above the galley and was torn away by the wind. For those who were spared from the seasickness, this meant that food would soon be available. This made them feel separated from the apocalypse at least by a meal. The captain stood on the quarterdeck in his tarpaulin, spoke to the steersman and gave him instructions for the next hour. If the storm were to reach and sustain its expected strength, they could exceed the 30° northern latitude in about seventy hours. Captain Bonn wanted to use this welcomed storm like a catapult to gain some time. From the end of October there would be no hope that the dreaded calms, the doldrums of the equator, would still be broken by monsoon winds. He absolutely wanted to avoid the long crossing of the southern horse latitudes in their windless season.

Lovis Verhoeven

Most of the soldiers of the contingent, different in build and height, but almost all blond, were farm boys and came from the interior of the Nether-lands. They did not have the experience of the coastal dwellers. So, it was their first encounter with the salty world of the Atlantic and the view into the open belly of the sea frightened them. With confused eyes they looked for something familiar, some spoke quietly to their creator or in spirit with their parents and friends left at home, inviting them to help them and not to forget them.

Those below deck who, choking bent over bowls and buckets, had no more strength for such thoughts and were also unable to look forward to the forthcoming meal, went through the harder school of navigation. One of the curious ones on deck had been wise enough to bring his own oil gear for the voyage but clung even more firmly to his wide-brimmed hat made of soft, black felt, probably the most inappropriate piece of clothing on deck in this weather. But Siebold was satisfied behind the grimace that the wet wind struck him. Now the ship went faster and made at least twelve knots.

After more than two weeks in which Siebold had spent most of his time in his cabin learning Malay and Dutch, the sky tore open in one afternoon and it was like entering another world. The sea calmed down, the sun shone down hot and the *Jonge Adriana* made good speed with an even, strong north wind. Passengers who looked as if they had escaped the inner circles of hell after a long time because of their seasickness could now also be seen on board. Like emaciated ghosts, they held onto the railing or simply laid down on the tailgates to relax in the fresh air. Siebold, who in his rank of surgeon-major was also the ship's doctor, took care that these weakened passengers, who were mainly severely dehydrated, ate and drank enough so that they would not be in mortal danger when the next heavy weather followed soon afterwards. The worry was unfounded, for from then on, the journey was smooth and calm, so that he would have preferred somewhat stronger winds. Siebold gradually encountered most of the passers-by. He was also dependent on conversations with his fellow travelers, because he had to advance his Dutch. He wanted to speak the language of his employers fluently when they arrived in Batavia. He also had the ambition to move to Java in the national language. To his regret, he couldn't find anyone on board to speak Malay. A young recruit of the contingent had been trying to attract his attention for a few days but was obviously afraid to address the higher-ranking German. Siebold had been observing him for some time and had followed a meaningful conversation unnoticed. When it was still stormy on deck and below, the recruit tried to bring the historical of the moment to his comrades. He proved his higher education, because hardly any of the other recruits had attended high school. He saw himself in the footsteps of Cristobal Colon, the great Columbus, as he explained. The uninterested listeners were instructed by their comrade that they were now and here on the route from which Columbus at the Cape Verde Islands, which they would soon pass, had turned off to the west in order to be carried from the north-east trade winds on a *broad reach* course to the New World as if on wings. The zeal of the young beardless soldier, presented in the unspoilt high-level Dutch language, made him not exactly popular, although his educational mission was well-intentioned and completely selfless. Those who watched him closely could hear the ingrained tone of despair generated by the struggle for recognition as his chances of success worsened. After ten days of sea voyage, he realized how deep the gap between him and his comrades was, and panic attacked him at night when he laid awake in his bunk. He, who considered military life to be the height of civilization, begged for being recruited in the hope of entering the colonies and crossing the Indian Ocean. He wanted to find his own character and then harden it militarily. He had this obsession that he could become his own teacher if the world only provided him with the necessary material. A long journey to the distant colonies seemed to be the solution for everything. Now he was afraid of the weeks and months that laid ahead of him. He would probably have fared better as a civilian, but he would never have raised the funds for the trip. He had already lost the support of his family, perhaps forever.

Siebold was curious and finally asked the officer of the contingent in the wardroom about the conspicuous recruit. He learned that the young man had broken out of a respected family, which for traditional, if not even religious reasons, showed no interest in long-distance trade. Captain Bonn had followed the conversation.

"You will see, Doctor von Siebold, that there are many of those and similar species who seek happiness in the colonies. In general, the colonies are full of adventurers, fortune knights, bandits, and cheaters. I recommend that you forget everything you think you know about culture, civilization, order, and values until you arrive in Batavia. Otherwise, I'm afraid you'll be on the passenger's list again on the first return trip."

"Yes, I can confirm that. I've been to Java before, but it was a real shock to me how life can look when it pulls faces," the officer assisted.

"Is this a problem that exists specifically on Java," Siebold asked cautiously, although he wanted to ask whether it is related to the way the Netherlands manages its colonies. Bonn answered him.

"No. I have visited many colonies, including the English and French ones, when our country was annexed by Napoleon and after France itself was liberated from him again. I have seen the same phenomena of decay and corruption everywhere. All in the sign of the greed of trade, often still saturated with a hypocritical religious missionary zeal. And you know, it's been that way for generations. My father went to sea and told me nothing else than what I later found myself. I cannot deny that the profits made by the East India Trading Company in our colonies are high, especially in our Crown Colony of Dutch India. But as a faithful, sea-driving Christian believer, it is always a torture for me to see what will become of the peoples and of ourselves when we conquer and subjugate these countries from the coast. You're very fortunate, young man, to come to Java on this transport. You can't imagine how much scum I've had to send out to Batavia. And that is exactly what all European countries that have mastered the art of weapons and seafaring do. They export criminals, adventurers, weapons, booze, and vices. They import spices, fine fabrics, tobacco, tea, slaves, gold, and silver. So, let me return to your question, how you would have liked to have asked it: No, the Dutch administration is not a special form of mismanagement. It is colonialism in its entirety, a terrible evil we bring upon humanity."

Siebold was deeply impressed and had the feeling that he had heard every word of this honest man with his heart. With the heart? He had never thought of anything so romantic.

The afternoon of the next day he met the young recruit again on deck.

"Mr. Verhoeven, could you please assist me for a moment?" he asked him as if they were old acquaintances. Verhoeven was surprised that the doctor knew his name, approached embarrassed and asked what he should do.

"Forgive me, I forgot to introduce myself. Philipp Franz von Siebold, doctor of medicine, surgeon-major and ship's doctor. I have just caught this little flying fish with outrageous luck, an Exocoetus volitans. I'd like to draw him, but he puts on his wings again and again if you don't hold them with both hands."

Recruit Verhoeven held the wings of the strange fish spread and Siebold let his gaze wander back and forth between his drawing pad and the fish.

"Did you know, young Verhoeven, that Columbus was in shock when he first saw this species? According to the teachings of Aristotle and the Holy Church, such beings were not allowed to exist. Except in the very place where the world ends, and monsters take over. Well, isn't that a cute little monster?"

"Yes, I've seen shoals of these fish fly this afternoon. That was impressive," he returned enthusiastically. Thus began a friendship between Siebold and the simple recruit Lovis Verhoeven, who from now on no longer left his side.

On October 16th, the *Jonge Adriana* crossed the equator at 10° west. That night, Siebold stood with Verhoeven on deck and they watched the night sky together. "Do you know what's different here from anywhere else in the world?" Siebold asked the young man.

"No. Tell me!"

"Here the stars and their images rise vertically on the horizon to the east. They wander directly over our heads and sink again in the west. Correspondingly, they also describe a perfect semicircle around the north and south poles. The orbit of the stars here is concentric to the latitudes of the earth. It is the opposite of watching the stars on one of the poles because the same stars dance around you day and night for all eternity. Let me put it in another way. There is no place on our planet where you can see more stars than on the equator. From here you can see the universe with your eyes like a signal light on the coast once around the earth's axis."

So, they stood there for quite a while and watched the constellation Orion first appear in the east, then around midnight the Unicorn, and they said goodbye to the night sky only when the Sextant appeared at the intersection of the eastern horizon with the equator.

Ten days later Siebold woke Verhoeven up at two in the morning and dragged him out of his crew quarters on deck.

"We naturalists often have to get up early, you know?" he said, laughing cheekily. "I didn't want to miss to show you the *Southern Cross* tonight. It was only added to the previously known constellations of antiquity in 1679. There, they're coming! Delta Crucis and Acrux. And how they shine. The cross is on the side."

Again, they stood under the shining roof of the gigantic starry sky over the Atlantic. In the northeast, the crescent moon rose.

"Major, do you know many women?"

"I beg your pardon?"

"Excuse me, but I thought maybe I could ask you something, since you're a little older than me and finally visit me in the middle of the night.

And then I see you, a handsome man on a long journey, wondering who you left behind." Siebold laughed.

"What makes you think I will give you an account?"

"Man to man? Why not? I'm telling you, too, which is why I'm asking. Besides the reasons you know, I chose the way to the colonies because the woman I loved married another", which Verhoeven underlined with a worried look.

"You see, we're kind of on the same path there. I'm going to the colonies to finally find a woman I like." And suddenly he thought that this young guy might be just the right confessor in a matter that had been bothering him for a long time. And the sea, which he saw glistening and heard whispering under the starry tent, opened the cage of his chest, where he had held this thought captive for a long time.

"I have not been able to love one of the women I have met so far. It had nothing to do with—as you rightly suspected—a lack of opportunity. Something's always bothered me. Whether it was the simple girls who offered themselves for the game or the ladies who already associated serious intentions with their open-hearted behavior—they were not able to captivate my attention. It's not that I enjoy standing there like an impregnable fortress. On the contrary, I also want to feel this unconditional emotion that is ascribed to lovers. However, I noticed that the women I knew and who could have been selected had male traits throughout. Yes, I must say, I find the women of my class pronouncedly harsh overall. So, it may be a question of opportunity after all. Cause, you know, a doctor doesn't count much where I come from. As a physician today, one has a knowledge and a culture that has been missing in the nobility for a long time. But that doesn't help, birth and ancestry decide everything and so the doors to the noble and beautiful women of the highest circles remain closed to a doctor like me. I'm not sure there's a solution. It is certainly not the decisive reason why I am on my way to His Majesty's Crown Colony. But to a certain extent, the Eternal Feminine has also contributed to the causes of my journey."

Verhoeven was surprised by this confession, which was, on the one hand, serious and confidential, on the other hand, had nothing more to do with his own concern. He was about to raise the sad story of himself and Adelaide Overdiek, but Siebold clearly waved off that he didn't want to hear anything about it. Meanwhile, Gacrux and Mimosa had also appeared above the horizon and the Southern Cross stood in all its glory in the night sky off the African coast.

The White Spot

Strong winds and heavy rain went with them once again as they passed the southern tip of Africa, the Cape of Good Hope, on 22 December. There they experienced a threatening spectacle of nature. From the deep grey north-east, no less than eight whirlwinds were moving towards them at the same time. These individual hurricanes danced like smoking columns in an unpredictable zigzag course across the troubled sea. The eight-times howling and roaring in different pitches approached the ship and swelled to a hurricane-like thunder. These screaming dervishes of wind and water, each at least twice as high as the top of the main mast, glided past the ship in unpredictable turns. Bonn cared astonishingly little about these mani-festations. Rather, he was highly satisfied, for he was pleased with the crackling rain, which he had collected in funnel-shaped tarpaulins of oil-impregnated material and poured directly into the barrels. The freshwater supplies were filled up without having to go ashore. Until then the *Jonge Adriana* was well in time. East of Mauritius the wind steadily decreased, and the heat increased.

One morning, Siebold came on deck and heard—nothing. The sea was as smooth as glass, the ship did not move, and the sails hung motionless from the masts and booms. For the first time since their departure they had fallen into a complete lull. The peace and quiet was relaxing and fascina-ting, for Siebold now realized how much noise seafaring is associated with. He taught Verhoeven to catch fish and they tried to make depth measure-ments with the plumb line to which they attached lead and sebum. But the line was too short. They then tied all the reserve lines together so that they could lower the perpendicular to a depth of half a mile. They still didn't touch anything. Position measurement according to longitude and latitude was more successful with an accuracy of arc seconds. The captain took the time to explain Siebold the *sextant* and let him practice with it. As Siebold knew a lot about geography and was also interested in the cartography of seafaring, they practiced constant bearings and measurements together. Then they entered the values in the maps. The captain's concern was not so much the lack of wind as the drift through the current. In a calm the ship can no longer navigate because it has no propulsion. The current can make it drift away from the course without you noticing if exact position measurements are not continuously made, explained Bonn, and showed Siebold further maps in his cabin.

"The seas of the world together form a vast underwater continent. In order to navigate there, I need not only the composition of the ground and the coastlines on my maps, but also the air and water currents. This map collection you see here, this is my great treasure. All my knowledge, yes, my whole life is recorded in these maps. There I documented all experiences and measurements I made on my journeys. This knowledge makes a captain powerful and irreplaceable. Do you know why there have been so few mutinies in the history of seafaring?"

"No. Please tell me."

"The crew is always in the captivity of the captain! The captain alone knows how to navigate, and only he knows the waters so well that the ship captured by the crew has no chance of finding the next port. Mutiny is no better than suicide, apart from the harsh punishments that every single mutineer has to face."

"How far have the oceans been mapped? What do you think?"

"Well, there are not many waters left uncharted. We have made enormous progress in the last thirty to forty years. The problem lies not in the areas covered but in the quality of the maps. See, every map is, like this one, a compilation. Generations of seafarers write their measurements and experiences on top of each other and often they contradict each other, or they are incoherent piecework. That's why I wouldn't trust a map I didn't draw myself. The most dangerous are the nautical charts, in which land masses are not indicated by exact coastlines and the water depths in their immediate vicinity."

"How about that in Japanese waters?"

"Japan? Shipping on the Japanese coasts is life-threatening, as we do not yet have a single suitable map. Since one may not go ashore there, so far no approximately usable measurements could be made. Seen from the sea, Japan is a white spot on our maps–and that means nothing good. All we know is the route to a bay where the city of Nagasaki is located. And that only because we are the only nation in the world still maintaining trade relations with Japan. But I haven't been there yet."

Later that evening, Siebold took Kaempfer's 'History of Japan' out of one of his book trunks and read up on it.

> "But this realm does not consist of one island, but of several islands separated by many narrow openings of the ocean. Nature has surrounded this empire with an impregnable protective wall and made it invincible, as it is surrounded everywhere by a sea hostile to the seafarer."

This was the state of knowledge in 1690, and obviously, nothing had changed since then.

Siebold was now busier than before as a doctor. Passengers suffered from fever, diarrhea, or purulent inflammation from minor injuries. Some of them came from fights that broke out among the crew. The men had nothing to do and spent their time playing games of chance, which led to repeated disputes. The boredom also affected the soldiers, women, and children and it became a torture to survive the days without events in the motionless heat. Siebold and Verhoeven were the only ones who were always busy. There were a thousand things to discover, even if it was the populations of vermin that settled in the camp premises, in the bilge, and in the provisions. There was nothing that could not be collected. Siebold discovered about one hundred species of insects, spiders, and worms, which he did not yet know and which he watched with Verhoeven under the microscope. Equally rich in life was the sea, and they were excited when a great white shark was spotted in the water, Carcharodon carcharias, a monster of more than twenty feet in length.

At night Siebold laid in his bunk and tried to imagine the depth below him and the living beings in it, from which only a few inches of tarred wood separated him. Some passengers had books with them like him and there was a lively barter trade because one never had so much time to read as in these calm, hot and humid days on the Indian Ocean. Even the sailors, at least those who could read, laid in the shadow of the sails during the day with knightly novels and seafaring tales. The most unpleasant consequence of the lull in this climate was the dramatic deterioration of the hygienic conditions on board, including the ever-increasing stench of feces and rot. The ship drifted most of the time in its own cesspool. Every two days a dinghy was dumped, and the sailors towed the ship rowing about half a mile out of the sewage puddle.

One evening Siebold noticed a faint light in the water, the source of which he could not locate correctly. It seemed to lie directly under the ship as if the keel were shining. Bonn laughed when Siebold took him to show him the phenomenon.

"These are algae. You'll see, this is going to increase quickly."

Bonn was right. After a few days, the *Jonge Adriana* was surrounded by a wonderful green glowing carpet at night, which continued to grow. Like a single large creature, it followed the ship when it was moved. Siebold observed dead fish swimming in the shining water. It seemed poisonous. Siebold asked Bonn for permission to let himself down with a rope on the side of the ship so that he could take samples of the water and observe the phenomenon at close range. He was then let down on starboard in a kind of swing of ropes. When he told the sailors to stop the descent just above the surface of the water, he was amazed at the sight. He discovered another reason for the foul smell that was spreading around the ship. Above the waterline, a thick layer of tiny, carnivorous mollusks had formed, which had died from the moment no more waves hit the hull and now slowly rotted in the heat. Below the waterline, he discovered a fascinating landscape of colorful tubular plants, shells, clouds of small, fast-moving crabs and seaweed threads gently floating in the green light. The entire hull was overgrown by a thick crust of weeds and marine animals, which grew even faster than usual in motionlessness during the doldrums.

The parasitic flora fed on the wood of the ship, the hull of which, unlike the newer ships, was not yet cased with protective copper plates. The fauna meanwhile lived on propelling algae and plankton. Siebold, who could hardly break away from this silent spectacle of nature, took a sample of the water and two dead fish with him, which had not yet passed into decay. The next day he examined both together with his young assistant, whom he meanwhile called Lovis by his first name. They found that this type of algae, similar to fireflies, had a cold luminosity in their bodies, but could occur in much larger and denser quantities than those. Late in the evening, something spectacular happened. Dolphins appeared and played in the green algae cloud. The marine mammals obviously had a lot of fun.

Each of their movements created elegant vortices and currents in the luminous substance, which otherwise remained hidden from the eye. They jumped over the water in high arcs, pulled the cool glowing snakes with them high into the air, splashed as far as possible around them when they were immersed again, creating a unique firework of exploding fluorescence. The passengers gathered on board and clapped to the animals' tricks. Siebold assumed that the algae poison did not harm the dolphins because, unlike the fish, they have no gills through which it can enter the bloodstream.

This small event improved the spirit on board considerably. The next day, Siebold proposed to Captain Bonn and the officers to provide the passengers and crew with a little more entertainment. They got wooden sticks from the ship carpenter and let soldiers and sailors alike doing exercises in safe fencing fights on the main deck. Siebold explained to the young recruits how duels are fought and diligently took part in the competitions. The whole crew was cheering and applauding in exuberant mood. The next day, after more than two weeks of calm, the redeeming wind finally came up. From then on Siebold again spent more time studying in his cabin. In the evening he registered the constellations of the southern sky with Lovis and now listened to the story of his disappointed love for Adelaide. Although a steady wind was blowing, it became hotter and hotter. They approached the equator again, this time from the south. The days passed quickly now, the crew was busy, and the soldiers regularly practiced the stick fight. One afternoon it happened. The crow's nest reported views of Sumatra and Java. Shortly afterwards, all passengers and crew were assembled on deck. They struggled for places at the bulwark, on the stairs and on the freely accessible superstructures. When the promised land finally rose from the sea on the horizon, joyful cheering and jubilation broke out.

Batavia

On the evening of 13 February 1823, after a journey of one hundred and forty-three days, the *Jonge Adriana* landed at the roadstead of Batavia. Siebold had the impression that he was now a different person. After almost half a year on the oceans, locked in this ship, which he now knew better than any other place in the world, and a distance of twenty thousand *nautical miles* traversed, he felt older and more experienced. Now came the farewell of all the people with whom he had met on the trip and sometimes even made friends. For Lovis, this was obviously a terrible moment. He would sorely miss 'his Siebold', he confessed to him. He would have wanted someone like him to be his big brother. Then he had to move with his contingent to the nearby barracks. Captain Bonn also awarded Siebold with a warm and heartfelt goodbye. It meant a lot to Siebold to be appreciated by this man who was so honest and straightforward.

The Governor-General of Dutch India had prepared everything for Siebold's arrival. He was first accommodated in a Dutch-operated inn, where he was mainly provided with good food and wine. They knew about the meager food on board on such a long voyage. After all, every single Dutch had arrived on this route on Java at some point and no one had forgotten the culinary delight when they could have their first piece of fried meat with fresh, steamed vegetables and a bottle of wine. Siebold had lost a lot of weight on the trip and was pleased with this attention. He was left alone for a few days so that he could strengthen himself and use the time to get to know the city. The first encounters were exotic. He faced a strange animal world. Geckos ran unabashedly across the walls of his room chasing fat beetles that fled from them. Magnificent butterflies the size of blackbirds flew by in front of his window and it seemed to him that nature here tended into the gigantic. Then he wondered during his walks about the similarity between Batavia and Amsterdam. There were the same generous bourgeois houses and Protestant churches, only that they somehow seemed degenerate in form. The whole city was strictly symmetrical and crossed by canals, like in Holland, over which small suspension bridges led. The whole impression was flashy and pompous. Meanwhile, the giant crocodiles swimming in the canals in the middle of the city were scary. Mosquito clouds covered these stagnant waters and the humidity was breathtaking.

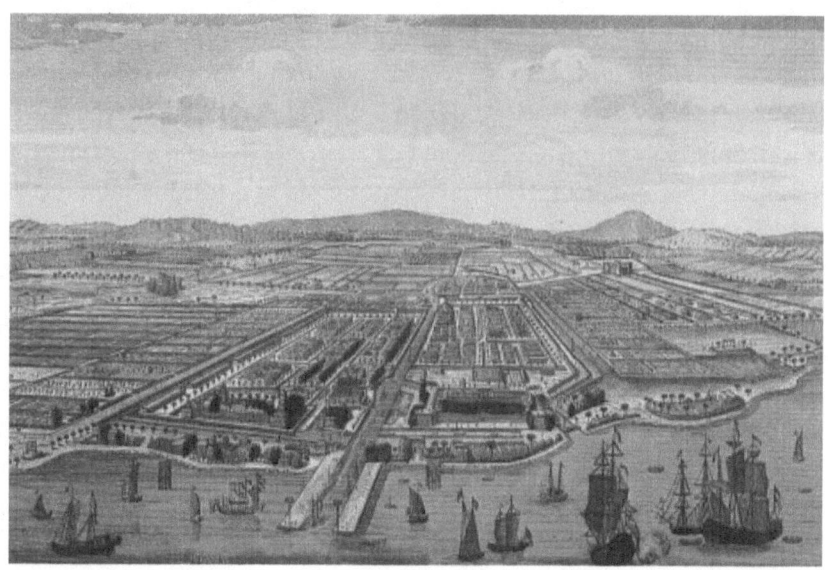

Batavia

Siebold went to the post office and visited several inns to watch the people. The local diversity of ethnic groups was also like that in Amsterdam, with the only difference that Europeans were a minority here. There were many people who looked Chinese, Thai, or Indian. But he saw no peasant settlers or white women. In contrast, countless soldiers, sailors, merchants, and subjects who obviously belonged to the riffraff. He was shocked by the way Europeans treated each other and above all by their behavior towards the natives. There was a brutal tone and, on several occasions, he witnessed widespread and unpunished violence against the Javanese. The Dutch behaved like loudmouthed knights on a raid and it seemed to be the worst kind of them that had come to wealth here. Siebold passed unreal, showy ornamental gardens and architectural monstrosities that could not decide whether they wanted to be huts or palaces. He suspected that they were the mirror images of the character of their owners. He saw fat, nouveau-rich nabobs plowing the streets of the city with an entourage of slaves, unleashing on every occasion deluges of insults on their grotesque company or other passers-by. The city was a Moloch, a horrible freak of civilization. Siebold was disappointed and disgusted. Now he understood what Captain Bonn wanted to warn him about months ago. At that time, he lacked the imagination to figure such a Sodom of colonialism.

He was therefore relieved when an envoy appeared at the hostel and transmitted his assignment as a troop doctor in the 5th Artillery Regiment in Weltevreden. He went there at once and was glad that he could leave the city. Weltevreden was only half an hour outside the city borders, but there was a civilized order as he had expected from a military base. He was given a spacious, bright house. The next day he began his service in a well-equipped practice in the main building. He was astonished at the number of sick people in the region. Many patients suffered from severe skin eczema, thrush in the mouth and throat, open inflammations, venereal diseases, or fever. One of his patients probably infected Siebold, for he was unable to get up after just a few days. He was gripped by a severe rheumatic fever and had to stay in bed for weeks, his body getting weaker and weaker.

In the meantime, the Governor-General of Dutch India, *Baron van der Capellen*, had received the letters of recommendation from the German scholars and the Inspector General Harbaur as well as a written testimony about Siebold's person from Captain Bonn. He was told how the young doctor settled in and when he heard that he had fallen ill, he immediately had him brought to his country estate in Buitenzorg. The eighteen-hour journey went to a mountainous region where the climate was like that of Europe. There Siebold should recover in the next weeks.

After spending a few days in bed, he took the first walks and admired the landscape in the midst of which Van der Capellen's spacious estate laid. This included a well-equipped botanical garden, which reminded Siebold of his native Würzburg. Van der Capellen soon invited Siebold to join him at the table, where he dined daily with the director of Buitenzorg Botanical Garden, Caspar Reinwardt, a commissioner of the Indian High Council, and Alexandra, the governor's teenage daughter.

"I hear you treated fifty-two patients in the crossing, and they all survived. There were no casualties on this journey, which is extremely rare", the Baron opened the conversation.

"Sometimes you have to force the sick to recover by nursing. Once they are exhausted, they lose their appetite and do not notice how parched they are. Then I sat down with them and spooned water and soup in, even if they didn't want it."

"Captain Bonn told me all about it. You've been very caring. He also reported that you were incessantly busy."

"I am pleased that the captain assessed me in such favorable terms. Yes, I have used the time to learn languages, continue my studies in comparative anatomy and create a collection of sea creatures. For the hardship of a long sea voyage, the best way to keep yourself safe is to talk to nature."

"Since I can't do that, what should I do if I have to go back to the Netherlands," the young lady asked.

"Take a box full of books and maybe a few plays with you. You can perform one or even two of these with crew and passengers. These people, no matter what their origin, will be grateful for any distraction. You may end up discovering your talent as a theatre director with such willing actors."

Alexandra was beaming at the thought and the other guests of the table felt well entertained by Siebold's ideas, who now clearly felt the return of his spirits. The Governor's beautiful, delicate, and lively daughter was like a tonic for him. After many months among mostly coarse men, she appeared to Siebold like an elf. Her further questions and remarks betrayed the intelligence of a slightly spoiled princess. She fired them coquettishly at Siebold, and he felt a little tickle in his heart every time.

The days passed in an alternation of social gathering, quiet rest, and renewed study. Director Reinwardt had several opportunities to marvel at Siebold's extensive knowledge of botany and zoology, and the Baron was also fascinated by the cosmopolitanism and the historical knowledge of his guest. The Baron's curious sympathy grew with each new meeting, and gradually a mild dose of fatherly love flowed into it. Van der Capellen soon discovered on Siebold the features of the son he had always wanted. As if to strengthen these imaginary family ties, he let Siebold know that he had studied together with his grandfather in Göttingen. Siebold basked in the male affection and friendship of this elegant, admirable man, who did not even hesitate to touch him and lay his hand on his arm or shoulder as soon as any pretext offered sufficient cause for it. Siebold noticed how this satisfied a strong desire, a long felt need in him. In their conversations, they kept coming back to Japan. Here, too, Siebold was well informed and the Baron supplemented his knowledge with reports on the latest developments from a political perspective.

In the Dutch colonial ministry, the opinion had been formed for some time that trade with Japan had been neglected too much and when comparing the documents and figures of the past one hundred years one had to register a clear decline. This was not an isolated phenomenon, for the entire balance of payments of the once infinitely powerful *Dutch East India Company* had deteriorated dramatically since 1770. After the company went bankrupt in 1800 and was taken over by the Crown, the fate of the colonies was no longer to be controlled from a purely economic point of view, but military, strategic and political goals were to be incorporated. The Dutch government had discovered that the colonies are of national interest. Java was placed under the administration of the Crown and its ministries, and all trade should now be planned according to political guidelines.

Then came the French occupation of the Netherlands, which was renamed Batavian Republic. The English then took over the Dutch colonies of Cape Town, Ceylon, and Java. Until Napoleon's defeat and the Congress of Vienna, where the Netherlands was restored, and Java was returned, the small island of Dejima, on the edge of the world in the port of Nagasaki, was for ten years the last place on earth where the Dutch flag was flying. In this consciousness, which also held a certain form of national gratitude, they wanted to revive relations with Japan.

On the evening of April 14, 1823, the Buitenzorg society gathered again at the richly laid table and this time some foreign guests had been added. Van der Capellen took the floor right at the beginning.

"Honored guests, dear friends, I have some news for you. After careful consideration and extensive consultation with the Indian High Council, I have decided to fill one of the most important positions in my administration. Mr. von Siebold, my young friend, I would be pleased if you would go to Japan on my behalf as the personal physician of the resident of Dejima. Everything I have heard and seen from you, including your literary work, the systematics of your studies and your impeccable manners, all that has strengthened my opinion that you are the right man for this important and demanding mission."

There was applause at the table and Siebold was speechless. When he had regained his composure, he thanked him and agreed. The Baron then informed him that he would travel with the newly elected resident as early as June.

That same night Siebold wrote a letter to Lotz, who was best suited to spread this good news among his friends and relatives in Würzburg.

"It could have taken me many more years to get from here to Japan–if at all! But I seem to be under a good star and just–maybe for a moment–to have what you call fortune, this magical form of happiness that makes the impossible happen. It was a lot faster than I could have imagined. I succeeded in what I wanted. I am now awaited by death or a happy, honorable life! Do you know, dear Lotz, what else the Baron van der Capellen said at the table in front of the assembled guests? *'We expect him to do an excellent job, for our Mr. von Siebold'*, and he turned to me, *'shall become a second Kämpfer and Thunberg.'*"

Siebold concealed the Baron's last words from Lotz, although it was precisely those that prevented him from sleeping that night:"...*if not even a second Alexander von Humboldt, the Humboldt of the Far East.*"

Chapter III

Japan

*The Journey Continues–An Aesthete with Stethoscope–Secretum
Tabularorum Magnorum–Aaron Mendelssohn–The Castaways–
The Great Storm–The Arrival*

The Journey Continues

The governor's secretary sent him a letter the following afternoon, regulating all the details. On the sidelines of the dinner, Siebold had discussed with van der Capellen what equipment and financial resources he would need for this expedition. Van der Capellen calmed him down and gave him notice that there was already a generous arrangement for this. Indeed, as of now, his salary increased from three thousand six hundred to five thousand three hundred guilders per year, he would receive a share of ten percent of his personally managed trading turnover as well as free accommodation and food on the island colony Dejima. In addition, the government provided him with a one-off sum of one thousand eight hundred guilders for the scientific preparations for the trip. In mid-May, he returned to Batavia from the governor's country estate. Rested and full of zest for action, he no longer felt as threatened by the city as during his first stay. He could even amuse himself about the grotesque figures he met there again. The houses and people seemed to have sprung from the wild, brightly colored pictures that children like to paint. He concentrated on assembling the equipment for his expedition. The chief financial director had the money paid out to him and got him material from the military medical camp in Weltevreden. The warehouse management also helped Siebold to get some physical and geometric instruments in the shortest time, including an air pump, an *electrifying machine*, and a *galvanic* apparatus to impress the Japanese. He was particularly happy about the purchase of an additional, significantly improved microscope, which he had long waited for to be completed. Since his studies, he knew that achromatic lenses could now be produced from flint and crown glass. They were already used before 1800 for the construction of telescopes. Achromatic lenses have the considerable advantage that the observed objects are no longer surrounded by a ring of rainbow colors, which was unavoidable until then. Siebold was aware that attempts were now being made to use these new lenses in microscopes as well. Now he finally had such a fabulous instrument.

He ordered a list of scientific manuals and the latest standard works from the military administration in the fields of biology, physics, medicine, geography, and botany. He also obtained the most recent travel reports on Japan, published in 1799 by the Frenchman Lapérouse, in 1812 by the German Langsdorff and in 1812 and 1817 by the Russians *Krusenstern* and *Golownin*. They had all tried to establish a connection with Japan at the beginning of the century. In vain. Golownin had even been captured. The last scientific report about Japan, the *Resa uti Europa, Africa, Asia förrat aren 1770-1779* of the Swede *Carl Peter Thunberg*, was already half a century old. Thunberg worked for a year in 1774 as the base's doctor on the island of Dejima and was thus one of Siebold's predecessors. Siebold still possessed the original of this book, which he had acquired years ago but could only read with great difficulty. This time he ordered the Dutch translation. Finally, he had a proper load of beer and wine put together, always anxious to keep the Japanese hosts happy at all times. The beer was bottled and stored in plaster so that it could easily grow twelve years and older. Of course, his fortepiano was not to be missed either, which he had brought from Weltevreden. He hadn't played on it since his departure from Würzburg, as it was stowed away in the hold on the first ship's journey and he also lacked the leisure to play the piano. Now he was looking forward to having it with him in Japan.

Two merchant ships, the *Drie Gezusters* and the *Onderneeming*, were ready at anchor for the voyage to Japan, but for unknown reasons, the departure was repeatedly delayed. Captain Jacometti of the larger *Drie Gezusters*, with whom Siebold was to travel, was not a bit talkative and so Siebold had no choice but to wait. But the wait was worth it because a ship from Rotterdam arrived and surprisingly brought a parcel for Siebold, which was delivered to him at once. It was a book with a message from Don Mastema.

Dear Major Doctor von Siebold, dear friend;

I was very pleased to hear that you followed the path I once showed you. In order to stay in your favorable consideration, I have once again looked in my scientific treasure chamber for an appropriate souvenir and found the enclosed. I hope it will provide you with the services you need to complete the stage ahead of you.

Your most devoted

Don Mastema

Gosh, he thought, only the devil knew how the Basque could follow his trail to here and fit him so precisely with this show. Neither the parcel nor the letter bore the sender's address—as Don Mastema did when he sent the Japanese work of Bernhardus Varenius. The book, separately wrapped in tissue paper, was a heavy, leather-bound folio. Siebold unpacked it, opened the book cover, and couldn't believe his eyes. The title was *Secretum Tabularorum Magnorum* by a certain Aventinus Meyerbeer. Siebold had never heard of the author or the title. What could that be, the 'Secret of the Big Maps'? Even more astonishing, however, was the fact that the frontispiece, on which a monk surrounded by angels, demons and geometric instruments could be seen in the cartographic work, was not printed but painted by hand. It was spotlessly beautiful and seemed to live. The spatial and sensual impression of the scene was so intense that he thought he saw movements in it. Siebold continued to leaf through the pages and his assumption was confirmed. It was an original! The whole book, artfully written by hand and full of detailed drawings of enigmatic maps, was possibly even unique. It was always reported that in the Middle Ages the monks had written and copied sacred books in this way. There were handwritten copies of ancient medical books from Hippocrates to Galen, which were diligently crafted in monasteries. Siebold had never held in his hands a work from the time before Gutenberg's printing press began its triumphal proliferation, but he could certainly say that this copy did not come from the Middle Ages. For it was written neither in Middle High German nor in Early New High German, but in common modern High German.

On June 28, 1823, the time had finally come. The *Drie Gezusters* and the *Onderneeming* were ready to leave. Siebold was to travel with *Colonel de*

Sturler, the newly appointed resident on the island of Dejima. He had met him at a Batavian officers' club just before departure. Sturler was in his mid-forties and, despite his burly frame, an intelligent man. He had distinguished himself several times as a gunner in the war against the French. During his career, which brought him to the Colonel as a permanent reward for his extraordinary military service, he had successfully compensated for the shortcomings of his simple background and education. He matured into a man who was highly educated by his standards. Now he was on the road as the top envoy in the Dutch Japan mission and as such Siebold's immediate superior. Siebold, who otherwise had a good access to various characters, could not cross the line between politeness and sympathy at Sturler. Sturler, for his part, showed no need to transform their formal relationship into a friendly one. He was interested in Siebold's plans for his stay in Japan and he also knew that this project enjoyed support from the highest authorities. It was therefore his firm intention to support Siebold in all points and to always be accessible for all scientific and cultural concerns of the mission. Compared to most of his predecessors, Sturler was a liberal, wise, and sociable resident. At the time of the *East Indian Company*, the Dutch were almost exclusively represented in Japan by merchants who were greedy for money, opportunistic and rough. Siebold knew this and was pleased with the new, enlightened trade policy, with which the volume of business transactions was to increase again, but this time accompanied by a lively scientific, cultural, and diplomatic exchange. He was also relieved that such a demure and pleasantly reserved personality as Sturler had been assigned to lead the mission.

The anchorage of the ships in the roads was about half a nautical mile from the mainland. Numerous fully manned rowing boats had accompanied the crew and passengers on board. They called out to their relatives, acquaintances, and friends, cheered and waved untiringly. When the anchor winch finally groaned and the massive chain links clank, the bells rang on the surrounding Chinese ships and called for morning prayer. Siebold watched the hectic activity on board and the hoisting of the sails with a naive heartbeat. It was the exhilarating feeling to have swaying ship planks under his feet again, to feel the sea day and night, to be in constant movement, again on a great journey that takes him even further away from his homeland. He was surprised how he had learned to appreciate life on the ship and had already missed it, even though in the short time and under the many impressions of his stay on Java this missing could not yet grow into an acute longing. On the first evening, he sat in the cabin, which would be his home again for months, reading the diary notes of the first journey and summarizing the mission once again with the due pathos.

"The forced idleness of a sea voyage leads involuntarily to deeper reflection, and the soul, wavering between hope and fear, deals with the most varied images of the future. Nine months ago, I left Europe, staggered on the vast ocean for five months and happily reached the land of destination. As a newcomer in a tropical climate, I was at once struck by a serious illness and found myself more often displeased as a military doctor. Unexpectedly I now find myself out of this situation. I am now being brought closer to the goal I had set myself on my trip to East India, for I am about to sail to the strangest and most distant country that Europeans visit. But unfortunately! not to a country where they live as free men; no, to a country where the state wisdom of an Asian nation keeps us excluded from all free movement with country and people! But the examples of enthusiasm and perseverance that history preserves for us from the lives of naturalists and travelers keep my courage alive. And when the already excited imagination of a young traveler decides, like the venerable role models, to endure all troubles and dangers, then he feels irresistibly driven to run towards this place, where also for him as an admirer and promoter of science a hearth of sacrifice is blazing, on which he may lay down his small gifts".

He noticed how his style was ostentatious when he wrote about himself, how solemn and almost heavy-blooded the melody sounded from the lines. But in the face of the history that he would now write and in which he would have an important place, this solemnity seemed to him nevertheless appropriate. He could now finally begin with his *bibliomorphosis*, with the transformation of his life into a great adventurer and explorer novel.

The next morning Sumatra, the main island of East India, came into sight. Along their coastline, they drove towards the smaller island of Bangka and passed the waterway between the two landmasses. The heat and humidity increased tremendously. Every day, yes, almost every nautical mile they approached the equator, the column of mercury seemed to rise further. The light and steady south-west monsoon wind provided the crew with some cooling. For Siebold, the journey was quite varied and distracted him from the suffering from the heat because the land was still in sight and the coastlines could be explored well with the strong telescopes. The crew and some passengers watched him with astonishment as he climbed barefoot into the crow's nest below the top of the mast. When he arrived there, however, he looked down and the height was scary for him. Suddenly he had to struggle with a fear he didn't know yet. But as soon as he had taken the telescope and searched the horizon, he was distracted, and the feeling of dizziness abated. Yet, that didn't spare him the way back, which was now much harder for him than the ascent. Less strenuous was the observation of the seabed, which shimmered green, yellow, or blue in a few *fathoms* of depth. He saw huge swordfish, *Xiphias*, and eagle rays, *Myliobates*, gliding through the water, whose weight he estimated at between five and six hundred pounds. He regretted not getting closer to these majestic animals and thought about a glass cage to be developed for this purpose.

They experienced the full force of the tropical climate when the mouth of the great river of Palembang came into sight on July 5th and the ships anchored at Fort Mentok. They were now protected under land in the calm. Siebold watched as the tar between the planks began to liquefy and the sun boiled the last remnants of resin from the wood of the hull. In the evening a surprisingly mild and fragrant breeze blew offshore. The sun set behind the mountains of Sumatra and on the coastline a tropical painting of splendidly shining bushes and lush woodlands, which were repeatedly surmounted by palm trees, appeared in this warm light. In between, the red roofs of the fort blinked on the hills. Shortly afterward, as every evening, Siebold followed the communication between the two ships, which took place with the help of voice tubes and flag signals, in order to prepare the mutual visits of the captains. This time it was Captain Lells from the *Onderneeming* who came over to the *Drie Gezuster*s. To celebrate the day, Captain Jacometti had the officers' mess staff set up the table on the foredeck so that the captains and officers could enjoy the wonderful view together over dinner. Colonel de Sturler turned to Siebold with a smile in an unobserved moment.

"This was my idea. A warhorse like Jacometti would never have thought of his own accord to spoil us with such comfort. I am also pleased that he has accepted my proposal to extend the usual round and to invite other passengers to the officers' table. As a South German, you should appreciate this informal conviviality, right? He pronounced the German word 'Gemütlichkeit' with a Dutch accent like a gargled 'chemuiitliich-chaiit'.

"Yes, absolutely right," Siebold replied amusedly. "I am very grateful for this idea. During my student days, we spent many afternoons and evenings with our professors in the beer garden in Würzburg." When they sat down with two dozen officers and guests at the table, which was covered with white tablecloths, gold-sheathed porcelain, and silverware, Sturler continued. "I'm going ashore tomorrow to pay a visit to the resident of Bankga. Usually, he's on an island we passed and he's digging for pewter in the pits. But these days he's in Fort Mentok. Tin is an important commodity for our business with the Japanese. That's why I wanted to talk to the resident about the expected prices and quantities in the coming years. There is also an interesting young man in Fort Mentok who, like you, is a medical officer. Won't you come with me when we ferry tomorrow? I will not make use of you for any protocol duties. I just thought you might take the opportunity to go ashore, gather some immediate impressions and meet *Surgeon Major Fritze*."

"With great pleasure," Siebold replied, although he understood perfectly that Sturler was not trying to please him with everything he did and said, but only wanted to deliver good and meaningful reports to van der Capellen in the end. Sturler thus cultivated a highly developed form of impersonal commitment, which Siebold was irritated by, but to which he believed he would have to get used. The open-air dinner was very well received. There was marinated beef with shallots, ginger, and prunes, going with red wine with cinnamon or beer on request. The atmosphere was cheerful, and the conversation was much more exuberant than usually in the wardroom below deck. Captain Jacometti did not let the sailors go to rack and ruled to open two beer barrels for them too. Siebold was surprised that both ships had loaded almost twice as much beer as drinking water. Sturler explained to him that in the heat of these latitudes, where eating is often simply not a pleasure, seafarers are kept strong and happy with beer at the same time.

An Aesthete with a Stethoscope

The next morning, they went ashore. Due to the mangroves, the two rowboats did not quite make it to the beach and Siebold had to be carried on the shoulders of a strong sailor through the shallow, muddy water, which he found embarrassing and almost humiliating. Sturler, who himself sat on the shoulders of a man who, however, was smaller and less solidly built than himself, looked at Siebold's unpleasantness and laughed slightly mockingly. From the beach, they went directly to the hospital, which was located at the edge of the fort on a hill. Sturler bid goodbye in front of the entrance and went on to his meeting with the two residents of Bankga and Sumatra. Siebold entered the flat, spacious wooden building. In the main hall, where there were about one hundred beds–less than half of which were occupied–he saw a delicate man with wild hair and an enormous mustache, who was in the process of *auscultating* a patient. He obviously listened to a patient's lungs, but he used a device that Siebold had never seen before. It was stuck in the doctor's ears like a big clip, from which a tube led to a can, which he slid jerkily over the patient's back. Siebold approached and introduced himself.

"Pray, Major Fritze, allow me, Major Doctor von Siebold, the doctor of the Japanese mission to Japan on my journey there." Fritze turned around, took the instrument out of his ears, stood up and looked at Siebold in amazement. Then he laughed broadly. "Pleased to meet you. Fritze, Chief of Staff to Mentok. I... you'll have to excuse me. I'm a little speechless. It gives me great pleasure to meet you so unexpectedly. Nobody told me you'd land here on your way to Japan. Do you know your reputation? And then... well, how should I put it? What an appearance you are! I must be careful not to do a Chinese three-quarter kowtow in front of you, which means that you almost kiss your own feet when bowing out of reverence for the other person. I know so many stories about the Siebolds, and now I face the youngest hopeful scion of this great family. Let's go for a walk, I want to show you my humble facility." He put one hand on Siebold's back and carefully pushed it in the direction he pointed with the other hand.

"Thank you very much for this compliment, even if it is still underserved. Because as a doctor, you are at least one step ahead of me. What is that device you just used?"

"Ah, you mean the *stethoscope*," taking the instrument off his neck and giving it to Siebold.

"This is a wonderful invention and arrived here just a few weeks ago. It is an excellent aid for amplifying organic noise. Above all, it serves, of course, to better monitor the heart and lungs."

"Can I give it a try?"

"Of course. Pick a patient." Siebold approached a young man who actually looked quite healthy and asked him in Malay to be allowed to do a brief examination on him. He opened his white, light shirt without a word and let Siebold willingly touch his chest with the device.

"Now I'm gobsmacked. You already speak Malay! You really live up to your reputation." Then he remained silent so that Siebold could concentrate on the patient's heart sounds and lung noises.

"This is indeed an extraordinary improvement. I can almost hear the sound of his blood."

"Yes, but you should not overlook that this instrument does much more than improving medical diagnosis. It also has the effect of a magic wand. Since I have been using the stethoscope, I have, especially among the natives who call themselves Orang Gunong or 'mountain people', the status of a real witch doctor with magical powers. My charisma and with it the patients' trust in my healing art have grown considerably with the instrument. I imagine that this process could be observed in all peoples who are not familiar with our Western medicine. He laughed compassionately at Siebold, who was much bigger than him. Siebold was, however, interested in another aspect of Fritze's remark.

"The Orang Gunong is the 'mountain people', as you said. Then the orangutans are 'forest dwellers' in their own language?"

"Yes, that's right."

"Does that mean the Malay people don't see a significant difference between themselves and the monkeys?"

"Indeed. The Orang Gunong even claim that the orangutans don't speak just so they don't have to work." They both laughed. Siebold, however, did not let go of the thought.

"I must confess that I am amazed," Siebold mused. "I have never heard of such intimacy between human beings and the womb of nature. The serious question is whether, if they cannot distinguish between themselves and the animals, they themselves are already human beings."

"Dear, esteemed colleague. You'd have to see an orangutan up close. They have to look this good-natured, hairy forest dweller in the eye and observe them in their dealings with one another. You will inevitably ask yourself whether these beings are as fundamentally different from us as academic teaching demands. Then you will reconsider your question."

Siebold looked at him thoughtfully and felt he had received an important lesson from this little, brightly awake man. Among all these rather harsh and unthinking colonists he has met so far on his journey, this modest, kind doctor was willing to open the concept of humanity to creatures from the animal kingdom as soon as they qualified themselves through their behavior. Suddenly, almost in the form of enlightenment in miniature, Siebold understood how little human the human beings themselves frequently are. He clearly remembered the disgust he felt when he arrived in Batavia. Hadn't he compared people with blind worms and vermin in moments of indignation? Of course, Christianity and humanism teach that there is a core of dignity that forms an inalienable part of humanity even in the most miserable and depraved subject. But wasn't Fritze right then that other beings, namely through their behavior, could also earn this dignity or even have always been part of it? At the same time, he respected the natives' view that there is no substantial difference between them and the orangutans, but only a gradual, an accidental one. Instead of explaining the natives for animals, which Siebold was also inclined to do briefly and which would inevitably have made join him the spiritual society of the cruel Dutchman of Batavia, Fritze saw living creatures among the animals that could be human in the best sense, even more human than many specimens of the actual human species. All this, thought in a short moment, caused admiration in Siebold for the unprecedented lack of prejudice of the little staff doctor Fritze.

They continued their walk through the hospital complex. "We mainly treat *dysenteries*, liver diseases, and foot oaths. There are also cases of *syphilis* and eye inflammation. Here's a patient I had to amputate two weeks ago." Together they looked at the already well-healed stump of the leg and agreed that the process of wound healing is progressing much faster among the Indian peoples than among the Europeans. Siebold noticed how neat and clean the facilities were and how the dry climate in the flat wooden buildings corresponded exactly to what he considered necessary for the recovery of patients. Fritze said that he had copied the English design of houses in India, where the colonists lived almost exclusively in such so-called *bungalows* because otherwise, they would not survive the humid heat. The openings on all sides of the buildings were important for constant ventilation, just like the position of the entire hospital on the hill, where it was exposed to the healthy change of land and sea winds. Thus, Siebold got to know in Fritze a thoroughly practical person who paid attention to these things and incorporated the latest developments in the fields of diagnosis, therapy, dietetics, hygiene, and nursing into his hospital operations.

After lunch, Sturler came back to pick up Siebold. Fritze apologized briefly and came back with two narrow boxes in his hand.

"My dear Mr. von Siebold, I would like to seal our friendship and ask you to keep in touch from now on. I am very curious how you are doing in Japan and I would be delighted to hear from you by letter. Take these two stethoscopes with you on your journey, because they will be useful to you. I'll give you two samples because in a foreign country you'll need one for yourself and the second one as a gift for personalities of high standing or other good friends."

"I would like to thank you sincerely and combine this with the promise to keep you informed of all important and interesting events in Japan," replied Siebold, visibly moved. Sturler watched attentively this small ceremony between the two men, which took place as if he were not even present.

Secretum Tabularorum Magnorum

The next day, the two ships set sail again and Siebold continued his observations of nature. The journey went slowly because the wind rose to a light breeze only in the morning and evening. During the day they often stood still, and the sails hung like wet sheets on the masts. When the sun went down, the South China Sea, which they had reached in the meantime, was laid out before them like a huge cauldron in which all the world's blood bubbled quietly. Siebold, unlike the rest of the crew, enjoyed this time because he was able to analyze every piece of flotsam and he was fascinated by the huge shoals of fish that swam under the ship, always followed by flocks of gluttonous terns, gulls, and petrels. He also started learning Japanese and perfecting his Dutch. His pronunciation was still colored with a southern German accent and he was still uncertain in his grammar. Now he also had enough time to deal with Don Mastemas gift, the *Secretum tabularorum magnorum*. Siebold wondered about the Latin in which the author Aventinus Meyerbeer had written the book. The style did not resemble the classic Ciceronian model, which, despite complicated hypotactic structures, was characterized by clarity and elegance, nor the scholastic, pedantic expression known throughout Europe since the Middle Ages. It was a simple and sensual language that stuck in the reader's mind at once. There was an anointing melody to it, which, when Siebold read the lyrics aloud for himself as a test, developed a sacred atmosphere. It was like a ghost that would lay down over the pages when they were read. It reminded him of–the Bible.

Meyerbeer told a great epic about the art of cartography since the time of Ptolemy, who worked in Alexandria in the second century A.D. In his book *Almagest*, Ptolemy had not only depicted the entire celestial building with all the stars on a map. He also tabulated the positions of the most important places of the then known world and provided the basis for the later scientific geography. Then there was the magnificent work of the Flemish geographer *Gerhardus Mercator*, who in 1567 assumed a spherical form of the earth for the first time and projected it onto a plane. This finally solved the problem of uneven distribution of lengths and latitudes. By this time, the great voyages of discovery had long since begun, but the captains always ventured to the supposed edge of the world without a single usable map. There were the Portuguese red *roteiros*, but they were strictly secret and only insiders could read them. These books, which had maps of varying quality and detailed travel reports of the navigators, contained the entire naval power of this proud nation. When the Dutch began to rebel against Catholic Spain and Portugal, they also wanted to rise to the rank of a maritime power. Although they were already excellent sailors and shipbuilders, they did not know the seas. They managed to get some roteiros into their possession. But almost a dozen expeditions with even more ships had run aground, crashed on the coast or their crews died of thirst and starvation on the open sea. The Portuguese had deliberately forged the stolen roteiros to mislead the Dutch. The Dutch East Indian company then produced and collected reliable maps for a century, which they compiled in a 'Secret Atlas' with which they finally broke the Portuguese domination of the South West Pacific around 1700.

Breathlessly, Siebold followed the history of geographical maps, for until then he had not realized how much power they had always held. Conversely, he had only judged them on their usefulness and accuracy. But they were, like the secret atlas of the Dutch, the highest state secret and many who had stolen, sold, or lost them had to pay with their lives. Siebold noticed that Meyerbeer's beautiful book was undated. Its content almost reached the present day, but its material design could have been five hundred years old.

The history of cartography was only the preparation of the actual topic. Meyerbeer wanted to penetrate to the secret of the maps as such. He wanted to show how the 'Great Maps' differed from all the others. His central teaching was simple. The secret of the Great Maps is not the struggle for power and wealth, but the search for God. They are the guides through creation to its Creator. That one can become rich and powerful with them is only a welcome side effect. In fact, however, the maps are the key to paradise, postulated Meyerbeer. He admitted that he knew well how much such heretical views would earn him the cleansing flames of the stake. But he believed that unlocking this mystery is a revelation that came directly from God to him and which he therefore could not keep to himself. The Great Maps, he continued, began, as in Ptolemy, with the measurement of the sky, and they will end there again. Mercator had written the most important work in this field on the basis of his first angularly projected world maps. His *Atlas Sive Cosmographicae Meditationes De Fabrica Mundi Et Fabricati Figura* of 1595, the 'Atlas or Cosmographic Observations of the Created World and the Shape of the Created', was a five-volume cosmography of creation that remained unfinished. But it showed the only true goal of all cartographic research.

When the earth as the here and now of creation is fully grasped, then the exploration of heaven and the hereafter continues. But this search can only begin once the earth has been measured exactly. According to Meyerbeer, this required three qualities that a geographer absolutely needs to create a Great Map. On the one hand, he must be able to measure its location well, which means that he must always be able to precisely record longitude and latitude as well as height and water depth. On the other hand, he has to draw error-free, because a wrong line spoils a whole card and thus the work of months and years. The third and most important characteristic, however, is the belief in the perfection of the Divine Creation and the completely unclouded will to uncover, measure and understand it down to the last, hidden corner of the universe.

Siebold provisionally kept to the obvious. The mastery of cartographic drawing can significantly speed up the creation of maps–and it enables the cartographer to make copies quickly. Therefore, drawing exercises and the listing of standard forms for guiding the pen in drawing took up almost half of the book. Siebold, fascinated by these practical instructions, practiced for hours every day on countless sheets drawing vertical views of mountains, rock formations, gorges, paths, roads, settlements, rivers, coastlines, reefs, and shallows quickly and accurately. After a short time, he had developed a remarkable skill in drawing maps.

Aaron Mendelssohn

These days a man appeared at the lunch table in the officers' mess who had already caught Siebold's attention during the great dinner on the deck off Fort Mentok. Like then, he was in a good mood and spoke almost incessantly. His fluent Dutch had a minor accent, a slightly harder stroke of the tongue, which proved him to be German. Nevertheless, the officers obviously enjoyed listening to him. He was, as Siebold learned, invited by the officers with the captain's permission to entertain them in the wardroom and he seemed to tell interesting stories with a sympathetic voice. Siebold sat down in a vacant seat closer to the action after some officers had already returned to their duties or to their cabins. The lecture of the stranger was about the natives of Greenland and the beauty of the crystals, the planetary orbits and the volcanoes in the deep sea. The officers and lieutenants made explanatory remarks and asked him questions. He repeatedly drew short lines of connection between his observations to illustrate their significance for the development of human culture.

Early that evening, Siebold saw the man on the foredeck. He sat on a three-legged folding stool in front of an easel with a view of the other decks and drew with charcoal pens. Siebold climbed the stairs and walked towards him.

"Good day to you, Sir," he preempted Siebold.

"You are the Bavarian doctor working for the Colonial Ministry, aren't you?"

"You're in the picture. Yes, that's me and my name is Philip Franz von Siebold, Surgeon-Major in the service of His Dutch Majesty."

"Pleased to meet you. I am Aaron Mendelssohn, merchant and traveler."

"Merchant? That's amazing. I was impressed by your conversation in the officers' mess. There was nothing commercial about it. Neither is the artistic activity you're doing here right now."

Mendelssohn laughed embarrassed.

"Thank you very much. Well, I don't manage to hide very well that my quality as a traveling salesman is only a means to be able to explore the world as unhindered as possible following my scientific and aesthetic inclinations. You see, it would have been difficult to make this trip to Japan on behalf of a university. I would have had to gather many patrons to make this possible," he concluded, while he jokingly pulled a sour face.

"What are you doing to finance this adventure?"

"I have been commissioned by several publishing houses in Amsterdam, Paris, and London to procure literary works from Japan, which may be translated and published in Europe. We have no knowledge of Japanese literature, philosophy, and science. But we know that the scholars there know the most important European works."

"How can you work for several publishers at the same time without getting into a conflict in the selection of books and manuscripts? Everyone wants the best if I'm not mistaken."

"It's quite simple because every publisher wants me to explore a certain field of knowledge or a certain literary genre."

"Do you speak Japanese?"

"This is not an unimportant point. No, not yet."

"Then how could you make it credible that you could even do the job?" Siebold noticed that he became too pushy with his questions. But Mendelssohn took it with humor and answered with a smile.

"I speak and write fluently Russian, French, Hebrew, Arabic, Portuguese, Latin–and as you have heard I also speak Dutch. I have been gifted by nature in this respect. The acquisition of a language is easy for me. It will take me an estimated six weeks to speak fluently with the Japanese."

Mendelssohn didn't seem much older than Siebold. His dark, half-long hair blew wildly around his head in the light evening breeze, from which two large, lively eyes looked at Siebold friendly and with curiosity. He was dressed in fine, grey cloth, thin and airy, which dressed his rather *leptosome* frame. Ideal for this voyage in the sultry Chinese Sea.

"Now let me ask you a few questions for a change," Mendelssohn remarked graciously after a short break.

"Are you really a doctor, so, just a doctor, or are you traveling in this disguise like me?"

"Mendelssohn, you amaze me again. Where did you get such a hunch? We've never met, and I don't know what source you could draw from to suspect hidden motives for my journey."

"Don't worry. I'm just a judge of character. And maybe a good observer."

"All right, then. I shouldn't make it inappropriately suspenseful. Yes, I intend to be much more than a simple doctor in Nagasaki. I have an extensive assignment and even more extensive ideas about the actual research I want to do in Japan. The goals of your project clearly converge with my plans. Besides, I don't know the Japanese language any more than you do. Maybe we could find a common theme here. That would make me happy, all the more so since I would certainly benefit more from it than you," he said with a smile and relief.

"Agreed. But only if you stop talking in that stalked fashion. The Germans, and therefore you too, tend to think that speaking and writing are the same things. Just relax! If you speak to me, please not in this official scholarly German."

"I'll do my best."

He liked this man and he could be useful, too. But in reality, Siebold felt, it was all about something completely different. After the cordial proximity of van der Capellen on Java and the short meeting with the surgeon Fritze on Sumatra, Siebold was looking for a continuation of such acquaintances. The fatherly soul of the old governor general had made Siebold receptive to this kind of male intimacy for the first time and he could hardly conceal from himself that he longed to get more of it with a certain melancholy. It was only a transparent attempt of self-deception to explain the usefulness of this man in detail so that he did not have to justify inwardly the feeling of a swelling sympathy any further.

Until then, the trip had been without any incidents or inconvenience. Siebold explained Mendelssohn, whom he now saw every day, what investigations he carried out. Together they watched gluttonous seabreams, chased after flying fish or a large shark that had been lurking behind the ship's rudder for days, caught sea snakes with the harpoon and took speed measurements with the logline. At its end was a wooden board that was attached like a kite. Once thrown into the water, the wooden board at once set itself up vertically and offered resistance, so that the line ran off over a drum. The length of the unwound line within fifteen seconds provided the basis for calculating the speed. They compared the results of this method with the measurements they made with the help of drifting seaweed or other flotsam as points of orientation.

Gradually the duration of the stay at sea began to become noticeable again. As with Siebold's last trip, the hygienic conditions deteriorated, the smell returned, and food became scarce. The latter was caused early on by the fact that the vermin had taken over control on board. The various cargoes the ship had transported in East India in recent years, particularly firewood and sugar, have created a permanent population of scorpions, centipedes, and spiders. These, in turn, had multiplied considerably after they had succeeded in accessing food supplies. But the real plague was the cockroaches, the Blattae orientalis. Hundreds of thousands of them were on board and their disgusting smell got stuck on everything they touched. Where they came into contact with food, everything was hopelessly spoiled. But also clothes, hammocks, ropes, and all utensils were infected with their stench. Siebold came into Mendelssohn's cabin one evening with a bowl in his hand. After unsuccessfully trying to chase away the animals with the strongest Cajeput oil, an essential oil from an Indonesian myrtle species that smells of camphor and eucalyptus, he had copied a simple trick from the sailors. He showed Mendelssohn how they hunted down the disgusting vermin. He half-filled the bowls with water and covered their rim with sugar dissolved in red wine. This offer was completely irresistible to the cockroaches. The next morning the bowl was full of the drowned beasts. It was not a pleasant sight, but when Siebold and Mendelssohn emptied their bowls into the sea, they felt a certain satisfaction that they had not only defeated the annoying enemy in this battle but could also feed the fish with their carcasses. In jest, they solemnly reached out their hands. The battle they won was a small triumph, but they would never win the war.

As they passed the small archipelago of Pulo Condore on July 18th, a Chinese junk crossed their course. Siebold was fascinated by the hulking sailing ship. It was plump and wide, had hardly any draught and was built raw. Captain Jacometti said that about eight hundred Chinese were crowded together there under the worst hygienic conditions. It was one of many ships on which the desperate were brought to Java to try their luck.

On July 22nd they crossed Macclesfield Bank, a huge reef of red corals. It was still deep enough that it could be travelled on everywhere. In a few years or decades, however, this would change as the corals continued to grow. Siebold wished nothing more than to be able to observe the underwater landscape better. He was hoping for a total lull. Even better would have been a construction he had thought of before when he wanted to watch the fish: a wooden box with a glass window embedded in the bottom. However, there were no devices for this on the ship and he did not even dare to make Jacometti this proposal. Two days later, the same high swell with surf was suddenly sighted on the open sea as before on the reef. This was a clear sign of shallow water. Jacometti rushed into his cabin, checked his maps, and leafed through his notes hectically. Then he ran up again just as quickly and shouted to the helmsman with all his strength to turn off at once. They were heading straight for the Praters Cliff under full canvas! The mate immediately fired a warning shot with the cannon for the *Onderneeming*. Both ships just managed to sail around the razor-sharp underwater rocks, which were lurking just a fathom or even less deep under the water surface. Only after the panic on board had subsided did Siebold realize that this was the most dangerous situation of his entire journey so far.

The Shipwrecked

In the following days, a first fine haze condensed into thick, cloudy mist, which was repeatedly traversed by strong gusts. The ship made a lot of speed at times, but the position could not be determined. Jacometti announced his concern that they could suddenly arrive or even collide with another ship. On 27 July the fog finally cleared, and the volcanic shores of *Formosa* came into sight. Longingly, the Dutch peered over to the coast of this beautiful island, which once belonged to the Dutch colonies. For the connection between Java and Japan, Formosa could have developed into a strategically important intermediate station. But in 1683 it fell under the rule of Chinese pirates. They were therefore not allowed to approach the coast yet wanted to keep it in sight to be able to orientate themselves on it for a while.

Then the weather changed in a strange way. Wind direction and current suddenly stood against each other. The waves became shorter and shorter and formed a surge around the ship. This created a loud, monotonous stomping that strained the crew's nerves to the extreme for several days and nights. The men couldn't sleep anymore. The whole hull of the boat served as a drum for the beat of the waves. On the morning of August 5th, just as they reached the cloudy northern tip of Formosa, the scout sighted slightly off course a floating ship without mast and sail. Jacometti decided to approach the damaged vehicle. When they had made sure that there were still people on board, the *Drie Gezusters* was brought about and lowered a sloop. Jacometti, who wanted to supervise the rescue himself and climb into the boat with him, gave Siebold permission to go with him after his urgent request. The wind was strong, and the waves went up. It was only with great effort that they managed to reach the small drifting wreck. Then Siebold almost took his breath away when he saw the crew. They were Japanese! The first Japanese people he was to see were shipwrecked. No one expected to find them so far off their own coasts. The Japanese had no seaworthy ships and limited themselves to coastal shipping.

The men of the disabled Japanese sailor cheered when they realized that it was Dutchmen who wanted to take them in. They knew that the

Netherlands were the only nation that their country still had good relations with. They could also assume that their rescuers were on their way to their Japanese homeland. At the same time, two more sloops that the *Onderneeming* had dropped were approaching. The Japanese captain struggled with himself and his crew for a while to decide whether they were allowed to leave the ship at all. Using sign language, he told the Dutch that they must make a hole in the bottom of the ship to make it sink. Jacometti did not quite understand what the purpose was, but he agreed. After the twenty-four Japanese sailors with the most necessary luggage were distributed on the three sloops, the boatswain beat the Japanese vessel so leaky that it sank quickly. Concerned, the Japanese watched as the sea swallowed their ship. Then the boats went back to the Dutch ships at once. One of the Japanese sat next to Siebold and laughed at him vividly. Siebold was a bit embarrassed, because he feared that his curiosity might be written on his face and appear rude. But although the thirty-year-old man with dark skin was marked by the effort and despair of the days in the storm and although his clothes were torn and dirty, he not only made a healthy, strong, and well-groomed impression, like his fellow fates, but he also still radiated dignity and self-confidence.

When the castaways came aboard the *Drie Gezusters*, they tampered with their belongings at once, rolled out mats on deck, took out their personal luggage and began quite naturally– what most of the surround-ding Dutch found extremely strange–with their body care and personal hygiene. They cleaned themselves thoroughly and shaved their faces and skulls with great skill, leaving a broad hair comb in the middle. Then they unpacked their provisions, ate pickled vegetables with rice porridge and drank from their rice wine called *sake*, which they also had rescued. Siebold now watched with undisguised curiosity the behavior of the strangers, for as soon as they had been cleaned and strengthened and had put on fresh robes, they also walked around on board with a friendly smile and looked extensively at every object that was unknown to them and attracted their attention. They admired the entire construction of the Dutch ship, for they had never seen anything like it. Siebold and Mendelssohn tried to commu-nicate with the Japanese by means of an improvised sign language, which they succeeded quite quickly. Siebold made it clear to them that he was the doctor on board and asked them to be examined. However, he could not find any disease or deficiency in any of the shipwrecked.

By late afternoon they had learned a lot about the origins and fate of the Japanese. They were from *Satsuma*, the southernmost landscape of the big island Kyūshū. On behalf of their prince, they had bought rice and sugar on the Ryūkyū islands even further south. With this cargo they had come on the way back in strong headwind, which swelled to the storm, tore away their sails, mast and anchor and let the small ship drift far to the west. They would undoubtedly have been driven out to sea and starved to death or died of thirst. The pigtails that some of them wore on their belts were their own, which they had previously cut off in their hopeless situation in order to sacrifice them to the patron god of the seafarers in the event of a rescue in their homeland. So, the time passed until the evening in a strenuous, but also amusing and interesting conversation with the cheerful Japanese. For Mendelssohn and Siebold these were their first lessons in the Japanese language. They could not let go of these cheerful, sociable people who had just escaped death and yet made the strangest theatrical gestures to tell their story, laughing loudly.

The Great Storm

Suddenly the *barometer* fell. The mate informed the first officer and the latter at once the captain. An enormous area of low pressure was moving right towards them. A few minutes later, a cool wind set in and the sky took on a ghostly, deep grey color. Siebold was asked to translate to the Japanese that they had to go below deck with their luggage. Tense Jacometti waited next to the helmsman for the further development of the weather. Then he decided that the storm sails should be set. However, the guests were already so strong that the sailors were almost unable to rescue the sails. Only after more than one hour the storm sails were hoisted. Heavy rain started and the stomping against the ship's wall, which had been following them for days, turned into a rhythmic thunder. Only with jib, foretop and fore topgallant they were now almost unable to maneuver before the furious wind. By nightfall, everyone had to leave the deck. Only the strongest and most experienced sailors stayed there, put ropes around their hips and tied them to the railing so as not to be washed away. The mountains of water became more and more massive and the ship, depending on how a wave hit it, tipped forward, backward, or sideways as if it wanted to roll over. The stem post dived long and deep into the water and the sailors feared every time if it would appear again. Wind and waves were one roar.

On deck, the men only communicated with a show of hands. You couldn't hear your own voice anymore. Siebold was restless. He wanted to go on deck to get an overview but could not open the hatch at first. The violence that faced him there took his breath away. Spray, splash water, and rain whipped through the air and hit his face like a thousand needles. Concerned, he looked up into the heavy rigging, which clashed against the masts. The foot of the mainmast groaned dangerously under the weight of the enormous lever, which pulled with a stirring motion at its anchorage. At that moment Siebold saw the jib ripped with a sharp hiss and after a few seconds, only its shreds fluttered like mad in the wind. Then the dinghy, in which they had rescued the Japanese just a few hours ago, flew whirling around its own axis across the deck and cracked asunder on the cabin wall below the foredeck. At that moment he felt fear for the first time. After the long journey from Rotterdam to Java, he had imagined that he had already bravely faced the power of the winds and the sea. But now he realized that so far, he had only experienced the quiet course of a normal sea voyage. He remembered wondering about Captain Bonn's stoic serenity as the sea raged over the *Jonge Adriana* in torrents. Things were different this time. The waves buried the ship in this pitch-black night and it was perhaps only a matter of time before it would simply burst under the influence of these forces. All hell broke loose below. Sailors and passengers were thrown around like dolls. In the cabins, the beds, shelves, and cupboards came loose and danced eerily through rooms and corridors. Siebold had to be careful not to be hit by heavy objects which, once torn from their anchorage, swayed back and forth like waves. He tried with great difficulty to get into the captain's cabin. When he arrived there, he saw an extinct man sitting silently among his standing officers. They kept asking him what to do next and what the prospects were, but he did not answer. When he also saw Siebold enter, he suddenly rose from his chair, went to his bunk, and simply lay down. The officers were speechless. They had never experienced such behavior before. Are they really that close to death that the captain surrenders himself to him in advance? Would they really have to go down and drown? Then the mate rushed in the door and breathlessly reported that the sailors were working hard on the pumps and that despite the terrible storm there were only sixteen inches of water. All eyes were on the captain, accusingly, who had literally turned his back on his crew and stared at the cabin side. The first officer took the initiative and instructed his men to take out the axes. In an emergency, they should cut the masts so that the ship is not pulled down by its own superstructures. This news calmed Siebold and ended the short moment in which despair had also won over him and he had been afraid for his life. He had the thought that if they survived this hurricane they would need him as a doctor. He had a responsibility and had to be rested when needed. So, he went to his quarters and tied a rope around his waist, which he tied to the bunk. Later, he should write in his diary.

> *"I tried to get to my place of sleep, fortified myself as best I could on the bed of rest and surrendered to fate with vivid memories of all that remained of love and value to me in the fatherland. Exhausted, I soon fell asleep, from which the call of the dawning day awoke me.*

It was still raging. The waves rolled house high through the eerie dawn, but they were not as steep as at night. Siebold first went into the crew quarters and looked at the injuries and bruises of the crew members. It wasn't as bad as he feared. He splinted one broken arm, turned another in and sewed several lacerations. There was no sign of the captain. On deck, the first concern of the officers was the sister ship. Had the *Onderneeming* weathered the hurricane? It wasn't until noon that she suddenly appeared. She stood motionless on a huge wave when Siebold saw her and shortly afterward fell into the next valley. Great relief spread, and it seemed that everyone had survived the *typhoon*. Wind and rain were so violent that it was impossible to think of going under sail. Instead, the boatswain and his assistants carried out the necessary repairs. Towards evening the weather calmed down. The wind now blew strongly and evenly from the south-southeast. The Japanese were happy when they saw Siebold and greeted him formally and cheerfully at the same time. They made him understand how much they admired the construction of the ship. They assured him, seriously and with great eyes, that they had once again prepared themselves for death, which they underlined by nodding their heads violently and saying "*Hai! Hai!*" Then Mendelssohn also appeared. Siebold was happy to see his travel companion again.

"My God, Mendelssohn, you look as if you have met the hobgoblin in the flesh! You're pale as death. And you've got a bump and abrasions. Let me see that."

"I confess, this was the least entertaining and aesthetic encounter with nature I have ever had," he replied with an exhausted smile. "I wanted to die in between. In a state of extreme nausea and deepest despair, I hovered for hours between life and death. It's so humiliating that you can't even keep a little posture when it comes to the end. I was as miserable as never before," Mendelssohn summed up last night.

"You weren't the only one. The captain was so resigned as I would not have expected from such a brave sailor. And I'll make you a confession, too. Last night I experienced the limits of my courage and confidence. Now I'd like to ask you to come and see me in my cabin. I need to clean and disinfect your injuries. There's nothing I can do about that bump, though. It'll adorn it for a while longer."

"Do you know when we'll see land again? Or more precisely: when will we arrive and have solid land under our feet again," Mendelssohn asked with a longing sigh. Siebold laughed.

"The Japanese think that tomorrow or the day after tomorrow we should reach the first islands. So, it's not weeks anymore, it's days."

The next morning, they spotted the Mesima group of islands and soon afterward the first mountains of the Japanese mainland. Siebold felt a sweet restlessness, a tickle in his stomach and a nervous happiness when he saw these sublime, cloudy peaks in the distance. But then thunderstorms with strong wind and heavy pattering rain started again. In this stiff weather, they were not allowed to approach the coast. Captain Jacometti, who had taken command again grumpily and obviously did not want to say a word about the incident, ordered to take down a part of the sails and to tack off the coast at a safe distance.

The Arrival

The next day, early morning of August 8, 1823, Cape Nomosaki finally came into sight, the landmark for the approach of the bay of Nagasaki. Captain Jacometti called the crew and passengers on deck, handed out Bibles and held the last mass. The Dutch were not allowed to practice their faith in Japan and were not even permitted to take a Bible ashore. The travelers sang fervently Dutch psalms together with the sailors and Siebold tried to tune in as best he could. His thoughts were somewhere else. There hasn't been a trace of the *Onderneeming* since the day before. As the mass was read and they approached the entrance to the bay, the rugged rocks of the two mountains Nomosaki and Osaki stood on both sides like guards. In the background, the mighty volcano Unzen, dominating the horizon, sat there enthroned as if to reinforce this outpost.

Jacometti had the Dutch flag and a secret signal pennant placed at the top of the mast. Minutes later they saw a flare rocket shoot high into the blue sky, signaling the arrival of the ship to the port guard of Nagasaki. At the same time, a large fire was lit at the highest point of the cape, which was to burn for a day and a night to carry the message to Edo over a long chain of further signal fires on the peaks of the Japanese mountains. The weather was clear and fresh again for the first time in weeks. There was a steady wind from the southeast and the bow of the *Drie Gezusters* made a silent, fast cut through the calm water.

When they passed the entrance and their first view of the great bay of Nagasaki was opened to them with the sun in the back of this early summer morning, Siebold thought, the arrival in paradise must be like this. What an immeasurably high compensation this sight was for all suffered efforts and privations! For years he had been eagerly awaiting this moment and had imagined it as vividly as he could. But now he noticed how many colors and forms of his palette had been missing to create something even approximately comparable in his imagination. The panorama of this coastal landscape presented to him was more magnificent and beautiful than anything he had ever seen. In the foreground on both sides of the bay were lively, green hills and gradually built mountain ridges, in between estates with flashing white houses and shimmering temple roofs rising above the cedars, firs, and spruces. In the distant background, the deep blue mountains laid like a benevolent, cool shadow. The smooth surface of the sea was broken by single rocks in changing colors. Small barges, fishing boats and strange sailing vessels with triangular sails could be seen everywhere. There was a lot of activity in this beautiful bay. The fishermen were almost naked, dressed only in a kind of loincloth and waved joyfully to the ship from all directions. The Japanese on board could not dissimulate how moved they were and that they could hardly believe their luck to see their country alive again. The wind gradually diminished until only a gentle breeze was still blowing. On one of the hills, a guard post drew attention by raising the Dutch flag at a high mast to greet them. The end of the bay gradually appeared on the horizon and one could guess the outline of Nagasaki.

Chapter IV

Nagasaki

The Japanese Procedure–The Mountain-Dutchman

The Japanese Procedure

The harbor was only a few nautical miles away. Siebold was surprised that Jacometti let all sails except for jib and mars pull in at such a great distance. The lot measured a depth of eighty *fathoms*. They couldn't drop anchor there. The chain wasn't long enough. But since there was no current and the wind had completely stopped, they could remain lying like this. The sails Jacometti left would be enough to navigate and to cruise at this height in front of the harbor. Then boats were spotted heading straight for the *Drie Gezusters*. The *sanpan* of the emissary of the port committee, long, flat barges with a high bow and two oars supported by rowlocks, glided smoothly over the water. Three officers and two crewmembers came aboard. They stood gracefully and sternly tripping in the middle of the main deck, where Captain Jacometti faced them with two of his officers. It was now very quiet on board. Then one of the Japanese officers spoke with a loud, almost imperious voice and without a trace of kindness. This impression was in painful contradiction to the warm and inviting atmosphere of the fascinating landscape, the first flag greeting and the gestures of the fishermen. The first translator then said in Dutch, in a less authoritarian but nevertheless indifferent tone, that the Japanese government had here the first instructions for the Dutch ship, which must be followed before it may be towed into port. The Japanese officer handed over a scroll to Jacometti, which he received with a stiff bow. The translator further explained that this scroll also contains general questions about crew and cargo, which must be answered in writing by noon the next day. At this time, he announced the arrival of the *Gobanjoshi*, the envoy of the governor of Nagasaki. Furthermore, the master of the ship or one of his officers must come along as hostage and be placed under arrest as long as the military security measures continue. One of the Dutch officers stepped forward, said goodbye to Jacometti with a nod and joined the Japanese formation. They bowed silently, turned away and left with their hostage as quickly as they had come.

Siebold and Mendelsohn agreed that it would have been Captain Jacometti's duty to prepare them for the meeting with the Japanese forces of order and this procedure. He hadn't said a word about it the whole trip. The mood was depressed after this surprisingly threatening scene. Two hours later, the *Onderneeming* came into sight again for the first time since the thunderstorm near Cape Nomo. She approached slowly. There was still near calm. Shortly thereafter the same sanpan appeared as before and came towards the sister ship. This time they were accompanied by a swarm of larger barges, which were identified by a wimple and the shape of their lanterns as armed guard boats. On the way to the *Onderneeming* the train split and about a dozen of these police boats headed for the *Drie Gezusters* and circled around her continuously from then on.

To Siebold's surprise, the fishing boats were still allowed to approach the ship and even talk to the crew. In the midships, where the hull was at its lowest, the shipwrecked and the crew were talking to the fishermen standing on their narrow boats, bent far above the railing. They put fish and shellfish from their catch into the lowered baskets. The rare guests should dine well on arrival. It was also a kind of compensation for the rough treatment by the Japanese authorities, which the common people of Nagasaki regretted time and again. The hungry sailors were deeply grateful for these gifts. The meals during the last three weeks were meager because insects had infested a large part of the provisions. The petty officer and Mendelssohn offered them coins for these delicacies, but the fishermen refused. The shipwrecked Japanese on board tried to explain and finally simply show what the fishermen would surely like to accept in exchange: ordinary green wine bottles! Anything else would have been suspicious as foreign contraband, especially here, under the watchful eye of the port police. When the ship's cook had his assistants carry bottles in boxes, enthusiasm broke out on the water, where the fishermen had tied their boats together to form a small, floating settlement. Siebold gradually relaxed and decided with Mendelssohn to ask Sturler what was going on and what was yet to come.

"Don't you know that? I'm sorry, I thought you knew. It's quite simple. A few years ago, in 1808 to be precise, the English warship *Phaeton* arrived here in this bay under the command of Captain Pellew–under the Dutch flag! It would have been too polite to say that the English had disregarded all the diplomatic rules of the Japanese and international shipping. It was piracy. A declaration of war, actually. *Hendrik Doeff*, the then *opperhoofd* of the factory on Dejima, sent his people on board unsuspectingly, accompanied by three Japanese delegates of the port guard. The English simply captured them."

"What was the purpose of this aggression," asked Siebold, who already knew what Sturler would answer and what connection could open up that explains the Japanese behavior.

"It's very simple. The Netherlands no longer existed in Europe. At the time of the Batavian Republic, which was founded on Dutch soil in 1795 under the protection of revolutionary France and later during the Napoleonic occupation, the country no longer had the strength to maintain its colonial system. The English believed they could seize the moment and take over our post on Dejima in the same way as they did it with our colonies Ceylon, Cape Town and Java. In this respect, it would have been a declaration of war against a state that no longer existed, except here on the small island over there that you will soon get to live on. The English didn't understand, however, that we had not settled here by force, but had even been appreciated as friends of the Japanese for centuries. As you know, we have been the only nation officially admitted to trading with Japan since 1639."

"And what happened to the English," Mendelsohn impatiently asked, preferring to hear the pirate story rather than the chronicle of Japanese-Dutch trade relations.

"Oh, yes. The Japanese closed off the whole bay with everything that went by water. They even ordered the heavy Chinese junks to reinforce the blockade. The English quickly realized that they were trapped. They had no chance against such opponents, because the fast, small boats could have simply set the *Phaeton* on fire with arrows. What are you going to do with guns and rifles against these nimble opponents? Then the Brits threatened to sink all ships in the port if they did not receive food, water, and wood. The Japanese saw this as an acceptable compromise because they knew how important it was to give the opponent a chance to save face. So, the English released their prisoners again, received the required provisions and a free withdrawal. Pellew's mission had failed. After the incident, Matsudeira Genpei, then Commissioner for Ports, decided to take full responsibility. He made his will and killed himself. Despite this mild outcome, the shogunate was in shock. It also ordered the seven officers who had been assigned to the port commissioner to commit suicide and strengthened the security precautions. Since then"– with his finger in the direction of the harbor he drew an invisible line across the bay–"there lies a heavy iron chain just below the surface of the water, which can protect the harbor basin from intruding ships if necessary. But I urge you to keep this to yourself, because the Japanese don't even think we know about this device. And one more thing."

This time he pointed to the hills on both sides of the bay at the height where the hidden chain should lie.

"Do you see all these flags on the sentry post? Shortly behind are large military deployment places in depressions that cannot be seen from the water. There, because of our arrival, the troops of the princes Nabeshima and Kuroda are assembled. They are personally responsible to the mighty shogun for ensuring that no one enters the port without authorization. All of Nagasaki is directly subordinate to shogunate in Edo because of its great importance for Japan's trade and traffic with other nations."

"Then all these measures are for our own protection?" asked Siebold.

"Yes. I'm asking you to look at it this way. We are very grateful to the Japanese because they protected us not only then. With the procedure we are going through today, they want to grant nothing more than our safety. You'll see. You'll see. When the formalities are over, and we are identified as friends of the Japanese nation, everything will change."

"I'm impressed. This makes the new sound we have had to bear so far more bearable. But please tell us one more thing, Colonel," Mendelssohn followed up, as the buccaneer story of the English seemed to be over. "Why are there Chinese junks and thus Chinese merchants here, when it is claimed that the Netherlands is the only nation with which Japan has trade relations?"

"That is also easy to answer. The Chinese traders are all here on their own account and, so to speak, privately. However, Japan and China have no official relations. This difference becomes most obvious in the big court journey to the shogun to Edo, which will take us in three years. Only the Dutch are allowed to enter the city walls with an official legation. So, the Chinese are tolerated, not as representatives of their country, but only as business travelers."

Siebold, who could hardly hide his astonishment at how well Sturler was informed, asked, "And what about the Chinese doctors who are supposed to work in Japan?"

"Doctor von Siebold, you will see, there are astonishingly many of them and they will be your worst enemies. Prepare for it right now."

In this statement, Siebold noticed a trace of satisfaction that made him listen attentively. He wanted to contradict Sturler in this matter, because why should Chinese doctors close their eyes to the findings of European medicine. But he held back because he wanted to respect his superior's greater knowledge and experience for a start.

Towards evening, when Jacometti and his officers were already filling out the extensive lists for the Japanese authorities, Mendelssohn and Siebold were sitting at the railing again, taking turns talking with each other and with the fishermen, who no longer wanted to leave their side. They made progress together in their Japanese lessons, which they now received from these simple people.

"Have you noticed", Mendelssohn asked, "that they don't use the word 'I' at all?"

"Yes, and not only that. They do not conjugate the verbs according to the person either. They don't say: I eat, you eat, he-she-it *eats* and so on, but there is for eating only one word, taberu, which is always used in the same form. Only in the past, it's tabeta. That makes it easy when you know this basic form of the verb."

"Very well observed. You're not as untalented in the exotic languages as you wanted to make me believe when we first met. Taberu is a good approach, by the way. I'm so hungry that I'm afraid I'll have to eat all alone the lovely little fish that these warm people have given us throughout the day."

"What am I supposed to say! Look at this." Siebold pulled the waistband and the belt, whose buckle was already hooked into the last hole, far away from the belly. He had lost so much weight since his departure from Rotterdam that his clothes were shaking. The long sea voyages and the disease on Java had melted away his rustic Würzburg build.

"Yes, you're right", Mendelssohn answered laughing, "a whole fisherman and a fat Englishman fit into these trousers. But don't think you can just sneak up at the table with it."

Soon the bell rang calling for dinner in the officers' mess. There was only a thin soup and pickled cucumbers with the fresh fish and the big crabs because the supplies of vegetables and fruits were either depleted or spoiled. At dusk, the watch boats lit their lanterns and on the surrounding hills, the large fireplaces were lit in the distant watches, which shone far across the bay. In addition, there were the small fires that the fishermen made in their boats on grates to start night fishing. The dark, mirror-smooth water surface of the bay was transformed into a fascinating flickering spectacle in the reflection of the many lights from near and far. Siebold and Mendelssohn watched until late into the night the fishermen, who collected the rich gifts of the sea with nets, fishing rods, stab forks and great skill.

The Mountain-Dutchman

The next day, as announced, the *Gobanjoshi*, the representative of the Governor of Nagasaki, came at noon, this time accompanied by four interpreters. Jacometti had prepared Sturler and Siebold that they would have to be present at the forthcoming meeting. Jacometti himself led the Gobanjoshi to his cabin, where a table was prepared for the legation, the officers, Sturler and Siebold to entertain the Japanese guests with the best that still existed on board. This included a wide range of liqueurs, wines, brandies, rum, whiskies, and beer. The Japanese were obviously delighted, even in the best mood. They were now granted a privilege of which every prince in the whole of Japan could only envy them. The Gobanjoshi did justice to the red wine. He was dressed in an extremely elegant fashion, or–as Siebold thought–"wrapped in fabric." All over, corners of a new type or color of fabric looked out of the Commissioner's robe, making it difficult to get an overview of the garments involved. The Gobanjoshi, who had darker skin and more slit eyes than the Japanese Siebold had seen so far, was a subtle man. After enjoying two glasses of red gold with his eyes closed, he spoke to Jacometti quietly and politely. The translators let him know how much the government and of course the whole city of Nagasaki are happy about the arrival of the ship. The Dutch have always been the only and best friends of the Japanese. There is great interest in increasing the scope of economic and cultural exchange. Jacometti let him know that the arrival of Dutch ships this year stood exactly in this very sign. He introduced Colonel von Sturler and Major von Siebold. He assured the Gobanjoshi, who used the break for another glass of wine bottled ten years ago in Bordeaux, that the Dutch government had sent their best men to the Japanese nation. The Gobanjoshi was in a good mood and cheekily asked back whether there used to be only cutthroats and convicts on Dejima. Jacometti laughed out loud and for the first time since Siebold knew him.

This could have been the signal to end the official part of the meeting, to move on to the unrestricted social part, which would have been only right for the Japanese, too. But an iron hand of duty called them from the invisible to order and the face of Gobanjoshi and his interpreters became serious once again. He turned to Sturler, who had the next claim to his attention after the captain. He let him know that he is looking forward to having a capable and respectable man as contact person in all matters concerning Dejima. He had his translators underline how much he personally appreciated the presence of the wise *opperhoofd* Jan Cock Blomhoff so far. When he said this, Siebold noticed that all members of the Japanese legation had changed color. Suddenly they were all red as cooked lobster! Siebold was worried that a great anger had secretly arisen in this friendly man and his companions. He thought hard whether anything of what had been said so far could have been a provocation for them. Or whether it was just a physiological reaction to the consumption of alcohol. Sturler remained unimpressed and replied fully relaxed.

"Dear Gobanjoshi-*sama*, I would never dare to replace a wise man. I am only a man on whose word one can rely and who was endowed by his mother with an unswerving sense of order. Wisdom is not my field. For this I brought along a man who, despite his young appearance, has been

repeatedly attested that he is already a wise man in the realm of nature."
He pointed directly at Siebold. The translators giggled, for they found this
answer witty and perfidious, but at the same time did not know how to
translate it appropriately without the Gobanjoshi laughing off. The idea
that there is a sage of nature was ridiculous for the Japanese because every
Japanese was at home in the lap of nature. It was almost as if Sturler had
said that the doctor and Major von Siebold recommended himself because
he was a plant. The translators whispered among themselves and agreed
that Sturler wanted to say that Mr. von Siebold was closer to wisdom than
he himself, because he knew many plants. The Gobanjoshi obviously did
not understand what was meant by this, but he did not want to insist either.
He turned directly to Siebold. He looked at him in a friendly and
explorative way. Then he spoke much longer than before. The translators
were concentrated to remember the whole speech. Again, they put their
heads together and whispered. Then one of them who hadn't even spoken
yet picked up.

"Shiboruto-san, the Gobanjoshi, welcomes you to Japan and hopes that
you and your fellow travelers will soon be able to move from the status of
prisoners of war to the status of state guests. We have had the best
experiences with the doctors on Dejima in several centuries. We want you
to know that Nagasaki is an open city for you within the legal possibilities
and there are many people who are highly interested in the news that you
will bring from the West. The Gobanjoshi also wants you to know that he
appreciates your gaze. You have what we in Japan call 'eyes piercing
through mountains'. There are few people who have this special gaze. That
is why the Gobanjoshi would like to believe Colonel de Sturler that you
are a wise man." Siebold was thunderstruck. In Sturler's exposition he had
once again perceived this fine, little dagger turned against his person. But
he couldn't have imagined that the Gobanjoshi would twist Sturler's words
in his mouth. Beyond that, he could not resist the sympathy he felt for the
Gobanjoshi from the very first moment on. He reminded him of the
portrait of a Roman senator with his posture and luxurious lower lip
despite his otherwise pronounced Asian appearance. He was also
surprised that such subjective impressions were allowed to flow into a
diplomatic conversation, which up to then had distinguished itself
through its formal character. He was amazed at the accent-free and

completely fluent Dutch that this translator spoke. He sounded like a native Dutchman. Now it was up to Siebold to thank him for this kindness.

"Dear Kurato-sama. You are a powerful man. Your tolerance and the pleasure that you take in our presence is the source of many favorable conditions from which we want to benefit in order to establish an even better relationship between Japan and the Netherlands. I will know how to behave as the most obedient subject of the Japanese people and thereby make our nation imppear as an example of discipline and order. We are deeply ondepted to you and your nation."

He was proud that he could address the Gobanjoshi with his name and the honorific address -*sama*, which he had heard in the earlier exchanges between him and his translators. Yet, the translators looked at Siebold with astonishment. He could see from the corner of his eye how Jacometti kept his breath.

"Excuse me, Shiboruto-san, what do you mean by 'imppear' and 'ondepted'? I don't know those expressions. Are these perhaps idiomatic expressions that have been coined in recent years," the translator asked in perfect Dutch.

Siebold felt a hot blush lay on his face. He was not prepared for this situation. It hadn't occurred to him that a Japanese man could expose him as a non-Dutchman. Why had no one warned him about those talented translators? He had also underestimated the Japanese, as he had to realize. He had not expected this precision of their logical thinking and of their linguistic expression. It was the cliché of the general retardation and naivety in which all non-European countries still had to find themselves that he blamed for his mishap. There he had an idea—also inspired by the whiskey, to which he had already done justice.

"Oh, forgive me, that's a dialect I speak. I am a High German and we partly use other prefixes. Of course, I meant 'appear' and 'indebted'".

Kurato insisted that the translators at once reported the irritation that had arisen. That's when he suddenly woke up. Could it be that they were in the middle of a trap? That the people at the table who pretended to be Dutch are all English or Russian? That the drinks that were given to him and his entourage were only meant to paralyze their resistance and facilitate their capture? His life was at stake because for such a capital mistake the shogun would require his head. Or rather, he would have to bring this sacrifice without being asked to save his name and the honor of the family, as Matsudeira Genpei did after the attack of the English. He sharply ordered the translators and officers to be extremely vigilant and to observe every movement of the strangers. The Dutch, who except for Jacometti had not understood the occasion, were horrified by the violent and loud gestures of the Japanese. Then Kurato addressed Siebold again with the help of the translator.

"Shiboruto-san, how can you make it credible that you are a Dutchman? How can you convince us that you are all citizens of the Netherlands and not disguised spies of England or Russia?"

"Kurato-sama, as far as I am concerned, I would ask you to believe that I come from a region of Holland that is not by the sea, that is located further south on the European mainland and where people speak High German, which has a few differences from Dutch. I suspect that the people here on the island Kyūshū speak a different Japanese dialect than the people further north on Honshu, don't they? And it's still the same language and the same country."

"Yes, in fact, the deviations are sometimes so great that people don't understand each other. So, if you speak High German, you live inland somewhere in the mountains where it's high?"

"Yes, you could say that."

"Then you are a Yamahollanda, a mountain-dutchman. All right, that convinces me. And what about your companions?"

"Do you think that if we had warlike intentions, we would arrive here with two plump merchant ships, each of which has only two cannons? I can assure you that the new European and American warships are so powerful and dangerous that we would certainly not do without them. Two of these ships could destroy Nagasaki with guns and..." he bit his tongue because he wanted to talk about the fact that even heavy underwater chains would no longer help there. But he had promised Sturler that he would keep the secret–which in fact hadn't been one anymore for a long time–to himself.

"And what?", the translator insisted.

"...and take the city with three hundred soldiers armed to the teeth. I personally vouch with my life that the Netherlands has no plans of this kind. Only the opposite is the truth. The Governor General of East India told me himself that this is the first mission to seek scientific exchange with the Japanese nation. The Netherlands itself has just been liberated from captivity and occupation by a foreign country. We no longer want to bring war into the world, but only peace, trade, and science. Your entourage will be next to search the ship anyway. Pay attention to how many books, medicines, and instruments are stored in my chamber and in the storage rooms. A large part of them are gifts for the best and brightest of your compatriots. We would be really weird spies who would share all their knowledge with the country before they scout it out."

While the translator told Kurata all this and he repeatedly let him hear an approving grunt, Sturler looked for Siebold's eyes and nodded to him in appreciation. Then, when the translator had reached the last sentence of Siebold, Kurato laughed out loud. He liked that. Spies who reveal more secrets than they learn. Thus, the ice was broken and as quickly as Kurata became suspicious and brusque, so quickly he found again the sociable tone in which everything had begun so pleasantly. "Yamahollanda, mhhmhhh," Kurato said several more times, looking at Siebold grinning and his translators laughing again and again.

The translator with whom Siebold had spoken asked him to occasionally be introduced to the rules of the Yamahollanda dialect, into High German. Siebold assured him of this with a smile, when in reality he only had attention for the whiskey he had just brought to his mouth. That was close. Then he asked him why the Gobanjoshi was so amused by the term Yamahollanda.

"Well, the word means not only 'mountain-Dutch', but also 'wild Dutchman' or even just 'wildling'. Without wanting to be rude, the Gobanjoshi finds the thought of a 'wild spy from the mountains who reveals more secrets than he learns' quite amusing".

Later, when six port watch inspectors thoroughly searched the entire ship, compared the stocks of weapons, provisions, and merchandise with the completed lists and the Gobanjoshi initiated a formal investigation with the interrogation of the shipwrecked Japanese, Siebold visited Colonel de Sturler in his cabin.

"Colonel, I don't want to interfere insubordinately in your plans or question your decisions. But there is something that keeps my mind working. Would it not have made sense to draw my attention to this interrogation and the dangers involved? I must confess to you that for a moment I felt my nerves tense like the strings of my fortepiano." With the last remark, he tried to amusingly alleviate the presumption that, despite the preceding testimony of respect, the question was undeniably in his mind.

"I thought it would only make you nervous. You have mastered the situation very well. Or to stick with your picture: you played a wonderful piece in which every note fell well in place." This thought amused Sturler.

"What if things had turned out differently? If I hadn't remembered the story of the High German and Mountain-Dutch?"

"Then you would have been like the Belgian doctor who was sent back four years ago by order of the Japanese government–because the translators of Gobanjoshi did not understand him. That's why you won't find a doctor here on Dejima to relieve you and take these ships back home. Didn't you know that your famous predecessor, the Swede Thunberg, also had the greatest difficulty being accepted by the Japanese as a Dutchman fifty years ago?"

"No. I'm new to everything you're saying. And maybe you're right. I would have been concerned to know how strict the rules are here. I certainly could not have speeded up the learning of the Dutch language anymore and therefore it would not have been possible for me to influence the course of the 'polite interrogation' if we want to call it that".

The entire inspection had gone satisfactorily, and the Gobanjoshi gave the captain written permission to enter the port with the *Drie Gezusters*. He said goodbye and drove with his people to *Onderneeming*, where he would repeat the same procedure including the social part. Shortly afterward, many rowing boats appeared that were more compact than the sanpan. They were towing vehicles. At first, there were twenty to thirty, but there were more and more until she was surrounded by more than fifty boats. They picked up the ropes that the sailors let them down so that they could pull the ship into port. The fully loaded ship was also difficult to move for this large number of rowboats. But after a short time, the contours of Nagasaki and the port facility became sharper. Then they saw the tiny island of Dejima in front of them and could see the buildings with their glass windows glistening in the sun and the green blinds. The Dutch flag hung from a high mast. Siebold was moved by this sight. The closer they came, the more breathtaking the view became. Embedded in the lush vegetation of evergreen oaks, cedars and laurel trees, majestic temple groves alternated with friendly houses. Cereal fields and vegetable gardens lay in front of rugged rock walls on the steps which had moved into the fertile volcanic hilly landscape and made the close coexistence of man and nature at this place obvious. The port facility looked to them friendly with the symmetrically arranged, white warehouses and the spacious landing stages.

Siebold could no longer calm down. He was so agitated at the sight of his destination that he had to leave aft for a moment. Behind the helmsman's back, he looked at the smooth track of the ship back to the sea behind them–and cried. He squeezed out some tears of excitement. How many hindrances he had overcome! How often everything, even his life, was at stake; and how often little was missing that he would never have experienced this great moment! He regained his composure and rejoined the crew waiting on the main deck for the first Dutch boats from Dejima. With nine cannon shots, the city has announced the arrival of the Dutch ship, while this time they measured twenty-five fathoms under the keel. Jacometti had the anchor thrown. Its impact on the water, followed by the deafening rattling of the heavy chain, was an unmistakable sign–the sounding symbol of fulfillment. They had arrived in Japan. Siebold was once again overwhelmed by his feelings. In the midst of the noise and the cheering of the crew, his eyes met those of Mendelssohn. They laughed at each other, both with wet traces of tears of joy on their cheeks.

Chapter V

Dejima

The Prison Island–Hokusai and Bakin–A Walk with Mendelssohn–
The Dutchmen's Talk–The Cataract Operation–Misuzu Inukawa

The Prison Island

This officially put an end to the state of war in which the die *Drie Gezusters* and the *Onderneeming* had previously found themselves and had to be treated as ships of an enemy nation with warlike intentions. The government-ordered mistrust at once ceased and even the strictly looking posts on the watch boats were now friendly and helpful. First of all, the officer retained as hostage and some Dutch suppliers, the Comparadores, as they were still known in the old Portuguese style, were allowed on board. They brought on board baskets of fruit, vegetables, and bread as a welcome gift with recommendations from the head of Dejima. The crew threw themselves at the fresh produce like starving wolves. A little later the translation to the island began. The Japanese had to organize this transport because the typhoon had destroyed both sloops of the *Drie Gezusters* off the Chinese coast and the Dutch were not allowed to own boats on Dejima. A dozen sanpan took the crew and passengers on several tours to the west side of the island, where the *hatoba* lay, the landing place for the arriving shipping traffic. The heavier Dutchmen needed a lot of skill to get out of the narrow boats of the Japanese. Not everyone succeeded. When one of them fell into the water, there was a lot of laughter every time, but even those who were involuntarily bathed took it with humor. The joy of the arrival made them forget everything else. The sailors, however, had to stay on board, they had no right to go ashore.

On the *Onderneeming* the inspection was less complicated, and so the Dutch crews of both ships gathered at the hatoba. Before they were accommodated, they had to be received solemnly. Siebold was amazed when suddenly a procession came around the corner with great fanfare and moved towards the gathered. At the head of this welcoming committee, the head of the Dutch trade in Japan, the legendary *opperhoofd* and knight *Jan Cock Blomhoff*, the luxuriant blond hair tamed under a heavy velvet cap and with a smile on his face, to which everything could be seen: relief, joy, emotion, and gratitude. With the arrival of these young men, who were to replace him and continue his work, a hopeful future spread before him. He would spend a few more years evaluating and writing down the results of his stay in Japan on behalf of the Colonial Ministry before retiring. Selling his private collection of Japanese items would improve his income. He would follow the further course of Dutch efforts in Japan with goodwill and support wherever possible with his knowledge and relationships.

The other participants of the procession were dressed no less spectacularly. They wore embroidered velvet skirts, black coats and feather hats, steel swords, and everyone held elegantly authoritarian Spanish walking sticks with a golden knob in their hands. The passengers of the two ships looked at each other with surprise and amazement. Some could not hold back and giggled audibly. Despite the seriousness and dignity of the uniforms, this parade of their compatriots, which still corresponded to the old ceremonial of the seventeenth century on Dejima, seemed grotesque to the new arrivals. It was obvious that not only in Japan but also on Dejima nothing had changed in two hundred years. Time had stood still here.

The opperhoofd approached Major von Sturler solemnly and they greeted each other with both hands. Blomhoff was a giant, but definitely not a handsome man. His soft, somewhat spongy, light-skinned face was covered with freckles or early age spots. When he laughed, and his bulging lips opened, huge yellow teeth appeared with a wide gap between the two front incisors. Siebold at once saw the physiognomy of a man tested by illness and perhaps additional suffering, whose aura of warmth and confidence overshadowed this blemish. His whole appearance stood in confusing contradiction to the old-fashioned and somewhat presumptuous outfit of his followers. Blomhoff asked Sturler to accompany him to the headquarters of the factory of Dejima, his future official residence and workplace. The carnivalesque human train followed the two. Only when the old and new leaders of the Dutch legation had closed the door of the House of Lords behind them, the procession dissolved, and the quartering began. Siebold was led into a small, two-story house of Japanese design, which was furnished according to European standards. The new arrivals had to wait for their personal luggage because, according to the regulations, all weapons and powder were first taken off board and transported to specially built warehouses on the mainland in the hills. Then the steering wheel was dismantled and taken to the port commissariat for safekeeping. Only then were the Dutch allowed to receive their luggage. When the porters had left the suitcases, trunks, and the fortepiano in the doctor's house, it was early evening. Siebold just made his bed, laid down on it and fell into a deep sleep at once.

The next morning, he woke up early. It was still quiet on the island. His house had a corner with two windows on the upper floor, each with a view of the bay and the landing stages of the port of Nagasaki. Outside he saw the Dutch sailing ships lying at anchor. The Chinese junks and Japanese cargo boats on the quay of the Chinese factory swayed quietly in the waves. Apart from the gentle beat of the surf in the distance, Siebold heard the soft clattering sounds of the rigging, a melody that put him into a hypnotic state against the background of morning silence. Sweet chills ran up his spine and crawled over his scalp. He got dressed and walked out of the house to the seaside of the island, where the first rays of the sun fell from the east through the mountains onto the bay and painted warm, shimmering spots. The first impression was incomprehensible, fleeting, like a fragrance.

After all the administrative efforts and the prosaic process of integration on the island had been completed the day before by both the Dutch and Japanese sides, the country began to develop its impact on him. Looking out over the flat basalt wall on the seaside, the white, flat beach of Oura laid in front of him on his right. On the left he saw the densely wooded coast of Inasa, which rose steeply over the bay. In between rested the sea, in which the mountains and the sky were reflected, like a true, calmly breathing elemental force. Siebold was stunned by the extraordinary atmospheric transparency, the clarity of light and the incomparable sharpness of all outlines. He felt as if he had finally been given glasses that made him see everything much more clearly and in more intense colors. This impression also stood out so advantageously from the memory of the many pale days on the Chinese Sea. It was as if he could see much further than before, because even the far-flung end of the bay in the south, where it leads out to the open sea, he saw sharply and as if within his grasp. So, he stood alone on the shore of this tiny island, which would now be his home for years to come and had the impression that it was not him who was looking at the quiet bay, the sky and the mountains, but rather them watching at him, this little man who had come from so far away to discover their secrets. Never before had he perceived nature as essentially as if it were a community of great personalities. He felt a great, all-encompassing tension diminish, which he had not even been aware of as such. Only with its disappearance did he feel this urge for the first time, which was much deeper than the simple desire to come to Japan. The sight of this landscape, or rather the way this landscape looked at him, released a bracket that had held his previous life together and was somehow connected to everything he had done or thought of up to then. A driving force had found its goal and now set him free for new tasks. He felt purified and ready for a new beginning, for another life.

He was walking around the island to get an idea of it. It was shaped in the form of a fan. The south side facing the sea measured about six hundred feet, on the land side it was five hundred feet and between the two just two hundred feet. There were about two dozen, mostly two-storied wooden houses, seven or eight of which were intended for Dutch officials. The others were shelters for the merchants, magazines, and warehouses. The largest of these was the sugar storage, because sugar had been the product for which the Japanese paid the highest prices since the beginning of trade relations. There was a small square around the flagpole and a walk-in, overgrown vegetable garden. There was a lot of work to do! He passed the only bridge where two silent guards looked at him emotion-lessly. On the other side was the harbor district, where pretty white houses with many windows and large sliding doors stood along clean streets. Behind it gradually rose the city of Nagasaki, which nestled against the mountain with its winding streets, narrow squares surrounded by houses and temples, and well-kept gardens. So, the island was a small and somewhat bleak world to which he had to adapt. It stood completely in contrast to the wonderful views that one had around on the sea and the mainland.

Dejima in the bay of Nagasaki

He spent the day unpacking. He had to organize and stow away his many instruments, medicines, books, and clothes. Siebold was lucky because he had been assigned an apartment of the latest standard with all European conveniences. His London fortepiano by Rolfs & Sons had survived the journey in the hold undamaged. Here he found for the first time since his departure from Heidingsfeld the opportunity and enough space to set it up. For his practice, which he began to set up at once, a separate house was planned right next door. Later Blomhoff came by and invited him to his house for dinner with Sturler. When Siebold left his house at dusk and went over to Blomhoff, the shrill, rhythmic singing of the cicadas filled the air from everywhere. It gave the humid-hot Japanese summer an unmistakable sound. In the light of a mighty candelabra, Blomhoff entertained his guests with wine and crispy roast lamb with all kinds of stories about the Japanese, the small island and its years during isolation.

"At that time, *Doeff* was still opperhoofd here and I was his assistant. A great guy, a legend of a man. You should have seen him when he met the English in 1813, refused to give up the island and to return to Batavia. The whole Dutch colony of East India was taken over by the English in 1811. Doeff insisted that this is the Netherlands and he would not leave this country."

"So, did the English come back here after the Phaeton incident?" Siebold asked.

"Yes, indeed, it was another attempt to deprive the Netherlands of its trading post. And again, it was the grandiose Doeff who did not let himself being ruled out by the English. He mistrusted them. They told the Japanese that the Netherlands no longer existed as a sovereign country and that England had taken control of the former Dutch colonies. Worse still, the English had bribed *Willem Wardenaar*, the former head of our factory, who conducted these negotiations for them. Wardenaar was still highly regarded by the Japanese. However, Doeff remained tough. He didn't trust Wardenaar either. Finally, he found a solution. A senior official of the factory should go back to Java to have the English provide evidence that they are telling the truth. The Japanese authorities agreed. So, it came that I was practically taken hostage to Java, because the choice for the envoy fell naturally on me. And what do you think was waiting for me there? I had a series of talks with *Thomas Raffles*, whom the British crown had appointed as governor. A highly educated, intelligent and liberal man in himself."

"He has also become a recognized researcher, discovering the two-thousand-six-hundred-year-old temple city of Borobudur during his tenure in Java. Georg IV has knighted him in the meantime", Siebold added. "I find his two-volume work History of Java exemplary, by the way. And let's wait and see what happens to Singapore, this city he founded for the East India Company on the Strait of Malacca."

"Yes, he is an interesting and ambitious adventurer, for which our club should certainly have more than just passive understanding," Blomhoff replied with a meaningful grin. "But I found out that the English had boldly lied. By the time they appeared in Dejima, French rule in the Netherlands had already ended and the Batavian Republic was dissolved. Raffles nevertheless, cold as ice, tried to bribe me too after Wardenaar— with the not to be sneezed at the sum of fifteen thousand Spanish dollars. However, my heart rejoiced at the good news from Europe. I recommended Raffles to discuss his request better with my king, who would soon ascend the throne again. Raffles foamed with rage and threw me as a prisoner of war into one of the terrible Batavian dungeons. I was taken by the next ship to England, where I waited in London prison for a court-martial. Raffles wanted me convicted there. But things turned out differently. Napoleon was already on his way into exile in Elba and the Dutch ambassador protested against my imprisonment at the British crown. The matter was extremely embarrassing for the English. I was immediately released, with an explicit apology from the government and the offer of a free passage back to Batavia. However, I no longer wanted to suffer English travel companions and drove home to the Netherlands.

You can't imagine what it was like here back then. You know, we had nothing left. Even Doeff walked around in shoes made of straw and coarse kidskin. Many had to sew trousers and shirts out of their already yellowed bed linen because their clothes hung down in shreds. There was hardly anything left to eat. And of this...", he took a break and held up his glass with the red wine from the noble grapes of Tenerife, which he smiled at longingly, "...there was nothing left at all. It wasn't like this condition only lasted a few weeks or months. No, it went on for three, four, five years. Can you imagine what the morale was like? And on top of that, day in, day out on this island, always in the uncertainty of how the families in the homeland are faring, yes, how the homeland itself is doing! It was horrible. What I saw after my return and what Doeff reported helped me to understand how the Japanese really are. For while they kept the strictest expression to the outside, they undermined the instructions and laws to treat foreigners wherever they could in our favor. So, the officers themselves secretly had simple, small sailing boats and rafts built, which they loaded with small bags of rice or grain and let drift from the beach to the island and through the barricade when the wind was favorable. Since they were not paid for it, it was not smuggling, and nobody had to set foot on the island or to favor a Dutchman personally. They could have said that these are floating offerings to their gods or something similar. Thus, under the mask of authority and rigor, our unfortunate colleagues discovered the great sympathy and compassion that the Japanese had with them. Since then I have been deeply grateful to these people. I may say that in the meantime some of the officials have become good friends and I will sorely miss them when I leave this country."

"Are you expecting a family at home?" inquired Siebold. But the effect of his question frightened him. Blomhoff's appearance changed within one glance. His facial muscles slackened and the many flesh in his face hung down gray. He suddenly looked like an aged hunting dog and answered with a tired and resigned voice.

"Oh, I hoped I could skip this chapter. But since you ask. Not everything went as well with the Japanese as I just told you. Six years ago, with the first ship after the long isolation, I came back here with my wife and my little son. *Titia* was her name. She was a wonderful person and for me the most beautiful woman under heaven. She was spirited–and stubborn. I couldn't stop her from going with me to Japan at the time. It was not only risky from the outset but impossible. The rules for Dejima and the traffic with foreigners expressly exclude the residence of foreign women here. But my euphoria was boundless, and I was absolutely sure that I could persuade the Japans to modernize these traditional rules. In my delusion, I even believed that they owed it to me because I had averted so much damage from them by being held hostage by the English.

On the day of arrival, it became obvious how presumptuous that was. You cannot picture the dimension of the scandal that followed. The Japanese lost their heads completely when they saw Titia. She was the first European woman in Japan and she was unlike anything that they could have imagined here. I formally applied for a right of residence for my wife and son. But the Bakufu was rigorous in its decision. Titia had to leave the country within two weeks on the same ship she had come on. Oh, what a goodbye, what a shame! We were both so unhappy and my little son didn't understand anything. Three sailors had to bring Titia back to the ship. She fought back with her hands and feet. She wouldn't admit to the last moment that we had lost the fight.

But that's not all. For days the ship could not leave the bay because of a storm. I could still see it out there and knew what more pain it had to be for Titia. The sea voyage to Europe must have been a long way from hell for them. Two months after she returned to The Hague she died, ill and desperate. She is the price I paid for the little glory that my local task has earned me. As a souvenir, my son is waiting for me at my sister's house."

Blomhoff, whose face looked like an abandoned quarry in the rain, struggled with tears. Colonel de Sturler felt uncomfortable with the prospect of having to endure the sight of his weeping colleague, whom he was to honorably replace here. He had no understanding for such senti-mentalities, especially not in front of guests who were invited to one's table.

Siebold, who sensed Sturler's growing cold, had beyond his sympathy now also pity for the kind Blomhoff. He felt called upon to protect him from the contempt that surfaced at Sturler.

"As a half-orphan, I'm very sympathetic to your loss. It is, of course, worsened by the physical separation from the loved one and from the actual event of death. A death without farewell and in the distance is still something different from the departure of a close person from life after a long illness. But why did your wife insist on the arduous and dangerous journey to Japan?"

"It was her temper—and her love."

Hokusai and Bakin

"'Mr. Iitsu! Mr. Iitsu!' What bloody nonsense! Why do I have to run around town like a fool to find you just because you've come up with another pseudonym? And then also such an ordinary name, behind which one would assume a fishmonger, basket weaver or candle turner. *Katsushika Hokusai* is a neat-sounding name, which one does not have to mess up with such childishness."

"Calm down, old friend. I had to pass my name on to a younger artist. Besides, I've laid out tracks for you everywhere! I told all the people to send you to me when you came. By the way, do you know how I described you to them to make them recognize you?"

"No."

"If an old man comes who's in a bad mood with yellow eyes and who looks and walks like he just must wade through all your shit, send him to me. That can only be *Bakin*-san," he mimicked himself like a monkey and laughed out of his stomach. "Sit down and drink with me. It's the right time for it," he then followed, soothingly, because Bakin couldn't enjoy his joke and he didn't want to upset his sensitive friend anymore. The servant of the inn, who had been sitting silently in the door until then, brought a carafe of sake, two small drinking cups and a bowl with slices of dried and salted eel

"What brings you here? I learned by chance that you were seen in the Suwa Shrine. "You still live in Edo and I don't remember you like to travel long distances like we do."

Bakin wrenched his face painfully, because for several years sitting has become almost as aching as walking. "Don't remind me. Hemorrhoids and furuncles have paved my way from Edo to here. I don't know what demon is after my ass." He grimly stroked his dry, bony hand over his bald skull. "I came here because friends had told me an agent from various foreign publishers was arriving this year on one of the Dutch ships."

Hokusai tied the belt of his kimono tighter together, which began to release his round belly. "So, are you looking for trouble with the Bakufu? Let me guess. You want to have your books published abroad."

"Of course. I've been annoyed about the local publishers for many years. The whole country reads my stories and all I get is an invitation to dinner, at best a hand money."

"Aren't you exaggerating a little? I hear you've been quite successful lately. They say you've started a great cycle. Forgive me if I don't read any of this. I paint from early in the morning until late at night–when I'm not sitting with old friends." Bakin looked at him inquisitively to find out whether this was seriousness, flattery or another sarcasm. They hadn't seen each other for many years and he wasn't sure if he knew Hokusai anymore. He also noted with some envy that Hokusai had held up well in this time and had been much less marked by age than he himself. Hokusai looked round and healthy, his skin was almost golden, and his hair was still thick and black.

"It's true. I have reached many people with my new work. It's tens of thousands. It is also true that for the first time I can finance a proper budget and my wife occasionally leaves me alone. But it's just as much as a bridge supervisor or a traveling salesman earns."

"I'm not interested in money. Tell me about your new work. And above all, drink."

Bakin obediently took his cup, drank it out, put it back down suspiciously, stretched his chin into the air, scratched his neck and then bared his teeth with a painful grimace–a multi-layered gesture that was inevitable when he had to tell about his work.

"It's called *The Legend of the Eight Dog Warriors* or simply *Hakkenden*. I started ten years ago and have written two dozen volumes. And I've got at least two dozen more to go. So, I can't tell you the whole story yet. It begins with the siege of Prince Satomi's castle in *Awa* by the army of Prince Anzai. The besieged are already starving for seven days. Satomi, who sees the downfall of his family, his entourage, and himself approaching, says to his hunting dog Yatsufusa at night with the bilious humor of the doomed man that he gives him his daughter princess Fuse to wife when he kills the enemy. The next morning Satomi wakes up and sees Yatsufusa on the *tatami*. Between the legs of the giant dog lies the head of Lord Anzai, who stares at Satomi with dead eyes. Satomi is more than embarrassed about this victory, because now he has to marry his daughter Fuse to a dog. For it turns out that Yatsufusa is no ordinary dog, but a dog-god. Fuse herself insists that the wedding takes place because she finds it unbearable when a promise of a ruler is no longer valid. The marriage takes place and the Yatsufusa takes Fuse to Mount Tomisan. There, shortly afterwards, Fuse dreams that she is pregnant, even though she was still a virgin. However, she can no longer bear this disgrace of giving birth to a dog's children. When she commits *seppuku*, her Buddhist rosary breaks out with hundreds of pearls, which a priest had given her exactly one year earlier and thus connected the prophecy of a unique fate for her. Among the many scattered pearls, eight begin to glow blue, rise and float away. They are the true sons of Fuse, born as human beings by other women from different provinces. Each of them has one of the magic pearls with a holy inscription and they become all warriors, the eight dog warriors, each embodying a Confucian virtue. Together and with the help of the magic pearls they are to create a new, fairer order in the province of Awa. They will pursue their task until and when the sacred inscriptions on the pearls disappear." Moved by his own words, Bakin looked with big eyes at the ceiling and through it into the sky, where he suspected the power he wanted to let work in this story.

"That's a damn good story here, a really great story, Bakin-san! Fill us up, woman, faster. We're old and dying soon, so hurry up, I don't want to be sober," he barked at the servant. "You've already told me more than you've written. That's what I heard. I realized that your dog warriors are no samurai, this snooty and useless bunch."

"Yes, that's right. The time of the samurai is long gone. They are no longer the embodiment of what was sacred to me as a young man."

"Thank you, my old friend. In my mind's eye, promptly dramatic, wild pictures emerge that are worthy of your subject in their size. I just wonder why you secretly asked my son-in-law Shigenobu Yanagawa to do the drawings. But let's drink."

"Don't give me that! Never again will you illustrate my stories! The experience with my *Chinsetsu Yumihari-Zuki* has cured me. You didn't want to understand what kind of pictures I expected of you. I am always annoyed when readers write me letters and congratulate me on the illustrations."

"You don't realize I imagined something completely different." Hokusai laughed. Bakin had fallen back into his old rage at their difficult collaboration from then as if all this had only just happened.

"You really are still the same disgusting pig bone you've always been. And you're probably right. We should stop working together. You've become as vain as I am. Although we're both just having a little fun with our art. No nobleman would ever see our work. Drink, come on drink!"

"No, no, that's enough," Bakin refused. He was afraid of Hokusai's pathetic attempts at fraternization when he was drunk—because he knew how susceptible he himself was. Then again, he drank his cup and Hokusai smiled satisfied. "What did you do in the meantime," Bakin asked, who, despite their quarrel at the time, knew he was working with the greatest painter of his time—whatever the aristocrats might think of it.

"Let me show you some pictures." He opened a large wooden box and produced several woodprints on paper wrapped in fabric. "This is one of my views of Fuji. I made almost fifty of them, and they're very popular. Here, this is also a frequently-bought motif from this series, 'The Great Wave.'

"Very impressive," Bakin just breathed and stroked without touching the paper, along with the ridge of the big wave in the foreground and down into the valley, where staggering boats could be seen and on the far horizon the Fuji, which appeared much smaller than the wave-mountains of the outraged sea.

"Then I did these studies on the waterfalls of all the provinces known as *Shokoku Taki Meguri*. Meanwhile, I even sell my sketchbooks, the *manga*.

Fortunately, I'm no longer on the market myself to offer my *ukyio-e* and manga. There are so many copies in advance that I can always hire other people to do it. And there are inquiries from dealers all over the country."

"Wouldn't it be interesting for you if our government were to expand and improve relations with foreigners? Maybe the barbarians in *Yōroppa* can get an idea of the higher values of our culture with your pictures."

"Why do you think I'm here! Last year, the chief-Dutchman of the troupe crammed into the harbor gave me a nice job. He has a fascinating face, looks like an old dog, what do I say, like a dog god, just like in your story. But... well, I'm not done with the job yet. Honestly, I haven't even started yet. I'm here for a very different reason. I want to see such a woman again as when the first female foreigner was on Dejima for a short time. We camped for days on the shore near the bridges to be allowed to take a look at her at least once from a distance. And what can I tell you! I saw her! You can't imagine! A woman like an animal, a demon! I couldn't sleep properly for weeks. She was very close to the bridge, surrounded by a crowd of our translators, whom she towered by more than one head. She was huge. Her eyes glowed like fresh lava and her mouth, from which she made incredible sounds, was so big that she could cut off and swallow a Japanese head with a bite. There were many large white teeth in it and its fringes were lined with fleshy lips like germinating fruits."

"You're making fun of me. You drank too much," Bakin threw in grumpily–and emptied another cup, which the mute servant filled again at once.

"Bakin, you have princesses getting pregnant with dogs. You have no idea what else nature has come up with. So, listen." Hokusai closed his eyes and let the image of the demoness rise again before he continued speaking.

"Her hair was like wild bushes in a storm. They whirled through the air in circles and were completely intertwined. She had swirls and proliferating curls like a man's beard. Her body was almost cut in the middle. It ran from her hips, which were approximately at the height of our interpreters' chest, wide lengths of fabric all the way down over her feet. Towards the top, towards the shoulders, her body also became wider, but the fabric snuggled tightly against the forms below. You can't imagine what breasts she had! Two big Fujis side by side, each certainly as big as a pumpkin. I thought I was gonna faint. I've never seen anything like it. This figure and the hell-dance she performed, that was so eerie and so exciting! I wished that demon would jump over the water on top of me and eat me. I only hoped that she would take much time when she devoured my longing flesh and that my bones would be sweet enough for her. For the first time, I could think of death with pleasure."

"You're abnormal, I always knew that. All the feminine beauty of our country is wasted on you. But thank you for the description, because it's true, I was interested. I am pleased to hear that nothing is like the lovely *urisane-gao* of our tender women. These wonderful melon seed faces, as they have been handed down to us by the painters from *Heian*, are for me the epitome of eternal delight."

"This is all aristocratic crap. I prefer every buxom *jorō* from the market to these affluent princesses, I prefer every hour in the house of pleasure to the tedious reading of these boring and redundant Chinese moral sermons, from which the noble views of our high lords are nourished. And you know what? Ha! They love my *shunga* and they buy them underhand, you understand? They send their servants dressed as merchants and pay without asking the prices I make up! I'd love to know what they're doing with it, hehe."

Bakin had emptied another cup and just set it down as he nagged off instantly.

"I have seen one of these books. What rubbish! Such infamous crap! Come on, show me if your *dankon* is as big as you draw it. That's what I want to know," with which he pounced on Hokusai angrily and tried to get a grip on his genitals through the *yukata*. The much stronger painter was surprised, lost his balance, fell on his back, drew Bakin practically on him and then tried to shake him off. So they grappled and rolled over the tatami.

"Stop it, you crazy old man! What got into you?" Hokusai shouted, laughing. "Are you jealous or what? Do you want me to draw yours like this? Is that what you want?" Then he got hold of Bakin and sat him upright again, which he let happen willingly with himself. Both were out of breath. The servant filled the cups unmoved.

Hokusai shook his head with a grin. "Where were we? Oh, yeah, the Chinese. Yeah, they make me boil. I wish our country would drift far, far

126

away to the sea, so they wouldn't come here again. I have to write their fucking characters, I have to let their medicine heal me, and then I also have to look at their pictures in this tedious and pretentious style."

"Really? Why? You still paint like the Chinese yourself!"

"What do you mean?"

"Like me, you only work in your house, in your workshop. You should see young *Hiroshige*. His pictures are already offered next to yours. He takes all his material with him and works outdoors when he paints nature. You're still a classic studio painter, and you're just a Japanese Chinese." Hokusai turned up his nose and pulled a face of disgust. Painting outdoors? What an absurd idea. Bakin rejoiced at his little malice.

A Walk with Mendelssohn

"Menduruson-san! Menduruson-san," Siebold called for Mendelsohn down the street where he had discovered him walking around indecisively, cheekily imitating the Japanese pronunciation of this name. They hadn't seen each other for the first three days after the long journey.

"Oh, Siebold, I've been looking for you. I need your help." Siebold came closer and was shocked at Mendelssohn's pallor.

"What can I do for you?"

"I don't feel well. Since we arrived here, I can't really get on my feet. I have a headache and I'm tired."

"Well, come right into my practice. It's already closed, actually. In such serious cases, however, I feel the sting of my Hippocratic oath on my chest. But I will only examine you out of opening hours if you take a little walk with me afterward! I'll support you, if necessary." Mendelssohn looked at him with a mixture of disapproval and astonishment. He was just not in the mood for ironical statements. The examination quickly came to a surprising result. Mendelssohn did not have Siebold's robust constitution. The exhaustion from the voyage and the shortage of food now took their toll, even though the adventure was over. But the headaches had another origin.

"Mendelssohn, I have good news and bad news for you. Which one do you want to hear first?"

"The bad please," he replied soundlessly. He was miserable.

"You need glasses!" said Siebold in all seriousness. "You've become myopic in the last few weeks without realizing it. That's not a problem. We have enough glasses on board. They are among the goods to be sold to the Japanese. I'll see if we can find a good lens grinder in town that can fit one of them for you."

"And what's the good news?" Mendelssohn asked.

"You don't have to die, and you're not even seriously ill. Only regular and healthy food should be taken care of. I would also like to prescribe you some exercise and physical training. I can hardly offer you anything other than walking or fencing."

"Jesus, fencing, no, you can't do that to me. Then let's take a walk around this pile of earth. I feel better already. It is interesting how a physical condition on the one hand and the concern about it, on the other hand, accumulate and can only be felt as a unit. The art of a doctor is not only to heal the physical causes of suffering but also to dissociate it as far as possible from the associated concern".

"That's more like you. As soon as the concern is gone, you are the philosopher again."

Siebold locked his practice and went with Mendelssohn to the seaside of the island.

There stood a weathered bench that was once set up by an aesthete who mourned his Paris years. But it was never used by the practical thinking Dutch with little inclination to random walks. They cleaned it with their bare hands and sat down in the warm twilight in front of the panorama of the bay.

"So, you are settling in well, as I can see from your unclouded mood," Mendelssohn stated with the intonation of a question.

"Yes, I'm surprised myself. It's as if I've reached my destination. Nevertheless, I also take care to get enough rest after the exertions of the journey. I'm just a little depressed by the spatial confinement of our prison. And I think about almost nothing else but how to get ashore and start my research."

"Tell me, what do you know about the history of relations between Japan and foreigners? Thanks to you, I now know a lot about the morphology of the respiratory organs of bony fishes and as your diligent student,

I have learned more species of vermin than I carry guilders with me. Yet, in view of the richness of nature, we have completely forgotten this historical topic at sea ".

"That comes handy," said Siebold and leaned back. "At a dinner at the Opperhoofd's two days ago, we talked about it. Blomhoff not only refreshed my memories but also told me a lot about our mission and its history, which was unknown to me so far. You have to figure this: The magnificent city of Nagasaki was still a small fishing village in 1543 when shipwrecked Portuguese first landed nearby. Captain Bernao Mendez Pintu had brought with him a Chinese man from Macau who could talk to a Chinese man living here. The Chinese man, who had washed up with Pintu, described the Portuguese as harmless traders. However, they had long metal tubes with them, which were soon of great interest to the Japanese–rifles. The import of firearms decided the civil war that had lasted for centuries because they fell into the hands of *Oda Nobunaga*, one of many rulers with their own lands–or *daimyō*, as the Japanese say–whose goal was the unification of the country. The Portuguese were therefore very welcome in Japan. They had the permission to trade and to move freely in the country. However, the European guests could not refrain from missioning, reforming and making the Japanese happy with Christianity. The Jesuit Father *Francisco de Xavier* began his missionary work in 1549, and astonishingly the Japanese converted to Christianity on a massive scale, even if they had only a highly inaccurate idea of our religion. But that must have been the case everywhere the pious brothers set their feet on new land."

"Are you a believing Christian?" Mendelssohn interrupted him. He had clearly heard Siebold's dislike of the Jesuits.

"Am I here before the Holy Inquisition?" Siebold asked with a treacherous smile. But he already knew how to understand the question.

"You embarrass me a little, you know. I admit, despite a thorough religious education, it is difficult for me to grasp the concept of that benevolent higher being that Scripture calls the Creator of heaven and earth. I have seen the Bible, especially the New Testament, more as a moving legend of a righteous hero coming to a bad end. And you, are you a believing Jew?"

"Oh, unfortunately, a Jew is always a believer, whether he likes it or not. I'd be happy if I had a choice. But a Jew is born into his religion. He does not have to confess to it, he does not need baptism, confirmation, or communion. The Jew does not escape the Jewish faith. My heart would have beaten much faster for a Christianity like the great Leibniz represented it. Or *Kant*."

"Shall we get back to the subject?" Siebold asked politely, with a touch of irony.

"Yes, yes, of course," Mendelssohn hurried as if he wanted to make the unnecessary question of faith superfluous retroactively. Siebold continued with his historical lecture.

"Well, where were we? Oh, yes. Gradually the influence of the Jesuits became uncanny to the shogunate. Soon it was not only more than a hundred thousand ordinary people who admitted to Christianity, but also a growing number of daimyō converted. The daimyō *Omura Sumitada* even gave the Jesuits the city of Nagasaki. Meanwhile the generalissimo *Toyotomi Hideyoshi* had effectively promoted the centralization of Japan and attacked Korea with one hundred sixty thousand soldiers. However, this campaign was a failure. Instead, he issued the first edict providing for the banishment of all foreigners. It had not yet been executed, but a few years later Hideyoshi had twenty-six Jesuits and Japanese who had become Christians executed as a warning. He also took Nagasaki away from the Jesuits and brought the province under his control. After his death, the great *Ieyasu Tokugawa* took over the government, destroyed all domestic opponents in the great *Battle of Sekigahara* in 1600 and thus concluded Japan's unification into a nation with a central government. He took over the title of shogun again. This was the foundation of the new Tokugawa dynasty, which still reigns today. Edo became the new capital of the empire.

The government of this newly found police stated was increasingly worried who this ruler in distant Europe was, whom the foreigners called 'Pope', and above all how large his armies are. Of course, it had not escaped to the shogun and his advisors that Christianity was a forerunner that announced the coming of colonial troops. What was decisive, however, was the fear that the loyalty of the Japanese subjects and daimyōs to an emperor of Christianity could weaken the central government, which was just becoming more powerful. Then the Dutch came into play. The first factory was built by us in 1609 about a hundred *nautical miles* north of here on the island of Hirado. Like the English, we had no interest in missionary work. Soon after, the Spaniards were the first to be expelled from the country.

Then a story occurred which I could not find in the scholarly proceedings before. Blomhoff told of the uprising of the farmers converted to Christianity in the neighboring province of Shimabara. That was in 1638. The daimyō of this fief wanted to build a castle and pressed the money from his subjects, who increasingly refused to pay. He even sent his troops, but the resistance was much fiercer than he had expected. There was a great battle at the fortress of Hara. After a long siege, the rebels gave up. There were forty thousand men, women, and children. They all, without exception, died in agony. They were stabbed, impaled, or cooked in the hot sulfurous springs of the nearby volcano Unzen, which we could see on entering the bay. Shortly thereafter, the Portuguese were also banished forever. The Netherlands has been given the privilege of remaining in Japan in a less glorious way. They supported the local authorities and fired cannons at the insurgents from a ship. This loyalty in the persecution of Christians was rewarded the Dutch with a right to stay on the island of Dejima. They had to dismantle the factory on Hirado and to move here. So, we took Dejima over from the Portuguese, who had to dump this pile of earth a few years earlier here in the harbor basin. For the Japanese government began to take its own former edicts seriously: 'No foreigner should set foot on Japanese soil anymore.'"

"Truly, truly, this was not a triumph of virtue," Mendelssohn sighed philosophically.

"That's a noble expression. Firing only one bullet at Christians was a betrayal of our own civilization. Do you think there is any virtue or reason at all in the colonial undertakings of our nations?"

"I have never heard of a people happier since they made our acquaintance. And I can only hope that our violence, our greed for trade privileges and our abuse of all forms of hospitality will not live on for centuries as a European shame in the memory of humanity."

"You know, I was very impressed by my stay in Java. There I decided that the only justification for our activities in foreign countries is the enrichment of science and cultural exchange. Of course, this also includes trade, but only for as long as it is in our mutual interest. That is why I am somewhat grateful to the Japanese because they have their own interests so rigidly under control that I can work here with a clear conscience. Even if I'm not really happy about the insurmountable obstacles ahead."

"Yes, that brings us back to the subject. What happened to the foreigners in Japan?"

"This is told quite quickly. From 1638 on, the country was completely isolated from the rest of the world. Officially there was only the contact to the Netherlands on Dejima. The Chinese you will meet here are not considered foreigners because they are not accredited. In other words, they are not considered to be under the protection of the Chinese government and are therefore impersonal. The clearest difference to the Dutch, however, is that they are not allowed to visit shogun in Edo every year. Only the Dutch have this privilege."

"I cannot imagine that such great seafaring nations and colonial powers as England will put up with this in the long run."

"Absolutely right. There have also been a whole series of incidents. Some French, Russian and English ships have simply stranded or crashed on the Japanese coast. Others wanted to open access to one of the ports with more or less violence. They all failed. The Japanese government is obsessed with the idea of maintaining the country's isolation. This must be seen against the background of a period of peace that has lasted for almost two centuries. The last war in Japan ended in August 1600 with the aforementioned *Battle of Sekigahara*. Japan's refusal to correspond with other countries and to enter into the global trade is seen with some justification as a proven model".

"And what do you know about today's shogun?"

"His name is *Ienari Tokugawa* and he has reigned since 1786. He is said to be a megalomaniac, to plunder the state treasury with his pompous lifestyle and he has already fathered stunning fifty-two children. The young emperor, called *Tennō* by the Japanese, is Ayahito and has reigned since 1817. He is the religious leader of the country and the highest priest of the Shintō faith. The two should get along well because the shogun married a noblewoman of the Shimatsu family, which inevitably brought him closer to the high nobility at the emperor's court".

"Thank you for these teachings. I can see much clearer now. So, we are at the end of the world in a very strange country that doesn't really want to know anything about us. If they do, the Japanese want the sugar we brought. These are not bright prospects."

"Wait and see, Mendelssohn. I have heard that there are many cultured people here in the city who are interested in Dutch knowledge. And I already have a plan how we can win these people over. Wait and see."

The Dutchmen's Talk

The new Dutch legation had already been accommodated on the factory island for a week when Blomhoff presented his successor, Colonel de Sturler, and Major Dr. von Siebold to the assembled College of Translators. The occasion was the traditional report on the world situation, eagerly awaited by the Japanese, which they called the 'Dutchmen's talk'. Of course, it was not allowed to be more than an informal exchange, which preceded the detailed written protocol, which had to be delivered to the shogun later by the executive committee of the legation during the large court journey to Edo. But secretly, the Dutch discussion anticipated the entire report, making the occasionally more than fifty translators Japan's best-informed foreign policy circle. Many of its members were already translators for the Dutch from Dejima in the third, fourth or even fifth generation. The families, who had a long tradition of translation work, were extraordinarily cultivated and became influential through this knowledge. Their advice was in demand far beyond the district of Nagasaki. Every translator and translator family had specialized in a scientific or artistic field over the years so that these people were excellently trained contacts for the Dutch and not simple handlers.

"I had already written to Colonel de Sturler on Batavia announcing that a sketch of world affairs was expected of him," Blomhoff explained, "and I thought it appropriate for you, Herr Major, to attend the event. You are also invited to share your own observations and knowledge of European politics if Colonel de Sturler agrees." Sturler nodded silently. "However, I would ask you to exclude the issue of colonial policy as much as possible. The Japanese are extremely attentive and concerned listeners. We must weigh our words carefully because there is a great sensitivity in this area. You must know that this news spreads from here all over the country. We also have to withhold some of our knowledge so that the shogun has not already learned all about his informers and secret services, which he receives in the written report on his visit to the court." Instructed in this way, Siebold and his superiors went to the factory reception hall, where the translators stood up and bowed to the triumvirate. Blomhoff and Siebold sat down, Sturler remained standing and began to deliver his report at once.

"Gentlemen of the College, we are pleased to report to you for the second time in a row on the favorable developments in Europe after the end of the French Revolution and the subsequent wars. To give you the most important information in advance: The earthly god of war, the French monster, the dwarf who ruled all of Europe, is no longer. Napoleon Bonaparte is dead!"

A murmur went through the room. Siebold looked at Sturler in astonishment and admired him for the theatrical way in which he seasoned this message. At the same time, he remembered the day he had learned of Napoleon's death. The news was on the first page of the local newspaper Würzburger Kurier. A sigh of relief went through Europe. Finally, the spook was over, the French Revolution had finally ended. In Austria, bonds increased by two thalers. Yet Siebold was depressed at the time. He thought of the beautiful speech of his fellow student Wellmann, the eagle flight of his thoughts to the island of St. Helena, where Napoleon stood angrily on the lips of the cliff. Yes, he thought it might be that Wellmann would be right if we left Napoleon and all his work to oblivion. He had reshaped Europe, introduced a uniform legal system, deprived the nobility, and abolished torture. But the most important thing, Siebold thought, was Napoleon's promotion of science. France became the European center of research through him, and not only because the other countries were covered with wars. Napoleon was a thoroughly modern man, a great, forward-looking personality. This greatness alone made his downfall immeasurably sad and pathetic. At that time Siebold felt condolence, as if something unjust laid in this end. He felt this compassion so violently and he took it so personally that he had to admit to himself a hidden mixture of fear and hope that a comparable fate could one day befall him. At the same time, he became fully aware that he was politically inclined towards liberalism, even that he was a liberal and a democrat. In contrast to the proponents of the conservative system that Metternich established in Europe, which was to restrict freedoms and protect monarchies from the demands for participatory rights, in short, to this system that tried to stop time, Siebold believed in the necessity of constitutions, in the sovereignty of peoples, in the inalienability of human rights, in the restriction of governmental and state power through institutions such as parliaments and finally also in free trade throughout the world. He had respect for the hereditary monarchies, he understood that power must not be left to the rabble and he saw the inevitability of colonial competition. But these were only transit stages on the way to a new epoch. Europe was not allowed to stand still there. Napoleon had become for him the symbol of inevitable progress, which could temporarily also show its terrible face.

"He died on 5 May 1821 in English captivity on the island St. Helena, in the middle of the Atlantic Ocean, abandoned by all", Sturler continued in this dramatic tone, which did not correspond at all to his temperament otherwise.

"The new order in Europe adopted at the Congress of Vienna in 1815 has proved its worth. There has been no war in Europe since our last report. The restoration policy, which aimed to restore the European order of 1792, was a great success. The Holy Alliance, founded by the great powers to ensure a balance of European forces on the principles of the divine grace, accepted France in 1818. The revolutionary, liberal and nationalist activities were stopped in all countries. In recent years, however, Great Britain has noticeably withdrawn from the concert of European powers. In their 'splendid isolation', as the British call their policy, they devote themselves to industrialization and the slave trade. However, the former Holy Roman Empire of the German Nation, which Napoleon had dissolved in 1806, has not yet been restored. There is no longer a German emperor, but only a German alliance of thirty-nine princes and kings, to which His Majesty, King William I of the United Netherlands, has also joined as Grand Duke of Luxemburg".

Sturler continued with his report until he finally came to the new direction of Dutch policy towards Japan. In addition to stimulating trade, the explicit aim of this mission was to raise scientific exchange to an unprecedented level. If these words were to rush through the country from now on, then no disadvantage could arise for his intentions, Siebold thought. On the contrary. He kept his own political observations wisely for himself. The horror that the Japanese had inflicted on him when they almost exposed him as a non-Dutchman and would send him back to Java or Europe was still too deep in his bones.

The Cataract Operation

A few days later, a commissioner entered Siebold's surgical practice and reported the visit of an old priest from the mainland accompanied by an accredited translator. Several Japanese had already crossed the bridge to the island and had been treated by Siebold. They had minor ailments such as skin diseases or ulcers.

"Good afternoon, *Isha*-san, and welcome to Nagasaki. I would like to introduce master Shigetsugu Yoshisada, the venerable priest of the Sofukuji Temple," said the young translator to Siebold in perfect Dutch. The old man bowed and muttered a greeting that Siebold did not understand.

"Master Yoshisada largely lost his sight over ten years ago. He wants to know if the honorable Dutch doctor can do anything for him. You should know that master Yoshisada is a highly respected person in Nagasaki and his fame reaches far beyond the city limits. He is the first priest in a long time to be allowed to enter Dejima."

"Please sit on this chair," Siebold said friendly to the old man and led him to the chair. The translator explained to the priest what a 'chair' is, for very few Japanese knew this Western invention. Carefully and stiffly he sat down on the seat of this piece of furniture, which he had never seen before and could now only feel with his hands. Siebold bent the man's head backward and spread the upper and lower eyelids of both eyes one after the other with his thumb and index finger to examine the pupil width and the condition of the lenses. The latter was pervaded by dense white veils. Siebold diagnosed a typical cataract but kept this for himself.

"Please come back tomorrow," Siebold said to the priest, "and bring a few men with you, as well as a local doctor from the city who can treat you later. I'm going to do a little surgery on you here. That will take no longer than about half an hour. Afterward, you can be brought home by your helpers." The translator repeated the words in Japanese and the priest just nodded devotedly in silence.

The next morning Siebold looked through the window full of expectation to the guarded bridge, which laid diagonally opposite his practice and separated him from the mainland like an invisible wall. It was his firm decision that this bridge would soon no longer be an obstacle for him. As agreed, the priest appeared with four companions, the translator, and a young doctor. Everyone had to undergo a rigorous search before they could pass. When they entered the rooms of the practice and bowed before Siebold, he asked the priest again to sit down. Then he brought out one of the stethoscopes Major Fritze had given him, thinking involuntarily of his words. In fact, those present muttered devoutly as he listened to the heart beats and the flat sounds of the lungs of the old man with the impressive instrument–a procedure that he could well have spared for the forthcoming operation, but which was to impress his audience, which happily appeared in such large numbers. Then he asked his patient to lie down on the operating table and explained what he would do. The translator repeated it in Japanese for everyone present.

"I beg you, honorable priest, to drink this juice first. It contains a sedative to keep your eyes from moving so much. Then I will disinfect your eyes with this solution and anesthetize them locally", pointing to the two bottles of medication on the cleanly prepared instruction table." And finally, you'll get a few drops of this drug in your eyes." He held up the vial with a theatrical gesture. "It is the most important drug for this treatment." He gave the priest the sedative juice, which he drank without hesitation and with a serious expression. Then he piped the different solutions one after the other into the eyes of his patient, who had to blink on them and some of the liquid ran out of the corners of his eyes over his temples.

"When these drugs take effect, I will start the operation. I'm going to use this scalpel to remove a piece of your eye. You won't be in any pain. Later, too, your eyes will only water a little. They have to stay under a bandage for a few days until the wounds on your eyes have healed." Siebold sat down at his desk and took some notes, while the priest lay still, and his companions could not keep to themselves with curiosity. The young doctor forgot his restraint and inspected the instruments, the medicine cabinet, the anatomical maps on the wall and the reference library with the standard medical works. He was particularly interested in the microscope, which Siebold had placed on a specially brought along table with a few selected specimens. The priest's companions whispered like humming flies, barely audible, yet very excited. None of them had ever seen the practice of a European doctor. It was a long time ago that the great Swedish naturalist *Carl Thunberg*, one of Siebold's predecessors in this room, treated Japanese patients.

Siebold took a look at the priest, who already made a relaxed impression. The *morphine* had taken effect. Siebold did not want to take any risks with this important operation and had therefore chosen a reliable sedative agent for his patient. He got up, went to one of the cupboards and took out a palm-sized concave mirror on a band that he pulled over his head so that the mirror was fixed in front of his forehead. The Japanese looked at each other in astonishment, for Siebold suddenly looked like a Shintō priest before a sacred ritual. Then he lit a bright oil lamp, which was equipped with another movable mirror. He aligned both mirrors so that the light from the lamp and the daylight entering through the window was directed as well as possible onto his patient's face. He took an eye clip and fixed it to the eyelids of the first eye so that the priest could no longer close it. Siebold was content with the slowed reflexes. Without the drug and the local *anesthetic*, the intense light would have blinded the priest strongly. Siebold now had his eye well in view. The *atropine* had worked. The pupil was maximally dilated and thus the most important prerequisite for an exact cut was given. He took the eye scalpel and removed the entire cornea with the underlying lens in a single, continuous movement. The priest did not move and seemed quite calm. But Siebold noticed the cold sweat in the sinewy throat pit under his larynx. He repeated the procedure unerringly on the second eye. Then he let him close both eyes and put on the bandage.

"Please rest and keep the bandage on for about a week. Then come back and we will see," he said to the priest. The translator did his work and again the old man nodded silently, but this time with his mouth open and his head in an attitude as if he wanted to see something in the darkness in front of him. He would now be completely blind for several days. The four companions of the priest all tried to escort him out and over the bridge at the same time, taking him like something very fragile in their midst and gently pushing him forward. When they had passed the bridge, Siebold was satisfied. Now all he had to do was wait.

Misuzu Inukawa

Less than a week had passed since Siebold received a written message, which was delivered to him by the deputy port commissioner himself. He was asked to go the morning of the following day to the home of the priest he had previously treated. He would be in pain and unable to come to the island of Dejima. In addition to his escort, the port commissioner's office would deploy three policemen. Siebold inwardly rejoiced with happiness. He was able to leave the island! If only for a few hours. But at the same time, he fervently hoped that there had been no complications in the healing process with the old man. That would have been unfavorable for his plans. An inflammation of the eyes that he could not control would be fatal. Additionally, in the evening, Blomhoff and Sturler summoned him not to make a mistake. This was the first land visit of an island dweller in a very long time.

The next morning, he stood in his practice in an impeccable uniform with polished boots, impatiently waiting for the escort. The three port police officers arrived just before lunchtime across the bridge, where they had to produce a letter from the Commissioner. They entered Siebold's practice and lined up with their threatening lances and sinister faces. One of them spoke Dutch and asked Siebold to take his instruments and follow them. Siebold took his doctor's case and left the practice with the police. He had to get searched at the bridge. Two *saguriban* controlled every passer-by, scanned him, searched all the bags, including Siebold's. On the side of the mainland, there was a sign with Japanese characters in front of the crossing point, which regulated the communication with the strangers in a strict tone.

FIRST

Women are not allowed in. Exception: courtesans

SECOND

To priests and *Yamabushi*, except the *Kōyasan*, it is forbidden to pass through the gate

THIRD

Admission is prohibited for fundraisers and beggars

FOURTH

Beyond the banned pole or under the bridge it is forbidden to pass through

FIFTH

Without special permission, no Dutchman is allowed to leave the island

He knew the translation from the Dutch command book for island life on Dejima. The original inscription he saw for the first time, because the sign was turned away from the island. Then it finally happened. He took his first steps on the Japanese mainland. Shortly after his arrival on Dejima, he had become painfully aware that he was still not officially on Japanese soil, that the artificially built island was a kind of territorial purgatory, nothing true and nothing false. And now: Japan! He was finally, really and truly on Japanese soil. How many people had been allowed to set foot here in the last two centuries, with the explicit invitation of a local authority? Siebold felt like an explorer who discovers on unknown shores that the land before him had not yet been entered by his peers. Rather, the country had decided to establish an exclusive relationship with him and he was a welcome guest because people were interested in him and his knowledge. This exception, which the authoritarian self-confidence of the Japanese nation made in his favor, ennobled him. He felt in an awkward way returned home and for the first time in his life fully accepted. At that moment, his deep longing for Japan was replaced by an even deeper love for this country. The goal of his wishes was achieved. He was from then on in a state of continuous fulfillment. He had to laugh, could hardly suppress a happy grin. He sensed—no, he knew that the new chapter in his story, which he had been expecting for weeks, would finally begin.

Moved in this way, he walked the road for the first time, the course of which he had previously only been allowed to follow from afar. His trained eye as a naturalist let him capture such a lot of detailed impressions that he hardly had the opportunity to look at the people in the street. They were amazed and amused by the dreamy *Orandajin* in this dazzling outfit, which had not been seen for a long time, whose uniform was so colorful and clean and whose animal skin footwear shone as if he were a king who deserved a sedan chair. Who was that man? The bright white women under their wax-coated umbrellas turned to him like the farmers in their light straw sandals, who had never seen anything like it before. The street was lined with shops and boutiques of all kinds, a whole series of fishmongers, whose astonishing displays had bizarre, sometimes still wriggling, sometimes sleepy-embroidering creatures of the sea which Siebold did not know, as well as fabric, ivory, spice and porcelain dealers, who called out to the passing crowd. Workers who were naked except for a loincloth grinned cheekily over to him. This was how Siebold had imagined an oriental bazaar and he was impressed by the hustle and bustle. When they passed a kind of pharmacy stand where herbs of all kinds were hanging out, a woman in a pretty kimono with a cloud motif stood in front of the display and spoke to the salesman. Siebold could not see her but told the Dutch-speaking policeman that he had to look for medicinal herbs in this shop that might be beneficial for the treatment of the priest. The latter had no objections and Siebold stood next to the lady on the wooden step from the stand. Then she turned around, looked at him and opened her face to an enchanting smile. The round eyes gave her a childlike and clear expression that he did not know in the physiognomy of adult Europeans. Long eyelashes and strong eyebrows were missing. The eyelids were smooth and ran like tense sails into the corners of the eye. The white of the eyeballs was hidden and the fawn-brown iris completely dominated her gaze. Her teeth shone even brighter. Her smile was exactly proportioned so that it did not reduce the size of her eyes and no wrinkles could be seen around her. This face was a work of art like Siebold had never seen before, framed by blue-black, straight hair, which she elegantly wore together at the back of her head with a tortoiseshell pin. It was the first woman in a long time that he really noticed and that enchanted him unprepared. Siebold was so captivated by her appearance that he could think of nothing. She greeted him with a smile to free herself from the embarrassment: "Konichiwa, *Ijin-san*."

"Excuse me?" he asked back in Dutch like an automaton, although he had understood exactly what she wanted to say.

"Good morning, Barbarian?" she repeated her words giggling in Dutch, hiding her smiling mouth behind her right hand.

"You speak Dutch?" he asked back instead of giving a reasonable answer, thus neglecting the required courtesy for a gentleman. Moreover, this question was superfluous and downright idiotic, since she had already answered it.

"Of course. Who doesn't?" Her Dutch was better than that of the policeman who was talking to his two colleagues during that time.

"Are you saying that all the people of Nagasaki speak Dutch?"

"Of course. Well, a lot of them, anyway. Didn't you know that?"

"No, honestly not," he said, while a suspicion grew in him.

"You mean, I could ask this gentleman here in Dutch if he has dried sage leaves?"

"I don't have sage, Orandajin-san," the salesman replied unasked, "but instead I could offer you ginseng root."

Siebold was speechless at first. That was surprising, although he could and should have known it. He had told Mendelssohn the whole story. For generations, the people of Nagasaki have been in close, albeit strictly controlled, contact with the foreigners on Dejima. The town, originally a meaningless fishing village, had become a large and prosperous city by the Dutch. So why shouldn't the Japanese have learned their language in this long time?

"May I ask you a question, Ijin-san?" the woman asked curiously.

"Of course, please. You're welcome"

"What are you doing on Dejima? And what's your name?"

"Those are two questions, young lady."

"Oh, I beg your pardon. How rude of me!" She was really embarrassed and looked as lovely as a repentant child. Nevertheless, Siebold would have liked to take back his stupid and self-opinionated reply.

"I am the surgeon-major and thus the doctor of the Dutch legation. My name is Doctor Philipp Franz von Siebold, madam." He wasn't sure if he hit the right note when he said that because the 'madam' was so young that he thought more of a girl. But at the same time, as far as he could see under the kimono, she was well developed and had self-confident, well-behaved manners.

"Hirippu Hurantsu hon Shiboruto. So many names! Which one is the most important one I can call you with when you walk through our town so loudly again?"

"Siebold, I guess."

"Well, from now on, you are Shiboruto-san."

"Yes, madam," replied Siebold in a hint of irony. The salesman had followed the back and forth of this conversation with hypnotic concentration and the corresponding head movement and laughed as if at the end of a funny story. She, on the other hand, struck her eyes down again, bowed and turned away to walk.

"Wait! What is your name?" Siebold shouted after.

"Shiboruto-san," she said gently and quietly, slowly turning back to him only with her head and shoulders, "in our country women are not called after in the open street. Didn't you know that? However, we want to be hospitable with our Dutch visitors. Misuzu Inukawa is my name. I hope you will honor our house, the *Hikidaya*, during your stay. And then please remember my name."

With these words and a last floating smile, she finally turned away, opened an umbrella and walked up the cobbled market street in small steps on her wooden slippers.

When he reached with his escort a magnificent temple with a pagoda roof, the policemen positioned themselves in front of the side entrance, following their instructions exactly. A servant opened the thin sliding door, asked Siebold in with a devote smile and told him that he ought to take off his boots first. Then he led him through several long corridors, some of which were illuminated by daylight from one side and some from both sides by walls made from parchment paper. The priest's apartment was in a remote wing of the Sofukuji temple. When Siebold entered, he found a company of no less than a dozen men, all of whom stood up and greeted him with a deep bow. The priest himself was sitting in front of a narrow table, bowing and smiling contentedly. He didn't seem to be doing badly, on the contrary.

"Sit down, Shiboruto-san," the priest asked him. Siebold sat down opposite him at the table and tried to get into a cross-legged position with his stockinged legs, as he saw the priest doing. So, it was true. Many people spoke or understood Dutch. The old man included. The other participants settled on the flat floor in a circle around the two of them, sitting on their heels in the *seiza* with their legs closed and bent. Soon a small, old lady came in, distributed petite cups and poured gently transparent tea.

"Welcome to my unworthy dwelling. It is far too great an honor for me to have such a great man with me." He took a short break. Siebold already knew that the Japanese got involved in long and submissive expressions of politeness before they got down to business.

"I don't know if you can give me back my sight, Shiboruto-san. But my companions have healthy eyes, and they have seen amazing things in the honorable doctor's house. They would like to inform you that they are interested in a close cooperation."

The situation still seemed like a ritual, for the blind priest spoke loudly and rhythmically, fixing Siebold and the others with his blindfolded eyes as if he could see through the pads of cotton wool and the cloth bandages.

"It is an immeasurable honor, master Yoshisada."

"You must know, my guests here are not only the best doctors of Nagasaki, some have also come from far away. None of them would have dared the operation you have put me through. We are all eagerly awaiting the result. And no doubt you have already understood that I only asked you here on the pretext of my indisposition. *Okagesama de* I feel very healthy. A man of my age no longer depends too much on his eyes anyway. I've seen everything. But now I don't want to talk too much, especially not about me. My guests are far too impatient. Allow me to introduce to you the venerable *Ryōsai Kō*, an ambitious young doctor who came to us from the distant province of Awa. I call him first because he is an ophthalmologist and because he made such a great effort to get to know you that I was afraid that if I refused him this privilege, he would turn into a volcano right here among us, in my humble house. And you should know—we are experts on volcanoes."

The guests burst into hearty laughter, but not all of them. Ryōsai Kō laughed at first, but quickly grasped itself and then spoke seriously.

"Venerable Shiboruto-san, we have long waited for an outstanding Dutch doctor to come to Dejima. You will be aware that our government has strictly regulated the treatment of foreigners. Nevertheless, we are eager to know what innovations the Dutch sciences have experienced in recent decades. Therefore, our colleagues had come to you with the foggy blindness of our honorable master Yoshisada." He nodded towards the three companions of the priest, who were also present and bowed before Siebold again. So, they were doctors themselves.

"They told us about instruments they had never seen before, about anatomical maps that are more precise than anything we know so far–and about the obvious ease with which you performed an eye surgery that would be impossible for us. We do not yet know the result, but we have little doubt about its success and we did not want to wait any longer. Can you give us, if you'd like, a brief report on the significant discoveries since your predecessor Kempuhueru-san was here on Dejima?" Siebold was moved by this reception–and struck by what an educated and accent-free Dutch the young doctor spoke.

"Dear Kō-san, dear colleagues, I have indeed news from the European sciences to report. Since *Engelbert Kaempfer's* stay in Japan, there has been amazing progress, especially in the fields of anatomy, surgery, pharmacy, physics, and botany, to name but a few. I have brought along many books and a variety of instruments that you may not have heard of. I will also provide you with a vaccine against smallpox for the first time. Have you ever heard of the principle of *vaccination*?" His audience looked at each other and shook their heads.

"It is a method to prevent dangerous diseases by infecting healthy people with tiny amounts of the wound secretion of patients. They may then develop mild symptoms of the disease, but they will quickly subside. Once they get through this phase, they can never be infected with this disease again." A soft murmur went through the room and the doctors nodded thoughtfully. This description made sense to them.

"This is only a small part of what I would like to offer you all. But it will take me months to familiarize you with the details. It will be difficult to give you these new insights and to demonstrate the instruments every time I come to you under these restrictive conditions."

"We know how many obstacles are put in your way, as well as in our own," Kō replied. "But we are not completely without influence. We will arrange for everyone here to meet regularly at your practice on Dejima if you agree. We will also ensure that you are called to the city as often as possible, for example in difficult cases. So, we can watch you at work and assist you if necessary." Siebold had just taken a sip of the green tea, which tasted slightly stained.

"That's an excellent idea," he rejoiced. "I also look forward with great anticipation to what I can learn from you. When do we want to start the exchange?"

"First thing tomorrow," said Kō with a meaningful smile.

Chapter VI

Sonogi

Embryectomy–The Breakthrough–Otaki's Marriage Proposal–
Wedding on Dejima

Embryectomy

"You see, the juices must flow. Otherwise, your ability to work here will
soon be impaired. This island life is not pure joy, as you may have noticed."
Colonel de Sturler wanted to give Siebold good advice on how to deal with
Japanese women during the morning briefing, while Blomhoff had to leave
the office for a short time. Siebold was clumsy enough to mention to him
his encounter with the lovely Misuzu Inukawa.

"I have already inquired. There are ladies here in Nagasaki who take
care of the Dutch legation professionally. It's not what you might think, so
ordinary prostitution. No, these ladies are getting married on a temporary
basis with their foreign... customers. The woman you met is one of those
so-called courtesans. The Hikidaya is the best house in Nagasaki, an
institution. It's in the *Maruyama* district. You should consider whether such
an arrangement for the next four years would not be best suited to your
needs and our tasks".

"Thank you for your concern and the good advice you'd like to give me.
For my part, I'm not interested in an arrangement of this kind. I have a lot
of work ahead of me, and I won't have time to amuse myself with one of
these certainly most entertaining ladies."

He really could have imagined a relationship with a woman like
Misuzu. Only the thought that he would do it on Sturler's advice and in
addition under his eyes took every desire away from him. Siebold was
offended by the indelicacy with which Sturler acted up as a pimp for the
foreseeable, typically male needs of his organism. And indeed, his
teaching and research projects had a far greater appeal to him than a
woman could possibly ever have. In this respect, he felt safe at that

moment and was convinced that he would not find himself in the embarrassing situation of having to follow Sturler's advice one day.

He had also told Sturler about his appointment with the Japanese doctors, which he acknowledged. In the afternoon, a whole delegation actually appeared at the bridge and the saguriban had to do a search of them all. When they entered Siebold's office and greeted him with bows, he realized that it was the complete gathering of doctors from the previous day.

"It wasn't really that difficult. We have all registered as servants of the head interpreter who supports our request. He himself just passed the bridge with us and has now gone to the director to do other things. So we have about an hour," reported Kō, who remained spokesman of the group. Without hesitation, Siebold set out to introduce his witty and inquisitive visitors to the latest scientific findings of the West. Sitting on one of the chairs alone became an experience for some of them. They were fascinated above all by the microscope with which Siebold showed them selected specimens such as living water fleas, fine sea sand, and incisions of rose petals, flawless images of a bizarre world in miniature of which they had no idea until then. He was particularly proud of this because it was the first microscope with achromatic lenses and was indeed the best instrument of its kind. The hour flew by and his Japanese colleagues were deeply impressed.

The next opportunity for an encounter was not long in coming. That same night he was taken out of bed by one of the doctors, who introduced himself as *Choei Takano*, accompanied by an interpreter and the second port commissioner. There was an emergency and he was asked to come to town. Takano spoke of a woman who had concealed her pregnancy and was now seriously ill. This was important information for Siebold. He put all the instruments for obstetrics in his doctor's bag. Written approval had already been obtained. They set off in a hurry. In the district of Doza, they came to a large house of an obviously well-to-do family. An elderly lady and a young girl were waiting for them at the entrance. The lady of the house tried to keep her posture, but her face was wet with tears and desperate sobs suffocated her voice. As she did not speak Dutch either, the young girl took over the greeting.

"Dear Isha-sama, please enter the unfortunate home of the Kusumoto family at this late hour. Our honorable father is away, and my sister is dying. The doctors said that only the Dutch doctor could help her. We subserviently ask you to use all your arts to save our daughter and sister. She's so young and beautiful. We don't want her to go to our ancestors yet. My mother told me to tell you this. If you'll follow me, please. The other doctors have arrived."

She didn't wear any make-up, but a simple nightdress and held her head low while speaking softly, without even looking at Siebold. Her long hair was carelessly pinned together at the level of her bladebones. Siebold took off his boots in accordance with Japanese custom and entered the house. The two port police officers remained in front of the door again, while Choei Takano accompanied Siebold into the hospital room, where Ryōsai Kō and two other doctors were waiting for them. Mother and daughter stayed on the floor in front of the room, sitting on their folded legs. In the room covered with *tatami*, a young woman of about twenty years of age laid on a *futon*, kneeling with her knees tightened and arms crouched in front of her stomach. Kō told him that no one had known she was pregnant until she fell ill. She was in a delirium, moaned quietly and was bathed in fever sweat. Siebold asked his colleagues to set up four oil lamps around the sickbed, to undress the patient completely and to put her on her back. There was still little light in the room. He put on the headband with the hollow mirror and began the examination by pushing up her eyelids and observing the reflexes of her pupils in the focused light. The result was worrying. She was already in the transition from delirium to coma. Then he palpated the oral cavity, thyroid glands, and armpits with his fingertips, placed the stethoscope on and *auscultated* the lungs and heart. When he palpated the severely hardened abdomen with his hands flat, he realized that the pregnancy was already well advanced. He wondered how the young woman's condition could go unnoticed for so long. But he explained this to himself with the wide robes that Japanese women wore. Then he spread her legs and examined her vulva and vagina. There he found a brown-aqueous, foul-smelling discharge. Takano told him it couldn't be menstruation. Siebold hadn't suspected that either. He asked his colleagues to bring warm water and towels. They passed the order on to the two women outside the door. With several rolled-up futons, the men bedded the patient higher, similar to a birthing chair, a piece of furniture the Japanese did not know. Siebold had better access to her abdomen and gravity was to support further treatment. He washed the vagina from the outside and inside, causing a foul odor to rise. Then he took a pair of pliers out of his pocket, the round leaves of which were beak-shaped.

"That's a speculum. "I can visually examine the patient's abdomen and don't have to rely on my sense of touch alone."

He inserted the speculum into the vagina, spread it with the common movement of the leaves, aligned the focus of his forehead mirror gel along the open vaginal canal and was thus able to recognize the cervix on its base. He would have loved to show the Japanese doctors this first sight of a female organ, but there was no time for it. It was more important to explain the diagnosis and the next steps.

"We need to operate. Her water broke, and the baby is already dead. I guess she was trying to have an abortion. It's hard to tell if she used an object or strong herbs. That's not important now, because we must hurry. Her disease is a poisoning from the fetus, which hasn't come off. She is in the sixth month of pregnancy and the death of the rotten fruit is several days ago. It borders on a miracle that the mother's exitus has not yet occurred. We will extract the fetus, which we call embryectomy in Western medicine. The Caesarean section is out of the question. The patient's too unstable."

His colleagues nodded reverently. Siebold knew that embryectomy was a completely new form of acute obstetrics for Japanese doctors. They usually knew the Caesarean section, but only very few controlled it and most had an almost sacred fear of the bloodbath that they caused by lack of knowledge.

"First, we must rotate the fetus in the uterus, because it is not in the required head position. Then the challenge is to open the patient's cervix so far that we can get to the fetus. If we fail, I see no hope for her. Finally, we will open and empty the head. Only then can we extract the fetus from the uterus. Gentlemen, prepare for a long night."

The doctors looked at each other in shock. None of them had ever made such a drastic intervention in a person's body. For Siebold, too, it was an extreme case that needed his entire medical art, whereby he would also have to improvise. He congratulated himself on being well prepared by the teachings and writings of his uncle Elias von Siebold, the now famous obstetrician and gynecologist at the Charité hospital in Berlin, who had also recommended him to the Dutch colonial ministry for service as a group doctor. On the other hand, he was delighted that the dead fetus did not put him before the most difficult moral decision he could imagine: Can a doctor kill the living child in the mother's body to save her life? Wasn't that murder? In his *Standard Textbook on Practical Maternity*, the manuscript of which he had given Siebold on his journey to Java for reading before publication, his uncle clearly stated: "The embryectomy on the living fruit is not indicated." In this case, there would have been no alternative to the Caesarean section.

The first task was to rotate the fetus in the uterus. Siebold massaged the hardened abdomen of the patient and tried to move the head of the child's corpse towards the birth canal. This proved difficult because the fetus no longer floated in the liquid medium of the amniotic sac but lay fixed in the abdominal cavity like an organ. Only with patience and strength did he succeed. Remnants of the patient's bladder and intestines emptied, and the cloths had to be changed. The saying 'inter faeces et urinam nascimur' of Saint Augustine came to Siebold's mind and the extended it to the point that we are no better off born dead. At that moment, the patient moaned loudly and whimpered in delirium. At one word she repeated several times, the Japanese doctors were shocked. Kō explained Siebold whispering that it was the name of a general of the powerful *Shimazu* clan that rules the principality of *Satsuma*. Siebold did not let this distract him and explained to the doctors that he applied an ether tincture through the canal of the speculum to the cervix with the help of a pipette so that the cervix would relax. Then he would massage the cervix with his hand to open it so wide that he could use the other instruments. First, he gave the patient a sip of water with a high dose of *morphine* and blindfolded her eyes. She was under no circumstances allowed to see the pending procedures and certainly not the dead fetus if she unexpectedly wakes up from the anesthetic. Then he started the operation. After applying the ether to the cervix and removing the speculum, he oiled his hands and the patient's vagina. He then worked on it with strong, massaging movements. He tried to push his hand deeper and deeper into the patient's abdomen. He had to widen the canal to the uterus in the narrow pelvis. But even with all the strength of his arm, he was unable to insert the hand. It was too large for the opening between the pubic bone and the bony pelvic outlet of the petite woman. He sat up straight and thought for a moment. Then he looked at his colleagues one by one.

"What is your name?" he asked the youngest and slightest of the four men.

"Mogami, *Isha*-sama," he replied frightened, "my name is Mogami."

"I need your help. My hands are too big. Yours, on the other hand, could reach the cervix. I'm asking you to do the massage and widen it." He moved aside and told Mogami to take his place. The young doctor slipped on his knees hesitantly closer. Then he too washed his right hand and oiled it. As he shaped his fingers like a stork's beak and wanted to insert his hand like this, Siebold could see it trembling.

"Be brave, my young friend."

Mogami also had to turn and push his hand, but soon his ankles disappeared in the vagina and it closed over his wrist. He had beads of sweat on his face and the shaved areas of his head.

"Do you feel the cervix?"

"Yes, Isha-san," Mogami replied soundlessly.

"Then try to spread it further with your thumb and forefinger. If it works, massage it with three fingers and try to pass it. Through this opening, we must extract the dead fetus. The bigger it is, the better."

Mogami did as he was told. To the fear now came the effort and drops of sweat loosened from his nose tip. Suddenly he cried out.

"Aaaaahhhhhhhhh! Aaaaaahhhh!" Panicked, he tried to withdraw his hand, but moved uncontrollably and was held in the vagina by the vacuum. Siebold reacted quickly, grabbed Mogami's forearm and slowly pulled it out of the patient's abdomen at the right angle. Whimpering he held the evil-smelling hand away from his body. Siebold washed it and asked what had happened.

"I felt the skull of the dead fetus! I touched the cadaver!" Mogami cried uninhibitedly. "I can't do it, Isha-san, I can't do it." He slipped away on the tatami and turned his face to the wall, where he sobbed with shame. Siebold looked at the other doctors with concern. Kō tried to explain the situation to him.

"We Japanese regard a person's dead body as the most impure thing in this world. In the past, we did not even have funerals or cremations; instead, the bodies were simply thrown into the forest and left to the wild animals. Forgive my colleague, he's young and inexperienced." Then Kō slipped closer between the patient's legs.

"I'm doing this. Mogami-san has done good preparatory work."

In the next few hours, Kō managed to open the cervix so far that Siebold could take over again. Now a new instrument was used, the *trepan*. It was a long copper tube from one end of which a circular saw blade was pushed out. With a handle at the other end, it could be pushed back and forth and moved in rotation. Hermann Friedrich Kilian, a brilliant young doctor, and professor of medicine from St. Petersburg, who often visited Würzburg, had introduced the prototype of the trepan to Siebold at his uncle's home. He also gave him practical advice for embryectomy and especially for the application of his invention. During his time in Heidingsfeld, Siebold had the device built with Kilian's permission but had no opportunity to try it before his departure. The Japanese doctors, including Mogami, who had calmed down after Kō saved him from losing his face, were fascinated by this instrument, which looked like a metal worm with sharp teeth.

Siebold instructed Takano and Kō to press on the patient's abdomen and fix the fetus in the opening cervix. Then he inserted the trepan into the vagina with the saw blade retracted so as not to injure the patient and placed it on the skull of the fetus. When he felt the hard resistance, he pushed the saw blade forward with the handle and carefully started to crank. After a few turns, the resistance had disappeared, and the saw blade had penetrated the brain mass. He pulled the trepan out of his vagina. The doctors should hold their position but give him some room. Siebold then laid both hands on top of each other above the pubis, sat up into a kneeling position and suddenly pressed with his straightened arms, all his strength and all his body weight onto this spot. They could not hear it, but all felt in their hands the collapse of the skull in the birth canal. Siebold continued to press with violent movements because the brain mass had to be completely emptied. The Japanese were appalled by the brutality of this approach. But they were far from finished and should remain in their blocking position. Siebold pushed a bar with a sharp barbed hook through the tube of the reintroduced trepan, which he rammed deep into the fetus through the crushed head. While he was pulling on it, the doctors had to keep pressing on the abdomen and gradually push it through the birth canal. Suddenly the fetus came off, shot out of the vagina, and poured in a torrent of blood and brain mass onto the sheets in a puddle that stank of decay and death. Siebold pulled the umbilical cord and the placenta followed in one piece. He breathed a sigh of relief. If this pressure and tension method would not have worked, then it would have been necessary to saw the corpse in the uterus as a last resort. He also had a new instrument for this, a special fetotome, similar to the trepan, with a serrated wire, the loop of which had to be placed around the fetus to saw it apart. In the hope that this additional, laborious and for the mother life-threatening intervention would not be necessary, he had not even taken it out of his doctor's case. Besides, his students had already experienced enough in those hours. He washed the body parts in a water bath and laid them out neatly arranged on a fresh cloth. The dislocated fetus, on which the face hung only as a skin flap, the fragments of the skull, umbilical cord and placenta were put together like a pattern to ensure that nothing had remained in the mother. Then he cleaned the uterus and vagina with water, which he shot in with a large plunger syringe with a movable *caoutchouc* hose attached to the tip. Finally, he asked his colleagues to have the women bring cloths in boiling hot water. He applied these to the patient in several layers as hot liver wraps. The operation was over.

Siebold presented the bundle of the child's remains to the young girl, who was still speaking with her head deeply bent and did not dare to look at him.

"Our gratefulness is immeasurably great. We hope that our daughter and sister *Tsune* will stay with us. But at least we can give this gift back to the *kami*. The child will have a beautiful place to be buried in the garden. Of course, we will pay you appropriately for your services. It is extremely unpleasant for us, but we ask you to be patient until our honorable father returns."

"Young lady, I expect no pay. It is my job and my calling to do so. I earn my money in other ways. Besides, your sister's not safe yet. I'll try to come every other day to check on her. Please only change these wraps every four hours, which you must put into hot water before. This supports her liver because her body is still full of dangerous toxins."

"I will do as you say, Isha-sama."

"My name is Philip Franz von Siebold. Call me Shiboruto, please. I like the Japanese pronunciation of my name. And what's your name, if I may ask?"

She looked up in surprise and for a short moment, he could guess her beautiful eyes and her pretty, clever face in the semi-darkness.

"Taki, my lord, *Taki Kusumoto*."

"Good night, Taki, go to sleep now. We'll meet again soon."

"Good night, Shiboruto-sama."

The Breakthrough

Two days later, an event of the utmost importance awaited Siebold. He had to go back to town and already had two different assignments. For each of them, he received a laissez-passer from the port commandant. The assistant interpreters had prepared everything. Sturler registered this rapid progress in Siebold's work with restraint. Siebold was only to learn from other Dutch officials that even the factory chief could only go ashore once, but at most twice a year, and only under the strictest guard. In a very short time, Siebold had acquired an unheard-of freedom of movement on the part of the Japanese, which was not hidden from his fellows on Dejima.

The first and very important task led him back to the Sofukuji temple. The policemen stopped outside the door as ordered and inside he met the assembled medical staff. Ryōsai Kō was present and his even younger colleague Choei Takano. The sliding doors and walls were opened with a short, linear sound of rustling velvet. The old priest was now sitting on the floor in the middle of the light-flooded room. Everybody knew what was coming. No one spoke. Siebold put down his doctor's case, knelt down as well and got out the instruments he would need now. He celebrated his medical art with decisive and almost ritual slowness. No breathing could be heard, only the cautious crunching of the scissors through the eye bandage of the old man. Siebold took the cotton pads from his eyes and rubbed an ointment on their edges. Then he asked the priest to open his eyes. He followed the instructions and at the same moment unintentionally opened his mouth, in which few teeth were still standing, and breathed heavily.

"Are you in pain, venerable Yoshisada?"

"No, not at all."

"And what do you see?"

"Lights! I see a lot of bright light. But I can't see anything."

"Of course not. First, jingle your eyelids a little and get used to the brightness again." Then Siebold took a frame from a soft leather case, put it on Yoshisadas' nose and clamped it behind his ears.

"What do you see now?"

The priest did not answer and breathed harder than before. Then he spoke something out in Japanese, two, three times in a row aloud into the room. Finally, he turned to Siebold again.

"By the souls of my ancestors, never in my life have I seen so much! Never in my life! My eyes are sharper than ever. I can see like a hawk, like an eagle," he exclaimed. He stood up and looked out like a lighthouse in all directions. Then he spoke again in Japanese, whereupon the doctors present bowed down in Siebold's direction with their hands folded in front of their forehead until they touched the ground. Finally, the priest knelt down again and bowed just as deeply to them.

How lucky! What a triumph! The operation was successful. Moreover, the priest seemed to have had a congenital sight defect that was never diagnosed. The star glasses replaced the sick lenses that Siebold had completely removed. There couldn't have been a better result. That was the breakthrough, he knew it. Then everyone rose and master Yoshisada began to speak solemnly.

"Shiboruto-san, you have returned the light of day to an old, insignificant man. You gave me the sun and I will see my garden again in this life. I didn't even have to suffer the slightest pain for it. You have convinced my friends here and myself of your outstanding ability. Of course, we all know about your treatment of the older Kusumoto daughter. She would certainly be dead today if you hadn't operated on her. Although I am not a doctor myself, it is therefore my great honor to inform you on behalf of the colleagues of your profession here and today: '*No doctor in Japan is worthy to compare himself with such a great healing artist as you are. You bring us new scientific knowledge and practices that we might never know about without you. You can heal patients who in our country would expect only a sad fate, perhaps even death. That's why, from today, your name is Sensei or Shiboruto-sensei. You are the master, here are your obedient students.'"*

Then they bowed to him again. Siebold was overwhelmed and so moved that he could hardly breathe. He struggled for countenance. Fortunately, the ceremony was over, and the meeting had to dissolve immediately. Each one thanked him once again with a deep bow as he went out. The priest then took him aside and asked him to sit down for a moment.

"Shiboruto-sensei, I already know you don't want to take money for treatment. But you will surely understand that a poor person like me, to whom you have done incomparably good, would no longer want to live if he could not show his gratitude. That's why I'd like to present you with this little gift. It's just a modest cake, but it's a sacred food. It is very rare and is produced by only a few people throughout Japan. It is forbidden for humans and is sacrificed only to the gods. In the past days, when I was completely blind, I spoke to the gods and ancestors and asked them to bless this food, so that exceptionally a chosen, great man may take it to make him strong and bring him happiness. Of course, I had to tell them about you, Shiboruto-sensei, at least as far as I knew. But that wasn't hard for me. I knew a lot about you, just from your voice. Now, please accept this gift and begin your great work for which we are all waiting."

When the police escorted the doctor to the Kusumoto house, he was still quite dazed. He felt courageous, strong and like a newborn giant, but at the same time small and full of fear of the challenge of filling this size in the long run. The success of his operation, which he had consciously staged from the very beginning, exceeded all his expectations.

When Taki opened the door, these thoughts were suddenly wiped away. In front of him stood a beautiful young woman, who he thought he had never seen before. She was wearing a fascinating kimono. On a white background, he showed the departure of light blue cranes from a reed into a horizon of orange and red. Her hair was stuck up this time and held together by a tortoiseshell needle. She was wearing make-up, but not as strong as he had seen with Misuzu and the other women he had met. Her mild smile showed the tension of highest restraint. As a greeting, she bowed deeply.

"Welcome to our humble home, Shiboruto-sensei."

"Konnichiwa, Otaki-san. How do you already know about my new nickname?"

"Please, Sensei, don't talk to me like that. Last time they just called me Taki. Stick with it, please. Then I'll tell you how I know about it."

"Good, Taki, I'm glad to see you. I want to say..." He was so stunned and embarrassed that he had to clear his throat and start over.

"I let myself be tempted to call by your honorific name because you look very different today than on my first visit."

"What do you mean, Sensei?"

"Well, I thought you were a little girl the last time you stood in front of me. Obviously, you're already a woman, and in addition a very beautiful one."

"You're too kind, Shiboruto-sensei. I'm a very simple girl, just sixteen years old. Well, I wanted to tell you how I can already be informed of your great success. Choei Takano is a good friend of the family. He's been worried about my sister from the beginning because he loves her, you know? After your meeting with the venerable Sofukuji priest, he came to us at once and reported on your success. He wanted to encourage us. Please, forgive him, will you?"

"Well, that's certainly not a crime. Let's go to your sister Tsune now."

They passed a room from which her mother smiled reverently at Siebold, and then found the sister in a comatose sleep. She hasn't been responsive yet. Taki settled in the corner of the room, so as not to attract attention or disturb. Siebold examined the sister. He looked at her eyes again, the mucous membrane of her mouth, and looked at her vagina, which he uncovered. Then he used a stethoscope to check her heart and lungs. He wasn't sure yet, but he had the impression that he could already hear the return of life forces in this damaged body. The discernment of hearing is amazing, he thought. Over time, he would learn to recognize many disease patterns with this device. The course of illnesses can also be followed excellently via the body noises. Only little secretion escaped from the vagina and the abdomen was already not as hardened as it was on the night of the operation. However, she had several bruises from the strong male hands that had broken the fetus and pushed it out of the uterus. The lymph nodes were already a little less swollen. However, the eyes continued to reveal violent liver activity. He was happy, because a positive prognosis was now justifiable. He didn't want to lose her at all, not now that he had just received such an advance of trust and recognition. If he lost her, he would inevitably feel miserable and overrated. She had to live.

"Otaki, can you tell me how this abortion happened? Was she executed secretly? Didn't your family know about this? I promise you, it'll be between us. But I should know so I can treat your sister's illness better."

Otaki was silent and didn't look at him. Then she raised her head and a serious, worried woman looked Siebold straight in the eyes.

"My sister is a prostitute, a *yūjo*. She started her training when she was my age now. As you can see, she is a desirable young woman. She had powerful and rich patrons. Her name as a courtesan is Chitose, which means '1000 years of joy'. Soon she would have been ready to choose her clients herself. All the way up to the courtyards of daimyōs. She was very ambitious. That's why this pregnancy was a great danger to her. You know, even if she had regularly aborted, many people would have been in on this and it would have gotten around that she owed the kamis something."

"What does it have to do with the kamis when a woman has an abortion?"

"In our Shintō faith, children are a gift. If this child is not born alive by the will of the parents, especially by that of the mother, then we speak of giving a gift back to the gods and ancestors. We call it *mabiki*, which means 'tree cutting'. There is no shame in that alone. But noble suitors fear that such debts could defile them. For they cannot know whether the gift was returned according to the rites. That's why the operation you did was a blessing to us. By ritually burying this unborn creature, my sister is blameless to the kami. But their noble clients won't believe it anymore. So, in the future, she will be a very simple courtesan, although she really could have been one of her greatest."

"Courtesans also offer their services to the Dutch. What kind of women are they?"

"We also call them yūjo. They are among the best in their profession. The Japanese government has ordered the Dutch to be the only foreigners to get a particularly good impression of Japan. In the early days, when the Dutch settled here, this was a terrible fate for these poor women, who had to give themselves away to the barbarians despite their talents. But gradually their reputation rose, because you must know the Dutch have many friends here in our country. For some Japanese, yes, even for some noble gentlemen, it became a privilege to marry a courtesan who had already laid in the arms of a Dutchman."

"What are your plans? What do you want to do with your life?"

"Oh, dear Buddha, some time ago I also wanted to become a courtesan and be registered in the venerable Hikidaya. This is the most prestigious courtesan house in town. My sister led a wonderful life. She was sought after by proud warriors and high councils. Even daimyōs were interested in her, as I already mentioned. But I have seen more and more their inner emptiness and complete dependency. She had changed since we were both young–I mean really young, like children. I also noticed how much it offended her when, by her profession, she met men with perfect courtesy and entertainment art, who treated her much worse than she treated them. Thus, doubts grew in me whether this is really the right way for me. I'm a humble girl. But I'm also proud. When my sister got sick, I suspected the worst. Now I'm sure I don't want to be a courtesan. I don't want to share her fate."

Otaki showed him the herbs from which her sister had brewed a stock, which had triggered the miscarriage but could not expel the fetus. It was, as Siebold had already suspected, a mixture of senna and mugwort leaves. Outside the twilight embraced the world, and with every moment Taki became more beautiful in Siebold's eyes. That girl he had almost overseen.

Otaki's Marriage Proposal

The news of the successful eye surgery on the old Sofukuji priest spread like wildfire in the city. The name Shiboruto-sensei was on everyone's lips, in every *izakaya*, the story was told with amazement and excitement. There had indeed come one of these Dutchmen who could teach the Japanese something. This increased the interest in the small Dutch colony in the harbor, which had disappeared from the center of public attention for many years. But that's not all. The tall, powerful barbarian with yellow hair and gorgeous uniform now sat on some evenings in the middle of the island outdoors on one of those strange pieces of Western furniture. In front of him stood an even stranger box on thin legs, from which sounds came that no one in the city had ever heard before. One day Siebold had his London fortepiano carried out and turned the island into a stage between the festive city and the open bay, where he played Handel's courtly fireworks music and Mozart's divine sonatas under the first flaring stars at dusk. Some listeners who gathered on the shore made an astonished face and wondered about the cascades of clinking sounds. Others cried without understanding why.

As announced, Siebold visited the house of Kusumoto every two days. To his great relief, the sister was clearly on the road to recovery within two weeks. She had woken up from the coma when the fever subsided and after a few days she could eat again. With Taki it was sheer happiness that shone from her face when she was allowed to watch her sister sip the soup. She never failed to lead Siebold into the garden room after the examination, where they could talk for a while without being disturbed. Thus, he learned that the clattering wooden slippers are called *geta*, how important the garden is for the soul of the people, or Taki played him a small piece on the *shamisen*, a delicate musical instrument with only three strings.

The father, a roundish, well-proportioned merchant and wood trader with a jovial appearance, had meanwhile also returned from his journey and offered Siebold several times money for his work. Siebold refused every time. He could not deny that he liked himself in this magnanimous pose. Soon Tsune was doing so well that she could get up. She had lost a lot of weight, her face had collapsed, and grey streaks had crept into her hair, making her very unhappy. But she had a strong will to live and left no doubt that it meant greater happiness for her to stay alive so disfigured than to be beautiful and dead.

But with her recovery, Siebold's time of regular visits to the Kusumoto house and intimate conversations with Taki came to an end. God knew he had much to do and every day that he let rise over the bay of Nagasaki increased Siebold's prestige and glory. In the meantime, he had treated many Japanese patients in his practice and his reputation went far beyond the city limits. Yet he noticed an invisible hook drilling deeper into his living heart. The thought of not being able to see Taki anymore from one day to the next, of having to give up her feminine, clever attention–and, yes, never smelling the scent of her hair of iris root again, this thought began to depress him deeply. In the evening he laid awake in his bed on Dejima, the duvet covered with documents and books. He thought feverishly about whether there was not a way out of this terrible situation for him. He began to curse the Japanese government first, then his own plans again. He thought of a new, unexpected combination that would make everything possible at the same time. Never before had he felt this power, this urge in his chest that seemed to drive him irresistibly into the arms of this woman. The longer he pondered, the more deeply he remembered this name with sweet pain: O-ta-ki.

When he was escorted to the last consultation at Kusumoto's, he thought this is how a gut shot must feel like. He suffered at the idea of how this time he would have to bid beautiful Taki an unendurable formal farewell while being forced to tolerate the empty courtesies of her parents. When he arrived there, he was received solemnly. It didn't look like his medical services were still needed. He was invited to settle down with the family in the main room, where the mother served him warm sake in a tiny cup and an amuse-bouche of marinated vegetables and grilled eel, decorated with sesame seeds. Taki looked enchanting as if she had made herself beautiful for a party. But she did not speak a word and did not dare to look at him.

"Shiboruto-sensei, it is an honor without equal to receive the famous Dutch doctor in my unworthy house," her father intoned. "You have saved the life of our beloved eldest daughter. Not even the gods could have done this in our country. As you know, I have offered you several times a high amount of money as a reward for your deed. You have always refused, and I have also had to learn from other patients that your services cannot be paid for with money. That's why there's only one way we can settle our debt with you. Would you do us the great honor of marrying our younger daughter Taki?"

Kusumoto looked him straight in the face. Siebold was thunderstruck, the earth swayed under him. He would have expected everything, he had thought everything through, except that. He tried to concentrate to hide his confusion and not to cut a bad figure.

"Honorable Kusumoto-san, I'm flattered by your offer. In this country, it is probably so common that parents decide the marriage for their daughters and also discuss them with the groom. I will not hide the fact that until not so long ago it was also a custom in my home country. But just as I bring your country the latest news of Western science, I have to tell you that men of my generation and my age are not satisfied anymore when the bride marries exclusively according to her parents' will. In our country, it is rather an increasingly widespread custom that the bride and groom discuss their intentions in detail with each other and only then inform their parents about them. I would, therefore, ask you to allow me a brief meeting with your daughter."

As determined as he had said that, the father had no choice, even though Siebold felt the confusion in the room when he left it with Taki. They went to another room and sat down on the floor at a small table. She didn't dare speak.

"Otaki, what does that mean? I... I don't know how to say it. I'm really honored by this offer. I would be the happiest person in the world if I could accept it. But for one thing, I don't know if it's what you want. Second, I know I would destroy your life. Please tell me what that means."

"Sensei, I've given a lot of thought. Since you first appeared here, and I had to face you unprepared and dressed in my nightwear. Between every glance, I thought more than in all the years before. Feverishly I hoped that the gods would show me a way leading to you. My father made you this offer at my request."

"But you know that I am a foreigner and that you could only live with me as a courtesan and then again for a limited time. Didn't you say you didn't want to be a courtesan anymore?"

Otaki suddenly burst into tears, sobbed, and could barely sit upright.

"Yes, yes, yes, I did say that. And so I wanted to. But now... I'd rather die if I may never see you again. You can't imagine. I've had such pain when you weren't here. I cried day and night and prayed that you would come back soon, that you would not turn to other, more important things. I saw my sister's condition improve so wonderfully and I wished death was back at her sickbed just to make sure you would return... Oh, that's terrible. All the days you've been here have been the best of my life. I've never spoken to a man like you before. And I must have a demonic power that prevented me from throwing myself on your shoulder at once, into your arms. I do, I do, yes, I do. I want to be a courtesan to live with you. Just as my sister is happy about her life, which she has paid with her beauty, so I want to pay by becoming a courtesan to be with you."

Otaki was completely dissolved in tears. Her makeup ran off and her hair came loose. But in this desperation, she was more beautiful to him than ever. He was moved that they both had such similar feelings for each other and yet it was she who dared to reveal herself despite all the etiquette. She had just made him the confession of love he owed her. But suddenly everything became completely clear before his eyes. Now he saw the way. Even if it wasn't he who found it, but this brave, tender creature. Siebold crawled around the table to her and took her in his arms. How much he had longed for this! She clung to his shoulders and could not stop the stream of tears.

"Otaki, I will marry you. Don't worry about a thing. I missed you all these days. And I ask your forgiveness for having to go this way alone, for leaving you to worry and fear of being rejected. You couldn't have known I loved you even though we barely knew each other."

When they sat down again with the family in the guest room, Siebold solemnly informed the parents that he would accept their offer with great pleasure. The parents and the sister laughed happily, and everyone lifted the sake cups to drink to the marriage. Then it was time to return to the island again in order not to risk any sanctions. Although Taki and he had now agreed to the marriage, the farewell was as polite and formal as before. They bowed to each other and Taki led him to the entrance. Only her smile had changed. It was tenderness and boundless happiness that spoke to him.

Colonel de Sturler was extremely satisfied with this decision, as Siebold had formulated his account so diplomatically that his superior could assume that his well-meant advice had achieved this. But the next steps were more difficult than he expected. Taki could only enter the island if she was a courtesan. Siebold had also been aware of this. However, he had imagined that a simple stamp in her passport would suffice. But since the courtesan's trade was highly respected and organized like a guild, Taki first had to be recognized and registered by one of the permitted houses. This would have taken years of training like the one her sister had gone through. Of course, this was not possible, so Siebold asked his doctors to contact one of the respected houses in his name to find out whether he could purchase the title of courtesan for Taki. Considering that Taki's later life after his departure from Japan would also be marked by the reputation of the brothel that acknowledges her as a courtesan, only the best, the Hikidaya in the Maruyama district, came into question for him. There the owner, a tough lady, signaled after some days that this possibility existed. Siebold was able to find out from his confidants that his request had led to fierce disputes. There was no precedent for this trade in the courtesan's title, and the women registered at the Hikidaya were extremely indignant and jealous. That drove up the price. Therefore, Siebold was shocked when he received the offer that Taki could be admitted as a courtesan for four thousand Dutch guilders. That was a fortune for him, almost a whole year's salary. But he did not hesitate, agreed and, with Sturler's approval, had the amount paid out by the treasurer of the factory. A week later Taki appeared at night accompanied by a servant of the Hikidaya and two porters at the bridge. The stoic-looking saguriban thoroughly examined all bags and boxes. In Taki's passport with the red stamp they read for the first time the name she had received from the Hikidaya as a courtesan. Her name was Sonogi from now on.

Wedding on Dejima

Sonogi was received by a handsome young man in magnificent uniform, who from then on would be her 'spouse pro tempore', as the Dutch called it. Philipp Franz von Siebold was on this autumn evening, which laid gently over the bay of Nagasaki on this autumn evening, twenty-six years old, an experienced doctor and major, had already travelled halfway around the world as a researcher—and he was afraid. This delicate, beautiful being, a girl of just sixteen years old, in a precious silk kimono with white and black cranes on their flight through a sea of plum blossoms on a red background, met him smiling in tiny steps as the promise of happiness and love made by the warm rays of the golden evening sun. As well as he has so far managed to deal with the matter of marriage objectively and to consider Colonel de Sturler's recommendation as a necessary stage of his stay on the factory island, so little could he now, in the sight of this nymph who Japan's gods had created for him, preserve his composure. Not only the knowledge of the boundless affection and devotion that this enchanting young woman had confessed to him and his own increasingly stormy love for her surged strongly against the Stoic attitude that he would have liked to have adopted. It was also the prospect of the hours before him until the next sunrise that unsettled him. Circumstances had not given them the opportunity to experience the first night of love now approaching them as an unexpected, in detail not exactly predictable consequence of seduction, as a natural-looking interplay of devotion and conquest, driven, as it were, by a rush of the senses. Yes, Siebold was nervous, for as self-confident as he was and decided to appear, he was anything but an experienced lover. He knew he made an excellent impression on women. Many female acquaintances in Würzburg would have liked to have favored the lithe, proud bachelor even then. But the sensorium of the by no means cold-blooded young man was too fine for women, his demands on the beautiful sex were simply too high. What his own ranks had to offer him in female appeal was simply not suitable to distract his passion from other occupations such as student comradeship and science, especially not at all to physically excite him. So, the Japanese girl Taki, who was now called Sonogi, was very lucky to have an adult, strong, good-looking, and virginal man from far away Germany. He became painfully aware of this fact, for he would by no means be able to present himself to Sonogi as a partner matured in matters of love. He could not offer more than precise anatomic knowledge. As a natural scientist he had heard a lot about the forms of the act and the mutual manipulation of the sexual parts, but as with any hearsay that does not deserve real trust, his ideas of it had only remained shadowy. As this troubling thought went through his mind, his assistants had taken Sonogi's luggage and were ready to follow the two into his house. Siebold offered Sonogi his arm. She saw her arm held horizontally and fixed it only as if she were trying to discover something about it. Then she looked at him with big, questioning eyes and it took a moment for him to understand. Of course! She had never seen this gesture before. He took her hand and wanted to show her what he had intended.

"You see, this is how man and woman walk together in the streets of Europe. The lady lays her hand on the inside of her arm and hooks into the man. This is to prevent the woman from falling and at the same time the man can proudly stand upright by her side as a strong support".

"*Anata-sama*, please, I can't walk by your side," she suddenly said in a hint of despair. "This is quite impossible. I'm Japanese. I must walk three steps behind you." Siebold was dismayed at his ignorance and the idea of having to let Sonogi run after him all the time. He did not want her to call him formally by 'anata-sama', the humble form of address for Japanese husbands. But it was not the right moment for objections. He did not want to unsettle his young mistress even more, whose poor heart was already beating like that of a frightened bird. So, he went ahead without further ado, even though he felt rude to a lady like never before. He thought of Orpheus, who could not turn back when he led his Eurydice out of Hades, and now he believed he understood the burden of this curse. Arriving at his house, he showed Sonogi all the rooms like a curious visitor and explained to her the use of the furniture she had never seen before. She stood fascinated in front of the fortepiano–and then with even greater amazement in front of the huge French bed, which Siebold had in the meantime made make. It seemed to her like a floating box, so strange to think that a sleeping pad was not lying directly on the floor, as she knew it from the Japanese futons. And she secretly wondered if she wasn't getting dizzy at night on that wobbly mattress-ship up there. They were both in a suppressed exalted mood. Siebold tried to be as relaxed as possible, but he roamed around Sonogi with the same embarrassment with which she moved through the rooms. They moved on like in a sort of dance, made inconspicuous pirouettes, escaped the other with a swing and tried to approach each other again and again. Siebold felt silly, but he didn't know how to act differently. He had no solution to this highly delicate situation. Sonogi was so beautiful and elegant, outwardly so composed and obliging that he could not help but discover a great shyness in himself at that moment. He showed her the dressing table and the cupboards that were now at her disposal. Full of admiration, she carefully touched the mirror on the chest of drawers with the tips of her slim fingers. She had never seen a real mirror, one of the goods the Japanese liked to buy from the Dutch, even if it cost a fortune. Siebold was grateful that she and her servant from Hikidaya wanted to first unpack her toiletries and store her laundry while he was still preparing for the evening on the ground floor. After a while the little servant came down, said goodbye submissively and crept away. Now he was alone with Sonogi. He was waiting to hear her footsteps. And then she came. Slowly she descended the stairs and walked towards him with her head bowed.

"Anata-sama, I'm ready for the ceremony. Would you like to ask the witnesses to come to us now?" she almost whispered.

"May I leave you alone for a moment? I'll be right back with you." Sonogi nodded silently, went to the large empire sofa covered in black velvet, sat carefully on the edge, folded her hands in her lap and seemed to want to wait for Siebold and the witness in this position. Siebold watched her every movement and was delighted by her uncertainty, which was carried with composure. Then he pulled himself away from that sight and left the house. A few minutes later he came back accompanied by two men who looked very different from himself. The first stepped up to Sonogi with an astonished and delighted expression, took her hand without asking her, bent over it and seemed to want to touch it with his mouth. But fortunately, he did not and Sonogi felt only a breath, a short warmth from his lips and his breath.

"Welcome to Dejima, dear Sonogi. We are very pleased to welcome such an ornament of Japan to our humble island colony. My name is Jan Cock Blomhoff and I am the departing opperhoofd of the Dutch factory. I would also like to apologize for the absence of our new opperhoofd Colonel de Sturler. He is unfortunately ill but sends you both his best wishes for the future." Then the second man approached her and repeated the on-the-hand-breathing, as Sonogi called this gesture in thought.

"I am delighted to make your acquaintance, dear Sonogi. My name is Aaron Mendelssohn and I am honored that you and Dr. von Siebold entrust me with such an important task."

"I'm sure Shiboruto-sensei chose the right man for the occasion and that he had good reason to ask you for this favor." How grown-up she speaks! And how beautiful she is! Mendelssohn and Blomhoff could not resist expressing their appreciation for Siebold's discovery of such an enchanting woman with an obvious exchange of glances. Blomhoff saw at once that Siebold was particularly lucky. She was very different from the traditional

courtesans who frequented the island. Sonogi was serious and distinguished, had a noble attitude despite her youth and was therefore very
different from the ordinary girls, who were often silly and insinuatingly
cheeky.

"Well, it was easy," Siebold replied somewhat delayed into the silence
that had filled with the admiration of his guests for his fiancée. "Mr.
Mendelssohn cannot play the piano. That's why he must take over the
clergyman's duties. I believe we are doing him a great favor, for in this
man there is a great spiritual ambition bubbling." This little insolence
amused everyone, and the laughter helped Sonogi to breathe some of her
tension away.

"Then it falls to me as master of ceremonies to ask the bride and groom
to come before me here. I would like to ask Colonel Blomhoff to perform
on the piano." Sonogi and Siebold stood next to each other in front of
Mendelssohn and Blomhoff sat down at the fortepiano, on which he
intoned a mass by Bach. Sonogi watched him with fascination, for she had
never heard so many strumming sounds at once, which spiraled higher
and higher into the air like a snake. Then Mendelssohn began.

"Dear Sonogi, dear Major Dr. von Siebold. You have appeared before
me here, as has been the custom on this island for centuries, to enter the
harbor of marriage for a limited time. Far from Christian Europe and yet
not entirely in the bosom of Japanese religions, you have decided to make
your own vows in the hope that all the gods of this world will see your
union with benevolence. I, therefore, ask you, Dr. von Siebold, to present
your promise. Please speak these words directly to your bride." Siebold
took a written sheet from the pocket of his frock coat, turned to Sonogi and
solemnly read the words he had prepared.

"Dear Sonogi, I stand here before you as the happiest man, for you have
awakened me from a long sleep. It was the sleep of love. I have never
known such feelings before and first had to come to this distant country,
to your homeland to experience them. You made me discover my heart.
This will not be the last discovery either and I hope that we will spend the
years ahead of us exploring your country. Because as much as I want to
live by your side and share everything with you at this time, so much do I
need your love and support for the work that awaits me here. That's why
I'm asking you to be my wife. I promise to be your faithful and caring

husband. Considering the great sacrifice you have made so that we can love each other and live together the years to come, I also promise you that I will always care for you after the end of my stay in Japan. And finally, I promise you that I will do whatever a man can do to ensure that our marriage will continue beyond this time until only death can divorce us." Sonogi looked at him concerned. She was not prepared for such a declaration of love. They had agreed that everyone would formulate a promise of marriage which they would not make known to each other in advance. However, Siebold's words had moved her so much that she was forgetting to deliver on her own promise, which was much simpler, more cautious, and more impersonal. Mendelssohn noticed her confusion and twinkled at her kindly. Then she read her words with a soft, high-pitched voice and a Japanese accent that made the coarse Dutch sound feminine and fragile.

"Honorable Shiboruto-sensei, Major-san and Doctor-san, I am an unworthy girl of simple origin..." she started, but then she lowered her hand that held the written vow, paused for a moment, and continued without reading. "...but the gods have decided to give me a special fate. When I first saw you, I heard a melody, a song. It told me the legend of this great man who stood before me. I knew I was with him. I knew it was destiny. And I was overjoyed that I was given such a clear signal. I want to become your wife because it is my destiny that I am grateful to. As your faithful, obedient, and diligent wife, I will be for you what you wish, I will be where you need me, and I will bear you children, so many as will bring you joy. I do not want to think about the fact that our covenant is only valid for a few years, because my promise is valid for all time. I want to belong to you as a woman as a woman can belong to a man at all, not only in this life but also in our next." As she spoke these words, the atmosphere in the room changed, everything dissolved as if there was just one shining thought left. It was only the two lovers who looked each other in the eyes. Mendelssohn and Blomhoff felt a gentle shiver of emotion, the revelation of a supreme will that brought everything together and elevated this couple before them. Siebold felt touched by something sacred, another feeling he had never known before. He sensed the presence of a spirit so much greater than anything else. There was horror and beauty in it, because it revealed the transience of his existence and at the same time his salvation, the love, the infinity, and the eternity that laid in the words and in the nature of this tender young woman.

As the magic of the moment gradually gave way, Mendelssohn handed them the gold rings, which they were supposed to put on alternately. Sonogi's delicate, light brown hand with the long fingers looked like a work of art when the ring found its place. Then the Master of Ceremonies explained the two to man and wife according to the good manners of the civilized peoples and was about to ask the bridal couple to seal the covenant with a kiss when the fortepiano suddenly drowned him out. Blomhoff had missed the transition in zeal and was already playing spiritedly from Joseph Haydn's third Sonata in E flat major. Mendelssohn did not dare to interrupt the colonel, especially since he was as impressed as Siebold was by the skill and elegance with which Blomhoff played. After the colonel had struck the last keys and the melody gradually faded away, everyone applauded, including Sonogi, who carefully imitated the gesture of clapping. Then Siebold asked next door to the table, where the Malay servants had solemnly served. In the glow of great silver candelabras, they dined excellently and enjoyed the best French red wine, a Cheval Blanc from St. Émilion, which was stored in the depot of factory for special occasions. They had great fun in explaining the use of dishes and cutlery, the ingredients of roast beef and pudding to the overwhelmed Sonogi and watching her drink and blush at the first sip of wine in her life. Mendelssohn and Blomhoff got along splendidly, yes, they even discovered a kind of spiritual kinship. Mendelssohn openly regretted that Blomhoff would soon leave. Sonogi followed the company as best she could and only spoke when she was asked something. She was busy with the countless new impressions that had invaded her since she had passed the bridge from the Japanese mainland to the Dutch island a few hours earlier and had thus immersed herself in another world. Since the men were in a good mood and drank a lot of the delicious wine, she did not want to be rude and had a refill. Siebold could not keep his eyes off her the whole time, even though he talked to the guests in an animated manner. That's why he soon noticed Sonogi getting tired. He discreetly signaled to Blomhoff and Mendelssohn that he would like to withdraw with Sonogi, whereupon the two of them rose, wished once more happiness and health, and left the place. Sonogi was already completely exhausted–and then he finally took her in his arms. They were now alone, and the double bed was waiting for them. He felt much more courageous than when they arrived, and the wine even made him audacious.

"You know, Sonogi, we have a nice custom. The groom carries the bride over the doorstep into the house when they come from the church. Since we cannot do this, I at least want to be able to carry you to our bed", whereupon he lifted her up with his strong arms and carried her up the stairs without asking. Sonogi sighed in protest, outraged and embarrassed, and tore her legs a little, but at the same time, she giggled with amusement at the exuberance of her euphoric, no longer quite sober gentleman-husband. She held her arms wrapped around his neck until he laid her on the bed.

"Will you introduce me to the art of taking off a kimono?" She said nothing and just looked at the lamps that lit the room brightly. He understood this time, got up and turned the wicks down until they went out. It was a bright, starry night, and the pale light of the moon shone in through the windows so that they could see each other well. Then he sat down on the edge of the bed. She got up from the bed, stood in front of him, untied a knot of her *obi* and gave him the end of the silk belt in her hand. He began to pull carefully, and she turned, spinning further and further along the lengths of fabric that were laid around her. Her naked arms, feet, and legs, then her thighs and finally her hips and buttocks appear again and again. Then she covered herself with the last remnant of the wide fabric hanging loosely over her shoulders, leaned forward, pushed away the jacket of his uniform and opened his shirt. Meanwhile, he tried to take off his boots so that they would not have to do this annoying heavy work. When he had done so, he also got up to take off his pants. She tried to help him but didn't understand the system of buttons that held them together. Then she gave a short sound of astonishment when she discovered another pair of trousers under his pants.

On this wedding night, Sonogi introduced her older yet inexperienced husband to love. Siebold felt how well she was familiar with the body landscape of a man, how exactly she already knew what touches he would like. He gleaned the tenderness of her wheat-colored skin and her long hair, which she had opened, and which now lay like a black river on the pillow they shared. She admired his strong build, gently stroked over his well-proportioned muscles, and sucked his masculine smell greedily. When he kissed her for the first time, he noticed how she reared under the first wave of sweetest arousal. He was captivated by the beautiful curves of her firm body, these seductive forms, which he had never been allowed to touch with pleasure before, by the fragrant, infinitely tender skin that clothed this wonder of nature. The Japanese custom would have demanded that at this moment she still adorn herself with a breathed 'No, no!' to arouse the man even more. But she felt his indecisiveness and understood that her job would be to stimulate him differently. As he stroked her body, she thought that the love services of women in Holland might be more in action than in passion and did not wait to see what would happen next. She wrapped her legs around his lap and skillfully pulled his member into her with all her strength, where it was enveloped by hot velvet. He was surprised by the initiative of his beloved, but even more by this tingle of lust, which shot through his body from his penis and took possession of his brain. She gently pulled him into a surging motion wherein he surrendered and gradually discovered his strength until he took the lead and whipped the waves higher and higher. This storm did not ease until both fell happily into a deep sleep from exhaustion.

"Sonogi, not that it meant anything to me, but you weren't a virgin anymore, were you?"

"Yes, my love, that's right. You sure you're not mad?" He wrested another promise from her last night, namely that she calls him Philipp, or 'Firippu' as she pronounced it, and that she addresses him in the first person, like a friend.

"No. I was just surprised that a girl as young as you is already so experienced in love."

"Would you like to know where it came from?"

"Of course, I'm dying to!"

"But only if you promise me you won't be jealous."

"I promise."

"And you must not betray me. Do you promise?"

"I promise not to betray you either," he replied with increasing curiosity.

She got up, went to her dresser, took out a bound notebook and sat down beside him.

"You know, the first time I shared the pillow with a neighborhood boy right after I had my first... bleeding?"

"Menses", he corrected.

"We were almost children, but we were in love. He came to me one night and more often afterward. My parents knew that or at least they guessed it. There's nothing bad about it either. We call this *yobai*, which means 'secret night crawling'. Then I later discovered these notebooks from my sister. They are intended for the training of courtesans so that they learn what their suitors like. Their name is *enpon* and I have heard that they are sometimes also given to young noble women for weddings. This is my sister's present."

She opened the loops of the booklet and unfolded a series of pictures– which took Siebold's breath away. They were shockingly detailed depictions of coitus in every conceivable position, the men with huge, veined sexual parts, the women, in the same anatomical accuracy and exaggeration, dripping with pleasure. The intermingled people seemed to feel the greatest joy in these partly wild love fights. Siebold was amazed and did not know how to react. He had never seen such grotesque and offensive images of human mating. Sonogi smiled at him and was visibly proud of her sister's secret wedding present. "We call these pictures *shunga*. Do you like them?" Sonogi had thus trained herself as a lover to introduce her husband to the same art. She was not ashamed at all, only worried that the possession of the enpon did not correspond to her social rank. "See, this is his *dankon*. Luckily, yours isn't that big. I would've gotten scared. And this is her *inmon*. Do I look the same?" she asked and giggled. "What do they call that in your language? I've never heard the words for it." Her impartiality gave him the courage to admit to her that this freedom was completely unknown to him, even that the whole Christian world did not know it, but that he might enjoy it. She was happy. His next confession, however, astounded her. She could hardly believe that her husband, ten years older than her, had given up celibacy with her last night.

A few days later he wrote to his uncle Lotz the first detailed report about his stay so far in far-away Japan. The longest time he worked on the sentence in which Sonogi was mentioned. How could he tell everything he experienced with her without embarrassing his uncle?

"I, too, submitted to the old Dutch custom and joined a lovely sixteen-year-old Japanese woman pro tempore, who I would not exchange for a European one."

Chapter VII

Narutaki

Learning Japanese–First Field Trip–The House by the Waterfall–
Moving to Narutaki–Siebold Teaches–The East Pole–Mendelssohn
Philosophizes–Matsudeira and Doctor Udagawa

Learning Japanese

In the autumn days after Sonogi's arrival on Dejima, Siebold realized how much this woman would change his whole life. He spent most of his time in his practice dealing with the ever-growing number of Japanese who were able to obtain permission to enter the island through the Translators' College. But as soon as he returned to his own home, where his library and all his study and research documents were located, Sonogi was with him. Her closeness was in a way soothing and stimulating that he did not know. Although she moved extremely reservedly, barely spoke and avoided any noise, she was busy all the time and never claimed that he cared for her. On the contrary, he felt completely taken care of by her attention and her existence. She soon became a great help to him. He frequently asked her questions about the Japanese language, its customs and her own life. The more he realized how intelligent and versatile she was and how much she enjoyed telling him about herself and her country, the more he asked. His new greed was soon almost impossible to satisfy, and he drew from it as if from a well. Gradually he got to know her and with his respect his affection gained depth. His initial desire, concentrated on the exotic oval face, the elfish body and the sweet, whispering voice, and his naive infatuation gradually took on a more mature, spiritual character.

Life on the island has been hectic these days. The trading period came to an end and the ships had to leave soon in order not to get into the winter doldrums on the Chinese Sea on their way back. But the negotiations about the sale of the last part of the cargo dragged on. The Japanese haggled incessantly. The waterline of the overhauled vessels was now considerably lower than when they arrived. A manageable quantity of copper crates had replaced the imported goods measured in cubic meters, hectoliters, and tons. The revenues from the sale of Dutch cotton, Chinese silk, Indian spices, port wine and beer, raw materials such as *caoutchouc*, tin, leather, ivory, tropical woods, and Dutch manufactured goods such as mirrors, watches, glasses, and glassware were considerably lighter than the goods brought in from afar by the Dutch. The Dutch would have liked to be paid again in gold and silver, but since 1671 there was a strict ban on using these precious metals as means of payment. The Japanese had noticed that trade with foreigners, ultimately only with the Dutch, had caused the money supply and thus domestic liquidity to shrink to the extent that they paid for expensive European goods in gold and silver. Japanese scholars had calculated the value of the outflow of funds at over one billion Dutch guilders. To illustrate their concern, they explained that minerals and precious metals are the bone structure of the country. In contrast to handicraft products and foodstuffs, which correspond in the national organism to its flesh, skin, and hair, however, this skeleton cannot renew itself. Later, even copper was allocated and thus restricted as a means of payment.

But this time the shogunate had paid an additional amount of copper, due since 1818, for sugar already delivered. This happened to Blomhoff's great joy because back in Batavia this would be regarded as another personal success. The goods that were not immediately sold in full, such as sugar, filled the island's storehouses so that trade could continue in smaller quantities in the time between deliveries. Only the negotiations about the tin from Banka dragged on, and that was no coincidence because it made up a large part of the cargo in tonnages and the two ships would not be able to leave until the tin was also unloaded and sold. The tin was too expensive to store for a long time. The revenues were expected immediately on the ships' return to Batavia, not next year. The Japanese knew exactly about the time pressure of the Dutch and made them with a smile to their hostages until the price was where they wanted it. The calculated profit margins thus melted in the warm Japanese autumn sun. This poor negotiating position of the Dutch was another reason, besides the ban on gold and silver, why trade with Japan had continued to decline since its beginnings over two hundred years ago. The Dutch were blackmailable, and so they often lost money in these transactions. They were fortunate to achieve a margin of twenty percent after deduction of all costs. This was a meager wage in view of the enormous risk of losing entire ships or even fleets in long-distance trade. How different it was on the Indian subcontinent or especially in China! There had been five hundred to a thousand percent profits in the best times. They were the basis of the East Indian Company operating from London and the now-defunct United Dutch East Indian Trading Company. The Dutch merchants in Japan could only dream of that. That is why the other part of the trade, namely the purchase of Japanese goods and merchandise for the European market, was of such great importance. Porcelain from Imari and Arita, two cities in the northwest of Kyūshū, was, particularly in demand. Siebold, who thought that he would one day return to his homeland, wanted to find out which Japanese cultural and natural products he himself would later be able to trade. He was fascinated to discover that in Japan there were neither dairy cows, and therefore no milk and cheese products, nor edible apples. In those days he remembered Don Mastema, who told him seven years ago in Würzburg about his interest in long-distance trade with Japan.

The following winter Siebold began intensive Japanese language studies. However, this caused him greater difficulties than he had expected. So, he almost went mad over the system of numerals. There were the simple cardinal numbers, which stood only for themselves or formed the root for the numerals of persons, and the numerals for things. The cardinal number 'eight' was therefore called 'hachi', but if you wanted to call things with it, you had to say 'yattsu'. In addition, there were separate counting suffixes for persons, 'nin', for books and booklets, 'satsu', cups or bowls with drinks, 'hai', flat objects, 'mai', long objects, 'hon', and four-footed animals, 'hiki',–but only if they are not too big! Then the Japanese alphabet consisted not of simple letters, but first of forty-five Japanese symbols, which could be combined into a system of one hundred phonetic syllables, the *hiragana*: -ka, -ki, -ku, -ke, -ke, -ko, -ga, -gi, -gu, -ge, -go, -kya, -kyu, -kyo and so on. Everything could be written with it, but one was only at the level of expression of the simplest people and children. In addition, there was another syllable alphabet with the same pronunciation, but only for foreign words, the *katakana*. So Siebold's name was written in Japanese instead of hirgana しいぼると in katakana シーボルト. He had the greatest difficulty, however, with the more noble form of written expression, the Chinese characters called *kanji*, whose complicated ideograms summarized the phonetic values of syllabary writing into words, pictures, or entire parts of sentences. The more distinguished a Japanese was, the more kanji he used in his writing. Aristocrats and scholars mastered at least six thousand characters—and he finally wanted to communicate with these persons without linguistic obstacles. Siebold set himself the goal of learning at least two thousand kanji characters within the first year. He studied day and night and practiced with Sonogi, who showed great patience and skill in teaching. In her apartment and in his large research room hung samples of the *iroha*, a mnemonic poem for the hiragana. He knew that his desire to learn the language of the host country could cause irritation. After all, an essential part of Japanese diplomacy was to leave strangers in the dark about the country's internal conditions. The Japanese opened the first door to their secrets if a foreigner was allowed to learn their language. But he remembered Blomhoff's stories about the great opperhoofd Doeff, who spoke Japanese fluently and is still highly regarded by the Japanese today. Then he was surprised at how much joy not only his students but also the interpreters received this message. For the latter, it would even have been understandable if they had regarded his intention as the emergence of an uncomfortable, perhaps even dangerous competition. But they didn't even seem to notice that. Siebold's reputation and popularity had grown so much that he no longer belonged to the category of foreigners to whom wise—and that meant: devious and tricky—political maxims of international politics and trade were applied. The head interpreter himself, *Sinsajemon Sujenaga*, finally insisted on the honor of being allowed to continue to teach him personally. At the beginning of his first lesson he painted the name 'Shiboruto-sensei' in a fine calligraphic manner with a brush in Japanese katakana characters and in Kanji, from top to bottom.

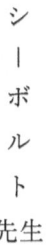

シ
ー
ボ
ル
ト
先生

Then he handed Siebold the brush and asked him to write his name himself. He was not satisfied with the result, although–or perhaps precisely because–Sujenaga smiled and said that even this was a start.

In the meantime, Fujiwara, the governor of Nagasaki, had been informed that the staff of translators had grown to over fifty people. He inquired about the reasons for this and heard many voices praising the Dutch doctor as a benefactor and friend of the Japanese. The news of Siebold's healing arts seemed to have traveled through the country on the back of the wind, for soon among the alleged translators were also doctors and scientists who followed the call and had come to Nagasaki from distant places. The governor, a liberal man in the tradition of the city that has always held in reserve unthinkable freedoms for other parts of Japan far from Edo, was in the difficult position that his person had to be the prolonged arm of a despotic government that had to strictly supervise the treatment of foreigners according to precise, centuries-old rules. Moreover, he found himself surrounded by a staff of overzealous lower civil servants who saw it as their task to be suspicious not only of the foreigners but also of their superiors. Despite the hostile political mood, Fujiwara sought ways and means to make it easier for the young foreign doctor, whom he did not yet know personally, to meet his patients, but above all the interested Japanese scientists.

He soon found a solution. On occasion of a visit by the envoy from the court of daimyō of Satsuma, he discussed the matter informally and asked him for advice. He inquired about the Satsuma clan's position on the problem of foreigners and asked for a written answer. The envoy, of course, understood the function of the letter Fujiwara had requested and supported him by writing it out immediately after his return to Kagoshima and sending it to him by express courier. On the arrival of the scroll, Fujiwara had all the secretaries meet and present the contents by his first secretary. Satisfied, the governor heard that it held everything he had dictated to the emissary without saying a word. The mighty house of the Satsuma, whose dominance not only shaped the south of the country but also remained the most dangerous challenger of the central power in Edo since the beginning of Tokugawa rule, made it clear that more can be won than lost in dealings with foreigners. Relations with the Dutch colony should be as intensive and at the same time as careful as possible. This was not an opinion of the prince himself, but rather an atmospheric picture of the court in Kagoshima, but it did not miss its effect. He gave the officials present at the reading of the document three days to spread it almost literally to all ranks of the administration.

Nobody underestimated the news from the court of the only prince who could possibly be the next shogun This gave Fujiwara some leeway, albeit within a narrow framework, in dealing with the Dutch authorities, in particular with the young doctor on the island colony. First, he allowed Japanese scientists and doctors to attend Siebold's lectures on the island without special applications and passports. From then on, Siebold taught in Dutch three times a week. Soon the governor's office extended the freedom of movement to the permission for Siebold to make regular visits to the sick ashore. His reputation grew daily and more and more people in the city knew about his deeds. Filled with his work, lectures, studies and Sonogi's loving support, this first winter passed like a cool morning. Spring came almost sooner than he liked because he had so much to prepare for the planned botanical studies during the flowering period. Not even the digging up and replanting of the garden on Dejima could be considered. Siebold simply did not have the time, and the Dutch islanders would not have done a handshake for such, in their eyes useless facilities.

This was already the only aspect of his stay so far in which he saw a quiet but suspicious shadow cast over his daily successes. The Dutch were indifferent or skeptical about his ambitious efforts to achieve scientific understanding. But they clearly begrudged him the growing extent of his privileges, from which nothing fell for them. Blomhoff had left for Batavia in December. Since then, there has been no mediating authority between Siebold and the constantly ill and ill-tempered Colonel de Sturler, who was soon more irritated by his surgeon's bursting health and enthusiasm than by his actual physical suffering. Soon suspicion arose in the clouds of his misanthropic musings that Siebold, the miracle doctor, would intentionally not heal him so that he would remain trapped in his illness and the doctor could enjoy all freedoms unhindered. Sturler believed that his rank as political and military head of the legation could be in danger. Siebold had probably noticed this, but the recognition he received from all other directions allowed him to accept this disgruntlement with serenity. Secretly, he also admitted a slight thrill of satisfaction, because it flattered him to get the Dutch with his successes so effortlessly upset without them being allowed to hinder him. Only Mendelssohn, whom he now saw less often, was truly friendly with him. But he regularly pointed out to Siebold to be more cautious, because he would have to endure it with the islanders for several more years. Fate could well turn against him occasionally. Since Siebold was extraordinarily busy, they could only rarely see each other, and if they could, then mostly at Mendelssohn's hospital bed. Like Colonel de Sturler, he had great difficulty getting used to food and climate. He couldn't to get on his feet right from the start and was often lying on his mattress dormitory for days on end with a slight fever, headache, or nausea. He had many thoughts, at least some of which he wanted to tell his doctor, who was the only one he could bother with such reflections born of ailing weakness. In these days little reminded of the fleet-footed, cheeky philosophizing cosmopolitan Siebold had come to know and appreciate in Mendelsohn.

First Field Trip

In the first week of April–in Europe it was the year 1824–one morning Siebold's most faithful students Ryōsai Kō and Choei Takano visited him at the practice. After the polite greeting, they could hardly hide their excitement. They had the honor of giving him such important and good news that they had to grin helplessly until Siebold asked them to speak after all.

"Sensei" began Kō, "through the mediation of three doctors, namely Kōsai Yoshio and the brothers Eiken and Sōken Narabayashi, your devoted discipleship has succeeded in acquiring two privileges that are unparalleled in history. First, we would like to inform you that mayor Takashima and, thanks to his intercession, again governor Fujiwara, will allow the Dutch legation's doctor to visit the hospitals, which are run by the aforementioned doctors, in order to carry out treatment there and, in addition, to teach students of medicine with practical exercises". This was followed by a short dramatic pause, for his visitors wanted to see the look on Siebold's face if he really would be as surprised as they had hoped. They could be satisfied because Siebold shone like they had never seen him before.

"The second message concerns your botanical studies. The governor has also authorized you to go on field trips to the surrounding area of Nagasaki under our personal supervision."

"Field trips...?" Siebold uttered soundlessly. That was truly more than he had hoped for. Of course, he had thought every single day about how he could expand his sphere of activity, because the imprisonment on the island was in the highest degree hindering for his planned scientific studies, despite the kind of release which had been granted to him with the occasional patient visits.

"Dear friends, this is the best news in years, exactly from the day I learned I was going to Japan!" he exclaimed, wanting to hold the men, who were considerably smaller, in his arms. He suppressed this impulse, however, because he did not want to embarrass his loyal but shy students with his impetuousness. By the evening, news had spread about Dejima. And once again, in the table conversations, there was a mixture of envy and incomprehension about this breakthrough, which enabled at least one of them to deal with the Japanese hosts in a reasonably dignified manner. Why of all things the doctor enjoys such privileges, who would at best have to offer emergency services on a commercial mission? The Dutch sensed another presumption of this man, who did not even come from Holland, a foreigner who had only achieved his rank through protection. Colonel de Sturler was particularly bitter, for he had been immediately ignored. Neither had he been offered this freedom of movement, nor had the governor contacted him in order to vote on this measure. Siebold, who had already suspected these resentments, also thought that this news and the inevitable subsequent bile release of Sturler would certainly not have a positive effect on the diagnosis itself, which was already problematic. Only Sonogi could rejoice with Siebold, and she literally trembled when he informed her. She had become accustomed to making his expectations and hopes completely her own, and so it came naturally that she soon doubled and strengthened all his feelings. As far as she could, she became a mirror of his soul, through which he always liked to come to her and report on everything, because the sympathy of his young wife allowed him to see a picture of himself that nobody could show him. He did not yet know that this was the very art of Japanese women's conversation that was taught to them to please their husbands. But it was no mistake on his part to take this kind of courtesy personally, because Sonogi was truly effortless in her learned role and was happy that her husband was satisfied and successful.

Three days later, the time had come. The governor's decision had been taken and a cumbersome, diplomatically formulated document had been issued to Siebold, which allowed him regular land walks and at the same time required him to respect the old laws for strict treatment of foreigners, which expressly and categorically excluded such freedom of movement. Kō and Takano came early in the morning to the bridge to the island, where they picked up Siebold. He had his practice closed for the whole day. With a knapsack on his back holding provisions, botanical tools and a series of containers for insects, snails and plants, he set off on a hike he had dreamed of for years. He thought of his famous predecessor Thunberg, who was the only one before him who managed to cross the city limits of Nagasaki. Thunberg, he recalled, was much worse off overall than he was, for in his day the Dutch mission in Japan was much more exclusively committed to the mercantilist spirit and only the most unpleasant and ignorant subjects were stationed on Dejima. Thunberg was the only one who managed to set up friendly contact with the Japanese during this difficult time. This time the omens were different, because the scientific and diplomatic character of the mission was in the foreground, so that Siebold's position in the legation was from the outset considerably better than Thunberg's.

Such thoughts still came when he crossed the streets of Nagasaki and his cheerful students, as well as the astonished glances of the inhabitants, accompanied him. Some people wanted to talk to them and ask the now well-known doctor for advice, but his overseers, although untrained in the matter, did not want to put the acquired favor at risk lightly and adhered to the instruction to strictly prevent contacts between Siebold and the Japanese in public. Gradually the population became sparser, here and there grass scars licked up again from the cold of the winter months into the city and on the slopes stood scattered dark conifers ready, as if to pick up the hikers at the entrance of their empire. The companions crossed mountain streams, which all carried a lot of water according to the seasons, over small bridges, whose arches reminded of hunching cats.

No more thought distracted Siebold. He immersed himself with all his senses in the most intense state of observation, open to everything that flowed towards him, at the same time searching for the connections between plant and animal life, without ignoring its relations to the mineralogical and geological conditions. In the mild coolness of the morning they climbed the hills in the northwest of Nagasaki, their backs always warmed by the April sun. Even before the sun reached its zenith, Siebold looked at the bay in all its size and expanse for the first time. The view was magnificent, a memory and deepening of the unforgettable impression when he stood on the shore of Dejima for the first time on that August morning after his arrival and looked out into the bay–and it into him. A short tingle crept over his scalp, accompanied by a slight dizziness. For the first time in his life, he had an unequivocal and immediate feeling of seeing a work of creation. So sublime, calm and beautiful laid it before him that for a moment nature, chance or evolution were no longer concepts to grasp the wonder of the existence of this miraculous formation of land, sea, and flora. It was more like a sign that went beyond itself, through which an infinite, timeless will wanted to manifest its intentions and show its original goodness. Seized in such a way by metaphysical feelings, for a time he lingered silently with his companions, who had sunk into their own meditation, of which he suspected that their center was closer to the great emptiness of Buddha, the natural gods of Shintō or their own ancestors.

Afterward, they took a break and ate their lunch snacks sitting in the grass, Siebold small wheat flat cakes with lard and pickled cucumbers, his students the typical rice balls in lotus leaves. Then they began with botanical and zoological work but also collected conspicuous rock samples. There was so much unknown to Siebold's eyes that he did not know where to begin. He studied grasses, flowers, bushes and trees, made quick, cryptic notes; dug up specimens of seemingly interesting plants here and there with a small shovel; analyzed the formations in which plants appeared; collected beetles and other insects; inspected tree bark, found larvae and dolls of new insects behind it; measured the length of roots and lit some cabbage with a lighted matchstick to check the smell; collected water samples, whose mineral and iron content he would later examine in his laboratory. Kō and Takano admired the concentration and thoroughness with which Siebold proceeded in his work. They understood at once that there had to be a system of field observation behind it, with which more and different knowledge could be gained from things than with their own Japanese methods.

That evening, exhausted from the first day's march since his departure from Germany, Siebold lay on the sofa, his head rescued in Sonogi's lap. They had become accustomed to a permissive, tender contact with one another, which was unthinkable between Japanese spouses, but which would also have been judged offensive, if not indecent, in the bourgeois circles in Germany. She stroked his hair, laughed at his slight sunburn on the forehead and bridge of his nose, while he was still breathlessly telling about his observations and finds.

"On the way back, my love, I made the biggest find. How I would like to tell you about it! But it is still a secret to be kept strictly secret. This isn't mature yet."

"You bastard! That's an infinite meanness. Speak up! You know how insatiably curious I am."

"Wait and see before you pull out the dagger. You'll be more than compensated for this little delay if all goes well. But I have an idea how I could compensate you for the time being..."

"You don't have to imagine you can wrap me up like that! But now that you've mentioned it..."

The House at the Waterfall

"Mendelssohn, how nice to see you so healthy! Are you ready?" Siebold had come to his door early in the morning to pick up Mendelssohn. Both were dressed for another excursion, for Siebold had managed to have him accompanied by a draughtsman. And so he had offered Mendelssohn, in order to revive his spirit, to accompany him on the next excursion to the surrounding country, if his health would allow it. In fact, Mendelssohn had already largely recovered, and he was quite well for the first time since his arrival in Japan.

"I am ready. But what surprise awaits me on our hike? I know you want to show me something. You couldn't conceal it."

"Patience, my friend, do not disappoint me. A philosopher is characterized by serenity and patience, isn't he? The wise men of Roman antiquity taught nothing of philosophical curiosity, even if I might be more interested in philosophy from this point of view".

"Well, then let's go before we start a disputation here that shortens the day and robs us of the beautiful views you raved about."

Kō and Takano were on time again at the bridge, the saguriban let Siebold and Mendelssohn after the usual double check of the laissez-passer and the additional permission for the draughtsman on the mainland and the small company set off again on the wanderings. This time the inhabitants in the streets of Nagasaki were even more amazed because they hadn't seen a long-haired foreigner like Mendelssohn for a long time. And they were guessing about the device he was carrying with him, strapped to the side of his backpack. A wooden object about two cubits long, which was composed of several parts. Was that a weapon? No, an easel.

They soon reached the hills, but they climbed further up than the last time. Siebold wanted to reach a higher viewpoint to be able to look at the neighboring landscapes. Mendelssohn was out of breath when they reached the highest point, the Himi-Toge mountain pass. From there they not only saw the bay of Nagasaki but finally also the Tachibana bay behind the eastern mountain chain. The air was dry and under the cloudless sky, the visibility was excellent. At a distance of about fifteen miles, the mighty *Unzen*, whose flat tip was covered by fine veils of mist, rose. This was the first volcano Siebold and Mendelssohn saw. They looked over there for a long time and Siebold told his companions what new insights European geology had gained into the formation and mechanics of volcanoes.

"You'll find signs of volcanic origin all over this area. We already collected basalt with a porphyry structure mixed with hornblende on our last trip."

"Volcanic mountains were also suspected on the moon," Mendelssohn added.

"Yes, that's right, *Sir William Herschel* reported it over thirty years ago. By the way, did you know that he died two years ago? I read about it in Rotterdam, just before we left."

"No, I'm sorry, I wasn't aware of that. I've been meaning to get to something else. His thesis on the volcanoes on the moon was published in 1783, and the following year the philosopher *Immanuel Kant* published a short and unnoticed treatise entitled 'About the Volcanoes on the Moon'. In it, he doubted that there could be volcanoes on the moon. And you know what else? He was right! It has now been proven that the mountains on the moon are not of volcanic origin but were created by gigantic cometary impacts."

"Interesting! A philosopher who can correct a famous naturalist without leaving his writing room. I honestly hope that this will remain an exception," Siebold replied with a wink. Kō and Takano followed the learned explanations about volcanoes on earth and the moon with stunned amazement and not a word escaped them. For a moment they got a feeling of how far the Western sciences were ahead of them and how much Japan had missed in centuries of isolation.

Mendelssohn built up the easel and began to make some drawings. He only made initial sketches, for his skill was not so great that he could have replaced the trained draftsmen from Siebold's entourage. One of them could work on these designs later. In any case, they had to bring some sheets with credible images with them if they were to be checked when they returned.

Siebold and his students continued the botanical, zoological and mineralogical works of their last excursion. This time he had an exact plan, which plants he would look for and which specimens he would collect. So, the time passed almost unnoticed until the afternoon. At a brook, they drank fresh water and ate their food with great appetite. Before dawn, they made their way back. However, they deviated from the paths on which they had come, and Mendelssohn noticed that the path no longer led straight down to the city, but along a contour line towards the northern slopes. He asked Siebold about the meaning of this detour, but he did not answer and laughed at him many times. Then the trees cleared, and they approached a kind of homestead with several buildings nestled against the mountain. Towards the main building, they soon saw a small waterfall fed by one of the mountain streams. Hedges were terraced around the property. Everything was well-proportioned, trees and bushes surrounded the complex in a loose arrangement, a bamboo forest grew further up, light and shade alternated invitingly everywhere, and nature radiated all its fertility and perfection. Mendelssohn would not have been surprised if some of Japan's countless gods lived in this true pearl of enchanted, fairytale property.

"That's it," Siebold finally told his unsettled and astonished companion. "This is Narutaki, 'the house by the rushing waterfall.'"

"This is an exceptionally beautiful country house. Did you come by here on your last trip?"

"Well, that too. But you know why I show it to you?"

"No, certainly not. Perhaps because it is uninhabited, and you want to tell me something about your most secret wishes," replied Mendelssohn, who wanted to find back to his lighthearted frivolousness.

"This will be my future place of residence and work," Siebold proudly returned. "Here I will set up a school and continue my practice. Yesterday, I heard, there was a decree allowing me to settle here on the mainland. I await the document on our return today." Kō and Takano smiled delightedly because they knew this plan from the very first moment and now saw it unfold.

"This is really incredible! How in the world did you do that? For over two hundred years, no foreigner was allowed to live outside the island."

"My Japanese friends here and many of their colleagues have done this. The governor has only given me permission to run a school, but I will soon acquire the house with his consent under a Japanese alias so that the government in Edo will not get nervous."

"Unbelievable. The Nagasaki administration is really risking a lot in your favor. And I must admit, I really can't overestimate you. But I already know how this is going to affect our fellow prisoners, especially Colonel de Sturler."

"Come on, let's keep moving. It's getting late. Yes, I know I don't make friends with that among the Dutch. But I hope you understand that I cannot be hindered by this. I am sure that I will soon receive further support from the East Indian government in Batavia. It is a major breakthrough for Dutch diplomacy, which has taken the path of science for the first time. Trade may be important, but our time also needs other links of interest between civilized nations. In trade, we will continue to fail for a long time because of the distrust of the Japanese and the isolation of their markets. In the sciences, on the other hand, they are almost eager to be taught by us. With our scientific findings, we have a raw material that they cannot replace in any way and do not want to do without."

In the evening Sonogi was beside herself with joy, when Siebold first silently presented her with the decree, which had arrived as hoped during the day. But when he explained to her the larger context, which did not emerge from the document, and the imminent move to the Narutaki country house, she burst into tears. Sonogi couldn't believe her luck. She had resigned herself to the fact that she was only allowed to live on the harbor island with her husband for a few years before returning to her company as a courtesan. Now she saw how the impossible became possible. Her husband's reputation, which she rarely experienced directly, had to be so great that it could even overcome ancient laws in her country. She was infinitely proud of him and congratulated herself again retrospectively for her wise choice.

Moving to Narutaki

"Major, I wish your mission every success. You report to me once a week as discussed. You continue to run your local practice three days a week for four hours each. Other than that, you will, of course, have free access to the island and your existing living and working space at all times. We will inform you as soon as we receive news from Batavia." Sturler sat grey and sick behind his desk. He had been passed over one more time, but he had resigned himself to it. There's no point in rebelling against Siebold's success in the current situation. Sturler was aware, despite all the affect against the parvenu, that such behavior would undoubtedly have to be interpreted as envy and malice by unbiased third parties in the event of a conflict.

"Thank you, Colonel," Siebold replied dutifully, while the cold formality of his superior had not escaped to him, including the feelings suppressed behind it. But Siebold had the upper hand, and he wanted to hear that again from Sturler's mouth.

"What are the chances that Batavia will grant my request?"

"Good," Sturler returned dry.

Shortly before, Siebold had written down a detailed report for the Governor van der Capellen, followed by a request for further financial means to acquire objects for the scientific collections and to create a botanical garden with greenhouses. It was a considerable sum, more than four times his first budget, which had been made available to him upon his departure from Batavia. But that was not all. Siebold had also asked that a draughtsman, a geologist–and another doctor be sent to his disposal. That was quite audacious because there was no precedent in the history of Dutch foreign relations. However, Siebold did not want to miss this opportunity to improve his status and expand his scope for action. He knew he wouldn't get another chance like this so soon. Sturler, on the other hand, naturally recognized the breathtaking presumption and hoped that Siebold had overstretched the bow so much that he fell from grace. Therefore, knowing the brief, he did not even think of calling on Siebold to exercise restraint. On the contrary, he rejoiced at the reckless exorbitance of his ambitious medical officer.

The next day the move began, which attracted a great deal of attention in Nagasaki. Even the ancients had never seen anything like it in their whole lives. For the first time, the people lining the wayside saw European furniture, carpets, household objects and suitcases. At the end of the trek Siebold walked among a group of soldiers of the governor in his magnificent gala uniform. Three steps behind him, , as required by Japanese tradition, Sonogi followed tripping on her *geta* in her blue crane kimono, accompanied by her servant from the Hikidaya. The solemn procession only reached Narutaki after more than an hour. There they were expected by Siebold's students, their families, and grateful patients. Everyone wanted to help and Siebold was moved when he was received with Sonogi by about one hundred people. This event was also unique for the assembled, because no open-air meeting of this size would have been allowed in the whole country. The police would have intervened at once. In this case, too, the governor again held his protective hand over the matter. Two hundred hands set up the whole house by the evening and it then looked as if Siebold and Sonogi were already living there for some time. Food was prepared, the beds made, and they were not allowed to even touch their household contents. Especially the former patients wanted to thank them. They still believed that Siebold did not take money for his treatments out of generosity. As a doctor on Dejima, however, he was strictly forbidden to collect fees for medical services outside his salary. A few times he half-heartedly tried to inform his patients about this ban. Nevertheless, they stubbornly adhered to their view that the Dutch doctor was a charitable man. Siebold knew that he had not really bothered to tarnish this beautiful appearance with the truth. But he was immediately supported by the justification that he always pursued this advantage in the sense of increasing scientific knowledge. His patients' many gifts were later to be important exhibits in Europe's museums and scientific collections.

The very next day Siebold opened his new practice and began teaching. Previously, he made an early morning tour of his new estate, once owned by the high priest of the great Suwa shrine of Nagasaki. It covered about two hectares and was, therefore, larger than the entire harbor island of Dejima. The housing complex was divided into two buildings and two annexes in Japanese style, which were now furnished with European furniture. The two-story main building opposite the garden gate had a large, foiled room on each floor. He would use the lower one as a workroom and the upper one as a study. They contained his research material, the collections of natural produce, medicines and his European and Japanese books. The rooms were closed off from the outside by semi-transparent parchment sliding doors called *shōji*, so that the rooms were extraordinarily bright, especially when they were opened wide during the day and offered a sublime panorama of the green valley populated by a few houses. Siebold had already noticed that the Japanese didn't know any window glass. From the records of his predecessors, he could conclude that there was no glass industry in Japan. To the left of this building stood the other, one-story main house, in which there were two spacious rooms next to each other, which now served Sonogi and him as living rooms, the larger of the two being at the same time a classroom, examination and treatment room. The other outbuildings were a fixed bookstore with an adjoining kitchen and a large shed. There were two wells, one in the treatment room, one in the kitchen. Narrow gravel paths connected the buildings. In between, bamboo bushes and trees were spread all over the property. Within the next two years, he planned to make a connected botanical garden with medicinal herbs and a collection of the most important specimens of Japanese flora.

Siebold Teaches

The first day was hectic because his many students came at the same time as the first patients. He set up a timetable to coordinate the various activities and to be able to work sensibly. From now on theoretical and practical medicine was taught in Narutaki, especially gynecology, pediatrics, ophthalmology, and surgery, as well as natural history and pharmacology. Siebold propagated a system of practical learning and his students worked together with him on the cases that came into practice every day. This had a great advantage for the patients because they did not have to be alone with the stranger in the treatment room. The presence of the Japanese doctors instilled confidence in them. Even if most believed that the Dutch Sensei had magical powers, they were afraid of the tall man with the big, strong hands. Especially the women. Siebold continued to take no money for his treatments. Since his patients did not want to owe him anything, they brought him many valuable gifts, works of art and utensils, but also rare plants, stones, and insects.

East Asian medicine was already at a high level, especially in the field of internal medicine. In anatomy and surgery, on the other hand, Europeans had a great advantage. The Japanese scholars knew this since the 'Anatomical Charts' of Johann Adam Kulmus appeared in 1774 under the title 'Kaitai-shinsho'. They were originally published in Gdansk in 1722 and reached Japan only because shogun *Yoshimune Tokugawa* had approved the import of Dutch books. The two translators Genpaku Sugita and Ryotaku Maeno attended the body section of a publicly executed criminal in a prison in Edo and realized that the anatomical teachings in the Chinese books were wrong.

Japanese medicine was strongly influenced by the Chinese tradition called 'kampo', which meant nothing more than 'treatment instruction'.

The healers imagined the human body as integrated into astrological and cosmological conditions. In addition, there was a teaching of elements comparable to European alchemy. Health was for them an equilibrium of these many reluctant forces and juices. The unrestrained circulation of the vital energy 'goto' was decisive. This healthy dynamic could be impaired by the effect of an unspecified poison 'doku'. The influence of European medicine began around 1600, when the Portuguese introduced surgical practices such as amputation and vascular suppression. Since the isolation of the country under the Tokugawa, only the Dutch have been able to bring medical knowledge to Japan. Caspar Schamberger, for example, who took part in the first court journey to the capital Edo in 1649, quickly became known and founded *Kasuparuyugeka*, a 'Kaspar school of surgery'. Engelbert Kaempfer, who lived on Dejima from 1690 to 1692, had made the first scientific record of Japanese medicine, but it was not taken seriously in his homeland. His book 'History of Japan' was only published posthumously in English in London in 1724 and finally in Germany in 1774. It treated acupuncture and moxibustion in detail for the first time. Siebold had read these chapters of the book with great attention during his journey to Java. Now he learned from his students the practical implementation of these Asian healing methods. Moxa was a heat therapy in which a small cone of dried mugwort or other medicinal herbs was burnt on certain regions of the skin on an area the size of a coin. This should strengthen the blood circulation in the tissues, but above all it should improve the organ functions and adjust them in such a way that the body is better able to defend itself against all kinds of ailments. Siebold noted with interest that the moxa was also used for education, as a last resort to calm wild and noisy children. The skin areas were the same that the acupuncturist needed to know in order to place his needles. Siebold was particularly fascinated by this method of healing and had the authoritative writings of the imperial acupuncturist *Sotetsu Ishizaka* translated at once.

Siebold learned an extraordinary amount about Japanese medicine in a very short time. He returned the favor by teaching his students how to use the stethoscope and the microscope, which gave the young men experiences that deeply impressed them. The clear hearing of organ movements inside the human body and the view into the microcosm of body fluids, plants and insects were of a new sensuality and higher sensitivity than they knew from Chinese medicine. Siebold was also able to inform them about important innovations in pharmacology. The drug that opened up completely new possibilities for eye surgery and gained decisive importance for his further work was *atropine*. He had already used it in the operation of the old priest Yoshisada. The success had surprised him, especially his ensuing fame as a miracle doctor. He was almost sorry that he now had to reveal the nature of his magic to his students. In Europe, the poisonous alkaloid was discovered around 1800 in all nightshade plants, especially in deadly nightshade and jimson apple. Atropine has an antispasmodic and relaxing effect and can be used against bronchial muscle cramps in asthma. In the eyes, it causes a strong dilation of the pupils. This was the first time the fundus of the eye could be observed. Siebold thus had considerably better visual control over the corneal layer to be removed during the cataract operation. The rest was a steady, sure hand–and no one compared to him in this regard.

In these first months, Siebold taught his students the art of the forceps birth, but above all the cesarean section. Regularly, women giving birth died in horrible pain because the operation was either not performed at all or was performed clumsily by frightened doctors. Siebold showed the students how they could save almost all children and most women with the cesarean section through small incisions in the abdominal wall and uterus. He taught them how to suck out from their lungs the amniotic fluid that would have been squeezed out of them in a natural birth in the narrow birth canal so that they would not suffocate. The students were also impressed by the truss or suspensory bandage into whose use Siebold introduced them. It was an elastic, belt-like band with pressure pad to hold back intestines, for example in the case of an inguinal hernia. Such fractures were particularly common with luggage and sedan carriers. Even swordfighters who were too old for the hard exercises of their art eventually suffered from it. However, the most important medical innovation that Siebold had in his luggage was the cowpox lymph, which he brought with him from Java. He was able to teach his students smallpox vaccination and at the same time to demonstrate the general principle of vaccination. He gratefully recalled the little speech of Sömmerring, who had told him about Edward Jenner's and Christoph Hufeland's experiences with smallpox vaccination and his own improvements.

Over the months, the topics that Narutaki was dealing with grew far beyond medicine. Siebold found more time for botanical and zoological studies, especially since he had to classify and catalog the plants and animals given to him as gifts. The climate, soil, and irrigation in Narutaki were ideal for creating a garden. At first, Siebold cultivated important pharmacist plants so that the doctors and his students, who had traveled from far away, could prepare their own remedies. In addition, he now also taught geology and mineralogy as well as linguistics. He soon wanted to turn to the humanities and cultural sciences to learn more about the history, art, religion, and politics of the country. He did this rather by chance by getting involved with his colleagues. The discussions with them gave him an insight that was otherwise difficult to obtain in a country like Japan. There were few books on Japanese history and culture, and politics was a secret matter anyway, just like the Arcana Imperii in Europe before the emergence of the press and the first parliaments. The most effective way to learn more about the Japanese state, cults, and customs was to open a conversation with one's own knowledge brought in from Europe, preferably combined with personal impressions.

The East Pole

Siebold invited some of his learned friends and students from Nagasaki and the surrounding areas to Narutaki. He asked Mendelssohn to join society. To obtain the passport for him went without difficulty. Siebold wanted to have an educated European at his side when he hosts his Japanese guests. They came at dusk and brought gifts, rare flowers, small lacquer works, herbs and fruits. They had made an appointment and had previously obtained information about which specimens were still missing from the garden of his house. For the Japanese it was an incomparable experience to sit on chairs at a European table, where beside the sticks a cutlery made of knife and fork was ready, if they wanted to try it. The Japanese servants—for the usual Malay cooks, waiters, and auxiliaries of Dejima the entry of the mainland was strictly prohibited—arranged the meal, while at the table the guests already talked lively about all kinds of trivialities and laughed a lot. Siebold and Mendelssohn were impressed by this informal, gregarious behavior which was unthinkable in the German bourgeoisie on such occasions. It was more like a meeting of carousing students, which is why it reminded Siebold of his fraternity feasts with a short sting of nostalgia. But when the food was served, his appetite prevailed over melancholy and he rushed almost unmannerly to Dutch specialties, first the hearty pea soup, then the young herring freshly caught in the bay, which had been pickled in a brine for five days and fermented, and finally the grilled beef steak. The latter was a sensation for Siebold's Japanese colleagues. Because of the Buddhist belief in the sanctity of life, the consumption of meat was officially forbidden for centuries and there were no animals for slaughter in all of Japan. Only in the countryside were wild boars, bears, monkeys, horses, and dogs secretly eaten and there were knackers. They used the carcasses of dead animals and mostly offered inferior, partly rotten meat. Pigs were not yet domesticated, and cattle were exclusively working animals that were treated as family members. Therefore, it took some good persuasion until the Japanese doctors dared to cut and eat the pieces of meat of the cattle slaughtered on Dejima. They were fascinated by the taste, with the good roast, salt, and pepper each playing its part. One of them, Sakamoto, was downright thrilled.

"If the gods had wanted us not to eat animals, they would not have made them of meat, would they?" he shouted out in ironically overacted ecstasy.

Siebold looked at Sonogi with gratitude as she served the guests. She had her Japanese assistants trained in the preparation and serving of European dishes and the result was delicious to look at.

Just as in this small company of a dozen Japanese there were some quiet fellows who wanted to stay in the background out of shyness and just listened with a smile, so there were also distinctive characters with idio-syncratic life stories and temperaments who liked to express themselves boldly. It was no secret that Jinichiro Sakamoto, for example, was a blasphemer who did not seem to miss anything that happened in the castles of daimyōs, in Edo and in Kyōtō. Or that the leather-skinned Sajūrō Baba was a drunk who quickly thawed after the second or third cup of sake, after which no eye remained dry because of his bizarre wit. Finally, there was Bansui Otsuki, who was said to have a philosophical inclination. But his Buddhist melancholy was intelligent and appreciated by his colleagues. He was already regarded as a kind of living saint, but one with a huge appetite that made him more sociable than some talkers.

"Tell us something about the outside world, Sensei! What does it look like? How big is it? Is there another country that is like Japan?

"Well, the earth is a big globe whose seas, continents and countries are already quite well explored. The Japanese island empire is certainly unique and at the same time the least explored the area between the North and South Poles".

"Uh-huh. Does that ball also have a West and an East pole?" Baba cunningly inquired. A brief silence followed. The Japanese wondered what he meant by that, while Siebold could not decide whether he should find Baba's question absurd or ingenious. Then he ended the expectant silence with a hearty laugh, which the guests joined in.

"No, dear Baba-san, there is no West Pole and no East Pole. But if the latter existed, it would certainly be here in Japan. East of the Japanese empire you're already in the far west."

"Whether it really exists is not so important, sensei. Just announce in *Yōroppa* that you have discovered the East Pole! Then more great foreigners like you will come to Japan looking for it. We can learn a lot and perhaps enjoy even more of these delicacies that you have brought to us."

The whole party rejoiced, for the wise Baba spoke from their hearts. It was the still sober Sakamoto who, after the dishes had been removed and the beverage bowls were filled again, wanted to switch from silly to serious topics.

"Shiboruto-sensei, let us learn a little more about the Christians tonight. We have some knowledge from earlier times until the Bakufu forbade the belief in Iesusu and Goddo. You probably know that the *fumi-e* with the 'Iesusu kicking' and the harsh punishments for refusing have cut us off from the newer practices in your faith."

"Yes, I would also like to know how you came up with the idea of letting the son of your God die on a wooden cross. If I remember correctly, you also had a choice between him and an ordinary thief," Baba added.

"That was a necessary part of the Son of God's passion, that means his sufferance," Siebold replied. "You must understand that his goal was death on the cross because he wanted to take upon himself our sins and reconcile God with men. He fought with *Satan*, performed miracles, and remained a faithful vassal of his father. And he died on the cross to save humanity as a whole. He is the most important kami in our culture, the *kamisama*, so to speak because the worship of his person can secure for the person who believes in him, after death, a place in paradise, which you call the 'Land of Purity.'"

"Who is Satan?" asked Otsuki with eyes only half opened, quietly taking a digestive nap.

Siebold hesitated before answering: "He is a fallen angel of the creator Goddo and brought evil into the world. To him, in his kingdom, a burning hell, come the souls of all evil men after their death. Hell is the other beyond. One could also call it the 'Land of Pain', where an eternal punishment of evil deeds awaits those who were sinner during their lifetimes."

"And what does Satan look like?" Otsuki asked unmoved.

"There are many ideas about him," Siebold replied, "which makes him so dangerous. Satan can change his form, has many names like Devil, Beelzebub, Belial, Lucifer, Mephisto or Lord of the Flies, and he is a powerful and cunning sorcerer. Often he was depicted in pictures with a split tongue, horns and a horse's foot."

"That sounds like our *Susanoo no mikoto*, the brother of the sun goddess Amaterasu. He is the ruler of the world of the dead and a giant, a huge wild man. The nail beds of his fingers and toes are bloody, for his nails were once torn out as punishment for his desperate deeds. And his teeth are sharp and sharp like those of a shark," Sakamoto replied and then asked with a smile, "Does this devil really exist? Does Shiboruto-sensei believe in him, the Shatanu?"

"An interesting question, dear Sakamoto-san. I never thought about that. It is hard enough for me that there should be a creator of the world and that this is the Christian god of all people. But no, there is no devil. Not really. That means I don't believe in him," Siebold replied.

Mendelssohn interfered and wanted to go back to the earlier topic. "The matter of Iesusu's death by cross can also be interpreted differently," he began, clearing his throat in embarrassment. Siebold looked at him in astonishment. What would he hear now, after maneuvering as *irenically* and harmlessly as possible between beliefs? Above all, he hoped that

Mendelssohn would not now make everything complicated from a Jewish point of view by denying the meaning of Christ as the Messiah.

"See, this story is essentially based on a single book, the Bible. This book consists of two important parts, the Old Testament, which tells the story of the world from its creation by Goddo to the age of Tennō Sujin, and the New Testament, which tells the story of Iesusu, born in this age. There are four great authors who tell this life story, and four times his path to death on the cross is also told. Well, it is so that even after reading these last passages of the so-called Gospels very carefully, I could not find a single word that came from the mouth of Iesusu that could prove his determination to die voluntarily, yes, to virtually provoke the fatal outcome of his passion."

"But, dear Mendelssohn, how do you interpret the evangelist Matthew when he reports that the assembled people demanded of Pilate that the blood of Christ be shed?"

"Pilatusu-san, a daimyō of the Roman emperor in Palestine, knew that Iesusu was betrayed and given to him out of resentment and envy. This Roman governor was the most righteous in all the saga, for he had shown fate a way out that would not have required a sacrifice of the Son of God. He wanted to see Barnabas convicted, a thief. His wife came to him before the judgment and begged him not to harm Iesusu, as she had dreamed of him the night before. Pilatusu even went so far as to wash his hands in front of the eyes of this same people and said, 'I am innocent of the blood of this righteous man! This is your lot' He saw the Jewish mob in front of him and it disgusted him."

Mendelssohn realized that he reached his limits as self-denial began to hurt so much that he had to think of retracting. But what did it help? Even if he and his Jewish fellows did not believe in Christ as the Messiah, in his arrival at that time: how could he contradict this tradition, which was also witnessed to in John's Gospel? Especially if he wanted to stick to the lyrics as faithfully as he had planned to. There was never any doubt for him that the Jew Jesus was a victim of the Jewish mob. He was also convinced that human sacrifice was the deepest root of human culture—and that Iesusu, as the Japanese pronounced his name so refreshingly naive, was an Enlightener who wanted to dissuade humanity from collective murder forever.

"What do you mean, Menduruson-san? Wasn't the conviction fair? Did the daimyō Pilatusu-san do so out of cowardice and opportunism? What kind of way is it to let the people judge a person's fate? Were there no strict laws," Sakamoto asked with palpable indignation.

"Yes, yes, there were strict laws. But it was a holiday when the daimyō wanted to spare a convicted criminal the punishment to prove his generosity and mercy to the people."

"And what about John's 'Revelation', where we can read right at the beginning about Iesusu '...who loved us and washed us from our sins with his blood?'" Siebold asked enthusiastically because he was not satisfied with Mendelssohn's criticism of religion.

"It is questionable whether the 'Revelation' can indeed be counted in the Bible," Mendelssohn began. "The Fathers of the Catholic Church had chosen to do so. Perhaps because this text only served the purpose of scaring people properly. Did you know that Erasmus of Rotterdam refused to translate the 'Revelation'? He thought it was an *apocryphal* text that had no place in the Holy Scriptures."

Then he continued by turning to the other guests: "Shiboruto-sensei and I, we obviously do not quite agree on this question. How and why should a holy man, who believes to be the Son of the creator of the world, voluntarily let himself be nailed to a cross? That was your question too, wasn't it, Sakamoto-san? I can't believe it. The Catholic religion also knows many other martyrs who were canonized by the Pope, the Tennō or the shogun of the Catholic Church. But if only a hint of suspicion had arisen that a martyr would have endangered himself and deliberately sacrificed himself, he would have been pronounced crazy instead of holy. Quite rightly, I think. That's sick fanaticism. *Eli, Eli, lama asabthani*–'Father, father, why did you leave me?' That were the last words of Iesusu before he died. Are these the words of a man who lets himself be crucified voluntarily? Who feels joy or perhaps even lust because he succeeds in his messianic plan? No, I don't think so. If this man existed, if he was crucified, if he really rose from the dead afterwards and if the Christians have been waiting for his return since his ascent to heaven, then this story can only have one meaning. Iesusu the innocent, the lamb, has lived a life of uncompromising justice, sincerity and truth. This sacred way of life has put him on the cross where he was to die. It was a causal chain of events, entirely in the logic of a sinful world that could not bear good. He did not want it and was desperate about the people who sacrificed an innocent man like him. He tested humanity, it failed. From then on, it had to cope alone, without a good God who has become man. His return can therefore only be at one point in time, namely when a Son of God like him can live unchecked and unchallenged among men".

Siebold, deeply impressed by Mendelssohn's portrayal, was still relieved that no Roman Catholic was sitting at the table. Before his mind's eye, he saw a Europe rising, which was destroyed by such religious questions of interpretation in the Thirty Years' War. Meanwhile, the Japanese guests looked alienated. They hadn't understood anything about this lecture, it didn't make sense. They did not understand why a son did not like to die for his Father and the honor of a divine family, why he wailed so unmanly at the hour of death and what the whole thing should mean with his resurrection and return. None of them had ever read the Bible, although some Dutch Bibles were supposed to have been stolen and smuggled from the barrels where they were collected and nailed by the Japanese authorities on Dejima every time a new ship arrived. Siebold had been proudly shown one of these specimens by one of his youngest students and was terrified. He advised him to destroy it if he cared about his life and that of his family. To know the secrets of Christianity is no longer so valuable that it would be worth dying for. After all, the Dutch were only tolerated by the Japanese government because they did not try to missionize their subjects.

"Many Japanese see this differently, esteemed Menduruson-san, especially the noblemen, the aristocrats and the samurai," the philosophical Otsuki interfered again with a calm voice. "Life is worth nothing in comparison to honor and loyalty. Sacrifice is a noble deed. It saves the soul and the reputation of the family for generations. This thought certainly did not play a role when tens of thousands of Japanese became Christians at the beginning of the Tokugawa dynasty. But then what was it?"

Mendelssohn remained silent, for he now understood that he had spoken to himself and perhaps to Siebold over the heads of the Japanese guests. Seeking help, he looked at him.

"As far as we know, these simple Japanese, in their majority of farmers, fishermen, and villagers, were particularly impressed by the Christian idea of paradise," Siebold took over. "In this land of purity, man is rewarded after his death for his ordained, diligent, God-fearing and obedient life. There all his wishes are fulfilled, which were denied to him before his death. In addition, the soul of the deceased lives on there for all eternity at Goddo's side. The soul and its salvation are much more important in Christianity than the body and its death. One could even say that it is a message from Iesusu–faith can defeat death."

"This is understandable," Otsuki went on, "because the land of purity is a Buddhist concept that many among the common people hardly know and rarely understand. They are more strongly influenced by Shintō. This belief knows no real country after death unless you live on in worship as kami. On the contrary, death itself is unclean. In ancient times, the dead in the forest were simply left to the wild animals and insects. Even the Tennō was discarded in this barbaric manner. Today the dead are at least cremated like with the Buddhists. But the place of death still must be purified with elaborate rituals. It's not very comforting to gradually lose one's parents and then the whole family in this way."

Outside the wind went around the house in the darkness and it had become cool. Sonogi came into the dining room and replenished everyone's glass, this time hot sake from an elegant porcelain bottle wrapped in a cloth. Then she put them on the table so that the guests could top each other up, little gestures of attention and friendship which the men did not want to be taken away. Tobacco was offered and so they continued their merrily drinking. After these serious discussions, the hour had come for the drinker Baba, who was already on the move and boasted of his adventures in a brothel. He did not forget to make fun of his own clumsiness and occasional impotence. There was bawling, cheering, coughing, and laughing. All Japanese had red faces and were as cheerful as they could possibly be on this side of madness. Siebold and Mendelssohn grinned conspiratorially and had the same thought–this kind of conversation and conviviality was completely unimaginable among well-behaved people in stiff Germany. They also shared the satisfaction that Germany and Europe were just far away. At a later hour, swordfish was served in wafer-thin slices with mild radish as a Japanese style midnight snack and drinking base. At the end, there was a ceremonial bowl of warm rice and some green tea for everyone. Happy and drunk, the guests left Narutaki well after midnight. The wind had died down, the lonely song of a single cicada came over from the bamboo forest behind the house. Fireflies floated through the calm sea of darkness, reminding them that summer would come soon.

Mendelssohn Philosophizes

Siebold made good progress with the garden, the greenhouses, the cataloging of his rapidly growing collections and the studies. His reputation as a miracle doctor now also attracted patients to Narutaki from higher strata of society and from ever more distant provinces. When summer took the stage, it became even hotter and wetter than the year before. European clothing was extremely inappropriate under these conditions because even before the double-row vest was put on the shirt was wet, not to mention the uniform jacket. Every movement increased the sweat flow, but even motionless the body, not accustomed to tropical moisture, had to sweat continuously. Siebold, therefore, dressed more casual and could usually be found in a simple, white cotton shirt with rolled up sleeves. To his surprise, this climate did not affect his physical energy, his concentration, or his sleep. On the contrary, something about this muggy summer weather seemed to inspire him. He moved here, unlike on Batavia, through the humid heat like a fish in water, which even the Japanese seemed to torture and limit so much that they could only do their daily work slowly and with difficulty. He performed his duties three times a week for four hours each in the doctor's practice on Dejima as agreed. Outside these set times he had to take care of the small garden on the island with his assistants, which he sometimes did alone because he regarded this time as his leisure hours. On an early August evening–the *civil twilight* was already in sight in the bay, while the surrounding hills and mountain tops were still glowing– Mendelssohn passed by, while Siebold still replanted tubers and was soiled with earth as far as the elbows.

"Good evening, dear doctor. I see you're all transported and lost in reveries while botanizing. I've been watching you for a while."

"Yes, Mr. Philosopher, it is true that here I can organize my thoughts."

"That's very wise of you because if you remember the end of Voltaire's *Candide*, any good philosopher will eventually become a gardener. Just not today, please! I don't feel like doing practical work right now. Let us rather philosophize."

Siebold laughed, jumped onto the fortification wall of the island, which bounded the garden, down onto the large stones and washed his hands and arms in the sea, which quietly splashed against the artificial island. When he came back up, he went to his doctor's bag and got something out.

"Did you bring your pipe? I'd like to end my day there on our wooden bench and join you in offering a pinch of tobacco to the gods of this country."

"Excellent idea! Yes, I am equipped with a pipe," he said and took it out of his box-shaped leather shoulder bag, which accompanied him everywhere. They dusted the bench, settled down and started stuffing their pipes. This vantage point and its seating seemed not to be used by anyone except the two, and the last time was almost a year ago. They looked out to the bay, which laid quietly in the dawn and they sucked on their small burnt offerings. "Have you ever thought about the origin of life?" Mendelssohn suddenly asked after a long silence. He obviously wanted to raise a topic for the first time on which he was not sure whether Siebold could be approached. Siebold looked at him and first thought about how he would have to understand the question.

"I will gladly try to answer you, but I hope you do not expect me to make a dogmatic comment on what is written about it in Genesis."

"You understand me quite well. I want to know what you, as an educated citizen and scientist, think about it."

"You see, I am an unphilosophical person and I have always stayed as far away from all metaphysical disputes as possible. This is one of the reasons why I did not want to study theology, which would have corresponded to my uncle and guardian's wish–probably because he is a canon. Fortunately, the tradition of medical work and research is so deeply rooted in our family that I did not hesitate in choosing this subject. But now back to your question. I believe that organic life is based on inorganic matter."

"Can you explain this to me?"

"Of course, I can't explain how this happens in detail. Who could? My teacher Professor Döllinger, certainly one of the most capable physicians in Europe and perhaps even in the world, still adheres to the philosophy of a certain *Schelling*. He may also teach a construction of living matter on dead matter, but he believes in a spirit that holds together the dead and the living of matter. I can't imagine such a thing."

"Do you see in life a blind force unfolding aimlessly?"

"This idea of an original life force has been around for a long time. Alexander von Humboldt believed in vis vitalis as a young researcher and hoped to be able to describe the origin of organic life. But he gave it up because he found that it could not be proven. I agree with him. What do I need a scientific theory for that I can't prove?"

"Do you know you agree with the philosopher Immanuel Kant from Königsberg?"

"Oh, please spare me the teachings of these Kants, Hegels, and Fichtes! I already thought Schelling's speculative philosophy of nature was exaggerated. But at least he was still understood. The other idealists, on the other hand, cannot be made accessible even with the best command of the German language. And didn't a writer kill himself reading Kant's philosophy? Von Kleist was his name, I think. He once had a phimosis performed by a friend of our family in Würzburg. In any case, the philosophers should stick to the research of the wisdom of the ancient world. I don't think they can really enrich the scientific knowledge of nature unless you add in the ghosts and powers they invent, erroneously to the benefits of nature."

Mendelssohn stood up and gave Siebold a cheeky and challenging look.

"Would you consider it a commendable achievement if a philosopher could teach mankind the origin of the stars and the shape of our galaxy?"

Siebold laughed and Mendelssohn heard an unpleasant note of arrogance in this response.

"Yes, I do. That would be a great achievement. As far as I know, however, William Herschel, whom we spoke of recently when we enjoyed this view of the Bay of Shimabara and the volcano Unzen, has already determined the shape of the Milky Way."

"That's right. Well, how would you like it if I told you that Sir Herschel, who published his observations on the spatial extension of the star population in the Milky Way in 1785, provided only the first confirmation for the theory of a certain philosopher named Immanuel Kant? In his book 'General History of Nature and Theory of Heaven' from 1755 he deducted and explained why the Milky Way must have the form of a spiral which we can only see from the side because of the position of our solar system in one of the spiral arms. If I told you that the same philosopher was the first to talk about the milky spot in the constellation Andromeda–he called it a 'cookie'–being possibly a huge cluster of stars and an island of worlds as big as the Milky Way? And that he was the first to show how all the suns and planets were formed by the interaction of dusty matter and gravity?"

Siebold looked at Mendelssohn in astonishment. If that was true, then he had reason to be impressed by the scientific achievements of this philosopher. At the same time, he was shocked at the extent of his under-estimation–and his ignorance. Why didn't he know? Why could an aesthete like Mendelssohn teach him, the doctor, researcher, and discover-er, on scientific questions?

"I admit that he must be a great thinker in the best sense of the word. But please help me. Explain to me how such discoveries can be made alone with philosophy, locked up with books in a dusty scholar's room."

Mendelssohn, who had been somewhat upset before, calmed down and was satisfied that Siebold actually showed insight.

"Philosophy, those are just words, you might think. But what are words? Are they just names for things and thoughts? No, some words are also concepts. And if you have the right grasp of something, then you can build on it and develop the next concept. In the end, you can demonstrate the whole nature with concepts and explore it yourself in this demon-stration. This is what Kant discovered in Königsberg. 'Give me only matter, and I will build you a world out of it'–you know this materialistic specu-lation that the philosopher Epicurus contrived more than two-thousand years ago. Well, Kant went on saying 'Give me only matter and I will show you how a world must create itself without me or anyone else–no God either–doing anything about it.' For, unlike Epicurus, he had not only the concept of matter, but also the concepts of movement, inertia, mass, and gravity. These terms stand for laws of nature, and since the ingenious Galileo Galilei we can combine these laws with figures, we can quantify them. We no longer need to copy the flight of a bullet from the flying object. Instead, we can calculate how that bullet *must* fly. Do you know the motto Kant used for his famous *Critique of Pure Reason*?"

"No, I haven't read it either."

"It is the preface to the *Instauratio Magna* by Francis Bacon, another philosopher. In it, he announced nothing less than that of his *Novum Organum*, a 'new form of science', was the end and the rightful conclusion of endless error, as he put it. He sought a new kind of logic, one that not only dissects individual sentences to find out how much truth is contained in them but one that discovers new truths that are not yet held anywhere. He did not believe that the treasures of knowledge from Antiquity already contained all the knowledge of this world, that the truth was 'wrapped up' in them and that one only had to 'unwrap' it. This was a revolution of thought that Kant quite rightly described as a Copernican turning-point. Not to mention that Bacon was also the inventor of what we now call 'experiment'."

"The experiment was invented by philosophers? That's never mentioned in the science faculties."

"That's exactly right. Even if you were unaware of it in the diverse scientific research you are conducting: the idea that you can approach nature and ask it questions with the authority of a judge, to which it must answer if you only do it correctly–this is a thoroughly philosophical and highly demanding practice. We, as the youngest children of the Enlightenment, have again forgotten how many millennia of knowledge lay in the dark and human curiosity has found something worth knowing only by chance here and there. Now that we are systematically expanding our knowledge in all directions, we are at an epochal threshold. You will see that the steam-powered weaving loom was only the beginning; soon there will also be steam-powered means of transport. And finally, one day all human work and existence will be mastered by sources of power such as steam and electricity. I met two young researchers in London, the Germans *Georg Ohm* from Cologne and *Michael Faraday*. These two will revolutionize the science of electricity, you can count on it."

"Sure, sure" Siebold replied somewhat overstrained, although at the same time somehow satisfied that he, for whom teaching had already become second nature despite his youth–he had only turned twenty-eight in February–was once again taught by someone whose authority was undoubted. It was exactly this position in Siebold's world of thoughts that Mendelssohn moved into during this intense conversation.

"But, and this brings us back to the question of the origin of life, the same philosopher Immanuel Kant stated in a book that few people know– even less understood it–that the whole universe with its bodies and forces could be explained rather than the creation of a single caterpillar or herb. So it is written in a footnote of his *Critique of Judgement*. This is the point where he surprised me because I would have thought that the mystery of the origin of life is only one of many for which a solution is already waiting. But Kant seems to categorically exclude that we will ever experience them. Why? Even if everything else can be experienced in time and space and is therefore accessible to knowledge! Therefore, dear doctor, as my scientific friend, I asked you so naively about the origin of life. It's a cry for help. The philosopher, whom I admire above all and who, as I have tried to convince you, deserves the highest merits of a naturalist, this very thinker puts a full stop to the possibility of scientific knowledge with the riddle of life. I don't understand. And I wanted to know how you feel about that." The offshore breeze drove the small clouds of pipe smoke out onto the water, where they stood like an indecisive herd, to be torn into veils and finally dissolved. Siebold took his time to answer because he felt that Mendelssohn was asking him one of the most important questions of all philosophical and scientific research.

"Your question reminds me of something I experienced when I started collecting insects. I was very young, maybe seven years old. I wondered why I had to dip the beetles and butterflies in vinegar ether before I could skewer them with the needles. I thought the solution was just to keep the animals from moving too much during needling. It was not clear to me that this treatment had already killed the animal and prepared it for centuries of conservation. I seriously expected the insects to start moving again once they had been needled into the glass collection boxes. When I noticed my misunderstanding, the border between life and death closed. Until then, death had nothing absolute for me, it was just a condition among others. I had to learn in these days to understand that there is no way back from death to life. Years later, as a teenager, I began to admire the phenomenon of life as such. I was amazed that something was alive and not everything was dead. Above all, I was overwhelmed by the diversity of life that had burrowed into every corner of the planet. The palette of colors and forms in plants and animals, it seems to me today more than ever, knows no limits. Do you understand? I am despairing of this task of documenting and cataloguing the phenomena of nature in all their forms. When I was a student, I still thought it was a finite task, because nature is finite too. Now I doubt it. I am happy about every discovery, but there are just too many of them! Could it be that the variety of flora and fauna is infinite? That my work here is vain delusion and that we can never collect exhaustive data and create corresponding registers?"

"Not bad, Doctor. You cleverly led my question to a field that interests you and from there you answered with a counter-question that has nothing to do with my original question. I would, therefore, like to ask it again and leave you no more options this time. Can you imagine that life will remain an inexplicable miracle for all time, which we will never understand, as the venerable Kant suggests?"

To his own surprise, Siebold's answer was very easy.

"Yes!"

Matsudeira and Doctor Udagawa

In the cemetery of the Sengakuji Temple in Edo, two old men stood praying with smoke offering bowls in their hands in front of the graves of the forty-seven *rōnin*. They quietly whispered a few sutras for the legendary heroes who were regarded throughout the country as the supreme embodiment of loyalty. They were once samurai who became masterless because their master, Lord Asano, was tempted to draw his sword in the palace of the shogun in 1700. It was an intrigue of the noble Yoshinaka Kira that had led Asano to commit this serious crime. He had lost his honor and could only restore it through *seppuku*. From then on, Asano's henchmen, who had become destitute, roamed the country as deplorable tramps, dice players, and drunkards. The suspicious Kira sent out spies to find out if these rōnin could still be dangerous for him. The matter was only settled for him when he learned that their swords had rusted in the sheaths. But two years later, on an evening in December, all forty-seven rōnin stormed the castle of Kira and beheaded him. The whole town was on its feet the next day and accompanied the rōnin to their master's grave, in front of which they laid Kira's head and finally, one by one, committed seppuku.

The two men had risen and walked with a serious expression through the shrine. "Your Excellency," Yōan Udagawa initiated the conversation, "have you heard the talk about the new barbarian doctor? It is still six months until the Dutch legation has to appear before the shogun, but the rumors about his miracles have already reached us long ago."

The personal physician of *Shogun Ienari* met with the venerable *Sadanobu Matsudeira* to discuss this political development with him outside the courtyard, where the walls had ears. Matsudeira, who had long since ceased to hold an official post, was still regarded as the grey eminence at court.

"I understand that you are worried," he muttered absentmindedly, "because the barbarian devaluates your Chinese art of healing. But frankly, my dear Udagawa, I am not particularly interested in your hurt vanity as a scientist. Let's talk about the bigger picture, about the well-being and the politics of our country. About how we must deal with the barbarians. Then... only then... perhaps.... we find a common theme."

Matsudeira was too old and too experienced to get involved in the short-sighted dodges of the political dilettantes at court. The physicians who followed the tradition of Chinese medicine already had a miserable reputation and it was not without danger for Matsudeira to meet one of them at all. They were considered devious and conspiratorial. Some even believed that Chinese doctors could control their opponents with magic and spells. Matsudeira was not one of them and he had little respect for these doctors, who tampered with mysteries and exploited every superstition when they treated the shogun. But he wanted to try and see if he could use the Chinese medical professionals as useful allies for his interests, for he was completely indifferent to their own concerns.

"We will not have an easy game," Matsudeira continued. The party of those nobles who want to break with the tradition of *sakkoku* in favor of closer cooperation with the barbarians has grown alarmingly in recent years. In this situation, it's just inconvenient for us that the Dutch bring such an ambitious and successful doctor to the shogun's audience."

"I promise your Excellency that his abilities are grotesquely over-estimated. People are gullible. If he comes here, we can certainly reveal his tricks and deceptions."

"You still don't understand, Udagawa-san. That's not the point. People admire him because they want to admire him. In the worst case, he would show you that his medical art is far superior to yours. No, you and your colleagues must not engage in such a scientific dispute. You will treat him with the utmost courtesy so as not to give the appearance of envy or grudge! Do you understand me?"

"Yes, Your Excellency, I understand. That's how we'll do it when you say it."

"I'll take care of the rest. Await further orders from me."

Udagawa bowed deeply, Matsudeira turned silently away. They left the cemetery in separate directions.

Glossary

of Japanese, medical, and scientific terms

Terms or proper names set in italics in the explanatory texts are cross-referenced and reappear elsewhere in the glossary or in the list of characters.

Achromatic

Deflection of 'white' sunlight by prisms without splitting it into its colored components; Greek 'achromasia' means colorlessness. A. lenses are the basic elements of microscopes and enable microscopical observation that is undisturbed by flairs of colored light.

Ainu アイヌ

Japanese natives living in the north on the island of Hokkaido, formerly called *Ezo*. Not recognized as Japanese on the mainland islands in the south for a long time, which is why their name is written in *katakana*, as for foreigners, instead of in *kanji* or *hiragana*.

Almagest

Major work of ancient geocentric astronomy, written by Claudius Ptolemy (probably *100, †175). Complicated circular models explained declining motions of some planets. Thus, the model was initially more reliable than the first heliocentric one by Nikolaus Copernicus (*1473, †1543), because it still assumed perfect orbits of the planets around the sun, but which are actually ellipses, as Johannes Kepler (*1571, †1630) later demonstrated and calculated.

Alum

A. is a salt used in papermaking, tanning and often in the form of a pen for hemostasis, see *astringents*. Since ancient Egyptian times it has also been known as a deodorant because it closes the sweat pores.

Amaterasu 天照大神

The sun goddess, highest of all gods or *kami* of the *Shintō* faith, also called *Ōmikami*. She is the legendary ancestor of the Japanese imperial family and is venerated in the shrine of Ise.

Anata-sama あなた様

'My Lord', polite and respectful address for the superior, such as the husband.

Anesthetic
Painkillers that cause physical insensitiveness. If the pain reduction also affects consciousness, it is a *narcotic*.

Apocrypha
Religious texts of the Jewish and Christian tradition that were not included in the Bible when it was canonized around 400 AD. Often the reason for this was that they were thought to be heretical.

Asama 浅間
An active volcano north of Tokyo near Karuizawa, whose largest eruption to date on August 3, 1783 killed over a thousand villagers by lava, steam, mudslides, and hot gases.

Astringents
A medical or chemical agent which contracts skin tissue and thus has a dehydrating, hemostatic and anti-inflammatory effect. Known astringents are tannin, *alum*, and oak bark.

Atropine
An alkaloid, extract of nightshade plants such as the datura and deadly nightshade, first isolated around 1805; used to relieve bronchial cramps and in *ophthalmology* to dilate the pupils.

Auscultation
Listening to heart sounds and the lungs, since 1819 with the *stethoscope* of Théophile Laennec.

Awa 阿波国
Old province on the main Japanese island Shikoku, today Tokushima.

Bakufu 幕府
'Tent Government', in the sense of an initially mobile makeshift military government that later on settled and became the government of the *shogun* in *Edo*.

Barometer
Device for measuring the air pressure and estimating the altitude above sea level, by raising and lowering a column of mercury.

Batavia
During the Dutch colonial period from 1619 to 1942 the name of today's Jakarta, the capital of Indonesia.

Bibliomorphosis
When one's life turns into a novel; psychoanalytic concept developed by

the Austrian neurologist and psychiatrist Viktor Frankl (*1905, †1995), founder of logotherapy, a form of existential analysis. In his definition, B. is a double-edged personality disorder because while the patient can subjectively enjoy his transition into his own literary narration (not necessarily; he can also suffer from it), he becomes objectively delusional. A famous example is Don Quixotte in the eponymous novel by Cervantes. His life turned into a campy romance of chivalry.

Broad reach
The course of a sailing ship in relation to the wind, if it comes obliquely from behind, i.e. from aft; also called downwind course.

Bungalow
Bengali and Indian construction for single-story houses with a large veranda and mostly a flat roof.

Caoutchouc
Part of the latex of some tropical plants. The Brazilians have used C. since time immemorial to produce elastic play balls and bottles. In 1744, the French scholar De la Condamine brought the first samples with him to Europe. Industrial significance, namely as tires, was not gained by K. until Charles Goodyear invented vulcanization in 1839.

Chinsetsu yumihari zuki 椿説弓張月
Kyokutei Bakin's first epic novel, published in 1791, with numerous illustrations by the painter *Hokusai*.

City on the coast of Yōroppa
Allusion to the great earthquake of Lisbon in 1754, probably with a magnitude of 9.0 on the Richter scale, in which up to one hundred thousand people died. It triggered fierce theological and philosophical debates throughout Europe about the theodicy, the question why an omniscient, omnipotent, and gracious Creator allows evil in the world.

Civil twilight
The astronomical expression for the brightness of dusk until the sun has set 7° below the horizon. It is called 'bourgeois' because it is associated with the idea that it is still bright enough for an educated citizen to read a book outdoors.

Daimyō 大名
Feudal and territorial prince in the *Tokugawa* period.

Dankon 男根

Radish; *fig.* phallus, penis.

Dejima 出島

Name of the island in the port of Nagasaki, derived from 'deru', 'get out', and shima, 'island', freely translated as 'the island that lies in front of the city'.

Dutch East India Company

The 'Vereenigde Oostindische Compagnie', abbreviated V.O.C. or VOC, was founded in 1602 as an association of several trading companies and received sovereign rights and trading monopolies. The VOC was the first multinational company and had to be liquidated in 1798 due to insolvency.

Dysentery

Various forms of intestinal diseases with slimy-bloody to purulent diarrhea.

Edo 江戸

The capital of the Japanese Empire and residence of the *shogun* from 1603 to 1868, whereby this epoch is called the *Edo* period; today's Tokyo.

Electrifying machine

Apparatus for generating electrostatic voltage by separating the charges. The E. was further developed into an electrostatic generator at the end of the 19th century.

Ezo 蝦夷

Ancient Japanese for the main northern island of Hokkaido

Fathom

A measure of length or depth in navigation; 1 fathom corresponds to approx. 2 meters.

Foot

The length or depth measurement (nautical), which was defined differently in the German states and cities before the takeover of the metric system in 1875. Here one foot corresponds to the length or depth of thirty centimeters.

Formosa

An island off the Chinese coast, which was a Portuguese colony in 1517 and a Dutch colony from 1624. In 1662, China reconquered the island. After the lost First Chinese-Japanese War, China had to cede the island to

Japan as a province in the peace of Shimonoseki in 1895. The resistance of the inhabitants who wanted to found a 'Democratic Nation of Taiwan' was brutally suppressed. With the capitulation of Japan in the Second World War, the island fell back to China under the name Taiwan.

Fumi-e 踏み絵

'Stepping-on picture', formerly an official examination procedure to determine whether someone was a Christian. The test mostly consisted of stepping and spitting on the image of Jesus on the cross, which was embedded in a copper plate on the floor.

Futon 布団

The Japanese word for 'blanket', which refers to a thin, multi-layered cotton mattress laid directly on the floor that is usually made of *tatami*.

Gaikokujin 外国人

The polite term for 'foreigner'; somewhat coarser is the abbreviation 'gaijin'; during the *Edo* period, all foreigners were still called 'ijin', 'barbarians'.

Galvanizing

Also called electroplating, it is the coating of surfaces of electrically conductive or made conductive objects with an even, very thin metal film by electrolysis. For this purpose, the object to be coated and the corresponding metal are suspended in a salty or acidic solution, the electrolyte. Between the object and the metal an electrical voltage and thus a direct current is generated in which the ions – electrically positively or negatively charged by lost or captured electrons – of the metal, which becomes the anode, move through the solution, deposit, and solidify as a uniform metal layer on the object forming the cathode. The anode must be made of a more noble metal than the cathode for the current to flow without an external supply of electricity.

Geisha 芸者

'Art person', artistic entertainer. Originally there were more male G. and only from the 17th century onwards, women took over this trade.

Geta 下駄

Wooden clogs resting on two small, transverse beams and held in place by a strap on the big toe.

Gobanjoshi

Representative or envoy of a governor, in Dutch 'Opperbanjost'.

Hai はい

"Yes"

Hakkenden 八犬伝

Short for *Nanso Satomi Hakkenden* 南総里見八犬伝, 'The Legend of the Eight Dog Warriors', a monumental serial novel by *Kokutei Bakin*, published from 1820 to 1842 in 109 volumes; probably the longest novel in world literature and to date not translated into any other language.

Hatoba 波戸場

Quay, pier, mooring.

Heian 平安時代

Japanese culture flourished from 794 to 1185, especially in *Kansai*, the region around Kyōtō and Osaka.

Herbarium

Plant collection

Hiragana 平仮名

Phonetic syllable alphabet developed around 800 A.D. consisting of fifty characters and further variations, with which all *Kanji* characters originating from China were transcribed in original Japanese. Today, there are only forty-six characters left. Siebold never learned more than H. and *katakana*.

Ijin 夷人

'Wildling', 'barbarian', 'stranger'; until 1868 the common designation for all foreigners, which was then replaced by *gaikokujin*.

Inmon 陰門

'Shady gate', vulva, cunt.

Irenic

I. was a mediating attitude between the Catholics and Protestants of the 17th century. Matters of faith were formulated in such a way that undisputed themes were sought and conflicts avoided as far as possible.

Iroha 伊呂波歌

An old poem of fifty characters that made up the Japanese syllable alphabet *hiragana*; today, the hiragana has only forty-six characters.

Isha 医者

A medical doctor, general practitioner.

Java

Island in the colony of the Dutch East-Indies from 1619 to 1949 with the capital Batavia; today the main island of Indonesia; Batavia was renamed in Jakarta.

Jigoku 地獄

"Hell"; *fig.* the name of the hot springs on the slopes of the volcano Unzen in which the Christians were cooked.

Jōmon 縄文

Japanese hunter-gatherer culture with rich art, beginning in the 5th millennium B.C.

Jorō 女郎

'Whore', 'hooker', rough word for prostitute.

Kami 神

Spirits of nature that were once humans and after their death entered the realm of the gods as the K. of a forest, mountain, river, waterfall, etc. A K.-*sama* is a 'supreme God', 'Lord of the Gods' or simply God in the sense of monotheism, e.g. in Christianity.

Kanji 漢字

Name of the Chinese characters, as used in Japanese since about 500 AD. There are also the simpler phonetic alphabets *hiragana* and *katakana*. There is an official list of the 2,136 most often used K., which are taught up to high school. Educated Japanese, especially when they deal with literature, master well over 6,000 K. The total number of K. is about 50,000.

Kantō 関東

The region of *Edo* (later Tokyo).

Kasuparuyugeka

School of surgery introduced in Japan by *Caspar Schamberger* in 1649.

Katakana 片仮名

Phonetic syllable alphabet developed around 800 A.D. consisting of fifty basic characters (since 1945 only forty-six) and other variations with which foreign names and terms are transcribed in Japanese as they sound to the Japanese ear (see Appendix); for example テープレコーダ is pronounced 'teepurekooda' and onomatopoetically translates the English word 'tape recorder'. Siebold never learned more than K. and *hiragana*.

Knot

Nautical speed measure; 1 knot = one nautical mile per hour = 1.852 km/h; voyage: 39,000 km to Batavia in 142 days equivalent to 275 km/day or 11.5 km/h or 6.2 knots average speed.

Kōyasan 高野山

A group of mountains in Wakayama Prefecture, where the Shingon Buddhist sect was founded in 819.

Kuge 公家

The emperor's most important advisory circle at court in Kyōtō, consisting of two to four experienced civil servants, most of whom have inherited the office.

Laughing gas

Colloquially for dinitrogen monoxide N_2O, a euphoric and *narcotic* gas whose medical effect the English chemist Humphry Davy discovered in 1799; yet, it had already been in use in England since 1772 for pleasure at so-called 'parties' by inhalation.

Leptosome

One of the three basic types of body constitution, defined by the psychiatrist Ernst Kretschmer (*1888, †1964): lean, tender, narrow or flat-chested, thin arms and legs, physically and mentally sensitive, often pale, narrow face; also known as 'asthenic'. The other two basic types are the pyknic and the athlete.

Mabiki 間引き

'Tree cutting', a euphemism for abortion. Practiced in Japan since the Middle Ages, it means 'sending back a gift from the *kami*' because it cannot be accepted.

Manga 漫画

Formerly the Japanese art of quick drawing; today the name for all forms of comics in and from Japan. The term M. was made popular by the painter *Hokusai* with his sketchbooks.

Maruyama 丸山

During the *Edo* period an entertainment and brothel district in Nagasaki with over seventy tea houses and more than seven hundred registered prostitutes and courtesans.

Mile

Old European distance measure, which varied according to historical epoch, country, duchy and in Germany also according to the free imperial city between 1,482 (Roman Empire) and 11,299 (Norway) meters. Here, as long as it is not referred to as a *nautical mile*, the London Mile with a length of 1,609.3 meters is always meant.

Morphine
Isolated active ingredient of opium with fewer side effects, improved dosage, and somewhat lower risk of addiction; discovered in 1805 by Friedrich Wilhelm Adam Sertürner, a pharmacist's assistant from Paderborn.

Narcotic
Blocks the sensation of pain in the central nervous system, switches off all sensory, motoric, and mental impulses to a large extent and thus usually impairs consciousness (narcosis). High doses of *laughing gas* and *morphine* are strong N.

Nautical mile
At sea a distance of 1852 meters.

Nengō 年号
Era name which is proclaimed after the accession of a new emperor (or, exceptionally, after special events such as natural disasters) and contain the motto of the upcoming reign, e.g. Meiji (1868-1912) 'Enlightened Rule', Taishō (1912-1926) 'Great Justice', Shōwa (1926-1989) 'Enlightened Peace', and Heisei (1989 until today) 'Universal Peace'. The Tennō forms the N. of two Chinese characters, which he selects from 216 Kanji. From then on it is officially used for the indication of years. The year 2018, therefore, corresponds to 'Heisei 30'.

Novum Organum
A major work written in Latin by the English philosopher and politician Francis Bacon (*1561, †1626) which for the first time describes a modern theory of science based on the experiment. It also contains the so-called 'Doctrine of Idols', in which the 'Idols of Thought' are depicted, i.e. the limitation of human thought through habits, traditions, authorities and the nature of the organs of perception.

Obi 帯
Wide, sash-shaped kimono belt.

Okagesama de お陰様で
"Thanks to the ancestors", "Thanks to your kind support."

Okā-san お母さん
Polite address for one's own mother and often also for the mother-in-law.

Ophthalmology
Medical discipline for the treatment and surgery of the eyes.

Opperbanjost
The Dutch name for the Chief Commissioner of the Japanese Port
Authority, see also *Yakunin* and *Gobanjoshi*.

Opperhoofd
Head and director of the Dutch crew on the island of Dejima in the port
of Nagasaki.

Orandajin オランダ人
Dutchman

Pyroclasts
Rock fragments of various sizes resulting from volcanic activities, from
bombs and blocks to ashes.

Rōnin 炉人 炉人
'Wave-men', masterless and mostly impoverished *samurai*, constantly in
search of a new livelihood and often troublemakers, who could continue
to exercise the privileges of their status over the peasants, craftsmen and
merchants.

Roteiro
Portuguese logbooks with nautical charts and personal records of several
generations of captains; the R. were treated like precious treasures and
state secrets.

Ryō 両
An old Japanese currency, see chapter *Japanese Units of Measurement and
Currency*.

Saguriban 探りばん
Sentry duty, guard.

Sake 酒
Name for a range of alcoholic beverages having 15 to 20% vol. alcohol,
whereas Japanese rice wine is more precisely called 'Nihonshu' 日本酒,
'Japanese alcohol'. In terms of the production process, S. is more similar
to European beer than to wine.

Sakoku 鎖国

The epoch of Japan's national closure from 1639 to 1854.

-sama 様

Polite and formal address for both sexes, "Venerable Sir", "Venerable Lady", which is appended to the family name.

Sanpan 三板

Flat, wide rowing boats commonly used in Japan and China.

Satsuma 薩摩藩

During the *Edo* period, a principality in southern Japan on the island of Kyūshū, which corresponds approximately to today's Kagoshima Prefecture. S. was ruled by the Shimazu clan and the princes of S. were the only rulers in the Japanese Empire who could have become dangerous to the *Tokugawa* regime.

Seiza 正座

Noble form of Japanese sitting on the heels with lower legs, with the instep touching the ground. Painful to impossible for the inexperienced.

Sekigahara 関ヶ原

Village in the old province of Mino, today's Gifu, where the fateful battle that brought *Ieyasu Tokugawa* to power took place on 21 October 1600. It is one of the three most important moments in Japanese history together with the opening of Japan in 1854 and *Genbaku*, the dropping of the atomic bombs in 1945. It marked the transition from *Sengoku*, the era of the civil war, to *Sakoku*, the era of peace and the closure of the country.

Sengoku 戦国

'Warring Land', age of the civil war in Japan during the Muromachi period 1338-1578 and beyond until the battle of Sekigahara in 1600.

Sensei 先生

Honorific term and title, originally used to address Buddhist priests and the instructors of Budō, i. e. all Japanese martial arts. Literally "the one born before", which means a person whose wisdom is built on age and experience. While today applied to artists, university professors, teachers, and any kind of person of authority or professional mastery, Siebold was the first physician in Japan to be addressed by this title.

Seppuku 切腹

It is also called 'Harakiri', a ritual form of self-disembodiment that arose in the 12th century by slitting the abdomen – in the old view the center of the soul – from left to right, while a standing friend strikes off the samurai's head at the same moment; originally limited to samurai. S. was officially abolished in 1873.

Sextant

Nautical and optical measuring instrument to determine one's position at sea by measuring the angle between a distant object, usually a star at sea, and the horizon. The S. can also be equipped with an artificial horizon, similar to a spirit level, so that the position can be determined even if no optical horizon is in sight.

Shamisen 三味線

A musical instrument with three strings, long neck and small sound body covered with dog or cat leather. Played with a plectrum, its mastery is one of the foundations of the education of bourgeois and noble women in the Edo period.

Shatanu シャタヌ

The Japanese name for Satan, the devil from the West.

Shimazu Clan 島津氏

Japanese noble family that ruled as *daimyō* the province of *Satsuma* in southern Japan for 700 years.

Shintō 神道

The 'Way of the Gods', an animistic religion in Japan that worships a huge variety of gods called *kami*; the highest deity or , Ōmikami' is the sun goddess *Amaterasu*; her brother is *Susanoo*. She is also the ancestor of all *Tennō*.

Shogun 将軍

Japanese generalissimo and chancellor; originally the title was 'Seii Taishōgun', which means 'Oppressor of the Barbarians and Great General' and corresponded to a European duke; but from 1603 on the S. took over all governmental power under the *Tokugawa* and delegated the *Tennō* into a purely religious function.

Shōji 障子

Sliding doors, movable partitions and room dividers covered with paper; an important element in the architecture of traditional Japanese houses.

Shokoku Taki Meguri 諸国 滝 回り 回り

'A visit to the waterfalls in the provinces', a famous cycle of paintings by the painter *Hokusai*, painted between 1827 and 1830.

Shunga 春画

'Pictures of spring', erotic and pornographic color drawings in the style of *ukiyo-e* for the instruction of men and women in love practices.

Silentio! Pugnat!

Latin for "Now be silent! Fight!"

Specimen

Latin and English for 'probe', 'sample'; this term is also used in German in biology and medicine.

Stethoscope

Medical instrument for listening to the sounds of all internal organs, especially the heart, lungs, and intestines. Invented in 1819 by the French physician Théophile Laennec (*1781, †1826).

Syphilis

Dangerous bacterial infection with a broad spectrum of symptoms and a complex course of the disease, which is usually transmitted by sexual intercourse, Latin *Lues venerea*, also formerly called 'French disease'. Until the Treponema pallidum pathogen was isolated in 1906, it was treated for centuries almost exclusively – and mostly unsuccessfully – with mercury, and since 1930 with penicillin with good chances of recovery.

Tatami 畳

Mats made of rice straw, with which the floors in traditional Japanese houses are laid. T. are 5.5 centimeters thick and twice as long as wide, usually with a surface area of 1.64 square meters. They are also used as an area measure. A standard room has a surface of six T. The *futon* is spread out on the T. for sleeping.

Tennō 天皇

Japanese emperor, whose ancestor is the sun goddess *Amaterasu*. There is a distinction between the government name of the living T., which corresponds to his birth name, and his posthumous name, which is identical to his government motto, the 'nengō'. Since his death in 1989, the former Emperor Hirohito has been called 'Shōwa Tennō'.

Trepanation

The opening of bony surfaces with a drill (French 'trépan'), mostly on the human skull, whereby a simple drilling can be made or a round piece of bone can be sawn out. The procedure is called craniotomy and has been used in Egypt, Europe, and South America since prehistoric times as a religious ritual and healing method; it was used to heal blood clots or to relieve painful intracranial pressure. In Japan's *Edo* period, this procedure was still unknown.

Tsunami 津波

A 'harbor wave', a tidal wave through volcanic eruptions or undersea quakes; T. flood the nearest coasts and reach a speed of 500 to 1000 km/h in the open sea, rising above sea level on the shore. It is called 'harbor wave' because the fishermen on the open sea do not notice it and believe that only their harbor has been affected. A tsunami can go under the boats if there is enough depth. The wave is always in contact with the ground, even when the water is several kilometers deep. It is a long wave, about 150 km long, and, like other waves, reaches half its length into the depths. The arrival of a tsunami can be announced by withdrawing water when a wave trough first arrives on land. On the beach, the kilometer-long wave becomes shorter, but all the higher.

Typhoon 台風

Dangerous tropical cyclones, which cause flooding in Japan and claim up to one hundred victims every year; at wind speeds of up to 300 km/h, T. are stronger than the hurricanes in the Gulf of Mexico and the cyclones in the Indian Ocean. The annual typhoon season in Japan is in May to June.

Ukiyo-e 浮世絵

Japanese genre painting that captures scenes from everyday life.

Unzendake 雲仙岳

Active volcano in Japan on the peninsula Shimabara.

Urisane-gao 瓜実顔

'Melon seed face', female beauty ideal of the *Heian* period from 794 to 1185.

Vaccination

A method developed by *Edward Jenner* for immunization against diseases.

Yakunin 役人

Civil servant, supervisor, commissioner of the court travel company.

Yamato 大和

An epoch in Japanese history from 250 to 710, when the imperial court ruled from the province of Yamato.

Yayoi 弥生

Japanese peasant culture from 300 B.C. to 300 A.D., strongly influenced by shamanism.

Yobai 夜ばい

'Night crawling' or 'window crawling' to lovers under the cover of night.

Yōroppa ヨーロッパ

Europe

Yūjo 遊女

Prostitute

Yukata 浴衣

'Swimsuit', light, comfortable summer kimono that can also be worn as pajamas or on the street.

Dramatis Personae

Names and terms in italics are cross-referenced and appear elsewhere in the glossary or in the list of persons.

Abaddon
Angel of the Abyss, Satan's right hand and King of Hell.

Bakin, Kyokutei
First professional writer in Japan (*1767, †1848) who was able to make a living from his income; author of the enormous serial novel *Nansō satomi hakkenden* or short *Hakkenden*, 'The Legend of the Eight Dog Warriors', which appeared from 1820 to 1842 in 109 volumes and has not yet been translated into any other language.

Blomhoff, Jan Cock
Dutch official (*1779, †1853) and *Opperhoofd* on *Dejima* from 1817 to 1823; author of a book about his court journey to the *shogun* in *Edo*.

Buddha
Asian founder of religion and saint, who himself is worshipped like a god. The historical person Gautama Siddhartha Buddha lived in India in the 6th century B.C. Buddhism came to Japan around the 3rd century B.C., where Zen Buddhism developed a highly spiritual form of this religion, in which no belief in the existence of the soul is held. Rather to the contrary, this belief itself is thought to be the real problem of human existence and suffering.

Capellen, Baron Gerard Philip van der
Dutch statesman (*1778, †1848), from 1815 to 1825 general governor of *Batavia*, Siebold's mentor and lifelong supporter.

Cretzschmar, Philipp Jakob
Anatomist (*1786, †) and initiator of the Senckenberg Society of Natural Sciences founded in Frankfurt in 1817; one of Siebold's most ardent supporters.

Doeff, Hendrik
Dutch official (*1764, †1837) and *Opperhoofd* on *Dejima* from 1803 to 1817. During his term of office, he had to deal with Napoleon's occupation of

the Netherlands until 1813, the Phaeton incident in 1808 and the conquest of Dutch East Indies (now Indonesia) by the English in 1811; he wrote the first Dutch-Japanese dictionary and his 'Memories of Japan'.

Faraday, Michael
English physicist and chemist (*1791, †1867), who, among other things, discovered electromagnetic induction in 1831–when an electrical conductor is moved in a magnetic field, an electric current flow is generated in the conductor–thus laying the foundation for generators, electric motors, and transformers.

Fraunhofer, Joseph von
German optician and physicist (*1787, †1826), who invented the spectro-scope to separate visible light into its spectral colors and discovered dark spectral lines in the sunlight, which were named after him.

Fritze, Johann
Surgeon at Sumatra, Fort Mentok; after Siebold's visit in 1823 on his way to Japan, he will remain in friendly correspondence with him for decades.

Golownin, Wassilij Mikhailovich
Russian seafarer (*1776, †1852), who published a book about his 'Voyage to Japan' in 1817. He was taken prisoner in Japan.

Harbaur, Franz Joseph
Inspector General of Medical Services of the Netherlands (*1776, †1824); protects Siebold and gives him a position as Chirurgyn Major at the Dutch Colonial Ministry.

Herschel, Sir William
English astronomer and musician (*1738, †1822); built his own mirror telescopes, discovered Uranus in 1781 and the movement of the solar system towards the constellation of Hercules in 1784; 1785 treatise on the spatial extension of the Milky Way; in 1787, he found the two outer moons of Uranus and in 1789 the two inner moons of Saturn.

Hideyoshi, Toyotomi
Japanese prince and general (*1537, †1598), who pushed Japan's agreement after Nobunaga's assassination and before the takeover by *Ieyasu Tokugawa*.

Hiroshige [artist name], Utagawa [family name]

Japanese painter (*1797, †1858); H. was the successor of *Hokusai* and became famous for his picture cycle 'Fifty-Three Stations on the Tokaido'. He didn't like *Hokusai*. His woodcuts were revolutionary because he painted in and after nature. Until then, all the pictures had been painted in a studio in the so-called Chinese style.

Hokusai [artist name], Katsushika [family name]

Japanese painter (*1760, †1849), one of the most important artists of genre painting style *ukiyo-e*. Best known are his 'Thirty-Six Views of Mount Fuji', from which 'The Great Wave of Kanagawa', and the erotically sinister drawing 'The Dream of the Fisherwoman'. He made the term 'manga' popular by publishing from 1814 on his sketchbooks in fifteen volumes.

Hufeland, Christoph Wilhelm

German physician and scientist (*1762, †1836); he is regarded as the founder of naturopathy and folk medicine.

Humboldt, Alexander von

German naturalist (*1769, †1859); together with the botanist Aimé Bonpland, he set off for a trip to South America in 1799. Until 1804, he did research in the area of today's states Venezuela, Cuba, Colombia, Ecuador, Peru, and Mexico; afterward, he returned to Europe via Cuba and the USA – where he made friends with Thomas Jefferson in Washington. From then on, he mostly lived in Paris until 1827, where he evaluated his expedition in the largest private travel work in history. In 1827, he had to move to Berlin and became an advisor to the Prussian king. His lecture cycle 'Kosmos' in Berlin in 1827/28 opened a new heyday of natural sciences in Germany. In 1829, he made another great journey through the Baltic States and via Moscow into the Urals to the Chinese border. Humboldt was the most influential patron of his time and helped many poets and writers, e.g. Heinrich Heine and Ludwig Tieck. Among his friends were Claudius, Jacob and Wilhelm Grimm, August Wilhelm Schlegel as well as Goethe, Schiller and their families. Charles Darwin described him as "the greatest scientific traveler who has ever lived".

Ishizaka, Sotetsu
Influential Japanese physician and imperial acupuncturist (*1770, †1841).

Jenner, Edward
English physician (*1749, †1823) and discoverer of controlled smallpox vaccination with lymph from cowpox blisters.

Kaempfer, Engelbert
German physician and natural scientist (*1651, †1716); as Siebold's predecessor, he traveled through Japan from 1690 to 1692 and became the author of' 'The History of Japan', which was published posthumously in 1727.

Kant, Immanuel
German philosopher (*1724, †1804), who revolutionized philosophy with his three works 'Critique of Pure Reason', 'Critique of Practical Reason' and 'Critique of the Power of Judgement' by pointing out the limits of possible knowledge and thus of reason itself, both with regard to knowledge about nature (mathematics, physics) and about the freedom of human action (morals, law). In his Critique of Judgement, Kant analyzed how the ideas of the beautiful, the sublime (aesthetics) and the idea of purposes (teleology) help us to explore, understand and orientate ourselves in the world, even though we (still) do not completely (mathematically, physically) penetrate it with our minds. The reflective power of judgment that this late work by Kant is all about is for man the true compass for exploring the world, which we always encounter as a 'foreign' world.

Kō, Ryōsai
One of Siebold's best and most eager students, a young doctor from the province of *Awa* on Shikoku Island; ophthalmologist, spoke fluent Dutch and was an outstanding botanist.

Krusenstern, Ivan Fyodorovich
Russian seafarer (1770-1846), who wrote the three-volume work 'Voyage autour du monde' about his famous world tour, which *Takahashi* received in exchange for Siebold's Japanese maps.

Kusumoto, Taki
Siebold's wife, (*1810, †1865), adopted the courtesan name 'Sonogi' to

marry him. The polite form of her name is 'Otaki'; Siebold also used the affectionate forms 'Taksa' or 'Otaksa'.

Kusumoto, Tsune
Sister of *Taki Kusumoto* (*1805, †1830); was saved by Siebold and married his assistant Heinrich Bürger in 1826.

Mastema
One of the many names of the devil; Prince of Demons, who causes God in the Old Testament to test Abraham with the sacrifice of his son Isaac; appears in the Apocrypha of Christianity; see main article *Satan*.

Matsudaira, Sadanobu
Japanese statesman of the Tokugawa family (*1758, †1829); prevented successor as *shogun*, reformer, capable conservative minister, and hardliner of the *sakoku*, the Japanese policy of isolation.

Mercator, Gerhard
Flanders mathematician, astronomer, philosopher, theologian and cartographer (*1512, †1594), who published the first world map in 1569, which, by a projection method developed by him, depicted the spherical shape of the earth true to the angle on one plane. As a result, the poles were extremely distorted, but for navigation in the lower latitudes these maps became irreplaceable. M. did not see himself as a simple artisan manufacturer of globes and maps, but as a cosmographer in search of the whole of creation.

Nobunaga, Oda
Japanese *daimyō* (*1534, †1582) and one of the warlords at the time of the Portuguese arrival in Japan; used their firearms and began to unite Japan.

Ohm, Georg Simon
German physicist (*1789, †1854), who discovered the law of proportionality of voltage and current in electrical conductors named after him in 1826.

Paraclete
Biblically 'the advocate', Jesus as the defender of the sinners, Holy Spirit; 1 John 2,1; John 14 ff; Rom 8,34; Heb 7,25.

Phanuel

One of the Archangels from the *apocryphal* Ethiopian book 'Enoch'; watches over the penance of those who may still hope for eternal life. His name means 'the face of God'. About him is reported: "A fourth voice I heard warding off the *Satans* and not allowing them to stand before the Lord of the Spirits [God] to accuse the inhabitants of the mainland.".

Raffles, Sir Thomas Stamford

British colonial politician and researcher (*1781, †1826), representative of the *East India Company* and British governor on Java from 1811 to 1815; discoverer of the 9th century B.C. temple city of Borobudur, later founder of Singapore. Published in 1817 the 'History of Java', which became the model for Siebold's 'Nippon Archive'.

Satan

In his 1624 'Quaestiones theosophicae', Jakob Böhme first described the principle of S. as that of a prevented creator: "He desired to be an artist, he saw the creation and understood the reason why he wanted to be a god of his own in it, and to rule in all things with Centralian fire-power and to form himself with all things, to form himself in all forms, that he was what he wanted, and not what the Creator wanted"; Daniel Defoe, the author of *Robinson Crusoe*, wrote the most detailed description of S.'s work in the world in 1726 under the title *The Political History of the Devil*.

Schelling, Frederick William Joseph

German philosopher of idealism (*1755, †1854), who strongly influenced Romanticism and the natural sciences, especially anatomy and biology, with his idea that reason does not only work in the subject of cognition, in the 'I', but also in nature itself, so that a systematic connection of development must be assumed in it.

Schlegel, August Wilhelm

German philologist, poet, translator, critic and early member of the Romanticist movement (*1767, †1845), best known for his ingenious translation of Shakespeare's plays into German.

Schwabe, Samuel

German pharmacist, astronomer and botanist (*1789, †1875), discovered the eleven-year periodicity of sunspots.

Siebold, Philipp Franz von

German physician, botanist, naturalist, and discoverer (*1796, †1866).

Sömmerring, Samuel Thomas

Anatomist and physiologist (*1755, †1830), was one of the most respected scholars of his time since his speculative dissertation on the brain, 'On the Organ of the Soul', and his treatise 'On the Beauty of Embryo's'. He introduced smallpox vaccination in Frankfurt in 1821.

Sturler, Johan Willem de

Dutch colonel (*1777, †1855), was appointed Factory Chief in April 1823; envoy on the journey to *Edo*; a highly educated man who fought the French; intrigued against Siebold.

Sujenaga, Sinsajemon

Chief interpreter of Nagasaki in all Dutch matters (*1768, †1835); taught Siebold in Japanese and accompanied the Dutch legation on the court journey to *Edo* in 1826; was removed from office in the course of the Siebold trial because of the many privileges he had granted him.

Susanoo no Mikoto

High *Shintō* deity, brother of the supreme sun goddess *Amaterasu*, the storm god and ruler of the realm of the dead; is described as 'wild man' and is most like the devil from the West among the demons of *Shintō*.

Tadataka, Inō

Japanese surveyor and cartographer (*1745, † 1818), who produced the first complete map of Japan from 1800 until his death. This astonishingly precise map was published in 1821 under the title 'Dai-Nihon Enkai Yochi Zenzu 大日本沿海興地全図', 'Complete Map of the Coasts of Great-Japan'. It was the basis for the maps with *katakana* inscription that Siebold received from *Kageyasu Takahashi*.

Takano, Choei

One of Siebold's best and most charismatic students; submitted a dissertation entitled 'From Whales and Whaling'. In 1839, he was arrested and sentenced to life imprisonment together with many other doctors who were attached to the Dutch school *Rangaku*. During this time he wrote a book on the history of the entry of European science into Japan,'Bansha Sōyaku Shōki'', 'A short report on the encounter with misfortune'. Then he fled prison and took his own life exhausted from persecution in 1850.

Thunberg, Carl Peter

Swedish naturalist (* 1743, †1823) and student of the great *Linné*; doctor at *Dejima* from 1775 to 1779; later published the 'Flora Japonica' and his report 'Journey through a part of Europe, Africa and Asia, mainly in Japan in the years 1770-1779'.

Titia

Née Bergsma (*1786, †1821), T. was the wife of *Jan Cock Blomhoff*, the *Opperhoofd* on *Dejima*, who was replaced by *Colonel de Sturler* in 1821. She was also the first European foreign woman to be seen by the Japanese. Despite the strict rules of the *sakoku* for the traffic with foreigners, which strictly forbade foreign women to enter Dejima, the governor of Nagasaki initially allowed her to stay on the port island with her husband. Five weeks later, however, he had to expel them because the *shogunate* had learned of this softening of the rules and ordered the immediate strict interpretation of the edicts. But in this short time, Japanese painters and sculptors had made over five hundred portraits of T. These pictures were immensely popular and sold better than all other prints throughout Japan for the rest of the century. Her face could be seen on four million pieces of Japanese porcelain.

Tokugawa, Ienari

Japanese *shogun* (*1773, †1841), who reigned during Siebold's first stay in Japan. Strongly influenced by his advisors, especially *Sadanobu Matsudaira*, he was a conservative hardliner. His reign was marked by political stagnation, corruption, nepotism, the massive waste of state finances and thus symptomatic of the decline of *Tokugawa* rule. It is assumed that he was mentally and intellectually limited despite his long period of government and his considerable propagation activities. The political agenda under his reign was developed and executed for many years entirely under the control of the circle of advisors. I. was therefore probably just a willing puppet.

Tokugawa, Ieyasu

Japanese *daimyō* and warlord (*1542, †1616), who concluded Japan's unification with the Battle of *Sekigahara* in 1600 and accepted the title *shogun*. The T. dynasty lasted until the *Meiji* restoration in 1868.

Tokugawa, Yoshimune

Japanese *shogun* (*1684, †1751) and reformer, who, together with *Ieyasu Tokugawa*, was considered one of the most capable rulers of this dynasty; under his government the import of European books, especially Dutch books, was made easier again.

Toyotomi, Hideyoshi

Japanese *daimyō* and warlord (*1536, †1582) who pushed forward Japan's unification after *Nobunaga*'s assassination and before the takeover by *Ieyasu Tokugawa*; his attack on Korea with one hundred sixty thousand soldiers was a failure. He issued the first edict against foreigners.

Villeneuve, Carl Hubert de

Dutch painter and draughtsman (*1800, †1874), came to Dejima at the age of eighteen with his wife Mimi, who was not allowed to leave the ship and soon had to leave again.

Wardenaar, Willem of

Dutch diplomat and *Opperhoofd* of *Dejima* (*1764, †1816); bribed by the English to lie to the Dutch on Dejima and persuade them to hand over the island.

Xavier, Francisco de

Important Catholic missionary in Indonesia, China, and Japan (*1506, †1552), co-founder of the Jesuit order and canonized in 1622 by Gregory XV.

Chronology

1543

Portuguese are stranded in Japan near Tanegashima.

1549

The Jesuit *Francisco de Xavier* begins with Christian mission.

1568

Oda Nobunaga, one of the many *daimyōs*, occupies Kyōtō and begins the unification of the country under a central state.

1579

The daimyō Sumitada Omura gives the Jesuits Nagasaki.

1580

Several daimyō on Kyūshū convert to Christianity.

1582

Nobunaga is murdered. His General *Hideyoshi* assumes the power of government and the title 'Kampaku', 'Ruler of the Majority'.

Alessandro Valegnano, the successor of Francisco de Xavier, organizes the first Japanese mission abroad; four samurai travel to China, India, Portugal, Spain and Italy as emissaries of the Christian daimyo; the journey lasts eight years until 1590.

1587

Hideyoshi's issues the first edict on the banishment of missionaries. But it will not be enforced.

1588

Hideyoshi takes away the Jesuit Nagasaki again.

1592

Japan attacks Korea and China with one hundred and sixty thousand soldiers but is thrown back.

1597

Hideyoshi has nine Jesuit priests and seventeen converted Japanese executed.

1598

After a second failed invasion of Korea, Hideyoshi dies. He is followed by his vassal *Ieyasu Tokugawa*, with whom the Tokugawa dynasty begins, which lasts until the Meiji restoration in 1868.

1600

Ieyasu defeats his enemies in the decisive Battle of *Sekigahara* and unites the country under a centralized police state. About three hundred thousand Japanese have converted to Christianity.

1609

The Dutch found their first factory on Hirado, an island some seventy kilometers from Nagasaki.

1624

Ieyasu's edict deporting the Spaniards is executed.

1627

Thirty-seven thousand Japanese Christians are massacred in the Shimonoseki uprising.

1638

Expulsion and banishment of the Portuguese. Only the Dutch and Chinese are still allowed to trade, but the Dutch are no longer allowed to do so from Japanese soil. They must move from Hirado to Dejima.

1758

John Dollond manufactures *achromatic* lenses from flint and crown glass for the construction of telescopes.

Beginning of the Nippon Trilogy - Part One

SHIBORUTO

1792

Eruption of the volcano Unzen.

1796

Philipp Franz von Siebold is born in Würzburg on 17 February.
Edward Jenner discovers smallpox vaccination.

1798

Siebold's father Johann Georg Christoph Siebold dies of pulmonary consumption.

1800

The philosopher Johan Gottlieb Fichte publishes his book 'The Destiny of Man', which is becoming highly popular, and Heinrich von Kleist comes to Würzburg to have a phimosis operated on.

1801

The Siebold family is accepted into the imperial nobility for the services of Philip's grandfather Carl Casper Siebold.
Lamarck considers a theory of descent for the first time.

1805

Alexander von Humboldt's book 'Journey to the Equinoctial Regions of the New Continent' is published.

1807

Johann Gottlieb Fichte gives his famous speeches 'To the German Nation.'

1808

Alexander von Humboldt publishes his famous book 'Views of Nature.'
The British warship Phaeton enters the port of Nagasaki under the Dutch flag and takes Dutch hostages.

1809

The young Siebold attends high school.
Lamarck publishes his 'Philosophie zoologique.'

1810

The artificial island of Dejima in the port of Nagasaki is the last place where the Dutch flag flies until the Congress of Vienna in 1815; the Netherlands is called the 'Batavian Republic' under Napoleonic rule.

1813

Napoleon's Russian campaign fails.

1814

Kyokutei Bakin begins his serial novel *Hakkenden*, 'The Legend of Eight Dog Samurai.'

Stephenson invents the locomotive; London is the first city in the world to receive gas lighting.

1815
Siebold enrolls in medicine and lives in the house of his professor Ignaz Döllinger during his studies.
The Japanese geographer *Tadataka Ino* measures all the coastlines of Japan for the first time and produces reliable maps.

1817
At the Wartburg Festival, the student corps demand a Germany unified as one single state and nation.

1818
Siebold's corps-brother Dr. Vincenz Wachter goes to the Netherlands as a military doctor.

1819
The first steamship crosses the Atlantic from New York to Liverpool.

1820
Siebold completes his medical studies with distinction.
Georg Friedrich Wilhelm Hegel's 'Basics of the Philosophy of Law' appear and there is a scandal because the philosopher polemicizes against the nationalist tendencies in the student fraternities.

1821
Siebold works as a general practitioner in Heidingsfeld, where his mother lives.
Napoleon Bonaparte dies on St. Helena.

1822
In spring, Siebold receives an offer to go to Java as a troop doctor on behalf of the Dutch Ministry of Colonial Affairs. Contacting learned societies.
12 May: Permission from the King of Bavaria to move into the service of the Dutch Colonial Ministry.
7 June: Departure via Darmstadt, Frankfurt, Hanau and Bonn. The brothers *Nees von Esenbeck*, the philologist *August Wilhelm von Schlegel* and the anatomist Eduard Joseph d'Alton pledge all their support.

19 July: Arrival in The Hague.

23 September: The *Jonge Adriana* will be leaving Rotterdam.

1823

13 February: Arrival in Batavia

Mid-March: Siebold has rheumatic fever, Governor General Baron van der Capellen brings him to Buitenzorg for recovery.

15 April: Siebold learns that he is going to Japan as the resident's personal physician.

28 June: The *Drie Gezusters* sets sail with the destination Japan.

5 August: Typhoon at the northern tip of Formosa.

8 August: Cape Nomo in sight, the landmark for Nagasaki.

August 10: Siebold is almost unmasked as a German and saves himself by posing as a 'Mountain-Dutchman'.

11 August: Official arrival and festive welcome parade of the factory.

September: Governor of Nagasaki gives Siebold permission to teach and visit patients ashore.

October: Siebold becomes famous with two spectacular operations and meets the sixteen-year-old *Taki Kusumoto*.

November: Siebold marries Taki Kusumoto, who has adopted the courtesan name Sonogi.

1824

Under a Japanese alias and with the support of the governor, Siebold acquires Narutaki, the 'house at the waterfall', and establishes a university there.

1825

Siebold sends his first tea plants to Java in iron-bearing clay balls.

The *Bakufu* confirms the ban on all non-Dutch vessels to call at the Japanese coast.

Japanese Government Periods

Nengō (name of regency and/or era)

With the Meiji Restoration of 1868 the shogunate was abolished. Since then, the posthumous names of the Tennō is identical to the era name of his own reign.

Temmei 1783-1787

Kansei 1788-1801

Kyowa 1801-1804

Bunka 1804-1818

Bunsei 1818-1830

Tempō 1830-1844

Kōka 1844-1848

Kaei 1848-1854

Ansei 1854-1860

Man'en 1860-1861

Bunkyū 1861-1864

Genji 1864-1865

Keiō 1865-1868

Meiji 1868-1912

Taishō 1912-1926

Shōwa 1926-1989

Heisei 1989-today

Shogun

Ienari 1786-1837

Ieyoshi 1837-1853

Iesada 1853-1858

Iemochi 1858-1866

Keiki 1866-1868

Tennō (birth name/posthumous name)

Morohito / Kōkaku 1780-1816

Ayahito / Ninkō 1817-1846

Osahito / Kōmei 1847-1867

Mutsuhito / Meiji 1867-1912

Yoshihito / Taishō 1912-1926

Hirohito / Showa 1926-1989

Akihito / Heisei 1989-today

Maps

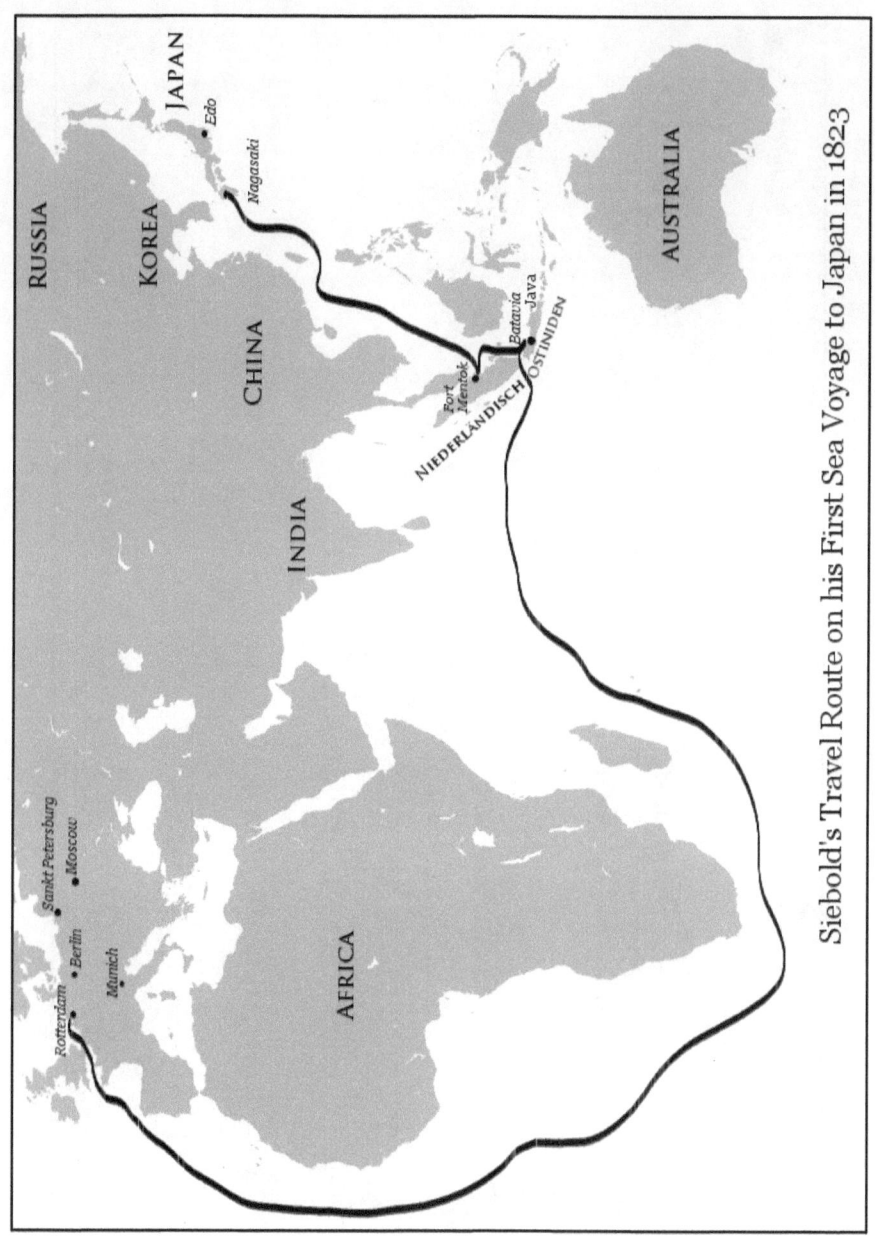

Siebold's Travel Route on his First Sea Voyage to Japan in 1823

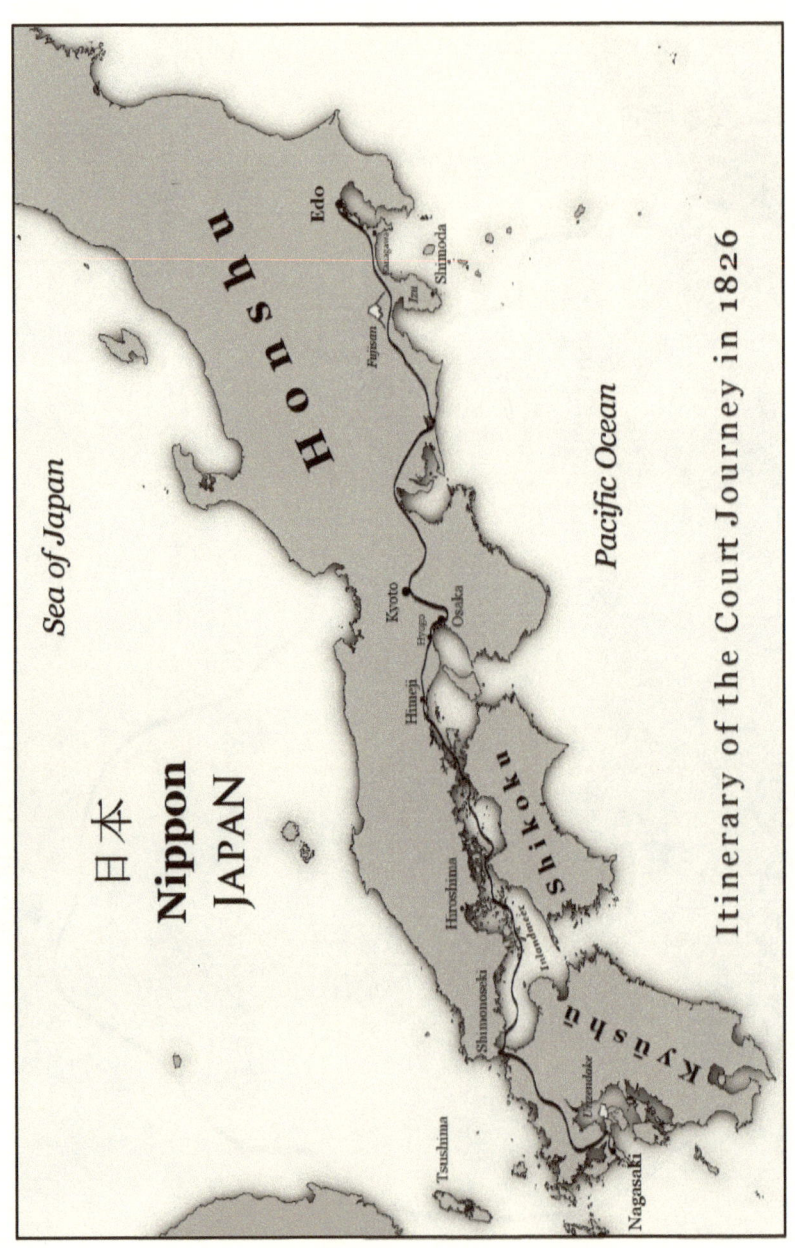

Sea of Japan

日本
Nippon
JAPAN

Honshu

Edo

Shimoda

Isu

Fujisan

Kyoto

Osaka

Hyogo

Himeji

Hiroshima

Shikoku

Shimonoseki

Island Sea

Kyūshū

Tsushima

Nagasaki

Pacific Ocean

Itinerary of the Court Journey in 1826

Units of Measurement and Currency

Units of Measurement

Fathom
Length or depth measurement in navigation; also called 'cord'; 1 fathom corresponds to approx. 2 meters.

Foot
Length and depth measurement (nautical), which was defined differently in the German states and cities before the adoption of the metric system in 1875. Here one foot corresponds to the length or depth of thirty centimeters.

Knot
Nautical speed measure; 1 knots = one nautical mile per hour = 1.852 m/h; voyage: 39,000 km to Batavia in 142 days = 275 km/day = 11.5 km/h = average speed of 6.2 knots.

Koku
Unit of volume for rice; 1 koku corresponds to the amount of dried rice grains consumed by an adult per year or about 180 liters. Koku was used to measure the rice harvest as well as all the assets of daimyos and the rice stipends for the samurai.

Mile
Old European distance measure, which varied according to historical epoch, country, duchy and in Germany also according to free imperial city between 1,482 (Roman Empire) and 11,299 (Norway) meters. As long as it is not referred to as a nautical mile, the London Mile with a length of 1609.3 meters is always meant here.

Nautical mile
A distance of 1852 meters.

Ri 里
Old Japanese measure of length; 1 ri corresponds to 3,927 meters.

Ounce
Weight unit, abbreviation 'oz', corresponds to about 28.35 grams.

Units of Currency

The conversion of the Dutch currency 'guilders' into Japanese coins or bars was simultaneously expressed in a fixed silver and gold rate. The Japanese currency units listed here are based on uniform weights for gold, silver, and copper. The Japanese yen was introduced in 1868 during the Meiji restoration.

The purchasing power of 1 gulden in the first half of the 19th century corresponded approximately to that of 8 to 10 euros. Examples: Siebold's initial annual salary on Dejima was between 44,000 and 55,000 euros and his Japanese collections were purchased by the Dutch government for 480,000 to 600,000 euros.

1 oban or bankin = 5.8 ounces gold = 165.4 grams gold; only for special occasions

1 koban or ryō = 5 guilders = 18 grams gold = 262 g silver; largest gold coin for everyday use

1 ichibukin = ¼ ryō = 4.5 grams gold; smallest gold coin

1 chōgin = 5, 7 ounces silver = 161.64 grams silver

1 guilder = 3.6 g gold = 49 g silver

1 zeni = 3.76 g copper coin; smallest Japanese currency unit

Japanese Syllabic Alphabets

Hiragana and Katakana

		ひらがな Hiragana					かたかな Katakana				
		あ a	い i	う u	え e	お o	ア a	イ i	ウ u	エ e	オ o
Seion		か ka	き ki	く ku	け ke	こ ko	カ ka	キ ki	ク ku	ケ ke	コ ko
		さ sa	し shi	す su	せ se	そ so	サ sa	シ shi	ス su	セ se	ソ so
		た ta	ち chi	つ tsu	て te	と to	タ ta	チ chi	ツ tsu	テ te	ト to
		な na	に ni	ぬ nu	ね ne	の no	ナ na	ニ ni	ヌ nu	ネ ne	ノ no
		は ha	ひ hi	ふ fu	へ he	ほ ho	ハ ha	ヒ hi	フ fu	ヘ he	ホ ho
		ま ma	み mi	む mu	め me	も mo	マ ma	ミ mi	ム mu	メ me	モ mo
		や ya		ゆ yu		よ yo	ヤ ya		ユ yu		ヨ yo
		ら ra	り ri	る ru	れ re	ろ ro	ラ ra	リ ri	ル ru	レ re	ロ ro
		わ wa				を wo	ワ wa				ヲ wo
		ん n					ン n				
Daku on		が ga	ぎ gi	ぐ gu	げ ge	ご go	ガ ga	ギ gi	グ gu	ゲ ge	ゴ go
		ざ za	じ ji	ず zu	ぜ ze	ぞ zo	ザ za	ジ ji	ズ zu	ゼ ze	ゾ zo
		だ da	ぢ di(ji)	づ du/zu	で de	ど do	ダ da	ヂ di(ji)	ヅ du/zu	デ de	ド do
		ば ba	び bi	ぶ bu	べ be	ぼ bo	バ ba	ビ bi	ブ bu	ベ be	ボ bo
HanD		ぱ pa	ぴ pi	ぷ pu	ぺ pe	ぽ po	パ pa	ピ pi	プ pu	ペ pe	ポ po

		Hiragana			Katakana		
Yoon	Seion	きゃ kya	きゅ kyu	きょ kyo	キャ kya	キュ kyu	キョ kyo
		しゃ sha	しゅ shu	しょ sho	シャ sha	シュ shu	ショ sho
		ちゃ cha	ちゅ chu	ちょ cho	チャ cha	チュ chu	チョ cho
		にゃ nya	にゅ nyu	にょ nyo	ニャ nya	ニュ nyu	ニョ nyo
		ひゃ hya	ひゅ hyu	ひょ hyo	ヒャ hya	ヒュ hyu	ヒョ hyo
		みゃ mya	みゅ myu	みょ myo	ミャ mya	ミュ myu	ミョ myo
		りゃ rya	りゅ ryu	りょ ryo	リャ rya	リュ ryu	リョ ryo
	Dakuon	ぎゃ gya	ぎゅ gyu	ぎょ gyo	ギャ gya	ギュ gyu	ギョ gyo
		じゃ ja	じゅ ju	じょ jo	ジャ ja	ジュ ju	ジョ jo
		ぢゃ ja	ぢゅ ju	ぢょ jo	ヂャ ja	ヂュ ju	ヂョ jo
		びゃ bya	びゅ byu	びょ byo	ビャ bya	ビュ byu	ビョ byo
	HD	ぴゃ pya	ぴゅ pyu	ぴょ pyo	ピャ pya	ピュ pyu	ピョ pyo

Picture Credits and Quotations

Cover: The coat of arms and seal of the Japanese emperor, Kiku no Gomon 菊の御紋, a 16-leaf golden chrysanthemum on a red ball.

1. *Vue de l'Île et de la Ville de Batavia appartenant aux Hollandois pour la Compagnie des Indes*, Daumont, Paris 1780, after a painting by Jan van Ryne, 1754.

2. Frontispiece of Gerhard Mercator's *Atlas Sive Cosmographicae Meditationes De Fabrica Mundi Et Fabricati Figura* from 1595.

3. View of Dejima and the bay of Nagasaki, lithograph by Carl Hubert de Villeneuve, from Philipp Franz von Siebold's main work *Nippon. Archive describing Japan and its subsidiary and protective countries*, 1832.

The quotations from Philipp Franz von Siebold's letters, diaries, and publications as well as those of his students are not shown individually. Some are taken from the monumental biography *Philipp Franz von Siebold. His Life and Work* by Shūzō Kure (*1865, †1932). It is 1760 pages long and probably unique in its genre. It was published in Tokyo in 1926 in Japanese and was translated into German in 1930 by the Japanologist Friedrich M. Trautz (*1877, †1952). I was able to view and study from 1988 to 1993 at the Bavarian State Library in Munich one of the two typescripts that had survived the Second World War. This biographical masterpiece was only published in German in 1996 on the occasion of Siebold's 200th birthday in an excellently edited two-volume edition by Iudicium Verlag, Munich.

Daniel Defoe's fascinating work *The Political History of the Devil* from 1726, that I have cited at several occasions, is a 450 page long, profound and wonderfully written study, in which Defoe explains how the devil has influenced the course of world politics since the beginning of time and incited peoples and religions against each other. It has not yet been translated into any other world language. Even internationally recognized experts on the devil and demonology do not know it. The e-book is available for free download at Project Gutenberg and on archive.org.

Note to the Reader

The Discovery of the East Pole is based on a long series of true events and represents the first novel in the new literary genre of True Historical Fiction. Almost all characters in the following drama—there are over one hundred of them—have lived, breathed, and wandered the earth in their time. Likewise, the chain of events in which they became entangled is not fictitious but was forged link by link by history itself. The natural disasters that you will read about occurred how they are described here, based on contemporary chronicles. Even the mythical and religious themes and their protagonists were living parts of that past historical reality. The share of fiction in this novel, therefore, is less than one-tenth, just as much as necessary to render this unbelievable series of events relatable in a literary form.

Part three of the Nippon trilogy, *The Road to War*, and its *Complete Edition* include an 'Afterword by the Author' that relates his personal backstory to the writing of this novel and the new literary genre that it represents, namely True Historical Fiction.

More background information, picture galleries, and research links are gathered on the novel's English homepage www.east-pole.com.

About the Author

©Jeronimus van Pelt

Reginald 'Reggie' Grünenberg (*1963) is a German novelist, writer-producer, entrepreneur, and inventor. He studied political science, history, and philosophy in Paris, Munich, and Berlin up to the doctorate. He also studied at Waseda University in Tokyo and became a certified expert on Japan in 2008.

His personal backstory to the novel is indluded as the 'Afterword by the Author' in the third part of the Nippon trilogy, *The Road to War*, and in its *Complete Edition*.

Reggie's homepage is www.reggies.world.

Table of Contents

Imprint

Nippon Trilogy

The Discovery of the East Pole

Part One: *Shiboruto*

Author: Reginald Grünenberg

Translated by: Bayard Taylor

Cover design: Kiewi Design

Publisher: Perlen Verlag, Berlin

ISBN 978-3-942662-28-4

© Perlen Verlag 2018

www.east-pole.com